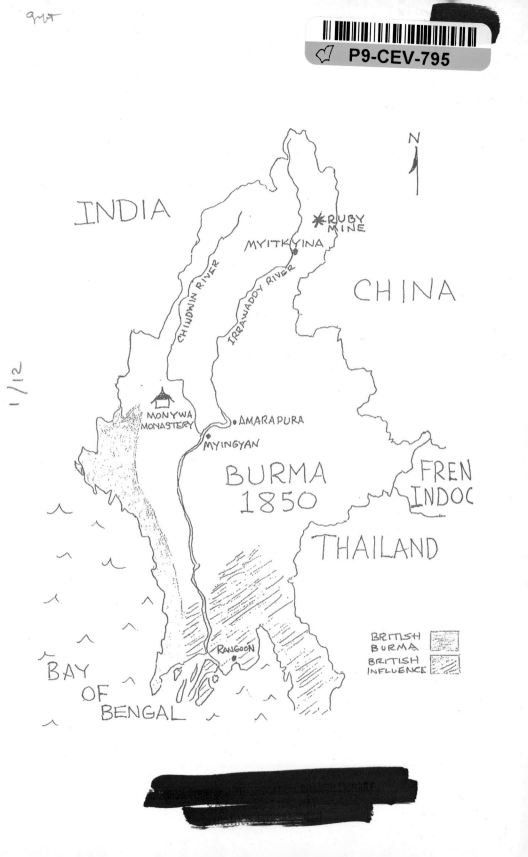

# MONTOOTH2

# MONTOOTH2

## *Race for the Ryland Ruby*

A CARTY ANDERSSON NOVEL BY

# ROBERT JAY

CLOVERLEAF

CORPORATION

Cloverleaf Corporation

1916 South Tamiami Trail

Ruskin, FL 33570

Text and cover design by AuthorSupport, LaGrange, KY

Author photograph in the Myakka swamps, FL by M. S. Christian

Book printed and bound by Berryville Graphics, Berryville, VA

Jay, Robert, 1943 –

Montooth 2: Race for the Ryland Ruby / Robert Jay.

p. cm.

1. Historical fiction. 2. Young adults – fiction. 3. Cuba – fiction. 4. Burma (Myanmar) – fiction. 5. Carty Andersson (Fictitious character) – fiction. 6. Montooth (Fictitious character) – fiction. 7. Alligators – fiction. 8. Armadillos – fiction.

I. Title

ISBN 978-0-615-40119-5

Printed in the United States of America

1 – 12

# DEDICATION

This book is dedicated to Hildegard, my wife of almost forty-two years, who has devoted a four decade effort – mostly unsuccessful – to rein in my eccentricities.

To my utmost appreciation, she immediately became an ardent supporter of the <u>Montooth</u> series and my most dedicated marketer.

# CONGRATULATIONS

Fans of <u>Montooth and the Canfield Witch</u> will recall that the book included a contest, "The Mystery of the Names."

The winner was Steve Todd of Costa Mesa, CA who realized that the first names of most of the upstanding characters in <u>Montooth and the Canfield Witch</u> were taken from the last names of past Cleveland Indian baseball players. Likewise, the names of the nefarious characters were taken from the last names of past players from the Evil Empire known to baseball fans as the New York Yankees. Mr. Todd even correctly identified the Haywood Dolder name as coming from Clew Haywood, the nasty Yankee first baseman in the best baseball movie of all time, *Major League*.

Mr. Todd will receive an autographed, leather-bound copy of <u>Montooth 2: Race for the Ryland Ruby</u> for his effort.

Readers interested in details may view the names on the official book website, www.montoothbooks.com. The website also lists new character names in <u>Montooth 2: Race for the Ryland Ruby</u>, which are linked to those from Evil Empire II, the Boston Red Sox.


Robert Jay

# ACKNOWLEDGEMENTS

As many fans of the <u>Montooth</u> series know, Cloverleaf Corporation's Publishing Division sponsored an international survey and contest that included students, nominated by their English teachers, from as far away as China. We sought input from over 24,000 readers about the book characters of <u>Montooth and the Canfield Witch</u> and what readers hoped to see develop in this second book, <u>Montooth 2: Race for the Ryland Ruby.</u>

The idea submitted by Jacob Cole of Grace Christian School in Raleigh, NC, USA, was selected by the managing editor for inclusion in <u>Montooth 2: Race for the Ryland Ruby</u>. His recommendation was incorporated by Robert Jay into a surprise ending to a plot line.

Jacob, an eighth grader at the time of the contest, was one of the younger entrants. He was nominated by the head of the English Department of Grace Christian, Debra Hentzell.

Jacob wanted <u>Montooth 2</u> to include a conflicted individual struggling to determine where his loyalties rested while encountering others in the <u>Montooth</u> series. In the end, per Jacob's wish, the confused character becomes an effective ally of his chosen side.

You will see the names of both Jacob Cole and Debra Hentzell appearing as fictitious characters in <u>Montooth 2: Race for the Ryland Ruby</u>.

The other nine finalists in the contest, ranging from the 7th to 11th grades, appear below:

| STUDENT | SCHOOL | TEACHER |
| --- | --- | --- |
| Monica Brown | Waukee Middle School, Waukee, IA | Nikole Monaco |
| Mackenzie Mills | Dover Intermediate School, Dover, PA | Margie Manley |
| Callie-Rae Nachtigall | St. Boniface Diocesan High School, Winnipeg, MB, CANADA | Jaime Riou |
| Bill Peebles | Cary Academy, Cary, NC | Briarly White |
| Jeremy Sayre | North Canton Middle School, North Canton, OH | Lindsay McCann |
| Avery Segal* | Barron Collier High School, Naples, FL | Christina Johnston |
| Allison Stegmaier | Lee's Summit Community Christian School, Lee's Summit, MO | Cody Persell |
| Julia Usiak | Middletown Middle School, Middletown, MD | Nena Allevato |
| Kevin Zhang | Concordia International School, Shanghai, CHINA | Eileen Bach |

*special achievement recognition

# PRIMARY CHARACTERS

*from <u>Montooth and the Canfield Witch</u>*
*Also Appearing in*
<u>Montooth 2: Race for the Ryland Ruby</u>

**Andersson, Catherine "Carty"** – Charter member of The Crew (group of friends), skilled archer, swamp expert, strong-willed tomboy, daughter of Michael and Bay Andersson, great niece of Lilly Andersson, boarding at Sarasota Preparatory Academy, sixteen as <u>Montooth 2</u> begins

**Andersson, Lilliquest "Lilly"** – Wealthy descendant of a Florida real estate and sugar mogul, influential citizen of the town of Winter Free, philanthropist, aunt of Michael Andersson and great aunt of Carty Andersson, sixty-eight years old as <u>Montooth 2</u> begins

**Andersson, Michael** – WWII Army Ranger, decorated veteran, expert tracker, engineer, operator of family limerock mining operation, father of Carty Andersson, late thirties as <u>Montooth 2</u> begins

**Canfield, Sally** – Also see *Elsmore, Sally* – Descendant of ancestors driven from Salem, Massachusetts during the Witch Trials of the Seventeenth Century, recluse, mischievous, formerly feared as a witch by most Winter Free townsfolk, thirty as <u>Montooth 2</u> begins

**Cruz Cruz aka "The Cuban" aka "Mr. Smith"** – U.S. Marine veteran, Tampa native, born to Cuban parents, emotionless, deadly behind-the-scenes power broker, superb military and operational mind, leader of the attackers of Sally Canfield; political power broker in pre-Castro Cuba, middle fifties as <u>Montooth 2</u> begins

**Dolder, Haywood** – Nasty rival of Carty Andersson, spoiled-rotten son of Winter Free's Chevrolet Dealer, devious but not particularly bright, thinks highly of himself, sixteen as <u>Montooth 2</u> begins

**Elsmore, James** – County Sheriff, WWII veteran, level-headed, fair-minded leader, principled, honest, middle thirties as <u>Montooth 2</u> begins

**Holmes, Blake** – Charter member of The Crew (group of friends), strong, courageous, gifted athlete, male, nearly seventeen as <u>Montooth 2</u> begins

**Hostetter, Clemens** – Former neighbor of Sally Canfield, dim-witted, lethargic, easily led astray, one of the attackers of Sally Canfield for which he was confined to Raiford State Prison, late twenties as <u>Montooth 2</u> begins

**Montooth** – Enormous alligator with large misplaced tooth, protector of ducks, denizen of Duck Lake, loyal, age unknown but believed to be well over one hundred

**Stein, Maximilian "Mack"** – Only non-charter member of The Crew (group of friends), post-WWII Jewish-German immigrant to Florida, well educated and cosmopolitan, committed to his adopted country, begins writing career as a cub reporter in the local Winter Free weekly newspaper, sixteen as <u>Montooth 2</u> begins

**Wending, Hale** – Charter member of The Crew (group of friends), leading student, from a large black family, good athlete, brave, resourceful, male, sixteen as <u>Montooth 2</u> begins

**Zeller, Carey** – WWII veteran of the Pacific Campaign, had difficulty adjusting back to civilian life, formerly employed by Cruz Cruz, shrewd, glimmer of a moral compass, skilled in combat, experienced in wilderness conditions, part of the attackers of Sally Canfield, early to middle thirties as <u>Montooth 2</u> begins

# NEW PRIMARY CHARACTERS

### *Appearing in*
### *Montooth 2: Race for the Ryland Ruby*

**Bappa** – Nepalese Ghurka mercenary, assistant to Mid-Nineteenth Century archeologist Ronald Ryland, brave, resourceful, easily bored when not under pressure, late thirties at the time of the Ryland Ruby adventure in 1852

**Canfield, Rev. Ezra** – Missionary Anglican priest, father of Elisabeth Canfield Ryland, adventurer, British Army veteran, upper fifties at the time of the Ryland Ruby adventure in 1852

**Elsmore, Sally** – Also see *Canfield, Sally* – Wife of Sheriff James Elsmore as <u>Montooth 2</u> progresses

**Maung, Htay** – Military leader working under Burmese revolutionary strong-man King Pagan Min (half-brother to Mindon Min), indeterminate age at the time of the Ryland Ruby adventure in 1852

**Min, Mindon** – King of Burma in the mid-Nineteenth Century after deposing half-brother Pagan Min, dispatched Ronald Ryland on the Ryland Ruby adventure, considered to be the "George Washington" of his country, resisted Pagan Min's military confrontation with British forces in favor of accommodation, ushered in major economic development of his country during a twenty-five year reign, middle forties at the time of the Ryland Ruby adventure in 1852

**Meier, Grant** – Distant cousin and admirer of Carty Andersson, from Cleveland, Ohio, math and business oriented student from an entrepreneurial family, sixteen as <u>Montooth 2</u> begins

**Novotny, Vosmik** – Former OSS undercover agent throughout Axis-occupied Europe in WWII, close friend of the Wending family, mid-1950s CIA hire, late fifties or perhaps older as <u>Montooth 2</u> begins (appeared briefly in <u>Montooth and the Canfield Witch</u>)

**Rafferty, Elena** – Close friend and classmate of Carty Andersson at Sarasota Preparatory Academy, daughter of Cuban banker Rafael Rafferty, adventuresome, headstrong, passionate, driven, sixteen as <u>Montooth 2</u> begins (appeared briefly in <u>Montooth and the Canfield Witch</u>)

**Ryland, Elisabeth Canfield** – Distant relative of the Florida Canfields, carefree daughter of missionary Anglican priest Rev. Ezra Canfield, wife of Mid-Nineteenth Century archeologist Ronald Ryland, early twenties at the time of the Ryland Ruby adventure in 1852

**Ryland, Ronald** – Mid-Nineteenth Century archeologist, resourceful adventurer, husband of Elisabeth Canfield Ryland, early thirties at the time of the Ryland Ruby adventure in 1852

**Toth, Flagstead** – Prissy, vindictive, U.S. State Department official, connoisseur of wines and food, formerly short-tenured principal of Cross Creek Elementary where he was inadvertently embarrassed by Carty Andersson, holds petty grudge against Carty, late thirties as <u>Montooth 2</u> begins (appeared briefly in <u>Montooth and the Canfield Witch</u>)

**Zapata, Castillo** – Mexican alias of Carey Zeller, one of the gang that attacked Sally Canfield in <u>Montooth and the Canfield Witch</u>, married to Easter Zapata, serves as resident handyman to Lilly Andersson and the James Elsmore family, early to mid-thirties as <u>Montooth 2</u> begins

**Zapata, Easter** – Wife of Castillo Zapata, domestic help for Lilly Andersson and the James Elsmore family, mid-thirties as <u>Montooth 2</u> begins (appeared briefly in <u>Montooth and the Canfield Witch</u> as Easter Huerto)

# CHAPTER 1

## *The Sighting*

*Courage is doing what you are afraid to do.*
EDDIE RICKENBACKER

**AUGUST 1952**

Across the wide boulevard from Cuba's University of Havana, Carty stepped abruptly to her left and grabbed Elena's hand to pull her behind a wide square concrete pillar. The rough column screened the girls from the few patrons seated at the coffee shop's sidewalk tables.

One customer, Cruz Cruz, also known as The Cuban, sat alone at a table barely thirty feet from them. Cruz was the redundantly named leader of the villainous band that had attacked Carty and several friends in Florida two years earlier. He took his eyes from a newspaper and snapped off an aggressive bite of a thick piece of bread.

To all those who had encountered him that eventful day, including Carty, he was known by a third name, "Mr. Smith."

Before Elena could say anything, Carty crossed her own lips with an index finger and hushed, "Shh."

"What is it?" Elena whispered.

"I'll tell you in a minute." Pointing in the direction of the doorway to the café, she said, "Find us a way out through the café. I don't want to be seen in front."

Elena led her into the building and beamed her most engaging smile at the young counter man. "My friend saw her old boyfriend near the front of your building, and she does not want an ugly encounter. Do you have an exit in the rear that we could use?"

Carty smiled at the boy, tilted her head downward slightly, and fluttered her eyelashes with just enough modesty to give him a glimmer of hope that he might have a chance at replacing the jilted suitor.

"Of course, *Señoritas*. I am Rodrigo, at your service. Come this way."

He led them through the stifling kitchen heavy with steam. They eased around boiling pots of sauces and past pans frying tastily scented food for the lunchtime crowd expected to begin arriving shortly. He unlocked the rear door to the alley and let them out with a small bow.

The confluence of odors outside was not nearly as recognizable as those in the kitchen, nor was the foul aroma in the alley at all agreeable. The two girls tried to hold their breath as they walked briskly to the adjoining street, watching their steps carefully to avoid dragging the unpleasant experience along. The large gray cat that scurried in front of them turned out, on closer view, to have the long, thin tail of a rat.

Before Elena could ask, Carty began talking. "Do you remember hearing about the four men who attacked Sally Canfield and The Crew a few years ago?"

The Crew was a group of four friends including Carty and two life-long pals, Blake Holmes and Hale Wending. About two years before, they had added a new member, Maximilian ("Mack") Stein. It was an eclectic group: respectively, a white, single-child female; the youngest boy of a large, white, motherless family; the oldest boy of an equally large black family; and an immigrant male German Jew without siblings.

Sally Canfield was the last descendant of a family that had been chased from Massachusetts during the Salem Witch Trials in the 1600s. In 1950, she was the first of the Florida branch of the family to give up the witch persona. For hundreds of years, the Canfields had encouraged outsiders to fear their mysterious ways as a behavior to remain isolated. Their rural enclave, located at the edge of Morose Swamp and Duck Lake near Winter Free, Florida, was seldom approached by locals.

"Of course," replied Elena. "The story about her and The Crew is a legend at school. Those friends of yours are great. I am always impressed at how the three boys give you so much credit for the part that you played. Boys here in Cuba don't think we girls can do anything."

"The only one of that gang who escaped from the swamp that day is sitting at a table outside of that café we just left."

Elena's eyes widened. "Are you certain you could recognize him? There were only a few people seated there, and from what I saw, their faces were all turned away from us to shelter their eyes from the rising sun."

Carty was not surprised that Elena had noticed such detail in the few moments that they stood there. Her friend could glance over an entire room in a few seconds, and hours later describe in nearly perfect detail the furniture, wall hangings, lamps, and other furnishings. She had won a large number of Cokes from unsuspecting fellow students and others who doubted her photographic memory enough to wager on it.

"I once experienced that man's profile from a few inches away with his gun at my head. A moment ago, though farther away, I saw him from about that same angle. I am as certain about him as knowing that you are Elena Rafferty. He is the stocky man wearing the powder blue suit and the white Panama."

In an excited voice, Elena suggested impetuously, "Omigosh! Let's follow him. Maybe we can find out who he is and where he lives."

"That is almost a good idea. *We* are not going to follow him, though. *I* am going to follow him. No offense, but he'd spot you before he wiped the coffee from his lips. Listen, you wait for me at the university bookstore. I'll come back there to meet you after I find out where he lives."

Elena was the sixteen-year-old daughter of Rafael Rafferty, a Cuban banker and former WWII colleague of Carty's father, Michael Andersson. Elena and Carty roomed together at the Sarasota Preparatory Academy (SPA), an all-girls boarding school in Sarasota, Florida. They had been alternating spending Easter vacations and parts of the summers with each other's families since becoming roommates in 1950.

Unlike most of her siblings, Elena had not inherited her mother's Spanish features. Instead, she, like her brother Roberto, resembled the Irish side of the Rafferty family. The brother and sister shared blond hair, light skin, and a sprinkling of freckles. In fact, she resembled Carty's Scandinavian features sufficiently that the two girls were often mistaken for sisters.

"That's not going to work. You haven't learned enough about Havana in a few visits to know your way around. You'll get lost."

"Silly, I don't need to know my way around. I can always find my way back to the university. It's one of the best known landmarks in the city. Besides, my Spanish is good enough to ask for directions."

"In two years of study, your Spanish is good enough to debate a native. I think it may be better than my English, and I've been bilingual all my life."

"It's been your tutoring that pushed me along. Anyway, we're agreed, right?"

Grudgingly, Elena relented. "All right, but I want you back at the bookstore no later than three o'clock. I don't want to worry any longer than that about you getting caught. Besides, we have to be home for an early dinner at six so we can see Roberto's game tonight. It's his first game, and he's really looking forward to all of us being there."

Roberto was a talented thirteen-year-old catcher. He was brought up to a team of fifteen- and sixteen-year-olds when the team lost its regular catcher to injury. If Roberto continued developing behind the plate and at the bat, a Major League career might become more than a youngster's mere dream.

"As it is, I can't believe that Mother let us out unescorted. Wait until she finds out what you're up to. She thinks that you are the responsible one." Her mother, Margarite, was unusually permissive for the times, especially in the Latin culture, but she was unlikely to countenance tailing criminals.

"It might be better to keep this between ourselves for now. Mothers have a way of getting overly agitated over nothing. Let's get going before he takes off."

Traffic clogged the narrow street, and exhaust hung heavy between the concrete canyon of mostly two-story, stucco buildings. They picked up the pace and turned at the end of the alley on to an adjacent street, Calle J, separating from one another at the next intersection.

Elena's worry darkened her usually bright disposition. She could not resist glancing back at the café as she crossed Avenida Universidad. The man in the light blue suit was still there, but so deeply involved in his newspaper that she could not see his face.

Carty, on the other hand, had disappeared. When Elena reached the other side of the street, she stopped and turned. She scanned the entire area but could not see Carty anywhere. She glanced back at Cruz and saw that he was standing with his back to her and had folded the newspaper to place on the table. He counted out pesos, anchored the money to the paper with his coffee cup, and appeared ready to leave.

She was baffled at Carty's disappearance but went ahead with the plan. Though she was worried, she had seen enough of Carty during their years at SPA to have confidence that Carty could do just about anything she set her mind to accomplishing. She entered the campus proper and made her way to the bookstore.

As Cruz was finishing his newspaper, he was curious about the young blond girl who appeared to be looking at him while she crossed the busy street. He was much like a bird, always checking his immediate environment no matter how engrossed he was in the matter at hand. It was a survival technique that had served him well. He had noticed Elena's attentiveness by barely looking over the top of his newspaper.

Cruz accepted that he was not a handsome rogue who might attract random notice from women, let alone a girl who was decades younger than he. So her examination was odd and worth his further attention.

Eerily, she had a passing resemblance to a younger girl he met in the swamps around Winter Free, Florida two years earlier. Clearly, the girl in the street was not Carty Andersson, but she was close enough in appearance to bring back unpleasant memories that were still guiding his actions years later.

As the girl turned away and walked toward the university, he wondered if he might be mistaken about her interest in him. Without moving his head, he glanced at the patrons seated at the other tables. None of the few late morning stragglers seemed any more likely than he to attract the intense stare of a young, pretty girl.

Of course, her gaze was likely to be innocent, he reasoned. Probably, from a distance, the girl thought that he was a professor or an acquaintance. Despite his rationalizations, he remained wary.

Blonds stood out in Havana. There were some of the artificial variety around, but their hair usually looked frizzy. This one looked like the real thing. He would remember her.

From Carty's hidden vantage point, she saw that Cruz noticed Elena looking him over. His prompt reaction – folding the paper, placing money on the table, and walking away – led her to believe that his senses were alerted. That was not a good prelude for Carty's plan to follow him.

Carty was an expert at tracking, but that was in the wild. She knew that she did not have experience tailing a person in an urban environment. Reluctantly, she decided on a more conservative tack. She remained hidden and did not follow Cruz as he left the café.

Though the limp in his gait was slight, she noted with satisfaction that he suffered lingering effects from her arrow that penetrated his leg two years earlier.

She watched from her distant location as he turned a corner. Then she remained motionless and waited. After about forty-five seconds, Cruz returned, rushing back around the corner at a brisk pace. If she had followed, he might have literally bumped into her, but at minimum he would have seen her with those squinty eyes that darted in all directions.

As he strode, Cruz acted as if he had forgotten something, patting his pants' and jacket pockets. Then reaching into a shirt pocket, he pulled out a small set of keys, gave a theatrical "aha" to himself, did a one-eighty, and retraced his steps around the corner.

Carty was tempted to follow, since Cruz would be less on edge after his corner gambit turned up no threat. But she decided that she was too much out of her element on city streets. Instead, she returned to the café, sat at a table, and ordered coffee.

To the young waiter she said, "I am planning to meet my uncle here this morning, but I am really late. I hope that I haven't missed him."

Recognizing her slight accent despite the well-spoken Spanish, and anxious to converse with the tall, pretty blond, he asked, "You are an American, *Señorita*?"

"*Sí*, I am taking a summer course at the university," she fibbed. "My Cuban uncle is coming to meet me here. If I miss him, he told me he would come back around noon. Now I do not know whether to wait or to come back later."

"What does he look like, *Señorita*? Perhaps I have seen him."

Carty described a man similar to Cruz but avoided being fully accurate. She wanted the waiter to believe that Cruz might be her uncle, but she wanted to be able to say he wasn't. If Cruz ever came back, she did not want the waiter mentioning the interest of an American girl.

"There was a man here a short time ago. He meets your description partially, but I do not believe that he is the right person, because he had squinty eyes – not the large round eyes you mentioned."

"My uncle's name is Oscar Melona. Is that the name of the gentleman who was here earlier?"

"I do not know his name, *Señorita*. He comes often for a morning coffee and bread and to read his newspaper, and occasionally to meet with students, but he has never given me his name."

"Oh, I'm sure that he is not my uncle then. He almost never comes to Havana. He is coming only to visit me. I will finish my coffee and return around noon instead. Thank you for your help, Carlos," Carty added, after seeing the name on his apron. Her dazzling smile brightened the rest of the day for Carlos.

At the bookstore, well before the appointed time, Carty found Elena paging through Salinger's Catcher in the Rye.

Sneaking up behind her, Carty admonished in a deep authoritative and apparently male voice, "You had better not let your mother find out you are reading that."

Elena jumped and almost dropped the book. She fumbled it back on to the shelf quickly. Seeing that Carty was the source of the scare, she pleaded, "You won't tell her, will you?"

"Of course not, Silly. Is it any good?"

"Actually, it's kind of boring and a little pretentious from the part that I read. I don't see what the fuss is all about," referring to the battles attempting to censor the book in the U.S. "Maybe it gets better later on.

"So, tell me. What happened with Blue Suit? You are back a lot earlier than I expected. Did you change your mind? I didn't see you anywhere."

"You didn't see me because I concealed myself. You should know that by this time. If I were readily visible to you, I would be readily visible to him too.

"Anyway, he is the same guy. I'm certain of that. He spotted you looking at him, and it spooked him."

"He couldn't have noticed me. He never looked up from the paper the entire time I watched him. In fact, I never saw his face."

"He saw yours. Trust me. That guy can see out of the bottoms of his feet. I didn't follow him when he got up and left, because he sensed that something was not right. It's a good thing that I didn't. After he went around a corner, he quickly retraced his steps, and I would have walked right into him if I had been following.

"Afterward I stopped at the café and spoke with a cute waiter. I don't know why you are so down on the boys in Cuba. He seemed really nice."

"Ha. Make sure that you always have someone nearby when they are around. They act like we girls are their playthings."

"Just tell them to watch it if they want to avoid a broken nose," she laughed. "That always works for me."

"For you that would work, because it is entirely believable. You are five-nine and still growing, with shoulders like Johnny Weissmuller[1]. But for fair damsels such as I, things are a little more difficult."

Carty indeed had strong shoulders from years of dedicated archery practice, but their width did not approach that of a dedicated swimmer, let alone the Olympic swimmer and actor.

"You are only a couple of inches shorter, Elena, and you know that I'm just kidding about bopping them on the nose. Just let them know that you aren't the kind of girl that they think they want you to be. They'll behave and like you better. And when they realize that you aren't going to give in to them, it'll cause them to chase after you all the harder."

"You mean like Blake?" she chuckled.

"Well, Blake is a special case. He's way too much of a gentleman and hasn't figured out that he is supposed to be a chaser. When he is with me as a buddy, he is as natural and fun as he can be. But as soon as something happens to make him think of me as a girl, he turns into a blubbering idiot. That's the reaction that frustrates every girl he meets. I think it has something to do with his mom dying when he was so young.

"Anyway, a little firmness is all a girl needs to keep things on a good footing with most boys – and the others aren't worth the trouble."

"I know. It's just their macho attitude. They can be nice when other guys aren't around, but when they get together, they can turn really crude. It must be some kind of herd instinct. But you got us off the subject. What about Blue Suit?"

"The waiter told me that he often comes for coffee and to meet with students, but Carlos doesn't know the guy's name. I didn't ask if he knew where Blue Suit lives, because I didn't want to show too much curiosity, but I think he would have offered the information if he had known it."

"'Carlos,' is it?" Elena teased. "No wonder you are sticking up for Cuban boys. Looks like one of them might be developing a relationship with you."

"I should wish," she laughed. "The closest thing I've had to a 'relationship' with a boy was at a Red Sox' spring training baseball game in Bradenton. Blake got so excited when Ted Williams pinch hit and doubled in Jimmy Piersall with the winning run in the ninth that he kissed me on the cheek.

"Then he spent the rest of the afternoon apologizing as we drove home. Finally, I had to kiss him back to shut him up. Fortunately, we were in his little Crosley[2], so we were close together. I told him, 'There, we're even. Calm down.' I don't think he has recovered yet."

The girls spent the rest of the day on the campus, getting a flavor of what they would be doing in another two years. Elena was destined for the University of Havana, and all indications were that Carty would be attending Purdue University. In fact, there was a possibility of The Crew being reunited on the West Lafayette campus in Indiana.

Coach Bill Normand's Keystone Combination[3] of Blake and Hale on the baseball field at Winter Free High was attracting a lot of attention from Big Ten college recruiters as well as pro scouts. Recently, the two ball player friends gave an interview to the local newspaper about their desire to stay together if they opted for college over pro contracts after finishing high school.

Working on the Andersson limerock mine during the past three summers, Blake had shown an aptitude for engineering equivalent to Carty's. Carty's father was working hard to get the two of them into Purdue's engineering program. If Blake attended, Hale was committed to Purdue as well, provided a scholarship came through – though Hale preferred political science as his area of study.

Since neither Blake nor Hale came from wealthy families, baseball scholarships – even partials – would help both regardless of where they went. However, few of the major southern colleges were accepting blacks readily, so Purdue appeared to be the likeliest location.

Mack had developed a fondness for journalism, so he planned to study the Classics with an emphasis on writing. He could have chosen about any university but enjoyed the camaraderie of The Crew. The prospect of four years with the four of them together was pulling him to Purdue.

# CHAPTER 2

## *Roberto*

*The kid doesn't chew tobacco, smoke, drink, curse, or chase broads.*
*I don't see how he can possibly make it.*
RICHIE ASHBURN

**AUGUST 1952**

After a quick bite to eat, Carty accompanied the large and boisterous Rafferty family who needed two full size Oldsmobiles to transport everyone to La Tropical Stadium. Roberto was playing his first game for the Havana Hurricanes.

Mosquitoes, attracted by the lights above and the perspiration of the crowd below, buzzed relentlessly as the last of the daylight escaped the summer sky. Few fans paid the insects much heed, though. Attention

14

was too focused on the young players on the field of Cuba's most famous baseball stadium.

These amateur athletes looked and played like professionals on the silky smooth dirt infield and emerald green grass. Both gave true hops to balls beat into infield chops or lined one-hoppers. The youngsters were accustomed on their previous fields to suffer bad, unpredictable bounces as often as those that were expected.

This was the last month of the 1952 season of the High Amateur League (HAL). Players who excelled at this stage of their development would likely be sought out for one of the Cuban professional teams in a couple of years. Most players would be seventeen or eighteen by that time and prime for a move up in competition. A tiny few – a very tiny few – would find their way to a minor league affiliate of a U.S. Major League team, and a rare player or two to a Major League roster at some distant time.

Four months earlier, Roberto, the new Hurricanes' catcher, celebrated only his thirteenth birthday. That fact of chronology made Roberto the youngest player ever to make an HAL team roster, let alone as a starter. He was a minor celebrity in baseball-crazed Havana and a favorite of the sports writers.

Roberto's great grandfather had pitched half a season with the Boston Beaneaters[4] before the turn of the century. Unfortunately, a torn rotator cuff led him to trade in his glove for a banker's pen and ledger book years before anyone had heard of that medical ailment.

Nevertheless, that ancestor went to his grave claiming that he would have given back all the money he made in his New York banking career for five years in the Big Leagues as even a mop-up pitcher.

Thus, baseball genes flowed through Roberto, and, if desire can be passed down, those genes as well. That would explain his dedication to perfecting his skill at the game. Possessing a rocket arm that intimidated most potential base stealers into staying put on the base paths, his defense was already being compared with that of young professional players on the island.

But it was his hitting that attracted the publicity. He held the home run records for each league he had played in, sometimes by half again the previous standard. Barely a teenager, he was equal the size of the other players in the HAL. He looked down on his favorite sibling, Elena – physically, not figuratively.

This night's game was a pitcher's duel, with only five hits for both teams combined. Going one for four, Roberto's double tied the game in the seventh inning, but he was not involved with the winning run in the ninth. Nevertheless, his pitcher lavished praise on the heady game Roberto called behind the plate, so the trip home with the family was as joyous as if he had been the hitting hero.

*FOR* the next three days, Elena and Carty returned to the university area where they enjoyed the academic atmosphere and the attention of the "college men." However, their real reason for returning to the area was to keep an eye on the tables in the café across the street in the hope that Blue Suit would return.

Periodically, one of them would peel off from the other and take a swift trip to a well concealed spot that had good sight lines to the café. Carty had provided Elena with a quick training course in staying out of sight. The instruction and the long distance between the café and the hidden site gave Carty confidence that Elena would not be spotted. The first two days went by without sighting their quarry.

On the third day, as they prepared to board the bus that took them into the city, Carty remarked, "This is our last day before we have to return to Sarasota. If he doesn't show up today, we will lose any chance of finding out where he lives – at least this summer. I really hope that the waiter was right about the man's frequent visits."

Carlos was vindicated when Cruz showed up at the café late that morning. This day he wore a beige suit, off-white shirt, cream shoes, and slim green tie. He wore the same white Panama. As an elderly waiter led him to a table, Carty was happy to see that Carlos was not on duty this morning. She dreaded that an off-hand remark concerning their conversation might tip off her quarry.

Carty walked briskly to the university coffee shop where Elena was waiting. As usual, Elena had attracted the attention of several of those Cuban boys whom she so frequently disparaged, and, as usual, she appeared to be enjoying their company immensely. When she saw Carty motion to her, she excused herself from the admiring throng and joined her.

"You seemed to be quite content with those fellows," Carty greeted in a lightly chiding voice. "Are they an exception to the Elena Axiom of Nasty Cuban Boys?"

"Oh, no," she laughed. "They are every bit as nasty as all the others, but I employed the Carty I'll-Bop-You-in-the-Nose Warning, and it seemed to set the right tone."

They both giggled at that response. Then Carty got to business.

"Blue Suit showed up, only he is Beige Suit today – same white Panama, though. I figure he lives nearby since he comes here frequently, so if we stake him out, we might be able to find out where he lives. The last time he left the café, he walked north to Calle J and then turned west. I've scouted Calle J and saw only two likely routes for him after that.

"I'll wait near the jewelry store further down on Calle J in case he goes straight, and you hang out in the flower shop on Bonita in case he turns right. Don't follow him, Elena. He will spot you in a flash. Just stay concealed and watch where he goes. If his final destination isn't too far and we are lucky, we may spot his home, even if we stay put and watch from the shops.

"If he lives too far, we will have to try again in the future. Worst case, we could plot his route further than we know it now."

The two girls returned to the concealed position briefly to be certain that Cruz was still there. They noted that Cruz had been joined by two young men around graduate student age. Elena did not recognize either student, and, because Cruz had his back to the girls, she still had not seen his face.

Carty led Elena on a widely circuitous route to Calle J so that they stayed entirely out of sight of the café.

About an hour later, Carty spotted Cruz in the distance as he turned on to Calle J and walked in her direction. He passed by the street where Elena was posted, leaving Elena out of the mix, and continued toward Carty. She recognized the gliding steps she first saw under more deadly conditions years earlier. Despite his sturdy physique, she thought he seemed more cat than human.

After he continued to close on her position for another half a block, her plans went awry. Cruz suddenly darted into the backseat of a car parallel parked against the curb. The large American Packard pulled into traffic, heading away from Carty, and almost immediately turned left on to Bonita where Elena waited.

Carty wished that she had one of Dick Tracy's 2-way wrist radios[5] so she could warn Elena that Beige Suit was approaching by car. Moments later, the car passed Elena's flower shop location. Elena failed to notice him, because she was expecting her target to come by foot if he used that route.

What was worse, she was standing boldly in the doorway, positioned to watch for him walking around the corner. As it was, Cruz observed her standing at the entry way of the shop as his car drove past. He recognized her readily – the same blond girl who showed an interest in him the last time he met with his university contacts. "Once was curious," he thought, "Twice is troubling."

Cruz instructed his driver to make the series of right turns to circle the block and return to the flower shop while he was deciding on a course of action. He was torn between following the girl and confronting her. By the second turn, he had decided on the latter.

Fortunately for the girls, the minor delay caused by Cruz's route gave Carty time to reach the flower shop and lead Elena away. They managed to vacate the area a few minutes before Cruz turned back on to the street.

Noting that the girl was no longer present, Cruz exited the car and entered the shop. He asked the clerk to prepare a bouquet of roses and spoke with the woman while she arranged the flowers.

"These are for my granddaughter," he said. "She is supposed to meet me outside of your shop. Have you happened to see her? She is tall and blond."

"Oh, yes," replied the clerk. "She was waiting for quite a long time, but another girl came just before you arrived, and they departed together. They're probably visiting one of the other shops nearby."

Cruz doubted that. "Oh, really? What did the other girl look like?"

"The two girls appeared to me to be sisters. Both were tall and blond. The second one had shoulder-length hair instead of the pageboy that the first girl wore."

Cruz paid for the flowers and told the clerk he would search the nearby shops for his granddaughter. As he left the shop, he pitched the flowers into a trash container and got into his car. "Let's take the long route, Elazar," he instructed his driver. "I have a lot to think about."

On the extended trip back to his Sierra Maestra Mountains plantation, Cruz contemplated the day's events. His meeting with Raúl and Fidel went well. Neither was politically practical at their young age, but they possessed just the right amount of passion to turn them into leaders and make them unwitting pawns to help Cruz prop up the current Batista Administration.

Cruz lived with constant concern that Florida police officials would identify him and seek his extradition for the attack on Sally Canfield in 1950. Thus far, Cruz had stayed a few steps ahead of Florida authorities, who had yet to learn his identity. But if they got closer, he wanted the protection that a position of power with Cuba's Government provided.

Guided behind the scenes by Cruz, Fulgencio Batista had seized power the previous March to head off an election that he was almost certain to lose. Batista offered better protection to Cruz than the Prío Administration.

Unfortunately for Batista, a group with strong ties to the University of Havana was agitating to overthrow him. So Cruz was secretly working to disrupt the budding rebel organization while giving the impression that he was helping it. This was the purpose of the meetings at the small café across from the university.

Cruz had no reason to suspect that one of the two blond girls was Carty Andersson, and, in fact, he did not believe that she was involved. But he was suspicious of coincidences, and two encounters with the first blond in less than a week was way too much coincidence to ignore.

Indeed, in the following several months, Cruz went into stalking mode prior to each meeting with his budding revolutionaries at the café. Instead of continuing to have Elazar drop him a few convenient meters from the café, he began stopping a mile away. From there he walked, taking care to view the surrounding streets from all directions.

He could have changed the locations of the meetings, but, if someone were interested in him, he wanted to figure out who it was and why.

Only after dozens of forays turned up no further sighting of the curious blond girl did he begin to believe that the previous encounters were coincidences that he need not distrust.

Unknown to Cruz, of course, Elena and Carty had returned to SPA the day after their abortive plan to track him.

# CHAPTER 3

## *The Winter Free Gazette*

*It's amazing that the amount of news that happens in the world
every day always just exactly fits the newspaper.*
JERRY SEINFELD

**SEPTEMBER 1950**

Mack began working weekends and one evening per school week at
*The Winter Free Gazette*, the town's weekly newspaper. He had spotted
the "Help Wanted – Part Time" sign a few days after freshmen began attending classes at Winter Free High.

Knode Geiger, the publisher, editor, and chief writer, greeted Mack
with a gruff manner that masked generosity and a soft spot for youngsters.
He appeared almost elf-like, being a curmudgeon bent over from arthritis

with thick, dark hair and wild bushy eyebrows that hid his advanced age.

"What do you know about the news business?" Geiger had challenged when Mack walked in holding the sign.

"I've read newspapers in Germany, England, and Florida, including *The Gazette*, sir, and I know that simply writing well is not sufficient – a newspaper writer must also write efficiently, sparingly, and to the point.

"My uncle David owned a small paper in Oberursel, Germany before the Nazis burned him out. I was too young to work there, but I was fascinated with the presses, listened, and always enjoyed the atmosphere."

"There's no writing in this job, Son. I simply need someone to clean up on Saturdays and to help me work the presses Tuesday nights to get the paper out every Wednesday. Eighty cents per hour – that's five cents above minimum wage. Eight hours on the weekend and six hours on Tuesdays starting at 3:15PM. Interested?"

"Yes, sir – I'd really do a good job for you."

"All right, I'll give you a try – just a try, mind you – to see how you do.

"You start this weekend – Saturday morning at eight. I'll show you what I want done the first day. After that, you'll be on your own. On the weekends, you can work either Saturday or Sunday or a combination. Just limit your weekend hours to eight and get everything done the way I want it. Can you handle that?"

"Yes, sir, but you don't even know who I am. How can you hire me so quickly? Don't you need references?"

"Son, everyone in Winter Free knows who you are. You're Maximilian Stein, 'Mack' to friends and family, one of The Crew who fought off the attack on the Canfield place a while back. *The Gazette* covered that story and ran several follow-up pieces about the trial. You are more famous than you realize.

"When you work for a small town newspaper, you know nearly everything important that goes on, a lot more that is unimportant, and," Geiger added, "even more that you shouldn't know. Our job is to inform and to highlight.

"Sometimes, we can actually help, for example when we wrote that Sally Canfield would be storing her financial bonds and jewelry in the Ensign Bank instead of her house. That was an interesting sidelight for our readers, but its inclusion, at the sheriff's request, was intended to dissuade any other prospective criminals from attempting a second attack."

Mack had started a few days later. Geiger soon learned that his confidence in Mack was well placed. Mack's weekend job seldom required as much as six hours, because Mack was so well organized and diligent that he completed his tasks in short order. Geiger had overestimated the time needed because he moved slowly in his physically impaired condition. Mack's ability to complete the work without help relieved Geiger of the most painful part of the business.

After a few weeks, Geiger asked Mack about his hours. "Mack, you keep turning in less than eight hours for your weekend work, but you complete everything I need done. Why don't you file for the full eight hours?"

"Mr. Geiger, I cannot cheat you. My tasks do not require more than five or six hours, so that is what I turn in." Geiger looked Mack over for a few moments and decided it was time to expand the job description without actually saying so. Slowly but steadily, Geiger assigned small writing tasks to see how Mack could perform and also to teach and guide him.

Mack started his additional duties by editing articles sent to *The Gazette* by stringers, people paid by the article. Later, Geiger allowed him to handle minor re-writes, correcting dates or times or citations, for example, without supervision. Mack performed flawlessly.

After another six months, Mack was allowed to write secondary items such as community meeting notices, the police report summary, and real estate sale transactions. Geiger's steady guidance had trained Mack well.

## MARCH 1952

*"MACK*, when you came to work here, you really wanted a reporter's job, didn't you? You couldn't hide the disappointment when I told you that the job did not involve writing. I was actually surprised that you took the position that I offered."

"It's true, Mr. Geiger, I do want to write. Many of my family died in Germany and Poland because not enough people stood up to the Nazis. Where were the newspapers when the Nazis stormed Jewish businesses on Kristallnacht[6]? Where were the investigative reporters when the Nazis burned the Reichstag?

"The Nazis first attacked the Jewish papers and any other critics who questioned where the country was headed. If reporters and newspapers had stuck together at the start, maybe the Nazis would have been defeated before they took power.

"Gradually, all the other papers were taken over and had to support the Third Reich. Inch by inch, small freedom by small freedom, the Nazis sliced another bit of power away from individuals. One day, everyone looked up and realized that the Government had all the power, and then it was too late to do anything about it.

"I took your job because it seemed the best way to work my way into a writing position. I figured if I did a good job at whatever task you gave me, you might be willing to give me a chance as a reporter."

"That was a good plan, Mack. I'd like to give you a chance at writing a real story. Are you interested? You can use those extra hours on the weekends to be a reporter – at least if you show that you can handle it. How does that sound?"

"Oh, *wunderbar*, Mr. Geiger. You won't regret this. I'll do a good job for you. I really will."

"You'd better, Mack. If you turn in an unintelligible jumble of incoherent gibberish with grammar so poor it would shock a Florida cracker[7], it won't be printed, and it'll be the last thing you write for me. Understand?"

"Of course, Mr. Geiger. Just give me chance."

"I've got the perfect story for you, Mack. Coach Normand at Winter Free High keeps telling me that his second base combination has Major League potential, and you know those two boys well, don't you?"

"Yes, sir – Blake Holmes and Hale Wending. They really are good."

"If you think that you can write a story about them that would interest our readers, you've got the assignment. It's due in the next issue, so I want to see your draft on Monday."

"Oh, yes, Mr. Geiger."

"And one more thing," Geiger chuckled, "Try not to mix in any German words or syntax." Geiger had noted Mack's tendency to revert occasionally to German when he got excited.

Interviewing Blake and Hale would be easy since he saw them at school every day. Moreover, Mack was a good player himself, so he could write with knowledgeable experience. In fact, Mack would have made the team had he not decided to use his time at *The Gazette* instead of on the ball field.

Mack sought out Coach Normand first. Normand had coached against or mentored almost a dozen past and present Major Leaguers over the last twenty years, so he had a solid frame of reference to judge the potential of his current prized pair.

"Blake, as a high school sophomore," Normand told Mack, "is already capable of competing in the low minors. Hale is not quite as far advanced, because he is a year younger and has still not put on the weight that he needs to hit with more power. Defensively, though, he is Blake's peer."

Mack got Normand to open up on how he convinced the school board to allow Hale into Winter Free High as its first black student. Normand acknowledged some residual discontent from a few on the board, but that Hale's scholarly efforts – already it appeared that Hale was the likely valedictorian for the Class of 1954 – as well as his dignity and good cheer won over most of the original objectors. Normand would not name the hold-outs.

Blake and Hale proved to be good interviewees. They told a story from earlier in the season about a team from Lakeford whose coach was unhappy to see Hale in uniform before a game. He was grumbling that his team might refuse to take the field if they had to play against a Negro player.

Jackie Robinson and Luke Easter had broken the color barrier in the two Major Leagues several years earlier, but a lot of bias continued in lower leagues, both professional and amateur, especially in the South.

"Coach didn't start me in that game due to a bruised knee I suffered in a game earlier in the week," Blake recalled. "So I was kind of relaxing around home plate, chatting with some of the Lakeford players during their batting practice. That's when I learned about the problem with their coach.

"The Lakeford kids were fine with playing the game. It was their old coach who was being the jerk. I told Coach Normand what I had heard, and he sent me back with a solution."

Hale joined in explaining, "Blake came out to my second base position as I started taking practice grounders and told me that Coach wanted me to boot every third one and to make a limp-armed throw to first on the grounders I did catch."

"Making so many errors was not as difficult as I thought it might be," Hale told Mack. "I just pretended I was Blake." Hale laughed as he took a glancing blow to his bicep from the unfairly maligned Blake.

"While Hale started his error prone display during fielding practice," Blake said. "I eased up to the Lakeford player I'd been speaking with earlier and put out the fib that Coach Normand gave me.

"'We've already won two games this year by forfeit,' I told the kid, laughing, 'when the opposing school refused to take the field. Coach uses the clumsy colored kid whenever we face a tough team like yours. He tries to goad the other coach into walking off the field.'"

"Well, sure enough, the kid scoots right over to his coach and points out to Hale, who is mangling the grounders like he was wearing a concrete block instead of a glove, and bouncing and sailing throws past Dexter at first who doesn't know what's going on and can't believe what he is seeing. We don't hear anything about Lakeford forfeiting after that.

"Then Hale led off the game with a soft liner to left center, and he catches the Lakeford outfield half asleep with lackadaisical fielding. Before the left fielder knows what's going on, Hale speeds into second on what should have been no more than a single.

"That caused the old coach to begin hollering at his outfielder so mercilessly that the pitcher was distracted."

Hale added, "When a pitcher is not paying attention, that opens up the running game. I stole third standing up because the pitcher was paying more attention to the coach's screaming instead of to me on base, and boy-oh-boy, did that set off their coach even more. He laid into the poor kid so hard that he balked me home before the next pitch.

"Their coach finally got control of himself at that point, because he could see he was hurting his team."

"Despite Hale's quick first run," Blake said, "the game turned into a pitcher's duel. The kid stepped up after that poor start and held us to two more hits and no more runs through the ninth.

"Dolder was pitching for us, and he was a lot better than usual, taking a shutout into the bottom of the ninth. Coach put me in for defense for the final inning after my substitute pulled a hamstring running out a grounder the previous inning. Up to that time, Hale had handled only one grounder all day, so their coach really did not sense that we had snookered him."

"Dolder began to tire in the ninth, loading the bases with one out, with Lakeford's best RBI guy, a left-handed clean-up hitter, coming up. Coach Normand brought in Lefty McGill to replace Dolder.

"On a three-two pitch, Lefty gives up a scorcher up the middle that looked like the game winner for them, but Hale launched one of his patented dives. He backhanded the ball on a short hop and flipped it to me from behind his back while still sliding on his belly. The play was borderline impossible."

"Blake nabbed the ball bare-handed, did a 270," Hale interjected, "and completed the double play like it was something we did every day."

"The runner I forced at second," Blake added, "was the kid I had spoken with before the game. He looked up at me from the ground and complained, 'I thought you said that colored second baseman was all thumbs.'"

"'Oh, he really is bad,' I told him. 'He can only make the easy plays like that one. Anything remotely difficult, and he is worthless.'

"I think he could have swallowed a swarm of bees as long as he sat on second base with his mouth wide open."

MACK'S story found a very receptive editor in Geiger, who read it while standing at the press.

In his head, Geiger reversed the order of two of Mack's sentences, broke up two long paragraphs, and added one marginal comma for clarity. Otherwise he planned to run the article as Mack had written it.

"Son, you combined the humor and social commentary better than I could have. You are a natural."

"Thank you, sir. My original article was about four times as long, but

I cut out a lot. I knew that it would be too long for the paper."

That statement caused Geiger to pause. "What things did you cut out?"

"I interviewed several members of the school board who voted on Hale entering Winter Free High. Only one refused to talk with me. I also left out comments from Mr. and Mrs. Wending and from two opposing coaches."

"You did all that in the few days I gave you?" Geiger asked. "How did you get time to gather all that?"

"The school board met Friday, so I was able to grab the members before and after the meeting. Politicians seldom turn down an opportunity to get their names in the paper. You taught me that, sir."

Geiger chuckled, "So I did."

"And Winter Free had two games last week, so the opposing coaches were readily available. I'm always out at the Wendings anyway, so that part was easy."

"You don't happen to have the longer version with you, do you, Mack?" Geiger asked, an idea slowly germinating in his head.

Mack reached into his leather case, pulled out a loose stack of paper, and handed it to Geiger. "Please notice that it's kind of a tangled mess, and I did not do final editing on it, sir. I only did that on the version that I turned in."

Geiger went to his cluttered desk and sat down to read the longer version. When he finished, he said, "Son, we are not going to run your article this week."

Mack could not hide the disappointed look on his face.

"Don't be so sad," Geiger admonished with a big smile, "Hear me out.

"These items you cut out: human interest with the parents, especially Harrison Wending talking about giving up his dream of playing for the Kansas City Monarchs[8] for his family, and Mrs. Wending insisting that her children outwork every other student in the class; plus conflict on the school board and the decisive split vote to allow Hale to attend Winter Free High. These are too good to leave out.

"But you are right. With all of that, there is too much for an article. This larger piece, though, has the feel of a series, a series of three or four articles. What do you say about that? Do you want to take on a series?"

"Gee, Mr. Geiger. I don't know what to say. Of course I want to do a series. Do you really think I can?"

"Yes, or I would not have suggested it. Next week we'll run your first article. You can use most of what you wrote in the short version. In the meantime, see if you can get to the remaining board member and more opposing coaches.

"The Lakeford coach would be a prime interviewee. Has he changed his attitude, or is he still stuck in the last century? You can use my office phone for the long distance call.

"Add some other teammates' comments and maybe a few from spectators at a game, and interview some of the boys' teachers. Are there any games this week?"

"Yes, sir – two."

"Get me a draft of Article One on Thursday, and give me a report on your progress at the same time. If we promise the readers a series, I need to make sure that we – you – can deliver the subsequent articles. Okay, then, don't keep standing here. Get going."

***BICK*** Bennington stretched out in a seat in the mostly deserted outfield stands at Sarasota's Payne Park. He had departed the chilly press box for the comfort of the warm sun in the cheap seats.

As usual, the aging Red Sox were trailing badly in the ninth, and Bick's already written story was ready to be filed – pending an unlikely miracle by the Sox.

He reached for a discarded local weekly, an unfamiliar *Winter Free Gazette*, which someone had abandoned on the adjoining seat.

"I wonder who broke a toe or picked up a littering ticket in the sticks," he thought idly about the expected content. Glancing at the first page, he noticed a baseball article – something about a high school short-stop and second baseman. He paid a bit more attention. He scanned the article as he waited for a final pitch from a wild armed Brooklyn Dodgers' rookie whose misguided missiles were prolonging the game mercilessly.

By the time the last out had been recorded, Bick was on his third reading of the article. "Man, this is good. We need to run this back home."

Glancing up for the first time in quite a while, he realized that the game was over. He made his way on to the field where players were being interviewed. He waited while a *New York Herald Tribune* writer finished with the Dodgers' Duke Snider.

Thrusting *The Gazette* toward the reporter, he said, "Hey, Al, take a look at this article."

"What? Did you get a new job writing for them, or did you pick up a paper route as a sideline?"

"Wise guy. Read the baseball article on the first page."

After a quick glance at the headline, Al said, "C'mon, Bick, what do

I want with an article about some kids playing high school ball? Let's get a beer."

"I'll buy the beer if you read the article."

"Deal. You haven't sprung for a drink since '49."

"Just read and spare me the insults."

Al devoted less than a minute on the article, just skimming the first page in a reporter's speed reading way. By the time he neared the bottom of the first column, however, he had become curious and interested. He returned to the beginning and re-read more methodically.

When Al turned the page for the continuation, he remarked, "This Stein's a good writer. Mack Stein – hmm, wonder why I haven't heard of him. You know the guy?"

"Nah. Never ran into him, but he knows his stuff and has a flair for getting to the real meaning in a way that anyone would understand it. This is a great article. Says it is the first in a series.

Bick added, "I'm going to recommend that we pick it up. Our readers will eat it up in Boston – at least the ones who can see past color."

"Maybe you ought to show it to Red Sox management, Bick. When are your guys going to break the color barrier?"

"No time soon that I can see. We've got no blacks in the minors who look good. The Sox seem to show no interest in scouting black players. I think they'd find some excuse to pass on Satchel Paige in his prime – too tall, too thin, too fast, too precise, but the real reason: too black. There'll be a half dozen more teams coming aboard in the next year or two, but the Red Sox won't be one of them."

"I think I'll pass this article upstairs myself, Bick. Thanks." Pulling out his pen, he said, "Let me jot down the details. It'd read well in New York too."

**BOTH** *The Globe* out of Boston and the *New York Herald Tribune* contacted Geiger and obtained permission to re-publish Mack's series. Most of the other large dailies around the country, reacting to the critical acclaim, quickly picked it up from United Press.

Though Mack's series was as much social commentary as a sports story, reflecting more on the changing social consciousness talking place in the South than on baseball, most papers ran it on their sports pages.

A lesser number printed the series on their first page. A paper in Cleveland that did so was the first to ask *The Gazette* for biographic information about the reporter, Mack Stein. That was the first time that Geiger had become aware of the widespread dissemination of his prize reporter's work.

He chuckled to himself as he drafted a bio for Mack and sent it to *The Cleveland Press.* "Wait until the country finds out that the reporter on the hottest current story is a high school kid."

**THE** news amazed readers and reporters alike. Not only was the writer a high school student, but English wasn't even his first language. A few over-enthusiastic commentators hailed him as the next Joseph Conrad[9].

Before long, *The Gazette* was inundated with requests from as far away as the *Paris Herald Tribune* for interviews of the famous reporter. Geiger controlled access to Mack. A youngster could get a "big head' mighty quickly if too much attention came his way, and Geiger was intent on making certain that this did not occur with Mack.

"Mack, it is easy to begin believing that you are like the sun, and that the world revolves around you. Stay as level-headed as you are now. You may go on to great things and be an enormous success – I rather think that you will – but anyone, you included, can wake up some morning and find that his hat no longer fits."

That made Mack chuckle. "I appreciate what you are saying, Mr. Geiger, but you don't need to worry. I'm always hanging around Hale Wending, and he already told me he'd slap me down in a second if I got too uppity about all the fuss."

# CHAPTER 4

## Prepping for the Coup

*It's not the voting that's democracy, it's the counting.*

DOTTY, IN *JUMPERS*

TOM STOPPARD

**JANUARY 1952**

Two months before Batista's coup, Cruz and Meyer Lansky[10] had finalized their plans with him. Lansky, a Las Vegas based gangster, wanted to expand his lucrative casino holdings in Cuba. Cruz sought political influence. Batista could almost taste the presidency.

"I will have the army support you, Fulgencio," Cruz encouraged. "It is the only way you are going to become president. If your campaign showed more promise, we could rig enough votes to put you over the top, in much the way big city vote fraud has helped candidates in the U.S. since the days of New York's Boss Tweed[11]. But you are too behind for that kind of effort to help."

"My people can offer some persuasion money to bring around army officers that need a financial push," Lansky offered. "Cruz has this lined up. Listen to him, Fulgencio."

"Thank you, Meyer," Cruz began. "As you know, the Auténtico Party has been staging violent protests. These are actually the work of my men in the Sierra Maestra. The protests are making many in the middle class uneasy, including army officers.

"In any event, both of the candidates running against you are from the two parties that are suspected by the army of evil intent. I have the army primed to help you pull off a coup."

"I need about two months to work my magic. Just say the word, and you will be president by March."

Batista looked each man in the eyes, watched the smoke curl up from his cigar, and nodded slightly in assent.

On March 10, he overthrew the Prío Government and ended Cuban democracy, imperfect as it had been, for what would eventually be the remainder of the Twentieth Century.

# CHAPTER 5

## *Prison*

*I would rather be a coward than brave*
*because people hurt you when you are brave.*

E. M. FORSTER (AS A CHILD)

**AUGUST 1952**

The door to the solitary confinement cell slammed shut with a solid metallic clang. Clem Hostetter allowed a long breath to escape as he reclined on the woefully thin mattress. He felt the cot's inhospitable springs pushing into his back, but took reassurance from the discomfort.

"Not the best room in the house," he muttered, "But a lot better than where I could be laid out about now."

Clem had entered the Raiford State Prison, Florida's largest, in February of 1951 after a brief trial. As the only culprit captured of the four men who attacked Sally and The Crew, he suffered the brunt of the Winter Free jury's ire. An unsympathetic judge sentenced him to fifty-five years on the many charges, including assault, battery, attempted robbery (armed), and kidnapping.

With good behavior, Clem might be paroled after thirty years. In any event, he was in for a long stay.

Actually, Clem tolerated prison life rather well. True, he missed the freedom to go where he wanted to go and do what he wanted to do when he wanted to do it. And he did miss his beer the most. But on balance, until the recent problem, he thought his life was not too bad at Raiford.

He received three free meals each day – not the best food, but filling and better than what he had been eating when he lived with Dredman, one of the criminals who died in the attack. Moreover, he did not have to put up with landlords complaining about his falling behind on the rent. In prison, the heat and electricity were never cut off for non-payment.

He did not get to pick his cellmate, and the wrong one could be a real problem to be sure. His fellow occupant, Quintana Montagard, seemed to be working out well enough, though.

Like other prisoners, Hostetter had to do a little work; Raiford produced the state car tags – or license plates, as he called them when he lived in Detroit. Clem disliked working on tags, but the production levels were low, and nobody complained about his efforts as long as he kept a reasonably steady pace. Anyway, the tempo was quite a bit slower than in the factories where he had worked intermittently in years past.

After a few months, guards and the warden regarded Clem as a "perfect prisoner." He was respectful, did what he was told, and caused no problems. So it was a surprise when Clem created a ruckus in the prison kitchen.

Without any apparent cause, he had scattered dozens of pots and pans against the walls and ovens, tossed racks of bread everywhere, and sprayed water on nearly every surface including the electrical fuse box. Then, with the other kitchen help standing back and staring incredulously, he had meekly given up when the guards approached.

"What have you to say for yourself, Hostetter?" the warden had wanted to know a short time later. "Was there a dispute of some sort? Did someone make you angry?"

Clem had refused to answer. He simply stared at the floor in complete silence.

"I have no alternative but to send you to Solitary," the warden continued. "You give us no explanation, and you caused quite a bit of damage."

Clem had not replied, and he trudged off to Solitary escorted by two wary guards, alert to the possibility of another outburst of bizarre behavior. But Clem had resumed demonstrating his usual docile demeanor. As the guards closed the cell door, they had given each other a shrug.

One offered, "It's hard to gauge these prisoners from one day to the next, but I thought I had Hostetter pegged as a reasonable guy. Wonder what set him off."

"Beats me. You just can't take these guys for granted. They wouldn't be in here if they were well balanced."

Clem heard the byplay as the guards moved away from the door. Unlike some dumb people who had inflated opinions of themselves, he recognized that he was not very intelligent. Unlike many lazy people, he knew that he lacked the energy of most men. But one thing that he did possess in abundance was a strong feeling of self-preservation.

For a few moments, his mind wandered as his eyes followed the spider web of cracks on the bare concrete walls. Then he recalled his many interviews with Sheriff Elsmore, the prosecutor, and other law enforcement officials before the trial. Clem saw no reason to lie, mislead, or deny. They had him cold. The witnesses were believable and numerous, and the attack was without mitigating circumstances.

While recovering from his injuries, and even though he was a bit woozy from all the pain killers and other medicines, he hung on to the fiction that he did not know that The Cuban's name was Cruz Cruz.

"Look, Clem," he remembered Elsmore cajoling, "You told us that 'Smith' has a double name. Why can't you tell us what it is?"

In fact, Clem had initially forgotten Cruz Cruz's name and had explained that it was Spanish sounding and duplicated. Only some days after divulging those facts did it occur to him that he was heading down a dangerous path. Cruz, he learned, had escaped and was not likely to take kindly to Clem sending the authorities his way. At that point, Clem clammed up about The Cuban.

"Really, Sheriff," he lied repeatedly. "I only heard The Cuban's name once. I was drunk. It was a noisy dive up in Detroit, and a bar fight broke out right afterward. I'm lucky I even remembered that it was a repeated name. I'm sure that I wouldn't even recognize his name if you told it to me.

"Since then, he was always The Cuban to me. Dredman never called him anything but The Cuban."

The truth of these latter two points helped Clem show sincerity.

It was also Hostetter who deflected the sheriff's attention to Detroit when the focus should have been the Ybor City area of Tampa. Clem was aware that Cruz was involved in some sort of fish wholesale business in the nearby Florida city, but Clem also realized that having The Cuban as an enemy was not a healthy situation.

Clem hoped that Cruz would eventually discover that he was the source of the misdirection that kept Cruz's identity secret. He reasoned that a grateful Cruz might offer him some assistance in the future but would at least refrain from coming after him.

Recovering in Cuba from two of Carty's arrow wounds, Cruz grasped rather quickly that the authorities had not identified him, and newspaper accounts of the story revealed that Hostetter claimed not to know his name. The tentative nature of the questioning of Gilbert and Maldonado about Cruz's Rex Seafood business was evidence that Hostetter had not pinpointed the business either.

Unfortunately for Hostetter, there were two overriding issues that he failed to consider. One was that Cruz could not be sure if Hostetter truly forgot the Cruz name with the risk that his memory might improve over time. The second was that Cruz did not care. Hostetter was a loose end, and the end was blowing in the breeze – sorely in need of scissors, preferably very sharp scissors, and scissors not to be used for the normal purpose intended.

Hostetter was enough of a realist, though, to stay alert for anyone looking to do him harm. He knew that Cruz might or might not come after him despite his silence, but in prison it made sense to always be prepared for unprovoked violence from other inmates for any reason or for no reason. After all, Raiford was not populated by members of the Mormon Tabernacle Choir.

*THE* attempt on Clem's life occurred on a typically sunny and warm Florida day, conditions Clem enjoyed. He finished a cigarette while talking with Quintana and a couple of other prisoners in the crowded exercise yard.

"It's a little too hot for me," Quintana said. "I think I'll head back in early." The others in the small group agreed, but Clem, as usual, said he would stay to get the full benefit of the nice weather. Clem used his last match on another cigarette and wandered aimlessly around the yard along the wall. He glanced up at the guard tower on the far corner of the red brick barrier and wondered if the guard had ever fired on a prisoner attempting to escape.

Probably no more than three minutes had elapsed since Quintana left, but in that short time, the entire yard of several hundred prisoners had been vacated – well before the end of the exercise period. As soon as Clem looked down from the tower and realized that he was alone in the vast yard, he realized that he was in serious trouble. All of the other inmates had obviously heard something and departed.

Instinctively, he knew that someone was coming after him, and he had little doubt that Cruz was behind it. "What do I do now?" his mind raced. There were only two ways back inside. "Would Cruz have someone waiting at both entrances?" he wondered.

"I'm probably safe here. No one would want to risk being seen by a guard in the two corner towers. He will want the isolation of the interior hall. There is always the chance that a tower guard is involved, but not likely two of them."

The exercise period bell rang, seemingly much louder than usual. It made Clem jump. He looked at the two entrances and decided on the farthest one. It was the better choice, but it only delayed the inevitable. As Clem walked toward that door, he noticed movement from the other entrance.

Though the assassin had chosen the wrong door, it was clear that he intended to correct that mistake. He came back into the yard with the intention of catching up to Clem in the other hall. Clem picked up his pace to a brisk walk. He refused to look at his stalker. He could tell that the following footsteps echoing in the empty yard's concrete floor were moving faster than his own.

Clem moved up to a jog, but the steps behind hastened to a faster rate. When Clem broke into a full run, it did him little good. He was not a fast runner, and his pursuer, apparently in better shape, was clearly gaining.

When Clem pulled open the door, he sensed that he had little more than a few feet lead. Inside, he passed a cart of dirty dishes that looked helpful. Rushing past, he reached back and swiped the cart into the middle of the hall. He took brief satisfaction at the crashing and clanging behind him but held little belief that his luck would hold.

There were guards around the corner at the far end of the hall, but Clem had no confidence that he could get that far before being grabbed. That is when he realized that he was at the back door to the prison cafeteria. Without a moment's hesitation, Clem stormed into the kitchen and began throwing bread, condiments, and every loose utensil against the walls. Then he grabbed a hose and began spraying water everywhere.

None of the prisoners working in the kitchen tried to stop him. They knew what was planned for the day – word gets around fast on the prison grapevine – and while these men were neither enemies nor friends, the fight was not theirs. If Clem chose this noisy method to avoid being killed, it was not in their interest to interfere on one side or the other.

The mystery man made no attempt to follow Clem into the kitchen when he heard the cacophony of metallic clatter and spraying water. Better to try another day than to risk too large a witness pool. He could rely somewhat on the prisoner code of silence, but with too many prisoners, the chances were greater that one might turn stoolie for a reduced sentence.

"Cruz isn't going to like hearing that I missed on my first try," Quintana thought to himself, "But I'll get a second chance tomorrow." That is when Quintana underestimated Hostetter's survival instincts a second time. Clem's ruckus in the kitchen got him a predictable fifteen days in Solitary where no one could get at him.

Of course, it would have been easy for Quintana to have taken Clem out at an earlier time in their cell, but Quintana had no interest in adding a death sentence to his current stretch, especially as he was likely to be paroled in a month. It is not easy to fake innocence when you are the only one in a locked cell with a dead man sporting a make-shift knife in his back.

Earlier, Cruz had dispatched his ever helpful accountant, Miguel Maldonado, to instruct Quintana at Raiford. Maldonado flew from Havana to Savannah and drove to the north Florida penitentiary.

"I don't want you flying through Tampa, even though that is an easier route. It's not a high probability, but someone might recognize you as the man who previously passed through Immigration under a fake Cruz Cruz passport. Appearing as Maldonado would be asking for trouble.

"Quintana knows that you are coming. I sent him a benign letter under your name but with enough references to his activities in the Sierra Maestra with me to know you will be my emissary. There was nothing in the letter to suggest what I am seeking, because the mail is examined by the guards."

In the years between the world wars, Cruz had provided military training for a small group of men in the southeastern Sierra Maestra Mountains of Cuba. The roving band served as a protector for Cruz's tobacco plantation while causing problems for his competitor planters. Quintana rose to second in charge during those years, and was one of the few men Cruz considered trustworthy.

During WWII, Quintana had helped at the American Embassy in Havana, and he was rewarded with a green card after the war. Unfortunately, his rum smuggling skills were less effective than his military abilities, and he was caught in a sting operation in Miami. The Feds considered him a minor player, so they allowed state officials to prosecute. He ended up at Raiford where he had another three years to serve unless he was paroled next month, and his clean record augured well for that result.

Cruz was patient. He knew that Quintana might need some time but believed that Hostetter had no way to avoid the inevitable. What Cruz failed to consider was the early stages of a social plague that was beginning to take hold within the American criminal judicial system.

# CHAPTER 6

## *Cash Corbane*

*Unfortunately, what many people forget is that judges
are just lawyers in robes.*

TAMMY BRUCE

**AUGUST 1952**

Cash Corbane received his law degree from a little known Missouri college that closed up shop two years after he was graduated. The quality of instruction was so poor that few of the graduates managed to pass bar examinations. Cash, though, had no trouble. He returned to his Florida home state and slipped through the bar examination by hiring a disgraced and disbarred attorney to take the examination for him.

That simple expedient set the tone for Cash's career. As a moderately successful criminal attorney, Cash was always one step away from joining his clients on the other side of the vertical bars. He learned as much from his clients as he did from the law books.

Nevertheless, Cash was a voracious reader of legal texts, court decisions, and Florida statutes. When there was a loophole, Cash exploited it. When there was no loophole, Cash created one.

Any moral person would have been appalled at the plaque on the desk in his office that read, "Lawyers don't do what is right; lawyers do what is legal." Cash, however, took pride in it.

Though Cash had no connection with the Hostetter case, he did know the public defender, Bill "Beef" Belson, who had been assigned to the penniless defendant.

Cash frequented lawyers' taverns near to the courthouses in a dozen towns and cities in southwest Florida. This day he sat on a tall barstool in The Bar's Bar across from the courthouse in Tampa. He looked at his barmate in the large ornate mirror that had been there long enough to reflect on some of Teddy Roosevelt's Rough Riders marshalling for the invasion of Cuba about fifty years earlier.

Beef was exactly what his name suggested: big, burly, and possessing a deep voice that resonated well beyond his immediate surroundings.

Cash's squeaky voice and thin, stoop-shouldered build contrasted sharply with Beef's. Cash wore a silver sharkskin suit that was almost a trademark for him. He sported a paisley tie, thin to match the jacket's narrow lapels. Topped with mixed black and gray slicked-back hair and long ears flattened close to his head, Cash appeared like a human form of Flash Gordon's rocket ship.

"I'm about ready to give up on Hostetter," Beef disclosed. "I've tried everything I can come up with, but it is as cut and dry a case as any I've seen: caught in the act, weapon recovered at the scene of the crime with his fingerprints on it; five credible eye witnesses, full confession. I'm concerned about the guy, though. He has been telling me that the other surviving man in the operation, the ringleader, is trying to kill him.

"I don't know if Hostetter is going batty or not, but he frequently creates disturbances in the prison in order to stay in solitary confinement, because it is the only place where he feels safe from the other inmates. He'll never get out early for good behavior at that rate, but he really believes that he is being targeted."

"What's the motive? He seems like a small timer, Beef."

"He is really vague about that. The best that I can guess is that they apparently left a lot of money on the table when the caper blew up, and the ringleader is afraid that Hostetter might get back his memory and identify him before he can return to finish the job."

"Do you believe any of that?"

"I really don't know, but the guy is truly scared. Of that I have no doubts."

The magic words for Cash were, "They apparently left a lot of money on the table."

"I feel sorry for the guy, Beef. What would you say if I agreed to take on the case and relieve the state of the expense? I'd like to take a crack at it."

"I don't for one moment believe that you have an altruistic cell in your body, Cash, but I'm grateful for anything to relieve my workload. You are welcome to the Hostetter case. I'll inform the judge and introduce you to your new client by telephone."

Cash gave Beef a thumbs-up sign.

"Sammy," Beef called to the bartender, "another Old Overholt for my friend here, and put that one on my tab."

A few days later, Cash drove up to Raiford and interviewed Clem in depth. Afterward, Cash advised him to carry on with his efforts to stay in Solitary. What Cash lacked in ethics, he overflowed in fake sincerity.

Clem took to him on the first visit. He opened up and gave Cash information that he had kept from Beef. Clem retained only Cruz's name in reserve, continuing the fiction that he could not remember it.

# CHAPTER 7

## *The Wedding*

*Mawage. Mawage is wot bwings us togeder tooday.*
THE IMPRESSIVE CLERGYMAN IN THE MOVIE,
*THE PRINCESS BRIDE*

**SEPTEMBER 1952**

September 6 was Sally's big day. She had accepted Sheriff James Elsmore's proposal on Christmas Eve the previous year, and September was the month they chose for the ceremony.

James and Sally had to sort out the financial situation before they were ready to marry. It had proven to be almost an insurmountable obstacle. Counting Sally's known wealth, she was the richest person in the county, and maybe Southwest Florida. An ancestor brought a fortune to

Florida in the early 1700s, and the family's careful stewardship over the following centuries expanded the wealth.

Sally insisted that the fortune presented no problem to their union, but James did not agree. On the one hand, he did not want or expect Sally to give up her family's wealth. On the other, he considered it unseemly to marry into a fortune and could not bring himself to take advantage of it. He had been brought up in an era when the husband was expected to be the family's breadwinner. The impasse continued with neither finding a solution as time moved on.

Sally had celebrated her twenty-ninth birthday the previous year, reaching an age where she feared she might soon be too old for children. In desperation, she sought advice from Lilliquest Andersson, her neighbor east of Morose Swamp and Carty's great aunt. Over tall glasses of Lilly Lemonade – the juice of five lemons to one orange – the two women discussed James' reluctance to marry into a fortune.

"Lilly, James wants to marry me, but he does not want to marry my money. If we do not find a solution soon, it will be too late for me to have children, and I really want a big brood," she laughed. "Besides, I love that man, and I'm not going to find anyone who could replace him."

Lilly looked around the Canfield house that she had seen only from the outside previously. The house was large enough to have sheltered the original Canfield clan of over twenty when they first arrived over two centuries ago to escape rumors of witchcraft.

Like the manor house that Lilly's father had left her, Sally's place was way too large for one single occupant. But neither woman wanted to leave the house where she had lived most of her life.

The main room in the Canfield Mansion was bordered by a massive fireplace with a seven by seven foot opening. From the 1700s until Sally put in electricity a short time ago, it had provided all the cooking area and most of the night lighting.

The back wall was lined with shelves of books in quantities that exceeded the county library's holdings. The rough exposed roof beams and rustic furnishings were reminiscent of a large lodge in a national park.

There were a few hidden tricks in the house, such as escape routes, that Sally had used to thwart the evil intentions of Cruz Cruz and his cohorts a few years earlier.

"Dear," Lilly replied, "I wish that I had had your problem when I was your age. At thirty and younger, I could never find a potential husband whom I thought had more interest in me than in the Andersson fortune. And your problem is that your suitor does not feel comfortable with the wealth that you have.

"As it is, I thought of so many scenarios for my own situation that I do have one possibility in mind that might work for you."

**SHORTLY** after Cruz's attack on Sally, James had bought the adjoining Hostetter farm that had served as the base of operations for the criminals. He saw Sally nearly every day since then, and by that time, was ready to grasp at any straw that could overcome the impasse. And so it was that Sally presented James with Lilly's solution.

The couple would live solely on James' income from his sheriff's position and on the rental income from the old Hostetter farm once he moved from it into her Canfield Mansion. Sally would be limited to using her money only for improvements to the mansion and property, gifts to friends, and for educational and charitable activities. She would not be permitted to use any for day to day living.

James thought about the concept as they sat in front of the fire on Christmas Eve, sipping grog that Sally had prepared from a Scottish family recipe. James was off duty, so he savored the hot aromatic rum drink that was heavy with cloves, cinnamon, honey, and other spices. Finally, James took her hand and shook it.

"Agreed on the business arrangements," he said formally. "And now the important part."

Dropping to one knee in front of her and still holding her hand, he looked deeply into her bright green eyes, and asked warmly, "Will you marry me, Sally Canfield?"

Sally raised an eyebrow, tilted her chin upward slightly, and replied solemnly, "What makes you think I would want to marry the likes of you, a poorly compensated law enforcement officer?"

She couldn't wait for a reply to her own silly question. Instead, she knelt on the floor next to him, kissed him warmly, and said, "Of course I will marry you! I've wanted to marry you since I first saw you when I was a teenager."

*SALLY* was the last of the Canfield clan, so she had no close relatives to help her with the wedding. Lilly, Carty, and Carty's mother, Bay, jumped in as substitutes. Carty and Bay served as attendants with Lilly as the Maid of Honor.

James asked Carty's father, Michael, to be his Best Man. They had grown close over the years as their WWII experiences created a bond typical of veterans.

On the wedding day, Gardner Ensign, the long-tenured president of the bank that his and Sally's ancestors had helped to establish over a century earlier, walked Sally down the aisle to hand her off to James.

Lilly offered her expansive yard as the reception facility. The manor house had been built by her father when he developed the sugar plantation that bordered it. It was a delightful location for the celebration.

The crowd was large and festive. As county sheriff, James was well known in political circles, so he felt compelled to invite prominent citizens and area politicians. Though he no longer reigned as the youngest of the sheriffs in Florida, he had held that status for several years and achieved more than a little fame in the state as a result. Even the governor took in the wedding at St. Mark's Episcopal Church.

Homer Hamlin, proprietor of the first and still most popular grocery store in Winter Free, supplied most of the food for the party, so he was happy to arrive early and eat as much of it as he could.

Vosmik Novotny chauffeured part of the large Wending family in his huge gray Checker, the yellow version of which served taxi fleets. He had grown very close to the Wendings since his retirement from the legal profession and a rumored undercover stint in the Office of Strategic Services (OSS) during World War II. The OSS was the forerunner of the CIA and the country's first formal spy agency.

A few years earlier, Winter Free's mayor had presented the town's Citizenship Medals to The Crew's members for their part in fighting off the attack at Sally's house. At that medal ceremony, Hale Wending publicly praised Novotny for his help. While still on stage with the mayor, Hale gave his medal to Novotny, and since then, Novotny had become almost part of the Wending family.

In most of 1952 central Florida, the sight of white and black families mingling in a festive social setting would have been shocking, or at minimum, distracting. But the Wendings had effortlessly melded themselves into much of the Winter Free social life. The family matriarch was as learned and cultured a woman as any, having been a teacher and part of a large land owning family in the Bahamas before marrying and moving to Florida.

The Anderssons, dating back to Lilly's father, Sven, led the way for racial tolerance in Winter Free. His sugar operation was the area's first major employer to pay equal wages to black and white workers. A delegation of the town's leading citizens met with him as he began operations around 1920. They sought to convince him to pay the blacks at a lower pay scale.

"If you don't," they complained, "Other coloreds will want the same treatment from all the other employers."

"Good," he had answered, adding to their consternation.

"But," he added, "If you think the practice is too disruptive, I will close down the sugar operation, and then everyone will still make the same – nothing."

It was not a bluff. He was serious and financially capable of following through, and they knew it.

"Well, no," came the hasty reply. "We didn't mean that. We can live with your scheme if you insist. We just wanted you to understand the ramifications."

"Understood," he had replied curtly. From that time forward, Winter Free developed a continuously improving racial harmony that always stayed steps ahead of the rest of the country, North or South.

Not the least important development in this movement was the election of James Elsmore as sheriff, promoted strongly by Lilly Andersson. James' even-handedness kept the community together when someone of either race ran astray. He won re-election without opposition and was rumored to be the Democrats' choice for a number of higher state offices if he chose.

In mid-century Florida, Democrats held complete power. Many white Floridians still resented Republicans for their strong support of the Union and blacks during and after the Civil War.

Few of the other guests were close friends of the bride and groom. Sally had never developed relationships with townsfolk because of legends that she was from a long line of Salem witches. Nevertheless, her circle of acquaintances was growing.

The fear that previously gripped most of the town with her presence was dissipating. In fact, that reputation, previously terrifying to most of the residents, was probably what drew many of the curious who were invited to the wedding. A chance to look at a witch dressed in white was too incongruous to miss.

Among the guests were Denton Dolder and his family that included his eldest son, Haywood. Sally had objected to their inclusion on the guest list even as James insisted.

"Dolder's Chevy Dealership is the town's biggest business after Ensign Bank, and Denton is the chairman of the Chamber of Commerce.

It would be an insult to ignore him, and I am an elected official. It makes little sense to create an enemy without reason. Why do you dislike him so much? You've never even met the man."

"I have no feelings one way or the other for Mr. Dolder. It is his son Haywood I dislike. He used unfair tactics against Carty and the boys on a school project. I really would prefer that he did not show up, and I'm sure that The Crew would feel the same way."

"Sally, the boys see him at Winter Free High every day, and maybe Carty would like to reacquaint herself with him after going off to school in Sarasota. Besides, whatever he did years ago couldn't have been too terrible. I don't recall hearing about any of The Crew having academic problems when they were at Cross Creek Elementary."

Sally thought back to the night she had foiled Haywood's plans. She used her witch persona one final time to frighten him into giving up the botany specimen that he stole from The Crew. Immediately afterward, Sally buried all of her witch paraphernalia and began to join civilization. Despite the lapse of time, she did not feel comfortable telling James about that night's activity.

"Oh, they managed to overcome the problem, James. It is just the principle. But if you really need to invite the Dolder family, we will add them to the list."

"Thank you, dear. I owe you one," he had offered.

"Yes, you do," Sally had laughed, "And I plan to collect."

From the time Sally was a young girl, she had sewed all of her witch dresses, most from black satin material. She still liked the feel and look of the smooth, shiny finish.

For the wedding, though, she purchased the most expensive dress that Tampa had to offer. She was not yet married, so she felt free to spend money she would not be allowed to access for personal items once James became her husband.

She chose a shimmering white satin with the only variations being the veil, the slightest use of lace on the cuffs of the mid-length sleeves, and a three-inch wide powder blue ribbon securing the long train to her waist.

Her shoulders were mostly bare to give ample exposure to another of the famous Canfield family jewels, a blue topaz and diamond display that caught the sunlight spectacularly as it beamed though the stained glass windows of St. Mark's.

The necklace had become a minor crisis when Sally realized that she had forgotten to retrieve it from her Ensign Bank safe deposit vault. If she had not thought to squeeze her giant Ryland Ruby for good luck the day before the wedding, she would not have noticed in time to retrieve the topaz piece. Once again she resolved to prepare an inventory of the hundreds of Canfield jewels but failed to convince herself that she would follow through. She had promised herself that duty many times before, but never found time to do it.

As she walked up the aisle to Mendelssohn's Wedding March, her wispy red hair flowed backward in the breeze, the overhead fans catching it just right. She never once looked away from James, who was standing at the base of the altar in his dress blue sheriff's uniform.

In turn he followed her every step until Gardner Ensign handed her off to him. Sally felt as though she never wanted Rev. Carpenter to finish the ceremony. She was floating on an emotional cloud.

At Lilly's for the reception, Sally literally glowed. The bright Florida sun reflected off of her dress so brilliantly that onlookers had to divert their eyes after fleeting moments. The best location was near enough to her so that the radiance encompassed the bystander as well. But James gave little opportunity for anyone else to stay close for most of the first hour.

Eventually, Sally broke away from him. "This party is for the guests," she urged. "Mingle." Then with a twinkled eye that made his knees weak, she teased, "You'll have me all to yourself later tonight."

As the day wore on, guests settled down at the long tables on the grounds. Places in the shade of the old oaks were prized, but the autumn day was not too warm and lacked the humidity of the earlier months. A small combo played on the porch as several couples danced to Glenn Miller tunes.

No one went hungry. They mounded their plates high with typically southern dishes of fried chicken, country fried steak, biscuits and gravy, and green beans. For variety, Lilly added Swedish meatballs from an Andersson recipe.

Grits were served with large gobs of butter or sausage gravy, though Mack Stein generated good-natured joshing when, as usual for him, he poured sugar and cream on his. A few people, though, surreptitiously tried it out for themselves and grudgingly admitted that it was as good as the traditional fare.

Several kegs of beer flowed for those who did not partake of the Lilly Lemonade made with citrus gathered from trees on the grounds.

By the time the sun began setting, coffee was served with the wedding cake. Everyone enjoyed the festivities – everyone except Haywood Dolder, who had quietly huddled near his mother for most of the afternoon.

Earlier in the day, Sally excused herself from a throng of admirers. "I have to change these shoes into something more comfortable, or I may never walk again," she joked. As she entered Lilly's house, she removed her shoes. As she padded quietly through the hall, she caught unexpected movement from the corner of her eye. Someone appeared to be sneaking through the house.

She stopped and quietly watched as Haywood Dolder entered the kitchen where more lemonade waited in a large galvanized tub. He unscrewed the cap from a shiny silver flask and prepared to pour its contents into the lemonade.

In a voice that Sally hadn't used for over two years, she rasped, "What are you doing, Haywoooood Doooolder?"

He jumped back from the tub. He had heard that voice from his bedroom window on that eerie night years ago. But that sound had come from an ugly, black clad, smelly old hag on a broom, not the angel in shining white who stood before him now.

"I was right," he stammered. "You are a witch."

Sally ignored his accusation and pointed at the bottle in his hand. "I repeat. What are you doing?"

"Oh, this?" he asked, holding the bottle forward stiffly as if it might ward her off. "It's just a bottle of water. The lemonade seemed a bit too strong to me. I thought it would taste better if I added more water."

"The lemonade is just fine," she replied. "That's just water?"

"Yes, just water."

"That's good, because you look a little red and hot. You need a good drink of water. Why don't you drink yours?"

"Drink this? Now?"

"I think that would be a good idea, don't you?"

"Uh, I'm really not that thirsty."

"You look thirsty to me. Maybe we should visit your father and ask him if he thinks you should drink it. What do you think?"

"Oh, no, that won't be necessary, Miss Canfield. I am a bit thirsty, now that you mention it. I'll drink it here."

"Actually, my name is Mrs. Elsmore now."

Dolder took a large swallow from the flask, grimaced, and coughed, as eighty proof vodka coursed down his throat. She stared at him with the same cold glare that she had used that night years earlier. He saw terror personified standing before him and felt the same fear as she stepped slightly closer. He took another swallow.

"That took care of my thirst," he pleaded.

She said nothing but intensified her stare. He took two more large drinks, draining the contents.

"There," she said, "You look better already. You should join your parents now."

Dolder staggered slightly as he made his way out the back door, away from where Sally stood. By the time he reached the picnic table, the liquor was taking its toll, and he could barely walk. He eased on to the seat and leaned into his mother.

"What's wrong, dear?" his mother asked. "You look like you've seen a ghost."

"Not a ghost," he answered in a hushed voiced as he curled up against her and dozed off. "A witch."

About sundown, the crowd began to melt away. Several festive lights kept the dark at bay but attracted mosquitoes and other unpleasant insects. Sally thanked Lilly, Bay, and Carty for all that they had done. The multi-generational bond had grown strong.

James threatened to carry Sally to their house through the swamp unless she got into his car right away. Bay gave a knowing wink to Sally and shooed them toward the driveway.

Except for when they ate, The Crew had spent most of the afternoon in the shade of the citrus orchard. They were grateful that Dolder had not followed them, even though it appeared to have been the result of his falling ill. Carty had wanted to bring the boys up to date on her sighting in Havana and did not want nosy intrusions or typically obtuse comments from Dolder.

"This is the first time we've been together since I was in Havana with Elena. I've been holding this news back, because I wanted to tell all of you together. One day, while we were near the University of Havana, I spotted our old friend 'Mr. Smith' who led the attack at Sally's house."

While Hale and Blake stared open mouthed, Mack asked, "Are you sure?"

"Of course she's sure," Blake interjected. "I've known Carty all her life. If she says she saw him, then he was there."

"Thank you, Blake," Carty said. "That was a nice thing to say."

"Uh, you did see him, right?"

"Ha ha, Blake. That vote of confidence didn't last too long."

"Oh, I'm sorry, Carty. I know you wouldn't make that up. But it seems so impossible. Tell us everything."

Carty explained the chance sighting and assured them that The Cuban had not seen her.

"He saw Elena, but she was not involved in the attack, so that doesn't matter. Unfortunately, our abortive effort to follow him died the last day we were there, so we did not get a clue where he lives. Since he was in a car, he might not even live nearby.

"I told Dad as soon as I got back, and we went to Sheriff Elsmore with the news. So guess where he and Sally are going on their honeymoon?"

"Really, Cuba?" Hale asked.

"Yep. They had booked New Orleans before I gave the sheriff the news. When he told Sally, she insisted that they change the trip."

"Isn't that dangerous?" Hale pressed, "What if 'Smith' spots them first?"

"He won't. Remember that he saw Sally as an ugly, black-haired witch. Even her voice is different. He'd never recognize her the way she is now, but she would recognize him in an instant. Moreover, his encounter in the swamp was with my dad and me. 'Smith' was long gone by the time Sheriff Elsmore arrived on the scene. They never saw each other either.

"That means that Sally and the sheriff can have total freedom looking for 'Smith', but 'Smith' could bump right into them and not know it."

"You have missed one thing, Carty," Mack said. "What makes you think that the two lovebirds will be looking at anyone but each other – assuming they even leave the hotel?"

"Mack!" Carty squealed with laughter. "You are so crude." Mack and Hale smiled, and Blake, as usual when such matters came up, blushed. "Regardless of the romantic circumstances, fellows, I'm sure that they will find some time to tour. The area around the university is prime tourist territory."

*AS* the evening drew to an end and the last of the guests had departed, Lilly looked in on Easter and Castillo working in the kitchen. "You two did a wonderful job today. Everything worked out perfectly. Thank you so much for your help."

"*De nada, Señora.* The pretty bride, she look very happy. They remember this day forever."

Lilly asked, "Will you be able to finish up tonight, or do you want to come back tomorrow morning?"

"Easter and I, we finish tonight, *Señora.* I have many more shingles to place on our house tomorrow and must get that done before we get rain."

"Very well," she replied. "I am tired, and I'm going to bed early. Remember to turn off the lights when you leave."

"*Sí*, Sra. Lilly, have a good evening."

Easter and Castillo Zapata had moved into a small building on Lilly's property several months earlier. Originally, it had been built as a house for the foreman of the old sugar plantation. Later, it was used for tool storage. Lilly had made them an irresistible deal when they applied for the job she advertised.

Lilly was nearing seventy, and she recognized that she was unable to handle the upkeep on the property by herself. She had suffered one broken arm convincing herself of that. She was so disillusioned with finding reliable men to work on plumbing, yard work, carpentry, and the like, that she decided to hire an on-site handyman.

The first four men to apply ranged from lazy drunks to foul-mouthed bums. When Castillo Zapata arrived, holding a copy of her newspaper ad, she thought her problems were solved. Not only did Castillo appear to be knowledgeable about plumbing, carpentry, electricity, and other crafts, but he came with a wife who could help with housework and cooking.

When Lilly was mending from her broken arm years ago, Carty had provided daily help around the mansion. Once Carty left for boarding school, Lilly realized how much assistance she needed. She hated to admit it even to herself, but age was catching up with her.

"I picked up Dad's genes for business sense and character, but I'm afraid that Mom's flowed through on the physical side." Lilly's brothers, including Carty's grandfather, died of heart ailments before they reached fifty years, so she felt blessed to be nearing seventy despite her depleted energy level.

Doc Brannigan said that her heart was getting weaker, probably from working so hard pumping blood through clogged arteries.

"Someday we'll have a medicine to clear out arteries, but not yet, Lilly. You were born too soon. Actually, we've all been born too soon."

"Bah, it'll just get more expensive, Duffy."

"You had better hope that it does get more expensive, Lilly. If medicine gets way more expensive, it'll get a lot better for just that reason. The more we are willing to pay, the more researchers will pour resources into finding cures. In fifty years, there will be medicines that we cannot even dream about today, but they won't be cheap, and they can't be cheap.

"When medical care is cheap, like now in the Fifties, that is when people die too young."

# CHAPTER 8

## *Recuperation*

*Be not slow to visit the sick.*

SIRACH 7:35

**SEPTEMBER 1952**

As the couple continued cleaning dishes and stacking tables and chairs, Castillo Zapata thought back two years to when he woke up in Easter's one room hut in Clewiston, in the heart of Florida's sugar country. Then he was a battered, torn, and nearly dead Carey Zeller of Detroit.

Only semi-conscious in the first weeks, he initially thought that he had died and was residing in hell. There was no all-encompassing fire, but the tin-roofed habitation in three-digit summer temperatures of south-central Florida was almost oven hot. Pneumonia filled his lungs, and he ached from severe pain of gouges, rips, and tears over most of his body.

Three broken ribs made deep breathing unbearable. He learned to take short breaths, barely more than panting, to ease the constant pain.

As he slowly healed and beat off the infections without the benefit of medicines, his memory began reappearing. He should be dead. He knew that. He should have been gator food.

He remembered that fateful day in 1950. His mentor, Cruz Cruz, and two losers from Detroit set out to steal a treasure from an old witch living in the swamps near Winter Free. One of the hapless pair – the older one, Dredman – had blown the operation.

"I almost had him," Zapata recalled. "Another fifteen seconds, and he was mine. But Dredman never made it. That monster gator – if I believed in fairy tales, I'd have said it was a dragon – seemed to swallow him whole. Ironically, Dredman saved my life by filling the gator's mouth before the beast came after me.

"I fell into an enormous pit that appeared from nowhere, and when the gator showed up, I believed I was through. I was able to maneuver away from the huge jaws as he snapped and hissed at me from above. But when he dropped into the pit, there was no escape. Nevertheless, I splashed around trying to avoid the inevitable.

"Seeing those huge jaws and long lines of large white teeth making for my head was the most frightening experience of my life," Zeller recalled with a shudder.

"Eventually, a misstep, a slip, and a solid whack from the powerful, swinging tail, and I was knocked unconscious for a short time. I awoke as the gator was lifting me out of the pit. He had my chest in his powerful jaws. Only my bullet proof vest saved me. But even with that protection, I felt and heard ribs cracking."

Zeller had commandeered a bulletproof vest during an attack on a Japanese-held island in WWII. One of his colleagues was killed by a Japanese soldier who had appeared dead, but whose experimental vest had saved him.

The Japanese soldier's good fortune was short-lived, however, as Zeller dispatched him in a quick skirmish. Then he stripped the vest from the dead soldier and wore it under his uniform for the remainder of the war. When he returned to a not always legal civilian life, he relied on that vest when extra protection was appropriate.

Zeller remembered trying to crawl away as the gator struggled with extricating itself from the deep pit, but the damage to his back had temporarily paralyzed his legs, and he was barely able to move a few feet. Soon the monster clambered out.

Nevertheless, Zeller had controlled his emotions. He realized that the gator, after swallowing most of Dredman, would no longer be hungry. Rather, it would be interested in keeping Zeller for a later meal. Alligators typically drown victims and store them under the water to snack on a day or two later.

Zeller had played dead as the gator slipped its lower jaw and tongue beneath Zeller's head and shoulders and clamped down like a crunching vise. Most of the force was absorbed by the vest.

Zeller's face was mashed deeply into the gator's tongue. If Zeller had not turned his head, he would have suffocated. As it was, Zeller had to hope he could hold his breath under water long enough for the animal to deposit him into a storage location.

Though a soft and cushiony tongue, its gravelly rough surface scraped Zeller's face as if it had been forcefully rubbed with coarse sandpaper. Most of the skin and millimeters of flesh tore off. Despite the excruciating pain, Zeller remained motionless, feigning death. With about a third of Zeller in its mouth, the gator began a side-to-side waddle, dragging him backwards toward Duck Lake.

Some of the gator's teeth worked themselves through the protective vest and into Zeller's flesh. His unprotected arms were badly flayed, and the towed legs left bloody tracks in the soft earth.

Zeller could not see anything but black inside the gator's mouth, but he felt the lukewarm water rush in as the gator backed into the lake. The gator gained speed once able to swim, and the additional pace is what saved Zeller. It arrived quickly at a submerged cavity in the lake's bank under the roots of a large cypress. The gator rolled Zeller into the hole for later feasting and swam away.

The small pocket of musty air in the hole was more delightful at that moment than the scent of a beautiful woman's expensive perfume. Zeller breathed deeply as soon as he sensed that the gator was far enough away so as to not notice, though realistically he could not have held his breath another second regardless. He remained under water, except for his face, for about ten minutes that seemed like an hour, in the hope that the gator was gone.

Slowly and quietly, Zeller swam to the surface. The gator was not in sight. He climbed out of the water and used the tree roots to pull himself on to the shore. After a few moments of rest, he regained some sense of movement and control in his legs and lurched eastward through the swamp until he collapsed well before emerging.

He slept without cover for nearly sixteen hours, during which any number of curious wild creatures looked at, prodded, or avoided the strange human form. Fortunately for Zeller, none were the carnivorous sort. The only animal that could have presented a problem, a rattlesnake, was content coiling up for the warmth of his body, and it left before Zeller awoke.

By that time, the excitement at the Canfield Mansion had quieted. No one was searching for him as everyone believed the gator had eaten him. Sheriff Elsmore's deputies, searching for Cruz, had looked in the opposite direction and lost the opportunity for a chance discovery.

Zeller struggled to his feet, eventually reaching Lilly Andersson's estate in late afternoon when he saw two men loading oranges into a covered truck. Lilly had sold the last of the year's modest citrus crop. When Zeller saw that the men were occupied paying Lilly for the purchase, he pulled himself on to the back of the truck, dug a small cavity in the fruit, and nested within. He peeled and ate two oranges, his first food since the ordeal.

With that accomplished, he collapsed into a mix of sleep and coma. When he came to hours later, his head pulsed with pain from clanging noise and bright red flashing lights. Only after several moments did he realize that the truck was stopped at a railroad crossing. At the time, he was otherwise unaware that he was on the outskirts of Clewiston.

Zeller slid out of the truck and crawled into the tall grass alongside the road, where he slipped back into a coma. It was there that Easter Huerto had found him.

After many months of Easter's tender care, Zeller gradually began to heal. He remembered his elation, ever as much as a small child's, the first day that she helped him to stand and walk a few steps on his own. Afterward, he steadily gained strength, though not reaching the level he had enjoyed before the gator attack. He was convinced that he would never heal that much.

Eventually, he was sufficiently repaired that he joined Easter toiling in the sugar fields. "I have to repay you for your kindness," he told her, as his additional small earnings improved her life. For each tiny treasure he brought in – some spices, a bolt of bright red cloth for Easter to sew a dress, a chicken – Easter sobbed in appreciation.

After a year, curiosity – or maybe a sense of self preservation – took hold of Zeller. He needed to find out what came of the attack that so changed his life. He hitched a ride to the Hendry County seat at LaBelle and found the library on Main Street. Inside, a helpful librarian, Debra Hentzell, offered assistance. That she spoke a little Spanish helped Castillo stay in character.

"*The Tampa Tribune* and a local weekly in Winter Free, *The Gazette*, covered the Canfield Attack and the aftermath extensively, *Señor*," she explained to him. She was mildly curious why a Mexican cane worker would be interested in the old case, but she was too professional to mention it.

"Clewiston Sugar Company had donated a microfilm system for the library only months before that case, so we were able to preserve all the articles."

Zeller said that he was able to read English reasonably well, so she showed him how to operate the reader and use the index. She left him to search on his own for every newspaper account discussing the attack on the Canfield estate.

He was relieved to learn that the consensus had considered him, along with the fool, Dredman, to be gator food. Hostetter was in prison with little hope of getting out until about the time he would be eligible for Social Security. Most intriguing was the status of The Cuban, the elusive "Mr. Smith." Authorities had discovered neither his identity nor his whereabouts.

When Zeller saw an old photograph of himself in an article, he was momentarily shocked. He looked around as if expecting the librarian or one of the library patrons to begin pointing and yelling "Zeller!" Then he remembered that the ordeal had altered his appearance radically. No one could possibly recognize him from that photograph.

Instead of dish-water blond hair slicked straight back, his hair now was pure white and cascading across his ears and forehead in a "bowl" cut shape that Easter had fashioned. Instead of a clean shaved face, he had a large, drooping salt and pepper mustache in the Pancho Villa style. Instead of a tall, ramrod stature, he seemed shorter, due to the slightly hunched-over carriage that Montooth's injuries had forced upon his body. His beak-like nose was unchanged, but it appeared different because his bowed posture softened the angle people viewed.

The realization that he looked so different gave Zeller an idea. "If I can team up with Cruz again, maybe we can return and salvage something out of that Canfield house after all."

On the way back to Clewiston in the bed of a pick-up truck, he pondered how he could find Cruz and how they could approach the Canfield place. Nothing came immediately to mind. The more he thought about it, the more he was inclined to leave Cruz out of the picture. He believed that he could figure out a way to move against Sally Canfield on his own, and trying to locate Cruz in Cuba would complicate things anyway.

There was time to formulate a plan, because it was apparent from the newspaper articles that no one was looking for Carey Zeller, and no one would ever think of him in his present state as Zeller's reincarnation. With a feeling of confidence he had not felt from the time he regained consciousness in Easter's hut, he was ready to take a step he had been contemplating for weeks.

So grateful was he for Easter's unquestioning kind heart that the next week he asked Easter to bring the priest to their primitive hut. When Fr. Garcia arrived, Zeller announced that he wanted to marry Easter, bringing uncontrollable tears to the devoted woman's eyes. When her first husband died at an early age, she despaired of finding another good man.

The priest tried to explain that there were procedures required that would take several weeks. Influenced by the emotion Easter displayed, though, in the end he agreed to perform the ceremony the following Saturday, bypassing many of the formalities required by the Church. Priests serving the migrant community were known to cut corners on the rules.

When the paperwork for the marriage was completed, the name on the certificate for the husband was not Carey Zeller. Instead, Zeller became Castillo Zapata, the name that he chose for himself months before when he became sufficiently aware that the name Carey Zeller was a prison sentence in waiting.

He had known a little Spanish growing up near a Puerto Rican section of Detroit, and he learned a lot more from Easter during his lengthy convalescence. To most Anglos he appeared as a Mexican, though Hispanics always recognized that Spanish was a second language for him.

# CHAPTER 9

## *Honeymooning*

*Whoso ever findeth a wife findeth a good thing, and obtaineth favor of the Lord.*

PROVERBS 18:22

**SEPTEMBER 1952**

Sally took in all the activity at the Tampa International Airport with the awe of a youngster. She had never been close to an aircraft, and outside of the windows she saw dozens, from small personal planes, to four propeller military transports, to large passenger craft.

"Which one will we be flying?" she asked James as they lined up to walk across the tarmac.

Pointing straight ahead, he said, "That DC-3 with 'Pan Am' on its tail. They are lowering the stairs now."

They waited a few more minutes while the stewardesses moved into position. Then the line began moving out of the terminal toward the plane.

He felt a sudden feeling of concern for her and said, "The DC-3 is the safest plane in the air. It was a workhorse for transporting soldiers during the War. I know you haven't been in a plane before, but there is nothing to worry about. Flying is not dangerous."

"Oh, I know that, James – you forgot about my broom." She said it so offhandedly and without the slightest hint of a smile that James almost believed that she meant it. He shook his head, took her arm, and guided her up the stairs.

As the plane approached the island country of Cuba, Sally marveled at the many shades of greens, blues, and turquoises in the varying depths of surrounding waters. "Oh, James," she exclaimed, pulling him across herself to the window. "Look how beautiful it is. I have never seen such color. And the water is so clear that you can see to the bottom. Thank you so much for bringing me here."

They had left warm temperatures in central Florida, but nothing like the heat and humidity that engulfed them as the door to the plane opened. "Gosh, this is hotter than back home," she remarked.

Outside of the plane, though, a brisk sea breeze moderated the environment. The wait in the immigration and customs office was painless for Americans, and they were hustled through to the line of waiting taxis in short order.

"To Hotel Riviera, please," he told the driver as they loaded luggage into the trunk of the white Buick.

They were greeted in the spacious hotel lobby by the concierge, who knew that the two were newlyweds. "We have you booked into the honeymoon suite, Mr. Elsmore. You and Mrs. Elsmore should find it very satisfactory," he said, with flawless English.

In that he was correct. On the second from top floor, the room overlooked the expansive pool so far below that the people lounging about looked like dolls. Sally could not stop looking at the bathtub which was three times the size of hers in the Canfield Mansion.

"First thing we do when we get back is put one of these in," she stated.

"I knew it was a mistake to take you away from central Florida. The house will be a shambles of renovations for years."

She gave him a playful swat on the rear, making certain that the bellhop did not see it. James gave him a dollar, a currency as readily accepted as pesos in the Cuban economy.

"What shall we do first?" Sally asked, but the glint in James' eye told her that she need not have asked.

They had room service send up a meal, and afterward took a nap so that they would be refreshed to try the night life around ten. They had many choices: singers, dance groups in bright costumes, Flamenco dancers, and even an American comic.

They opted for the dance group. James' generous tip assured them of a table near the front. The two-hour show was loud and energetic, and they were as exhausted as the dancers when it ended.

Sally marveled how the costumes managed to stay in place over the vital areas of the female dancers despite forceful and vigorous movements. She was as interested in the workmanship of the outfits as in the performance.

The show ended shortly after midnight, and the tired pair was asleep within the hour. They awakened earlier than they had expected the next morning, though, and were dressed and in the hotel lobby before nine.

"We'll take a taxi to the university area, Sally, and have breakfast at the café that Carty described. Apparently, 'Smith' shows up only in the late mornings, so we'll make that café our regular breakfast stop while we are here. Then the afternoons will be all ours."

They arrived at the café about 9:40 and ordered Cuban bread, eggs, and coffee. "Whew, you know that you are drinking coffee when you put this to your lips," Sally commented.

"It is strong. Even the coffee in Ybor City is not this bold. Once the Cubans become Americanized, they seem to like their coffee toned down a bit. Fortunately, they don't change the great breads, though."

They did not spot anyone who resembled The Cuban that morning and later toured the university campus. Sally was captured by the atmosphere of the setting, the buildings, the students hustling from class to class lugging books, and the bucolic serenity within the bustling city.

"It looks quiet now, Sally, but this is a hotbed of anti-Government sentiment. It would not take much of a catalyst to turn this quiet setting into the site of a riotous demonstration."

"I've been thinking about taking some classes in Tampa. What do you think of that?"

"You would enjoy it. I'm not sure how you finesse not having a high school degree since you were schooled by your grandmother at home. However, your knowledge rivals a typical college grad already, so an interview with admissions people and an entrance exam will probably be enough to get you in.

"We could try to schedule our classes so we could drive together."

James was nearing his degree. He had been going part time since before the War. When he became sheriff, he was able to double up on classes because he could organize his schedule to accommodate class times.

The mornings passed by without incident, and the love struck pair enjoyed themselves and the rest of Havana's sights and night life for the remainder of the week. With three days to go before returning to Tampa, a development set in motion a series of events that would affect people in the U.S. and Cuba.

*CRUZ* approached the café on foot from Calle J in typically dapper attire. He wore a dove gray suit with a light blue shirt and white tie. His gray shoes with blue laces complemented the blue band on his white Panama.

From a distance he saw the Castro brothers already seated, waiting for him, paging though a newspaper. They had not seen him as they faced the opposite direction. Fidel continued commenting to Raúl about the sports page.

"Sometimes I think I should have concentrated on baseball, Raúl. These guys today are not nearly as good as I was."

Raúl knew that statement was not true. He knew that Fidel's fastball was below average. The break on his curve usually was less than the width of a hand, and it tended to slop on a flat plane in a way to light up a hitter's eyes.

Moreover, Raúl once sat behind a St. Louis Cardinals' scout and watched him check almost every box in the below average and poor category on a chart with Fidel Castro's name on top. Raúl never told Fidel what he had seen, and he was not about to prick his brother's balloon today either. Besides, Raúl believed that Fidel had more of a political future than sports would provide.

"You could have been a great pitcher," he lied, "but what would that have gained you or Cuba? Camilo Pascual[12] is probably moving up to the Washington Senators soon, and how will that help Cuba? Not at all.

"No, you have a chance to change history if we can toss Batista out. Cuba is your destiny, not the ball diamond."

Cruz had reached the edge of the seats in the outdoor section of the café when an eerie feeling made him stop short. He could not imagine what was wrong, but he had such feelings before, and they always proved to be critical warnings. He had ascribed his reactions not to some magic or mystical power but to something that his eyes had seen but that his brain could not fully process immediately.

He held steady like an animal that has reacted to danger by freezing in place to limit the risk of being noticed. With no movement except with his eyes, he examined the surroundings. Nothing seemed out of place.

He saw Carlos, the young waiter, bussing some cups and saucers. A few tables, in addition to the one where the Castros were seated, were occupied in the slack time of late morning. All seemed normal.

Then he saw the danger: a young couple, both at profile, with hers less full than his. She was a beauty, mid- to late-twentyish, model quality, with red hair and sparkling white teeth he could see even at that angle. But she was not the problem. It was the man. Cruz knew him from somewhere, but he could not place where. Yet something told him that the stranger was someone to avoid.

The man had noticed Cruz and sat back in his chair to take a longer look. Instinctively, Cruz took a small notebook from his suit coat pocket and acted as if he read some important item. He tapped his forehead lightly with two fingers as if to say, "I've forgotten something."

Cruz turned and walked back toward Calle J, abandoning his intended meeting with the Castros for another time. When he turned the corner, he stopped to search his memory bank. "I know that man from somewhere, but where, and why am I apprehensive? I see many people that I vaguely know, and they do not cause me alarm."

He walked briskly to his car parked along the curb. "Let's go, Elazar. The meeting was cancelled." Cruz continued to wrestle with the identity of the mystery man. "It is like seeking a word that is on the tip of my tongue," he muttered aloud.

Elazar responded with, "Pardon me?"

"Oh, nothing, Elazar. I was just trying to think of something."

"I picked up a newspaper while I was waiting, sir. Would you care to read it?"

"Newspaper – that's it!" Cruz shouted, startling Elazar who was attempting to hand the paper over the front seat to Cruz.

Cruz took the paper but did not read it. What his mind needed was not in that Havana paper. It had been in a Tampa paper two years earlier. He recalled the photo in full detail: Chief Fireside and Sheriff Elsmore stood on the courthouse steps after the inquest of the deaths in the fire at a Standard Oil service station.

Cruz had a mail subscription to the Tampa Tribune. The paper arrived several days late in Cuba, but Cruz did not need information to be timely. He simply wanted to know what was going on in Tampa Bay. Though he was no longer a frequent visitor to the area, he owned extensive properties south of the city.

He remembered reading about the gas station fire. He had torched the gas pumps to mask the deaths of the two men he had killed to hide his identity from Florida authorities.

He had nearly run into Sheriff Elsmore in the café moments ago. "What's he doing here? It cannot be a coincidence. He must be looking for me."

He searched his memory for the identity of the red-haired woman but came up entirely blank with her. "No, I've never seen her before," he concluded erroneously.

"*STAY* here for a moment please," James stated in a command voice that he rarely used, but that she never resisted or questioned when he did. She had learned that the voice was used only involving her safety. "I want to check something out."

He rose from his chair and walked toward Calle J. James felt that there was something odd about the way that the man in the gray suit acted, and he did seem to meet the description of the mysterious "Mr. Smith."

By the time James turned the corner on Calle J, Cruz was ducking into the backseat of his car, and James was too far from the vehicle to read the license plate. The car pulled away and turned on to a side street before he could close the gap.

He returned to Sally and ordered another coffee. Quietly he said,

"I believe that I saw your 'Mr. Smith,' Sally, but something spooked him, and he took off. He left in a car before I could get close.

"Are you sure? Why didn't you tell me so I could get a look?"

"No. I am not certain, but the guy sure meets your description, and there aren't too many people that do. Witnesses usually give us, 'medium height, medium weight, medium brown hair.'

"But the consistent description from you and The Crew – 'short, no neck, built like a fire hydrant, thick arms, excessively squinty eyes, short black hair' – nailed the guy I just saw.

"I can't figure out why he left, though. He couldn't recognize you without your 'witch' hair and makeup, and you were mostly turned away from him anyway. And he did not see me on the night of the attack."

"Maybe he was still lurking in the woods after you arrived, and he saw you from the distance."

"Maybe, but it seems unlikely that he would have risked staying in the area. He was in escape mode when Michael let him go. Even if he had stayed, he could not have been close enough to see my facial features. This guy definitely knew something was up, but I do not know why.

"On a positive note, I think that we can take in an isolated beach and an excursion into the island interior if you'd like for the last few days of our honeymoon. I doubt that he will be back here anytime soon."

THE Castro brothers stayed another hour before they decided to leave. They were not upset. Cruz had given them standing instructions to expect a phone call at their apartment from him within two hours anytime he failed to show up.

"*Hola*. Raúl here," he answered.

"Cruz here, Raúl. I apologize, but I'm at the airport heading for Miami. There is a development involving the hardware shipment that needs my immediate attention, if you know what I mean. I will call you next week to set up a meeting."

In fact, there was no code between them to indicate that "hardware" meant "weapons." But Cruz believed Raúl was clever enough to interpret the statement to indicate that Cruz was travelling to Miami to secure guns for the first battle in the revolution. That would be more than sufficient salve for potentially bruised egos as a result of the missed meeting.

However, guns were not involved in the trip to Miami. Rather, Cruz wanted to find out what he could learn about Sheriff Elsmore's presence in Havana. There was no direct dial service from Cuba, though, and a long distance call identified as coming from an international telephone operator in Cuba would be too risky.

Later that evening, a phone rang in Winter Free. "Sheriff's Office, Winter Free."

"Hello," Cruz replied from a pay phone in the Miami Airport. "This is Harvey Lippman of *The Miami Herald*. I am doing a story on Florida sheriffs who are under the age of 35, and, of course, that includes your Sheriff Elsmore."

When Cruz engaged in impersonations, he chose a name that might sound somewhat familiar to the other party – not an actual name that might tip off a knowledgeable person, but a similar name that seemed vaguely recognizable. In this instance, he chose Harvey from radio newscaster Paul Harvey and Lippman from renowned newspaper columnist Walter Lippman.

"Might I be able to speak with him for a few moments?"

"I am sure that Sheriff Elsmore would like to speak with you, Mr. Lippman," the desk officer, a cheerful sounding woman, replied, "but he is not available."

"Will he be in later this evening? I am running into a rapidly approaching deadline and need to wrap up my story."

"I understand, Mr. Lippman, but Sheriff Elsmore is on his honeymoon in the Caribbean and is not expected back in the office for another four days. Could I have him return your call when he returns?"

"No. That would be too late, I'm afraid. But I am intrigued about his marriage. Maybe I will do a follow up story about that. May I ask whom he married?"

"His bride's name is Sally Canfield."

That revelation stopped Cruz short – the sheriff's companion in the café was surely not Sally Canfield – but he recovered quickly. "Sally Canfield? Why does that name seem familiar to me?"

"You may have read about the attack on her property a couple of years ago. She and four teenagers fought off a band of four felons. It was the biggest story in southwest Florida for months."

"I do seem to recall something about that. But wasn't that Sally Canfield an old recluse that everyone thought was a witch? Surely young Sheriff Elsmore did not marry an old woman."

"One in the same," the officer laughed in reply, "except the old recluse turned out to be quite a beautiful young woman. The sheriff is the envy of every man in the county."

"I see. Thank you for your time, Ma'am. I will contact the sheriff if my editor gives me a go on a follow up story. He is due back in four days, you said?"

"Yes, sir, in four days."

"Thank you. You have been very helpful."

Cruz hung up the phone, but, lost in concentration, he made no effort to exit the phone booth. An impatient middle aged businessman knocked on the door to the booth. "I need the phone, if you are done," he said importantly. It took no more than Cruz's malevolent glare to send the man backing quickly away.

"It is really difficult to believe that the red-haired woman in the café is the same Sally Canfield I spoke with in that house. I really did not see her well enough today to accept what the officer told me, but she surely had no reason to lie."

However, any residual thoughts Cruz might have hung on to about making a second attempt for the Canfield treasure dissipated in those few moments. He was not about to attack a sheriff's wife or property.

On the other hand, the explanation about the honeymoon satisfied him that the sheriff's presence in the café was benign, a one in a million coincidence that did not represent a danger. He would be able to resume meeting the Castros there without fear when Elsmore and his bride returned to Florida later in the week.

# CHAPTER 10

## *Loopholes*

*It is easier to make certain things legal than to make them legitimate.*

NICOLAS CHAMFORT

**SEPTEMBER 1952**

Cash had no highly active cases at the time he took over Hostetter's, so he dived deeply into it. Three weeks to the day he took the case, Cash had devised a strategy, though it took many months to get the result he was seeking.

He first filed an appeal with Judge Warren Lord, a bleeding heart liberal who always looked for a way to "help the downtrodden" and please the cocktail circuit he so loved. Cash based his appeal on Hostetter's condition at the time he confessed to the crimes.

"Defendant had suffered multiple fractures, a punctured lung, and the loss of several teeth. The attending doctors had administered multiple strong and narcotic pain killers to Defendant immediately upon reaching him, and they continued doing so during the next several weeks in the hospital. Clearly, Defendant was not entirely in control of his faculties at the time he made incriminating statements nor when he signed the confession."

Cash had given a fleeting thought to propose to Judge Lord that Hostetter should even have been advised that he had no requirement to talk at all to the police before having an attorney present. "No," he thought, "I'd better not get carried away. Even Judge Lord wouldn't be stupid enough to fall for that."

However, the judge accepted Cash's position that the confession was tainted, given the defendant's impaired condition at the time, and agreed that the presiding judge should not have allowed its admission. Although the other evidence was overwhelmingly damaging to the defendant, Judge Lord felt that the jury might have been unduly influenced by the confession.

Therefore, Judge Lord ruled that the defendant deserved a retrial in which the confession would not be allowed. Moreover, Hostetter was to be released from Raiford. No bail would be required, given that he had already suffered years of incarceration and, without financial resources, presented little risk of flight.

Clem seemed not as overjoyed as Cash expected when he drove up to Raiford to explain the good news that he would be released in a few days when the paperwork was completed.

"But where will I live?" Clem asked, with desperation in his voice. "I have no money."

"That is the second piece of good news. As you know, you lost your farm property in a tax sale. Since you did not pay taxes for several years, the property was at risk of someone else paying the taxes and receiving title. I discovered that the same sheriff who arrested you bought your farm by paying the back taxes."

"It was a stupid place anyway. I tried for years to sell it without as much as a bite from a potential buyer. What do I care if he bought it? Good riddance."

"Well, yes and no, Clem. You do need a place to live, and what better place than the old farm?"

"What? The sheriff isn't going to let me stay in his place."

"Just listen for a moment," Cash said with a sigh. "The sheriff being involved actually worked out well for us.

"After someone pays the back taxes and generates a pending change of title, the original owner has the right to cancel it by paying the late taxes, interest, and penalties himself."

Clem started to object again, but Cash gestured a stop signal, and Clem quieted.

"State law requires that the original owner must be notified so that he has a final chance to make the payment. Generally that means the tax office sends a certified letter to the owner's last known address. In your case, the 'Final Notice' letter was mailed to the farmhouse on Hostetter Cutoff."

"So what is the problem? That was my last address."

"No, it wasn't, Clem – your last known address at the time the letter was mailed was right here at Raiford State Prison.

"I chose to file a tax case appeal with another judge, Judge Rock, because he scrupulously applies the law and always sides with property owners when an issue does not suggest a clear choice."

Clem could hold back no longer. "How do you get to choose your judges, Cash? Don't the other attorneys try to get judges that are on their side?"

"Let's just say we've been lucky, Clem."

In fact, the cases rotated randomly so that attorneys could not "judge shop," but Cash was not above a clandestine meeting with the Clerk of Courts who was in charge of the rotation.

Cash resumed his explanation. "In this case, the Government in effect claimed that your last known address was on Hostetter Cutoff. But that was the very same Government, though a different agency, that was responsible for sending you to Raiford.

"Therefore, the Government technically 'knew' that Raiford was your address, not the farmhouse on Hostetter Cutoff. Accordingly, I contended that the 'Final Notice' letter should have come to you in Raiford. The judge understood my argument that the Government was negligent in sending the letter to an address it technically knew was wrong – even though the actual Government workers who knew you were at Raiford were different than the clerk in the tax office who mailed the notice.

"This judge is a highly ethical man – something that occasionally works to the advantage of us 'practical lawyers.' I could see that he was giving my position serious thought, so I hit him with the final point, i.e., the sheriff buying the property.

"I told the judge that I was not suggesting that the sheriff had anything to do with the misdirected notification letter. Nevertheless, I pointed out, 'Shouldn't the Government err on the side of the owner under such a circumstance? It looks suspicious, even if truly innocent, when the man who arrested a homeowner turns around and buys the owner's property through a tax sale.

"I added, 'It is especially appalling after the Government sends the 'Final Notice' to the wrong address when the Government knowingly had the correct address.'

"The judge agreed and ordered the title transfer rescinded and deferred. The farm is back in your name, at least temporarily. You can move back as soon as you are released."

"But I don't have enough money to pay the taxes anyway, Cash. How will this help?"

"I can delay the process for about eight months with motions, vacations, 'illnesses,' etc., so you have a place to stay until then. Your retrial should come up about that time too. When you are discharged from here, you'll get a little money from the prison. That is your pay for working on license tags. That'll be enough for you to live on for a month if you are really careful.

"I even managed to get your old Ford out of the impound lot. It's not in good running condition – that's probably why it did not sell – but you should be able to keep it going if you keep pouring oil into it. I even had a good used battery put in for you."

Clem stared at Cash for several moments. Then he said, "Cash, I appreciate all the work you have done, but even with the little prison money, I don't have any idea where I'll get enough money to pay you for the car battery or for your fee."

Cash smiled. Most of his clients did not have enough money to pay his fee when he took the case. But he learned to carefully choose clients who had good prospects of eventually obtaining money. Thus Cash favored burglars and embezzlers to murderers and thugs.

If Cash won the release of the former, they could fall back on their unlawful profession to acquire money for his fee, whereas the latter did not look upon crime as a money making activity, just a way of life. He had learned the hard way that the latter usually returned to prison, penniless, without paying him.

He really liked Hostetter's prospects.

"You'll think of something, Clem. After all, you'll be living next to a treasure, right?"

## OCTOBER 1952

*JUDGE* Rock greeted James with a smile and a handshake. "Hello, Your Honor," James said, with obvious warmth and a little confusion as to why he had been summoned. He respected the judge and wished that other judges had the same temperament and logical thought processes, instead of making things up as they went along.

"Hello, James. How is your beautiful wife? I heard from Lilly Andersson that Sally may be pregnant."

"Yes, Your Honor – Doc Brannigan says we might have an addition in July. Sally is so excited and doing well physically. Of course, she is as strong as a horse from all those years working the farm by herself."

"I hope that you are getting her some help, young man."

"We've cut back the farm to a large garden and chickens. She hated giving up her cow, but I told her that those 4AM milkings had to stop. Lilly Andersson hired a Mexican couple to help on her place, and we share them three days a week. There isn't enough to keep them busy on either place full time, but this works out well for them and us."

"I'm glad to hear that.

"James, I asked you to visit today because you are probably not going to like a ruling that I issued an hour ago, and I wanted to explain myself to you. It affects the old Hostetter place that you bought. I'm vacating the title transfer that was made to you."

Judge Rock went over the logic and explained that he wanted to avoid any possible suggestion of a conflict of interest.

"To say that I'm disappointed, Judge, is an understatement, but I would have done the same had our roles been reversed. Will I lose my investment?"

"No, that won't happen. Hostetter still has to come up with the payment, of course. If he does, you get your money back for the tax payment you made. What you would lose are any improvements you made to the property, such as a new roof or windows, for example. Moreover, you won't get any interest for the time that your money was tied up. However, you are allowed to remove any items like furniture that are not fastened to the walls and floors, but anything attached stays with the house.

"On the other hand, Hostetter has now received the 'Final Notice' letter at Raiford. If he fails to make the payment, the transfer reverts to you, and I will finalize it expeditiously."

"How long will it take before I know?"

"Four or five months at the shortest. With motions and delaying tactics by Hostetter's lawyer, it could stretch out further. If he gets too frivolous, I won't stand for it. I'd say five months, six at the outside.

"Of course, there is no telling what wear and tear Hostetter will inflict on the place while living there."

"At least I don't have to worry about that, Your Honor; Hostetter is locked up at Raiford."

"Omigosh, James. You haven't heard? Yesterday Judge Lord ordered Hostetter released. The grounds were dubious, given the overwhelming evidence against him. However, he will be getting a new trial.

"He'll be released within forty-eight hours, and he may be looking to move into his old place – I'm afraid that you cannot stop it. You do realize that you cannot stop it, don't you, James?"

"Judge, possibly losing the house is a big disappointment, but Hostetter's release is far worse. He fired a gun at Sally and the kids who were defending her. The idea that he will be living on the adjoining property is difficult to accept."

"James, I want you to be careful. If you do anything to harass Hostetter while he is out, it may help him in his retrial, and it will certainly do you no good, personally or professionally."

James shook his head slowly as if trying to shed his thoughts. "I understand, Your Honor. I'll leave a note on the door to tell him to stop by the sheriff's office for the key."

It turned out that Hostetter's release date was delayed until the following Monday, so James was able to enlist Blake's help over the weekend to move out all the personal items. When he moved in, he had stored Hostetter's furnishings in the barn, so he returned enough of them to make the house livable for Hostetter.

Late Monday afternoon, Hostetter appeared at the sheriff's office. James had left word with the desk officer to show Hostetter in when he arrived. When Clem knocked tentatively on the door, James got up to meet him.

"Hello, Clem. C'mon in and have a seat. How was Raiford?"

"It's not my favorite place, Sheriff, but it could be worse."

Clem seemed to be holding his breath as he took a quick look at his surroundings. The sheriff's desk was piled with neatly organized file folders. Several framed certificates hung from the walls. The print was too small for Clem to read, but they enhanced the intimidation that Clem felt.

"I saw your note on the front door of the old house. It said I could pick up the house key from you?" Clem more asked that stated.

"That's right, Clem, I have the key here," James said, holding the key in his hand but making no effort to hand it over. "I thought it might be a good idea to have a little discussion first since we are going to be neighbors and all."

"Neighbors, Sheriff?"

"Yes, Clem. You do know that Sally Canfield and I were recently married, don't you? We live on the Canfield Estate next to your old place."

Hostetter was struck dumb for several seconds. Hostetter had always been nervous around James dating to when, as a young deputy, he had picked Clem up on a shoplifting charge. Clem was never actually afraid of James, though, probably because James always treated him with respect.

But that was before James married a witch. James noticed Clem's fearful reaction, and it gave him an idea. He had intended to warn Clem to stay away from Sally before giving him the key, but a better thought came to mind as he watched the blood drain from Clem's face.

"Things are a little different than they were when you lived in Winter Free, Clem. It's important for you to know that. You may hear odd things from the Canfield Estate while you are in your old house. I want you to ignore them. You may notice strange visitors from time to time heading past your place. I want you to ignore them as well." Of course, this was all bluff.

"It would be best for everyone if you simply forget that the Canfield place is at the end of Hostetter Cutoff. Of course, if you do get worried about anything, you can always call the sheriff. Oh, wait. I am the sheriff. Ha ha haaaaa."

He mimicked the laugh that he had heard Sally use on a few occasions with good effect, and it nearly threw Hostetter into a faint.

As the sheriff reached out to hand the key to Hostetter, Clem recoiled as if the key were a venomous snake.

"Now don't you worry about anything, Clem. I put several improvements into the old house, and it is spic and span. I still have a claim on the house in case you decide not to pay the taxes, and I would appreciate it if you kept it in good condition in the event I do get it back. You can do that, can't you Clem?"

"Oh, yes, Sheriff. Oh, yes. I'll keep it in good shape. You can count on that. Maybe I should be going now. You must be busy."

"Not so busy, anymore, Clem. Since I married Sally Canfield, the county hasn't had a bad spell of criminal activity. A bad spell – ha ha haaaaa."

Clem hopped up from the chair and snatched the key from James' outstretched hand. "Goodbye, Sheriff. Thanks for the key."

After Clem scooted out of the station, the desk officer ducked her head into James' office. "Where'd you get that creepy laugh, Sheriff?" she asked. "I doubt Hostetter will be visiting you and Mrs. Elsmore after hearing that. Shoot, I doubt if I'll be visiting."


*CLEM* coaxed the old Ford to Homer's recently expanded grocery store where he picked up some basic food items: milk, raisin bran, bread, butter, sugar, bacon, eggs, beer, pork & beans, and pretzels. He did not have much money, so he needed to conserve it as much as possible. Homer shook his hand and steered him to a couple of items on sale.

"I was sorry to see your mother pass away and haven't had an opportunity to give you my condolences, Clem. She was one of my favorite people."

"Thank you, Mr. Hamlin. I should have made it to the funeral."

Cash's battery seemed to be the only part of Clem's car that operated properly. Purple smoke belched from the tailpipe, and the eight cylinders seemed to be operating as seven. Clem had to struggle to get the gears to mesh, but once the car got going, he found that he could maintain a forty mile per hour pace without difficulty.

Entering the house alone gave Clem an eerie feeling. When he had occupied it with Dredman a couple of years earlier, he did not give his childhood in the house a second thought.

This time it was different. He was alone, totally alone. His father had died before the War, and Clem had trouble bringing him to his memory except in a vague sort of way. He did think of his mother, Cora, though, and he found that odd as he had not thought of her once in all the time he was in prison.

He glanced upward as if looking to heaven and whispered, "I should have been a better son to you, Mom. I don't know why I wasn't. You certainly gave me all the love I could have asked for. I am sorry that I did not return some of it." With the last few words, he choked up as tears welled up in his eyes and rolled down his cheeks.

Clem set the groceries down and wiped the tears with his shirt sleeves. He took a look around. He noticed that some of the dusty living room furniture was in the same place where he had left it. The walls were now painted instead of papered, and they looked bare because the old pictures were no longer hanging. The carpet was new and clean.

In the kitchen he found a new range and Frigidaire. He noticed that the sheriff had left salt, pepper, canned soup, and a number of boxed food items such as macaroni and cheese.

"Must have been too much work moving it away," Clem thought. Actually, James had stocked the staples in the cupboards, figuring that Clem could use the help.

Tomorrow Clem would have to come up with a plan of action to solve his financial dilemma. Tonight he was too tired. He trudged up the stairs and, relieved to find a bed in his old room, plopped down and went to sleep.

*WEEKS* later, Hostetter watched from behind a curtain in his living room as the sheriff's car drove past. The sheriff had not contacted him since the meeting when he arrived in town. Clem was happy about that, but Cash seemed disappointed every time Clem said that the sheriff was not bothering him.

"If he gives you a hard time, let me know. I'll figure an angle to sue him," Cash said on more than one occasion.

Clem looked at the remaining money of the small stake he started with when he left prison. He was beginning to feel pressured and decided that he had no choice but to put his desperate plan into action.

# CHAPTER 11

## *The Meiers*

*I can see where I've been, a lot easier than where I'm going.*

G. THOMAS MEIER

**OCTOBER 1952**

The screen door slammed behind him before Grant had a chance to shut the sturdy wooden door of the Spokane Avenue house. The family home nestled in the Brooklyn area of south Cleveland, Ohio. Stately elms, one in every lawn near the curb, lined the entire street.

"How did it go today, Grant?" his mother called from the kitchen.

"This was the greatest day yet, Mom. I picked up a Mickey Mantle rookie card and a DiMaggio in his last year. I think that Mantle might end up being almost as good as DiMag, so that one will be very valuable, but the final DiMaggio – wow.

"And you won't believe what they cost me – a Hal Naragon, a Bill Glynn, and five of the bubble gums. It's like taking candy from a baby dealing with Pete Wysocki. He's in love with the Cleveland Indians and hates the Yankees so much that he can't see the long term value in cards from the New York teams. And I don't even like those slabs of pink gum that come with the cards."

"Grant, I wasn't referring to your wheeling and dealing baseball cards. I meant, how did your trigonometry test go this morning?"

"Oh, Mom, you know that I aced that. Why would you even ask?"

"Grant, I'm only trying to show interest. Your father thinks that we have to pay attention to your school work or you may slack off."

"Oh, right, Mom. Have I ever slacked off?"

"No, and I know that you never will. I'm just trying to keep your dad happy. He always wants to know that I'm on top of you, just in case. He wants you to follow in your brothers' footsteps. He is looking forward to another doctor in the family."

"You still haven't told him then, Mom? I don't see why I can't explain it to him. Why do you have to be the one to tell him?"

*GRANT* Dennis Meier, baseball card trader and highly motivated student at Cleveland's St. Ignatius High School, was born in 1936 to Grant Thomas "Tom" Meier and Rita Sherwood.

The original Meier in the United States, Otto, arrived in 1868 from Baden Baden, Germany as an eighteen-year-old. Four years later, as a modestly successful business owner, he married Penelope Bartlett in Our

Lady of Good Counsel Church within easy walking distance of Spokane Avenue in the German section of south Cleveland, Ohio.

Penelope was part of the Cleveland branch of the Bartlett family that included a small contingent in the Sarasota area of Florida. The Andersson clan of Winter Free, Florida was descended on the maternal side from a Bartlett.

When Grant came along a full ten years after his next older brother, it gave Tom a chance to rectify an omission in the family custom. Otto had arrived in the United States when Ulysses S. Grant was president and later decreed that one son in each generation thereafter should be named Grant.

Tom, however, had always disliked the name and had insisted on being called Tom. Though Pres. Grant himself was an honest man, his Administration was rife with corruption. "Why would I want to be named after that president?" he declared as a young man entering college.

Furthermore, he refused the name Grant to any of his first three sons. Tom relented only when one more son arrived so many years after the first wave of children, and only a few months after Otto's passing. But Tom never failed to insist that Grant act in an ethical manner as if the mere name might inspire corrupt behavior.

Grant took so readily to his father's training that he learned to go out of his way to be fair and upright with all of his relationships. No one questioned his honesty, and when he gave his word, nothing would make him renege.

Ironically, his solid reputation for fair dealing made it easier for Grant to get the better of his fellow students in any transaction. They knew that they could rely on his word, so there was seldom any skepticism with whatever he said.

"I keep telling Pete that New York City players' cards will be worth more than Cleveland Indians' cards, but he says he doesn't care. He likes the Indians and could not care less about New York's Giants, Dodgers, or Yankees."

"Do you really believe that your baseball cards will become valuable?" Rita asked.

"Sure, Mom. Remember the old mechanical coin bank that Uncle Leo sold for one hundred and twenty dollars to the antique dealer? When it was new, it sold for about a dollar. Many old things gain value, especially things that are unique and that remind adults of their childhood.

"Yankees' cards will be worth the most, because there are more kids in New York than any other city, and the Yanks are the only New York team in the American League. The other two split the National League allegiance, so there will be more adults who remember cheering for the Yankees. I like the Indians too, but this is business, and you have to think logically if you want to make money," he declared solemnly.

"There are exceptions. Future Hall of Fame players like Feller or Williams or Musial will be valuable regardless of the team. However, many barely above average Yankees will probably sneak into the Hall of Fame because of the greater number of baseball writers in New York City who are eligible voters. When those players reach the Hall, their cards will gain value."

"Oh, then it's a good thing that I didn't throw out all those old cards of yours when I was cleaning out your room in the spring," Rita said, in a serious tone of voice.

"Mom, you wouldn't."

"You should see the look on your face," she laughed. "No, I wouldn't throw out your cards or anything else of yours unless you agreed, but that does not mean I won't give you a fright every so often."

"You got me that time, but for that I get an extra cookie," he countered, grabbing two peanut butter cookies from the pan that was cooling in the brisk air on the window ledge. Indian Summer had faded away barely a week earlier, and the first hint of colder temperatures brought out Rita's baking interest.

"Okay, young man, but two is the limit. Dinner is at six, and I don't want you to spoil your dinner."

"Have you ever seen me fail to eat any of your delicious cooking? Besides, I smell roast beef, and I could eat every cookie on that pan and still dig into one of your roasts."

## NOVEMBER 1952

*"DON'T* forget to pack tonight, Grant. We leave for the airport at six in the morning."

"I'm really excited about the trip, Mom. I haven't seen Carty since I was twelve. She wrote that everyone will be coming to Aunt Lilly's for Thanksgiving dinner, including some neighbors."

"That's right. We will be staying with Aunt Lilly, so I'm expecting you to pitch in for the dinner. She has a big house, and I am sure that she can use the help.

"I'm really looking forward to a week away from the snow. It arrived early this year. We should get warm temperatures in Florida, but I am not looking forward to an airplane ride. I'd really prefer the train."

"Oh, Mom, planes are way faster, and they are really safe. You have nothing to worry about."

"Grant, you've never been in an airplane either, so you can't tell me you are not nervous about it."

"I've read all about planes, though, and I know there's no reason to be nervous.

"The only thing I was nervous about was whether Dad could get permission for me to get out of school for three extra days to make this trip. And all I have to do is write a description of the animal life I experience in Florida while we are there – and of course finish all the homework they piled on."

Tom had recently developed a rubberized track that could be retrofitted on to the wheels of a Ford tractor, giving the farm vehicle military tank-like traction. Michael Andersson had asked Tom to send a sample to Florida to see if the invention could be modified for some of the big equipment he used in his limerock mining operation. One conversation led to another and then to an invitation for the Meiers to spend Thanksgiving week in Florida.


*ANYONE* who knew the Meier family would spot Grant as a member of the clan from appearance alone. Nearly every male Meier had the same slender, almost too thin, body frame of medium height, seldom reaching five-ten. Shoulders were broad and straight; noses were a bit large for faces; and ears were far away from the head.

Thick dark eyebrows matched either black or dark brown hair. By early evening, every adult male Meier face could have used a second shave of the day.

Meiers were generally athletic but not exceptional at any particular sport. Few ever played on college teams or excelled for their high schools, but they were enthusiastic on the sandlots and as spectators.

At a time when most men had long ago retired, Tom Grant continued to expand his business, Grant Automotive Machinery Company. He was an exceptional businessman and had been since his mid-teens.

As a youngster before the turn of the century, in an era of relaxed liquor laws, Tom realized that he could make good after-school money selling the only bottled beer on Cleveland's West Side.

At the start, an uncle with a small tavern made purchases of kegs of beer on Tom's behalf from the Leisy Brewery at Fulton and Vega Avenues. Tom tapped the kegs in his uncle's back room and painstakingly filled his own glass bottles. Then he delivered the bottled beer under the label Cleveland Meier Beer to taverns whose owners were pleased to be able to sell bottled beer to-go when their patrons headed home. The deposit he charged for the bottles was sufficient for Tom to get the bottles back so he could wash and refill them.

When Tom started his business he delivered the beer near his Cleveland home, pulling two children's wooden wagons. He outgrew that humble start in the first month and put his uncle on the payroll as plant manager. Within five years, he had twenty men delivering his bottled brew with large horse drawn wagons. He had become Leisy's best customer and marketed Cleveland Meier Beer over most of the city.

His operation became nearly self-sufficient with a semi-automated bottling plant, horse stables, and a wagon repair shop.

When Tom sold his bottling business at the age of twenty-three, he invested the proceeds into machinery to supply parts to the growing automobile industry. His experience in wagon maintenance led him to anticipate that the fledgling automobile businesses would soon replace the horse and carriage. He wanted to be on the ground floor of the transformation.

Tom had been so single-minded about business over the years that he did not think about marriage until he was in his forties, and then he married Rita who was nearly twenty years younger.

"Stop this nonsense," she had told him after an extended courtship. "Ask me to marry you before I'm the one who is too old."

Despite his acumen for business, Tom did not want his sons and daughter to follow in his footsteps. From the earliest days of their childhoods, he encouraged them to study medicine.

"Business is too much work, and it is too easy to make a bad decision and go broke," he remarked, though he seldom did the former and never did the latter.

"I'm just being selfish," Tom often joked about his desire for his children to be doctors. "When I get old, I want someone I can trust to take care of me." Few in the family ever expected him to get old.

# CHAPTER 12

## *Visiting Florida*

*Practice makes perfect.*

JOHN ADAMS

**NOVEMBER 1952**

"Carty will be here for breakfast shortly," Lilly said to Grant, who awakened first after the long, three-stop plane trip from Cleveland that required an overnight in Atlanta due to bad weather.

"I'm looking forward to seeing her. It has been almost five years since we've been together. I'd really like to talk to her about the Canfield attack. She wrote to me about it, but that's not the same as a face to face conversation.

"Do you think that I could meet Sally Canfield, Aunt Lilly?" Lilly was actually a distant cousin, not his aunt, but because of the age differ-ence, Grant always called her "Aunt."

"Sally is Mrs. Elsmore now. She married our county sheriff. I'm sure she would enjoy meeting you, Grant. Ask Carty to take you there after lunch."

As if on cue, there was a knock on the screen door. "I heard that re-quest, Grant. In fact, I've already arranged for you to meet her."

Carty bounded in and gave Aunt Lilly a hug, and then stood back to appraise her cousin. "Grant, you've grown up, and you're more handsome than ever. Can I get a hug from you too?"

"After that nice compliment, Carty, you can get two." As they re-leased each other, Grant reacted to the crushing she gave him. "Holy cow, you are not only pretty, you are stronger than I am. Where did you get those biceps?"

Laughing, she told him, "Actually, I'm turning into a weakling. Years of daily archery practice built me up, but I seldom take up the bow any-more since I am at boarding school."

Thrusting her Hoyt Professional recurve bow forward, she said, "I brought it today, though. I thought that we could go to Sally's place after breakfast. You wrote that you were interested in a lesson, and it dawned on me that I never gave Sally the lesson that I promised her over two years ago. We had a little excitement at her place back then that interrupted our plans.

"She's expecting us for lunch. Is it okay if we leave you after break-fast, Aunt Lilly?"

"Leave for where?" Tom asked, as he and Rita entered the dining room.

"Uncle Tom, Aunt Rita!" Carty squealed, rushing to envelop them in a strong embrace. "How little you have changed."

"Wouldst that it were true," Tom laughed, while delighting in her assessment. "But you have become quite a fine young lady."

"If it's okay with everyone, I'd like to take Grant on a hike over to the Canfield Estate. Even though Sally is an Elsmore now, the property retains the historic Canfield name. He can meet the former Canfield Witch there. Of course, she isn't a witch, but that's part of the story."

At the table, Grant downed four glasses of fresh squeezed orange juice. "This is amazing. We get that horrible frozen concentrate in Cleveland this time of year. Yuck."

"Save room for the grits, bacon, and eggs, *por favor*," Easter said, while she delivered those items on a large serving platter, also thumping a large bottle of Tabasco Sauce on the table with emphasis. Easter insisted on trying to introduce the hot sauce as a regular part of breakfast, but she seldom found any takers. This morning was no different.

"Castillo is bringing the coffee." He arrived just then, and the couple was introduced to the Meiers.

As they ate, the cousins compared notes on their all boys' and all girls' schools and concluded that separating genders was conducive to learning. "No one is trying to impress the other sex, and our minds are on our studies – well, most of the time."

"Why don't you drive over to Sally's, Carty," Lilly asked, "instead of walking?"

"I thought it would be more fun for Grant to hike the hammock trail. We're sure to see a lot of animal life. Grant wrote that he has a school project to report about animals that he sees on this trip.

"Later, Sheriff Elsmore will drive us to town in the Pierce Arrow, which will be a treat, and Blake will squeeze us into his old Crosley and bring us back here this evening about six for dinner. Can we add him to the table?"

"Certainly, Carty. If he keeps growing, he won't be able to get into the tiny car much longer. That boy appreciates a good meal."

"I'll say. Everyone, remember to grab some food before he does tonight, or there might not be anything left."

"Carty will be staying here overnight to keep you company," Lilly explained, "and to bring in a turkey tomorrow. It'll be good to see the old place full of people for a change."

"Didn't your machinery company supply some of the parts for Pierce Arrows, Dad?"

"Don't remind me, Grant. That auto company left me holding the bag for over a thousand dollars of brake parts when they went belly up in the Thirties. The Crosley brothers were a lot better. When they shut down their automotive line, they made sure that everyone was paid. I met those two brothers several times. As different as they could be, but both are quality people."

**THE** two teens gave the Zapatas a hand with the dishes and set out for Sally's. Carty carried her bow and a quiver of arrows. Passing the old tool shed that Castillo had rebuilt into a small but tidy house, they reached the rusted gate in the fence.

Carty hopped it easily, impressing Grant who followed a bit less smoothly. "Is there anything you can't do better than me?" he asked, half in jest.

"Hmm, nothing I can think of," she joked back, earning a soft punch in the bicep.

"Wow, that's like hitting a tree trunk. I sure don't want to get into an arm wrestling match with you."

Late November days were enjoyably warm in Winter Free, the stifling heat of the summer a distant memory. A gentle breeze added to the pleasant feeling as it swayed the tall grass that bordered the swamp in the distance, but suggested rain might be headed their way.

"We'll walk in single file. Stay close, keep your eyes open, and don't wander off the path. Some of the things you might run into are not as friendly as I am."

Carty walked deliberately while maintaining a steady pace. She glanced to the sides continuously but in such an unobtrusive way that Grant did not realize she was doing it.

"It has been two years since I last took this route, and that led to the most eventful time of my life.

"Hale, Blake, and I were on a botany school assignment with Mack Stein. You haven't met Mack yet, but we'll see him later today when we get together with the other guys. We needed one last plant specimen to complete the project when we spotted it outside of Sally's house.

"In those days, Sally dressed like a witch, black pointed hat and everything else. She even wore a little make up to make herself look older and meaner. Now she is the prettiest woman I know, not counting relatives."

"Weren't you afraid?"

"Afraid? We were terrified. I'm certain that none of us would have approached her house alone. We were ready to run like rabbits despite the safety in our numbers. I've thought a lot about that over the years. There we were, four strong, healthy kids, and there she was, one lone unarmed woman – and she wasn't scared, we were.

"It shows how much the brain is capable of working against our best interests. Even though we knew – well everybody except Mack knew – that witches don't exist, we allowed our imaginations to outwit our common sense. I try to keep that little lesson in mind whenever I need it."

"What happened when you went to her house?"

Carty was about to answer when she stopped and put her hand out to keep Grant in place. A family of Bobwhite quail emerged from the grass about twenty feet ahead. They marched on to the path in front of Carty's intended course, Mama in the front and a line of five youngsters in a cute, single file procession behind her.

Only the last in the line, the smallest, noticed the humans watching. The little guy picked up the pace while keeping a wary eye on Carty and Grant as he scurried ahead. Thereupon, he bumped into the quail in front of him and sent that bird into the one next in line.

For a few moments, the quail falling like dominos was amusing, but suddenly a brown blur shot from the tall grass, and in one motion the mother quail was snatched into the wide mouth of a fat diamondback rattler. In a second, snake and quail were gone. The babies scattered in confusion and fear.

"Life changes quickly in the wild, Grant," Carty sighed. "Let's stand here for a few moments to give that snake time to move on. He's a big one, and I don't want to startle him."

"I've never seen a rattlesnake, except in the Cleveland Zoo. I thought they were supposed to make a rattling noise. I didn't hear anything, did you?"

"That snake was stalking prey. He needed to avoid making noise. If he had seen large creatures like us approach, he probably would have slithered away, and we would not have noticed him. He might have stayed put, though, and then he would have had the rattle going as a warning. I wouldn't want to tackle that one. He was big, maybe six feet long."

"What kind was he?"

"An Eastern Diamondback. It is the largest venomous snake in North America. You don't have them as far up as northern Ohio, though. Their range stops in the Carolinas."

"What'll happen to the little quail, Carty?"

"They were very young. Without Mama to guide them along, I'd say that they have very little chance. They will all probably be dinner for a fox or coyote or another snake before too many days pass. It's sad. Bobwhites are cute, and I love the bob-bob-white sound that they make."

"It looks like I'll have an interesting report for school. I hope that my teacher will believe that I'm not making it up."

While they stood stationary, Carty answered Grant's earlier question.

"When we knocked on Sally's door that first day, she nearly scared us to death. We only got into her house because Aunt Lilly had been kind to her in the past. As fearful as we were at first, we were well on the way to a firm friendship within an hour. It was a really amazing turnaround.

"She was a recluse from generations of other recluses, but, as the only one remaining, she was aching for companionship. When she realized that we represented no threat, she opened up to us, and we quickly lost our fear."

"That's when the gang showed up?"

"No, not that day. We came back the next day to hear the rest of a story she read to us from family lore, *The Legend of Montooth*. That is when they attacked.

"We were lucky. They were good – well, two of them were good: The Cuban and Zeller." For a second, Carty paused. She had an uneasy feeling.

"Is anything wrong, Carty?"

"Uh, no, Grant. I just had an odd image of Zeller flash into my mind for some reason. Beats me why. It's nothing.

"Anyway, the other two were kind of dumb, but even dummies when they have guns are formidable opponents.

"I think it's safe to move on now. Stay on the center of the hammock as we enter the swamp."

"Someone put up hammocks in the swamp?" he questioned.

"Not the sleeping kind. Hammocks are dry land areas slightly above the water level in a swampy area. The path we will walk on is a hammock all the way to Sally's. The water may be a little higher than when I was here last, since the rainy season ended only a short time ago.

"I don't want you stepping off and into the swamp. Some of the critters can be unpleasant. Stay close now."

Having seen what lay off the path, Grant said, "Close is my middle name." Carty had to laugh. Grant was much more comfortable in the wild than Mack, but Grant reminded her of him.

As they walked, she pointed out several birds and more snakes, but nothing dangerous. One small gator swam nearby. At a large downed tree she paused. "This is where I first encountered the real Montooth and two of the gang, though I didn't know who they were at the time, and they didn't see me."

"Yikes," Grant said, pointing as he froze in place. He had learned his lesson well. Carty had told him to stay still when he saw a snake until she could identify it. "What kind of snake is that?"

Carty turned around and walked back a few steps. "Good spot," she complimented him. "I missed that fellow."

She reached down to gently pick up an eighteen-inch scarlet king-snake. Its yellow, black, and red banding made for an attractive design. She allowed it to curl around her arm as the snake looked at her more with curiosity than fear.

"This is a good one, Grant – a scarlet kingsnake. They don't get much larger, maybe another fifty percent tops. Obviously it is not venomous, or I wouldn't be messing around with it. They are rather gentle, which makes handling them easy. I'd have one of these as a pet, but Mom can't quite get past the Garden of Eden story when she sees any snake.

"There are lots of non-venomous snakes that are very aggressive, like the black racer which can get to six feet long. Even small black racers dislike people, and they will strike at the slightest provocation, such as trying to pick one up. Even though they are not venomous, it is not fun to get a bite from any large snake, and I've got the scars to prove it."

She slowly reached her arm out to Grant, who allowed the snake to move from her arm to his.

"Lots of snakes seem to like the warmth of our bodies. As long as you don't make any sudden moves or hurt it, the scarlet king is usually one of the friendlier snakes. There is one problem, though, and that is a similarly colored coral snake that produces one of the most deadly venoms.

"There are several ways to figure out what kind you have. The easiest way is to remember that the black and red bands never touch on a venomous coral snake, and those colors always touch on the scarlet kings.

"Corals are usually not found in swampy areas around here but you never know. Sally's grandmother almost died from a coral snake bite when Sally was a young girl. That snake should never have been in this area, but it was. That is why it is always best to know what you are looking at rather than guess.

"You can let that one go now."

Grant knelt down and gently directed the snake to the ground.

She pointed to her left. "We're coming up on Sally's house. Do you see that palmetto with the red poison oak leaves wrapped around it?" When he nodded, she continued, "The large tree to the left is from where I shot my first arrow that day. It immobilized one of the gang – Dredman – but pinpointed my position for The Cuban, the leader, to come after me.

"We did a cat and mouse for a long stretch until I made a mistake and he got a hold of me. "If Dad hadn't showed up when he did, I wouldn't be here today." Carty felt her heart beating faster than normal just from the memory, and she figured that was the source of her earlier unease.

Changing the subject, she said, "Let's see if I can get us on the other side of that water without getting soaked." She was mostly successful, but, as the water was high, the best way forward put them calf deep.

As they sloshed over the pasture, the Canfield house came into full view.

"Wow, that's formidable," he remarked.

"It was built more for defense than aesthetics. It's really a lot larger than it looks from this angle because you can't see the depth. The inside is a lot nicer than the outside – just like a rustic, national park lodge. You'll really like it."

As they approached the house, Grant experienced a sense of foreboding. The dark gray walls and dense background vegetation combined to boost the effects of the witch rumors. He forced himself to resist the feelings, remembering what Carty had said about the negative effects of the mind.

"I can see why you were apprehensive," he remarked.

The door was open to take advantage of the pleasant dry air and moderate temperature. Sally was waiting for them in the doorway.

"Hello, Sis," Carty said, as she gave Sally an affectionate hug. "This is my cousin, Grant Meier. He is from Cleveland. Grant, this is Sally Elsmore, formerly known as the Canfield Witch and now my 'adopted sister.'"

Grant was not expecting an ugly woman, because Carty had told him that Sally was pretty, but he did not expect anything like her irresistible beauty. Sally was dressed in loose beige slacks and a pink satin blouse.

She had taken to wearing moccasins since she retired her laced-up, black leather "witch" shoes. Unruly red hair poked out from under a Detroit Tigers baseball cap with the unmistakable letter "D."

"Hello, Mrs. Elsmore. Carty has told me a lot about you. She admires you a lot. I see you are a Tigers' fan."

With the latter comment, Sally looked confused, so he pointed to her cap.

"Oh, not really, Grant. I'm just partial to Old English lettering. It's nice to meet you at long last. Carty has mentioned her favorite cousin on more than one occasion.

"Would you like to come in for a cool drink before Carty gives us our lesson? I've just discovered something new. It's called Coca Cola. Have you ever tried it?"

Carty and Grant exchanged surprised looks. "Oh, yes, Sis. It's really popular at school."

Seeing their look, she continued. "Of course. I keep forgetting that things that are new to me have actually been around for quite a while. Do you know about Pepsi Cola too? I discovered that I can get a ten ounce bottle of Pepsi for the same five cent price as a six-and-a-half ounce bottle of Coke, but I like the Coke better."

"It's always a battle of money and taste preference for me too, Sis, especially when I was younger and that nickel meant a lot more to me."

The teens removed their wet shoes and socks at the door and followed Sally inside.

"I see what you mean, Carty," Grant said, as he entered the great room and looked around. The orange and brown autumn decorations abounded. "Your house is beautiful, Mrs. Elsmore."

"Why, thank you, Grant. Grandmother and I always put a lot into changing the seasonal motif, but that is more enjoyable now that there are so many others to enjoy it."

"This is the first time I've ever been here when you didn't have a fire going," Carty remarked wistfully. She missed the smoky aroma of burning oak.

"We always had a fire even in the summer, Grant, because we did our cooking over it. Since we modernized the kitchen with a new Hotpoint range, we use the fireplace only to heat this large room now. I miss it sometimes – it was like a friend – but the room is more comfortable in hot weather now, and it stays cleaner without the smoke."

Handing them Cokes from the new Frigidaire, Sally suggested that they head outside near the barn. Carty demonstrated how to pull the bowstring while aiming the arrow. After several minutes of technique and safety, she noted nodding heads that suggested that the lessons were going well, so she let fly with an arrow into the side of the barn.

"Ahh, that felt good," she remarked. "For years I practiced this nearly every morning before the sun rose: rain, cold, fog, notwithstanding. Being away at SPA, though, I seldom have the opportunity."

For about twenty minutes, the two pupils improved their performance under her competent tutelage. Then Carty pulled a rolled-up paper from her quiver that proved to be a target.

"Stay here while I retrieve the arrows and tack up the target – a series of circles in different colors with a black bull's eye in the center."

When she returned, she remarked, "You know how now. You've been hitting the barn. Let's see if you can hit the target. I'll go first with one arrow to give you the idea and so you'll know that I'm not all talk. Then you."

As she drew the string back, they noted how quiet and calm Carty became, almost in a trance as she stared at the target. She held her breath and let go. They were a mere fifteen yards from the target, so Carty's arrow hit the black bull's eye seemingly without effort.

Carty shook her head disgustedly. "Look at that. No more bragging for me. It is amazing how quickly you lose a skill when you do not practice."

Sally and Grant looked at each other in confusion. Sally was the first to speak. "Weren't you aiming for the bull's eye, Carty?"

"Yes, of course, but look how far off the center of the bull's eye the arrow is. At this short distance there is no excuse to be so inaccurate. Oh well, I guess it's to be expected.

"Sis, you are first." Sally's first two arrows hit the square of the target but outside of the circles. Then her third caught the outside circle, causing the other two to cheer and Sally to smile brightly. Four and five were slightly better, but by the sixth and seventh arrow, she was missing the target altogether.

"Your arms are getting tired, Sis. You are strong from your years on the farm, but the bow requires different muscles than you are used to using. You did very well for the first time."

Grant proved a better archer. All of his arrows hit within the circles. His first two were high, but he corrected that when Carty explained the adjustment he needed to make. None were in the bull's eye, but two barely missed.

The pupils continued for another hour, alternating with one another to rest their weary arms and hands. Finally, Carty gave a display that demonstrated that she had not forgotten anything. Every arrow clustered within the bull's eye, and her latter arrows were dead center, including one that split an earlier arrow ala Robin Hood. That brightened her mood.

"You two will have sore hands, fingers, arms, and shoulders tomorrow, but you are tremendous pupils. Believe me, it is not normal for rookies to do as well as you did."

"It probably had something to do with the teacher, Carty," Grant said, and Sally agreed.

"Oh, look, James is home."

Carty and Grant stood back while Sally rushed to the sheriff's car and the still newlyweds greeted one another fondly.

"Hello, Carty," James greeted. "This must be your cousin. It's Grant, right?"

"Yes, sir, it's a pleasure to meet you. Carty sings your praises all the time, if it is possible to sing in a letter."

Viewing the barn side peppered with arrows, he added, "I see that the lesson is ongoing. How are your pupils doing, Carty?"

"Really well, Sheriff. I'm almost ready for the apple on my head stage. Would you like to take a try with my bow?"

"I think I'll stick to my gun, Carty. Besides, with all those arrows in the bull's eye, I'm already intimidated.

"Sally told me to plan for chauffer duty today. Give me a few minutes to change into civvies, and I'll get the Pierce Arrow running."

"It's really nice of you to give us a ride to town, Sheriff, especially in the Pierce."

"Nonsense, we have to go to Homer's for weekly shopping anyway."

After a light lunch of bacon, lettuce, and tomato sandwiches and Lilly Lemonade, Sally said, "Grant, why don't you and James take a look at the Pierce while Carty and I clean up? It won't take but a few minutes."

The 1923 Pierce Arrow was a long four-door, red, except for the black fenders. The rear "suicide" doors opened from front to back. Large headlamps jutted forward from sloping front fenders that covered tall white walls on wood spoke wheels. Grant walked around the car, admiring every detail.

"Hop in the front seat, Grant. I'll negotiate the car over the cutoff's ruts and potholes until we get to Mocking Bird Road. Would you like to drive from there into town?"

"That would be super, Sheriff. Do you think I can do it?"

"You are a licensed driver, aren't you?

"Yes, sir, but it is more intimidating than Dad's Lincoln, especially that tall gear shifter."

"The sequence is just like a Lincoln's. It's just a bit more awkward, and sometimes you may have to double clutch between second and third gears. Carty had no problem when she tried it."

"It's really easy once you get the hang of it," Carty added, as she and Sally climbed aboard.

"Sure, Carty, but you can do everything well."

Carty laughed and replied, "Well, I am having a little challenge with trig this semester."

"Ah, my best subject. I finally found something that I can do better."

Grant mastered the balky clutch without difficulty and followed James' directions to Dairy Queen where the males in The Crew were waiting. After thanking the Elsmores for the ride, they headed toward the boys, who were already in line.

"Grant, it has been a long time," Hale said in greeting, as hands were shaken all around. "Mack, this is Carty's cousin, Grant Meier, whom we've been telling you about. Grant, this is Maximilian Stein. He goes by 'Mack' among friends."

"It's really cool to meet you, Mack. You're famous in Cleveland for the series you wrote about Blake and Hale. I recognized their names when I read your first article. It was cool to read about guys I knew. I can't imagine how it was to write about them."

"These guys make writing easy, Grant. There are such talented ballplayers, and they have so many great stories that the words just flowed."

"How did you like driving the Pierce?" Blake asked, embarrassed at the attention and anxious to change the subject.

"It's a little different than driving a modern 1953 car, but in a way, I like it better. There is something nostalgic about old cars."

From behind them they heard a voice, "'Nostalgic' is nothing but another word for obsolete, old, and worthless. My dad says everyone needs to buy a new car at least every other year, preferably more often."

"Oh, hi, Haywood," Carty said, with forced politeness. "Haywood Dolder, this is my cousin, Grant Meier. He's visiting from Cleveland this week. Haywood's dad owns Dolder Chevrolet, in case you hadn't figured that out."

"Cleveland, huh?" Dolder pontificated, ignoring Grant's outstretched hand. "They're not going anywhere. They can't hit their way out of a paper bag."

Grant had the kind of personality that led him to like nearly everyone he met, but he was having difficulty fighting off negative feelings about Dolder in only a few seconds' time.

Realizing that Haywood was referring to the Indians, Grant responded tactfully. "You have a point, Haywood. They could use more power at first base than they get from Glynn, but the pitching is without peer. Except for Feller who is nearing the end, the others are hitting their prime. That gives them a good chance for the next three or four years."

"We'll see," Dolder countered sarcastically, as he tossed his cigarette butt to the ground, "I'm figuring last place."

By this time their chocolate dipped cones were ready, and they left Dolder ordering at the window. "He seems to have strong opinions," Grant remarked as diplomatically as he could, generating rueful laughter from the others, including a spray of ice cream from Blake.

They explained to Grant that Dolder was their nemesis. He often connived to get the better of them, but it nearly always backfired on him. They recounted a number of instances, especially involving Carty, when Dolder had lost face and how, ironically, Dolder helped to get The Crew together originally.

Carty explained, "Before the Dolders moved to the new, fancy section of town, they lived on Rag Weed Road, the street behind Periwinkle where the three of us live. Haywood's yard abutted Hale's orchard, but Haywood hung out with kids on his street and had nothing to do with us.

"The girls in our neighborhood were too sissified for me, so I was craving friendship with these two guys, but they didn't want anything to do with me."

"Right," explained Hale, "We were pretty well convinced that she had cooties." That got him a laugh from Mack and Grant and a playful shove from Carty.

"One sunny day, Hale and I decided to play catch in his back yard. As we hustled out back," Blake explained, "we didn't notice Haywood hiding in one of Hale's orange trees."

"Haywood made a practice of stealing oranges from our orchard. When Blake and I arrived abruptly, it apparently caught him by surprise during one of his raids, so he climbed the tree to hide."

"In the meantime," Carty added, "I was in my front yard across the street and noticed them playing catch. I ran in and got my ball and glove. I raced across the street and tried to join in, but they wouldn't let me, no matter how much I pleaded.

"I remember Blake saying, 'Girls can't throw. Stay in your own yard.'"

Blake grinned at the memory and said, "After a few minutes, I made a wild throw to Hale, and the ball rolled under Haywood's orange tree. He panicked and dropped out of the tree, holding a sack of oranges. He grabbed our ball and ran for his yard. We yelled and gave chase, but he had too big a lead.

"Then another ball came flying from behind us and whacked Haywood in the back of his head. He went down in a big lump – he was a bit hefty even then."

"I really wasn't aiming for his head," Carty told them. "I was only about seven years old, so I wasn't capable of that kind of accuracy. I just reacted instinctively at the escaping thief and heaved a throw in his general direction. Gosh, was I scared when I saw what I had done.

"By the time the three of us got to Haywood, he was sitting up and rubbing the big bump I put on his head."

"We could see that he was not seriously injured, so I grabbed my oranges and his sack and told him he'd better not come back. There was more of that waiting for him from our good friend, Carty."

"After Haywood left, the boys invited me in to get some Kool-Aid, and we had a good time reliving the excitement. They went on and on about my great throw, and I kept quiet about the luck involved. I did admit to worrying that I had really hurt Haywood, but they assured me that Haywood's hard head couldn't be harmed. From that day on, the three of us have been nearly inseparable."

"Except for Sarasota Prep," Blake added ruefully.

# CHAPTER 13

## *Turkey Time*

*There is a passion for hunting something deeply
implanted in the human breast.*

CHARLES DICKENS

**NOVEMBER 1952**

Carty saw that Grant already had a simple breakfast set for the two of them.

"Good morning, Carty," he said, stifling a yawn. "Even for Dad, 4AM is early."

Carty poured milk on to her Shredded Wheat and spooned in so much sugar that the biscuits took on a gray hue. Sugar was an Andersson obsession, probably because of the heritage of the sugar mill.

"I was afraid that I'd have to knock on your door and wake everyone else up too, Grant."

"Actually, I usually get up at five on school days, so this isn't too much different. I have to ride city buses to St. Ignatius, and it's better to avoid the traffic during rush hour. That way I get there early and get a lot done before classes start."

They were dressed in army surplus olive drab except for gray baseball caps. Carty was allowing Grant to use her recurve bow, and she was carrying Michael's older style. She wanted to give Grant a chance at bagging a turkey this year, so she gave him the better bow. As they headed for Morose Swamp, Carty explained the turkey tradition to him.

"Before the War, Dad always supplied the wild turkeys for Grandpa Sven's Thanksgiving bashes. Grandpa always expected Dad to supply half of the turkeys and for the rest to come from Homer's general store. That way if Dad failed to produce, there would be some turkey to fall back on. Of course, Dad never failed.

"When he returned from Europe in 1945, he took me with him that first Thanksgiving, and I accompanied him each year afterward.

"When I was eleven, I thought that I had learned enough and that I knew everything. I told Dad that it was time for me to take over Thanksgiving responsibility from him. I half expected that Dad wouldn't let me go on my own, but he didn't resist at all so he could teach me a couple of lessons.

"That first Thanksgiving, hunting by myself was the biggest failure in my life. I know you think that I am infallible, but believe me, I can mess up as well as anyone, and I sure did that year.

"I went out on Monday, Tuesday, and Wednesday and did not come back with a bird. Down here, turkey hunting is an allowable excuse from school."

"Oh, man. The best we can hope for in Cleveland is a snow day and a half day off for the Indians' opener every April."

"I couldn't seem to track as well as I normally did when I was with Dad, and I was way too noisy. Turkeys are among the cleverest of all game. They are wary and alert. I knew that, of course, but I could not seem to get control of my emotions. The pressure of having Thanksgiving depend on me was more than I could handle at eleven.

"I saw only two male turkeys – we don't want to take the females – and both times they were too far away and in too much cover before they sensed something amiss. They left before I could line up an arrow.

"That year we had to settle for Homer's turkey, so the meat portions were really small. I tried to pass on the turkey when it reached me, but Dad made me take some. It made me feel even worse eating it. Of course, everyone told me not to worry about it, but I will never forget my disappointment at failing. It always takes a little out of the holiday for me."

"It must have been tough for you to go out the next year with that pressure."

"Actually, it wasn't. Dad really mentored me all during the next year. I learned as much that year as I had all the time before, because I was really motivated.

"He made me understand how difficult the pioneers had it. If they did not bring home their game, they did not have Homer's turkey to fall back on. They went hungry. That was real pressure. But they overcame every trial, or they did not survive. He wanted me to learn how truly easy we have it in these modern times compared with our ancestors.

"Dad told me that he really had not expected me to bag a turkey that first time on my own. He believed the pressure would be too much and that I hadn't learned enough from him. He said I was getting a bit too conceited, believing that I had learned it all. So when I bragged that I could go after the Thanksgiving turkey on my own, he let me learn my own lesson. I know now to recognize the limits to my abilities.

"After several months, I told Dad that I coined the Carty Motto: 'If you don't know what you are doing, you are going to do it wrong.' That's when he said he knew that I'd have no problem hunting for the turkey the second year."

"You are lucky that Uncle Michael wants to teach you what he knows. My dad won't teach me anything about business. I learn a lot from him just hanging around and listening to him when I work at his office in the summers and when he is on the phone at home. He wants me to be a doctor just like my brothers.

"I'm a whiz at math, chemistry, and physics, but I have no interest in biology. I hated slicing up frogs. Can you imagine a doctor who can't operate on his patients?"

"I really want to invent things and follow in his footsteps in the business, but Mom won't let me tell him. She says she wants to break it to him gently, but she never does. I was beginning to think that she was hoping I'd change my mind before she had to tell him. But she knows that college decisions are looming, so she promised that we could have a family meeting to talk about it before Christmas."

Carty thought about Michael and his limerock mine. He wanted her to follow in his footsteps, but she wanted to go a different route – just the opposite problem from Grant's. Life was confusing.

"Have you chosen a college yet, Grant?"

"I'd like to live away from home but not too far. Dad wants me to follow my brothers' footsteps to Princeton, but the East Coast is too stuffy for me. Michigan, Ohio State, and Notre Dame have science and business programs, so they look good. Is it true that you are going to Purdue?"

"Probably. With me living away at SPA, Mom is learning to accept the idea. There is a good chance that Blake, Hale, and Mack will all be going there as well. That would be so cool with all of The Crew together again. Have you ever thought of Purdue, Grant?"

"No. Not really. It would be fun in college with you guys, though, that's for sure. Do you think I'd be horning in if I went there?"

"Are you kidding? The guys like you a lot. It would be great if you were there too."

"Hmm. Maybe I'll look into their programs. They have to be good in science with all those engineers. I don't know about their business curriculum, though."

It was still pitch black with not a hint of a sunrise when Carty pulled up at the fence to give instructions. A misty rain added to the gloom.

"We're going to get wet today, but it's a warm rain. The good news is that it will mask any slight noise we make.

"Previously, I hunted the fields and swamps on the other side of Dad's limerock mine. Hunting in Morose Swamp will be a first. Normally, I wouldn't look for a new spot at such a crucial time. However, I've been in Morose Swamp three times in the last few years, including the day we went to Sally's. Each time I saw quite a few turkey feathers along the hammock, so it looks like a good location."

Grant had not noticed any feathers on the trip through the swamp, but he was not surprised that she had and he had not.

"Foxes have the reputation for being wily, but turkeys, especially the Florida Osceola, have them beat. Once we get set up, we have to avoid any unnecessary movement and maintain strict silence."

She ran through a number of hand signals that she expected they might need: a rising hand to indicate standing; a mimic of pulling a bow string; a vertical flat hand to indicate no movement; and several others.

"I'll find a spot in the tall grass so that we will each have a tree and the expected location for our turkey between us. That way we will be able to stand and get ready without being seen.

Recalling that they encountered the rattler in tall grass, Grant asked about that possibility.

"That won't be a problem. When I set us up, I'll check out the area first. If a snake comes later, just stay still, and it'll leave when it senses you. On the outside chance that one keeps coming, you can always use your bow to keep it away and encourage it to go elsewhere."

That answer did not give Grant much comfort, but he had confidence in Carty's ability to keep him safe.

From a pocket, Carty removed a small rectangular wooden box and held it comfortably in her hand. A thin piece of wood was attached to the top of the box in a way to allow it to pivot. Both wood sections showed wear.

"This is a turkey call. Depending how I use the striker, I can make a sound like a purr or a cluck to attract the Tom. I don't think that we will need it today, given what I have seen of the feathers, but it's my back-up plan." Michael had taught her to always have a back-up plan in everything important.

After hiking a couple of miles, they were in the high grass at the edge of Morose Swamp. Carty stooped to pick up an iridescent, copper-colored feather that she handed to Grant. "That's from a male turkey. The girls' feathers are not this bright. We only go after the males so the ladies can keep the population up."

She selected two positions behind large oak trees as she had explained. They were about thirty feet from one another, too far away to allow for discussions or oral instructions. Grant refreshed the hand signals in his mind, though they were obvious in their meaning.

Carty showed him how to keep within the tall grass and how to slowly and steadily stand, using the tree for cover when a turkey arrived. They settled down for a long, quiet wait.

By mid-morning, the sun was above, but they could barely notice the difference as the thick clouds masked most of the light. Thankfully, the clouds and drizzle kept the temperature down.

Grant continued looking forward, hoping to see their quarry, but so far only rabbits, squirrels, and small birds ventured into the zone. Whenever he glanced at Carty, he noted that she seemed like a statue, despite the bugs that were beginning to stir. In fact, Carty occasionally did look at Grant and was pleased that he had taken her instructions well.

Around noon, Grant was getting hungry, so he reached into a

pocket for some beef jerky that Castillo had prepared for them. As he looked down at it, he noticed a short colorful snake moving toward him. It looked like a scarlet kingsnake, but he remembered that the coral snake looked similar.

"What was the difference?" he questioned himself. "Oh yes, 'red black together' is good. When they don't touch, that's the problem snake." He realized that he had been holding his breath when he told himself that this one was okay. The scarlet king continued slithering in Grant's direction until it reached his shoe. At that point, it stopped and looked up at Grant. As if to say, "oops," it immediately reversed and departed in the direction from where it had come.

When Grant looked away from the snake, he saw a large turkey walking on the path. Excited, he readied himself and looked at Carty for instructions. She gave him a slight shake of her head to indicate that this turkey was not one they were looking for. Grant was confused. He did not know what size this turkey was, but it seemed plenty large enough. Likewise, its feathers had the iridescent sheen of the males.

He settled himself back into his natural blind. He was getting cramped and wanted to stretch. The big Tom eventually left the hammock and disappeared into the dense forest, and all was quiet, save for the buzzing insects that had found Grant.

About two-thirty, Grant noticed movement ahead. Straining his eyes, he saw a second turkey strutting along, stopping to peck at things on the ground. It appeared to be a male, but somewhat smaller than the first. He glanced at Carty to determine if she saw the turkey too. He found her smiling back at him and nodding.

Carty gave him the "stop" sign to keep him quiet and to relax him. The turkey was out of Grant's range with the bow. Fortunately, the turkey continued in their direction, less wary than he should have been. Though predators like fox and coyote posed a danger to turkeys, human hunters did not frequent Morose Swamp. Perhaps this turkey was a bit too confident as a result.

When the turkey was in range, Carty signaled Grant to stand. She was pleased to see that he kept the tree as cover perfectly. When he was upright, she gave him the signal to draw back the bowstring. He did so while still behind the tree. Then he placed a foot to the right of the tree trunk and slowly eased the bow and the right side of his body around until most of his body was facing the turkey.

Carty had explained that a front angle was preferred, but that he should aim for the upper wing if he had only a side angle. Fortunately, this bird continued its leisurely pace directly toward Grant's position. For a moment, the turkey stopped and raised its head as if an instinctive sixth sense kicked in. That heightened pose worked to Grant's advantage, however, and he let the arrow go.

The arrow sped to nearly dead center before the turkey could react to the sound of the bowstring. The big bird sprawled backward and was motionless. Grant, who had never before killed anything save a bothersome insect, had a sudden pang of guilt.

Carty saw this in his hesitation. She walked over to him.

"Well done, Grant. You've taken to lessons well."

Placing an arm on his shoulder, she added, "To tell you the truth, I felt the same way my first time. But, you know the turkey we will be eating from Homer's store? Someone had to kill that one too. Don't feel bad. God made us omnivores, and it is nature's way for us to include meat in our diets – and there is no way to do that unless an animal gives its life."

Carty tied the turkey's legs together so that Grant could carry the big bird over his shoulder on the way back. "This one will be about seventeen pounds after plucking and preparing, Grant."

"Why didn't we go after the first turkey? He was even larger, wasn't he?"

"Quite a bit larger. He went over twenty-five pounds. I have a theory about leaving the larger animals alone. It applies to fishing too.

"A hunter is told to release the small animals in the belief that they are not fully grown yet, and to take only the largest. That seems unproductive to me. If we allow the largest and most robust to repopulate a species, the offspring should get bigger and stronger too. If we keep throwing the small ones back, they may be runts, not youngsters. If so, we will be expecting the runts to regenerate the species.

"Anyway, whenever I see a prime specimen like that first turkey, I leave it to help future generations."

# CHAPTER 14

## *Thanksgiving*

*The Pilgrims made seven times more graves than huts. No Americans have been more impoverished than these who, nevertheless, set aside a day of thanksgiving.*

H. U. WESTERMAYER

**NOVEMBER 1952**

The two early birds, Lilly and Grant, were up before sunrise as usual. Grant was enjoying another morning chat with her. Lilly held so much unwritten Florida history in her head that he could have spent a year in these morning coffee klatches and still barely tapped her memory bank.

In the vast dining room of the Andersson Manor House, the table was set for fifteen – of whom fourteen would be seated. Following the dictates of Sven Andersson's will, the seat at the head of the table was reserved for him as it had been each Thanksgiving since he died in 1938.

He bequeathed to Lilly the mansion and a generous acreage of citrus, with the proviso that she hosted an annual Thanksgiving feast to include everyone living on the property on the November date. She was required to continue the tradition as long as she lived. Failure to comply would result in her forfeiting the property to the state of Florida.

Dr. Duffy Brannigan was named in the will to witness the event annually, for which he received a stipend of three hundred dollars each year from Sven's trust.

"Easiest money I've ever made," he told Lilly on many occasions. "All I have to do is show up, jot down the names of the guests, note that Sven's place is set, and send my report to the trustee at the bank. On top of that, Mrs. Brannigan and I get to eat our best meal of the year in your beautiful house."

When Sven was alive, the feast was often held outside because of the large number of guests. The sugar mill operated at its peak employment at over a hundred, including as many as a dozen employees in temporary and permanent quarters on the property. Sven invited every employee who lived on the property plus family members to join him on Thanksgiving.

"Fourteen seats at the table may seem like a large group today," Lilly told Grant, "but we often had as many as sixty when Dad was alive and the mill was running at full scale."

"Why did your father close it down?"

"Though he had no known family in Sweden, he had many friends from his early days in Göteborg. He also had kept in touch with former shipmates retired in England. So he was well aware of what was going on with Hitler in the Thirties, more so than most in this country who were paying little attention to Europe."

"Dad realized that it would be a matter of time – and not too much time – before we were drawn into the conflict. He believed that sugar would not be considered a vital industry, and he would lose most of his workforce to the military.

"Anyway, he wanted his best men to be prepared to help in the war effort and to contribute more than they could either as foot soldiers or sugar workers. The Army, Navy, and Army Air Corps had a number of cadet training programs at the time. Engineers were among those in high demand, and the sugar plant had plenty of men who knew machinery.

"Dad encouraged his men to sign up for these programs. Initially, a few took his advice, but most wanted to continue working for him. Finally, in order to move them along, he announced that he would be closing the sugar operation, and he invited military recruiters to set up in this dining room. Each of Dad's men came in and listened to the pitches and made the choice right then and there.

"Off they went into training programs. Most became officers and saw active duty in every major theater after Pearl Harbor. Nearly all survived the War, and many have become prominent citizens in Winter Free and elsewhere in Florida. Almost to a man they have mentioned to me how much they appreciated Dad pushing them into those officer training programs where they learned to be leaders.

"Only two decided against signing up that day, and both were later drafted and shipped off to the Pacific where they faced enormous hardships – not the least of which was seeing many of their colleagues killed before their eyes. Both have since come to me saying they rued not listening to Dad.

"Dad's biggest regret was failing to convince the recruiters to sign up his black employees. But there was no convincing the Government in those days. Once Government develops one of its 'we know what is best' attitudes, there is little that ordinary citizens can do.

"So Dad kept the mill operating on a limited basis for almost another year so he could gradually find jobs for his black workers. It was not as difficult as it might have been because his workers were well trained, and other businesses knew it. Of course, by 1942, blacks were being drafted too, and finding a job was the least of anyone's worries."

*CARTY* joined them just as they heard, "Good morning, Sra. Andersson, Srta. Carty, and Sr. Grant," from Easter in the kitchen. "We see you have awakened before us once again. Castillo will be along shortly. He is picking some oranges for juice. I recommend a small breakfast of eggs this morning. The meal later will be big."

They greeted Easter and agreed that eggs and toast and strawberry preserves on Wonder Bread toast would be a suitably light breakfast that morning.

Preparation of the Thanksgiving meal was a community event, and everyone in the household was expected to pitch in to help the Zapatas, who would be joining the others at the table.

The Brannigans were bringing a rainbow of pies including mincemeat, cherry, key lime, and pumpkin, but Lilly was baking her own rhubarb with the fruit that Tom Meier had harvested before the first snows pelted Cleveland.

Sally promised to contribute unusual vegetables from her extensive garden. She was not satisfied with traditional vegetables and always planted exotics to keep the family table interesting. She was also supplying the cranberries in a special Canfield recipe that dated back sixty years.

One of the ships financed by the Canfields brought back a sampling of mandarin orange seeds from Tangiers in the Nineteenth Century. Several trees descendant from those seeds grew on the Canfield estate. No Canfield Thanksgiving was complete without mandarin orange sections liberally sprinkled into a serving dish of whole cranberries.

Tom and Rita arrived as the first eggs were being served. "Sunny side up, *Señor*," Easter said. "I will have yours scrambled shortly, *Señora*."

"Excellent as usual, Easter," Grant complimented, as he cleaned up the remaining yolk on his plate with his buttered toast.

"What time will everyone be arriving, Aunt Lilly?"

"We are eating at two. I expect Duffy and Pat Brannigan will be here about one, and the Elsmores the same. Michael and Bay are due about ten so they can give us a hand. Could you and Carty pick some flowers from the garden and arrange a centerpiece for the table?"

"Tiger lilies, Aunt Lilly? I know lilies are your favorites, but there aren't any white ones in your garden."

"Yes, tiger lilies, indeed. I wouldn't want white today regardless. The roses are in bloom. Add several of the orange roses to go with the autumn season. Those would be nice for this time of year."

Grant silently hoped that Carty was good at arranging flowers. He could pick them, but putting them into a nice display was pushing his creative talents.

Castillo brought a pitcher of freshly squeezed orange juice full of pulp and poured large glasses all around. Grant helped himself to a second glass. "I cannot get enough of this. It is so good. If we were home right now, it'd be apple cider."

"Sra. Andersson, will we use both ovens or squeeze both turkeys into the big oven?"

"Let's use both, Easter. It's easier to figure the time needed when they are kept separate. Grant's bird is just under eighteen pounds, and the store-bought turkey from Homer's runs twenty-two. We'll give Homer's an hour head start so the turkeys finish about the same time, and give the stuffing time to cook well in both."

Lilly and Easter had prepared two recipes of stuffing the previous night. Lilly used her traditional recipe, but Easter's version added spicy Italian sausage and a small dash of chili powder. Lilly was skeptical about the hot version, but Easter assured her that it would be well received. Of course, Easter always believed that something hot and spicy would be well received.

"Hello, everyone," Bay greeted as she entered. "We got an early start this morning, so we came ahead of schedule."

She carried a massive garden salad of lettuce, bell peppers, mild red peppers, cucumbers, shallots, tomatoes, mushrooms, sliced olives, eggs, and slivers of ham and cheese. Michael brought the salad dressing in a large cruet. Castillo's offer to provide the dressing had been unanimously rejected by everyone as they knew his preference for straight vinegar.

Homer had run a special on jumbo shrimp and oysters for the holiday. His little general store had grown to a large grocery with many specialty items by 1952. Michael had loaded up on those shellfish appetizers, and Castillo was allowed to prepare a cocktail sauce as a way to make up for his rejected salad dressing. His recipe, though hot in his wife's tradition, was delicious: Heinz Ketchup, grated horseradish, Lea & Perrins Worcestershire, Tabasco Sauce, and a dash of lemon juice.

Carty and Grant headed for Lilly's flower garden, with Grant confessing to no style sense as they walked.

"Don't worry," Carty answered. "I'm not too good at most of that domestic stuff myself, but I can handle a floral display. It has always seemed like a version of the out-of-doors to me, and that is my bailiwick."

First they cut enough red roses with short stems to establish a bed.

"Okay, now we need the orange roses. Leave a longer stem on these so that they can create a layer higher that the reds."

After some time, they gathered the roses and tiger lilies and brought them into the house.

"That took a long time, kids," Michael commented as they came in.

"Oh, we found a nice scarlet king and watched it for a while."

"Carty sure knows her snakes, Uncle Michael. I could never learn all that she knows."

"Sure you could, Grant. The swamp is her environment. You know every baseball statistic, but Carty doesn't. She couldn't tell you who has the highest lifetime batting average, for example."

"Ty Cobb – .367, Dad. Everyone knows that."

Grant stifled a grin.

"Yes, well, you get my point, Grant. You know a lot more about some things than Carty does. Don't sell yourself short."

"I know what you mean, Uncle Michael, but I've always been in awe of Carty. She is special, isn't she?"

Giving his daughter a hug, he answered proudly, "She is that, Grant. I did not mean to criticize Carty. I just want you to know that you have a lot going for yourself too."

Carty placed a base of Spanish moss into water in a deep, oval crystal bowl. She arranged a layer of red roses first, anchoring their short stems into the moss. Then she added a double layer of medium-stemmed orange roses. She topped it off with tiger lilies whose stems were cut to the exact height to extend beyond the top layer of the orange roses. She left a few of the tiger lily leaves to add a small green offset. Then she and Grant carried it to the dining room and set it in the middle of the table.

The ladies rotated basting the turkeys, not on any schedule, but with the typical nervousness that a major meal might go awry if not constantly fussed with and watched.

Carty and the men were in the parlor with the television tuned to some unremarkable show. Lilly had purchased the Muntz TV so she could watch film of the coronation of Queen Elizabeth II scheduled for June. The coronation was to be the first televised in England, and the plan was to send film of the event via jet airplane that night to the U.S. and Canada for viewing in North America.

"The Dumont Network televised the NFL Championship game last year," James mentioned. "It's too bad they aren't televising the Detroit-Green Bay Thanksgiving Day game."

Castillo surprised the others with a comment displaying an unexpected knowledge of football teams from Michigan and Wisconsin. "I am not sure why anyone should bother to watch. Detroit always trounces the Packers. Green Bay will never top the Lions."

Carty did not expect such conviction, and she looked at him with curiosity. As a rule, his demeanor was introverted, almost subservient. She was happy to see that he had a strong opinion about something, even something as trivial as an NFL football team from over a thousand miles away. Detroit did follow Castillo's script that day, though not on television, clobbering Green Bay 48-24.

Lilly called to them to come into the dining room. Castillo and Michael were drafted into lifting the big birds from the oven and carving them.

Grant claimed both birds' large hearts when no one else asked for them, and both Grant and Carty took hold of a drumstick from the wild bird. Carty stuck with white meat from the wild turkey, but Grant took some white and dark from both birds. Others selected nice slices of white meat to anchor plates full of the various vegetables, breads, and casseroles.

Lilly bowed her head, and the others followed suit. The Meiers and Brannigans made unobtrusive Signs of the Cross.

"We gather one more time, Lord, under your protection and in your generosity. We are thankful for the bounty that you have made available to us and our country. We ask you for peace on the Korean Peninsula. We know that this wondrous food is not a gift and is something that you expect us to work for, but we acknowledge that without your beneficence, our work would be for naught."

She added the traditional tribute to her father, "We also give thanks to Father, whose drive and character added so much to Winter Free and to all of us who descended from him.

"As some of us grow older, we recognize that we may not be present next year or the next following, but we are ever grateful for the time you have granted us on this beautiful earth. We hope that when our time is done, you judge that we have been good stewards of your land and contributors to its people. Amen."

"Amens" rang out from the assembled in response.

Carty saw her parents exchange knowing looks at Lilly's words, and she disliked what she was seeing. She made note to inquire later. She was old enough now to hear bad news if there were any to be heard.

The meal was accompanied by nonstop conversations, laughter, and reminisces. "It is sad that we don't see your children at these events anymore, Pat," Lilly said to Mrs. Brannigan.

The Brannigans' children, once a mainstay of Thanksgiving at Lilly's, were all living outside of Florida, including Sean who was an Air Force colonel stationed in South Korea. Duffy passed on tales of the difficulties U.S. pilots were facing with the Russian MiG aircraft.

"After WWII, we let down our guard and allowed the Russians to move ahead of us in some areas of military technology. The only thing that saved us was that we had not yet fallen too far behind. We certainly have learned our lesson. We have a much smaller population than the Russians and the Chinese. The only way we can remain safe is to use our technology to stay ahead of them."

James offered, "You all know that as county sheriff, I am a Democrat officeholder, and there is no way Florida voters would elect a Republican sheriff. But there are times when I look at the national Democrats and wonder what they are thinking when they insist on cutting back on our military. It's as though they are on a suicide mission. But enough about politics."

James asked if the new Gunsmoke[13] show that had debuted on the radio in April was being heard in Cleveland too. Grant said that it was his favorite show, and that it was probably broadcast everywhere.

Carty suggested that the reason for Grant's enthusiasm was Miss Kitty, a woman of dubious morals. That caused good natured chuckles and a blush to Grant's face.

He quickly changed the direction of the conversation. "There is even a rumor that it might be turned into a television show someday."

Bay, a dedicated fan of newspaper gossip columns, demurred. "William Conrad is Marshal Matt Dillon's voice on the radio. He has a great baritone, but he is really hefty. I don't see how he could be believable as Matt Dillon on television."

"They'd just have to get someone else for the part, Mom."

"It wouldn't be the same without Conrad's voice, Carty. I don't see any chance of a successful TV show."

When the meal was over, the men were banished to the parlor to light up their cigars and cigarettes away from the women. Although there was no football game on television that Thanksgiving, the score of the game in Winter Free was Anderssons and Guests: 14, Turkeys: 0, as little remained of the two large birds.

# CHAPTER 15

## *The Request*

*We can draw lessons from the past, but we cannot live in it.*
LYNDON BAINES JOHNSON

**NOVEMBER 1952**

Bay and Carty were up early the day after Thanksgiving. "Carty," Bay Andersson called from the laundry room, "I think I hear Mr. Donelee coming. Be a dear and bring in the milk – but don't skim the cream from the tops of the bottles."

"Oh, Mom, I haven't done that since I was five. Don't you ever forget?"

"Carty, you did enough mischievous things to fill a book, and I remember them all just in case you become famous and I get to write them all down for *The Saturday Evening Post.*"

That drew a laugh as Carty headed out the front door to meet Don Donelee and Greta, Donelee's horse. As Greta drew to a stop, Carty held out her hand flat with two sugar cubes in her palm. Greta nibbled the treat from her, and Carty rubbed the old mare's face gently.

"Hi, Mr. Donelee. What's our order today?"

"A bit more than usual now that you are home. Three quarts of milk, strawberry ice cream, and a pound of butter. You're not meeting me so you can skim the cream off the milk, are you?" he chuckled.

"Gosh, not you too, Mr. Donelee!" Carty exclaimed. "I could use a chunk of your ice, though. Somehow it tastes better than the ice from our Frigidaire[14]."

He reached back into the wagon and handed her two from the chunks that were strewn among the milk bottles to keep them cold. "You'd better take both. This may be your last chance. Next week they retire Greta, and I start driving one of those fancy new refrigerated trucks – no more ice to keep the milk cold. I guess it'll be better, but I'll sure miss Greta. We've been running this route together for sixteen years."

A melancholy mood descended on her as she took the dairy products into the house. She muttered to herself, "If change is for the better, why do I so often feel bad about it?"

"Did you say something, Carty?"

"Oh, no, Mom. Nothing important. Grant and I are heading off to see Sally when he gets here. I think I'll stop in to see Mr. Novotny too." In fact, the visit to Novotny was the prime reason for her bike ride.

"We'll be back in plenty of time for dinner."

*AT* the beginning of Hostetter Cutoff, Carty pointed the way to Grant. "I'll join you in a while. You remember that I wanted to stop in and say hello to a friend, Mr. Novotny, first."

At the beginning of Novotny's driveway, she absently noted his name on the mailbox. She knew that it was Vosmik Novotny's house without needing to see the printed name.

Riding up the narrow concrete driveway, she recalled the story Hale Wending told many times about making the run up this same driveway two years ago.

Her life and those of the rest of The Crew and Sally Canfield balanced on a small tipping point that day. If Novotny had refused Hale's request to call the sheriff – some locals had already turned Hale away – The Cuban would have killed the five of them and made off with Sally's fortune in financial bonds. Carty thought many times how one small occurrence can determine the fate of major events – "For want of a nail a kingdom was lost" carried special meaning for her.

Her solid knock soon brought Novotny to the door. "Carty, what a pleasure. Please come in. You said that you wanted to discuss something when you phoned?"

"I came to ask a favor, Mr. Novotny."

"You won't find a seat in all this clutter," he said, sweeping his arm toward stacks of boxes and piles of papers, each taking up almost every horizontal surface in the room. "Let's go to the kitchen. I apologize for the mess, but I'm in the midst of packing."

"So I see. Are you moving away from Winter Free?"

"Not exactly, Carty. I've been asked to return to Washington to help out an old friend. I'll keep the house here for vacations and," he laughed, "for my next retirement."

"Oh, that might mean you won't be able to help me, Mr. Novotny."

"Not necessarily, Carty. I don't leave until January. Why don't I get some lemonade for us, and you can tell me about it."

Carty followed Novotny through the house, glancing at several photographs of famous people on the walls – always with Novotny included: Novotny on a ship with Winston Churchill in profile in the background and Pres. Roosevelt seated in a wheelchair; Novotny laughing as Gen. Patten displayed his ivory-handled revolver in front of a half-timbered, German-appearing building; and Novotny with stuffy Charles de Gaulle, the Eiffel Tower between them far in the distance.

She vaguely recognized some of the others but could not place their names, though she did know the man who was dressed in an army colonel's uniform in a photo evidently taken in London.

Carty admired an unexpectedly large kitchen, well-provisioned with shiny copper pots and pans hanging from hooks and neatly labeled canisters organized by size on the ample marble counters. She did not know why she was surprised, other than she was accustomed to a kitchen being a woman's realm. It appeared that the kitchen would be the last room packed, as it remained in perfect order.

She took a seat on one of the straight-backed Shaker[15] chairs that Novotny gestured her toward. It was one of eight located around a basic table of similar design. The arrangement centered in a large alcove on the east side of the kitchen. Sunlight streamed through the floor-to-ceiling windows that formed nearly a semicircle exposing the yard in the back of the house.

Carty saw two adult goats roaming the expansive lawn that fanned out from the house.

"I see that you've spotted my automatic lawn mowers, Adolf and Josef. I named them after my two least favorite people, Hitler and Stalin, both of whom, like my goats, ravaged most all where they roamed.

"In the goats' case, however, I can control the devastation by relocating them every few days. If I didn't, they would eat the vegetation to bare ground, much the way those two tyrants devastated whatever they got their hands on.

"Would you like a turkey sandwich? I have some leftovers from the Wendings' big dinner yesterday."

"Oh, no, Mr. Novotny. I'm 'turkeyed out' by this time."

"Have lemonade then, Carty. It's not the tasty recipe of your Aunt Lilly's, though," he said, as he put a glass on the table. "How is she, by the way?"

"She has slowed down a little, Mr. Novotny, but she is as alert and as driven as always. Fortunately, she hired a Mexican couple to help with the property and housework. They refurbished the old sugar refinery tool shed to live in, and they seem to be working out well. I'm no help living in Sarasota most of the time."

"And how do you like boarding school?"

"I was a little homesick when Mom and Dad dropped me off, but that lasted all of about a day. Then the work piled on so much I didn't have time to feel sorry for myself. And I made a very good friend who is my roommate."

"Oh, yes. The young lady from Cuba, Elena Rafferty. Your friend Hale has told me a lot about her. I hope that her family is not suffering from Batista's coup."

"She says her dad is not political and rolls with the constantly changing politics by staying out of the way. He is content to run his bank, regardless of who is in charge of the country. He has his beliefs, but he confines them to the privacy of the voting booth – when voting is allowed.

"At SPA, Mr. Novotny, Elena keeps me laughing and sometimes leads me into trouble."

"Hale did say something about you and Elena almost being suspended. That does not seem like you, Carty. What happened?"

"It was not funny then, I must admit, but a year later I'm beginning to laugh about it.

"We were the only freshmen on the softball team and looking forward to the big game against our chief rival, Sarasota High – the Sailors. We always have a big pep rally when we play them, and that year it was especially intense as we were playing our final game of the season against them for the league championship.

"A pep rally was held at noon in the school courtyard where the team set up a temporary stage. The band played loudly, and the coaches riled up the crowd of students. The cheerleaders had us all chanting for victory in the Sunday contest.

"For the Sarasota game, Mrs. Tutwiler, the headmistress, even lets her hair down. She grabbed the bullhorn and exhorted us to beat them. She was on the original SPA softball team that lost its inaugural game to the Sailors 59-0 back in ought-something or earlier, and she has never forgotten that humiliation – partly because the Sailors still refer to us as the 'Fifty-Niners.'"

"Mrs. Tutwiler is a widow, and she lives on the top floor, the fourth, of SPA's dorm building facing the rally courtyard. The floor where she and several of the unmarried teachers reside is strictly off-limits to students.

"Elena got the idea that we should do something special for the rally since it was such a big game. It was not too smart of her to concoct the scheme, but I have to admit that it was even dumber of me to go along instead of talking her out of it, or at least, refusing to participate.

"Anyway, we had found an old beat-up manikin that a local men's store had thrown away. We dressed him like a sailor and called him Spud. Later we found a long board from the school storage area and two stiff poles.

"As the rally was reaching its fever pitch, no one noticed when Elena and I slipped away. Back inside the school, we donned cheap black wigs over our blond hair as disguises, just in case, and made our way upstairs into the forbidden area – I felt a little like Eve approaching the Tree of Knowledge.

"We had to enter Mrs. Tutwiler's apartment, because it has the only window that faces the rally. We opened her window and pushed out the board, like a plank on a pirate ship. I sat on the back end of the board so it wouldn't fall.

"Elena eased out on the board and pushed Spud forward with one pole. She held him upright with the other pole roped to his neck. When he reached the end of the board, he stood motionless for several minutes with the toes of his shoes hanging over the edge.

"Another girl, Sandy, had agreed to help us. We needed her because she was the mistress of ceremonies at the rally. At the appointed time, she yelled into the microphone that the Sarasota High Sailors were nothing but dirty pirate scum and needed to walk the plank.

"With that said, she pointed to Mrs. Tutwiler's window four floors up. As the crowd turned around and looked, Elena edged out on to the plank a little and used the pole to push Spud off of the end, from where he fell to a heart-stopping thud in the courtyard. Of course, he looked like a real sailor from the distance, so there were several moments when dread and shock overcame everyone on the ground.

"Before he landed, Elena was already crawling through the window so we could make our escape. Unfortunately, just as she was half way through, the window came sliding down and pinned the backs of both of her legs.

"She was screaming, 'Carty get this window off of me; I can't move!'"

"I was already out the door, so I skidded to a stop and almost flew back to help. Well, whatever originally allowed the window to go up so effortlessly and had allowed it to fall so easily to pin Elena was no longer working. Try as I might – and I am strong from years of archery practice – there was no budging that window. Elena is convinced that Mrs. Tutwiler had it booby-trapped to catch unwary students.

"It probably did not help that I started to laugh, especially when Elena began calling me strange Spanish names I did not recognize and probably should not learn.

"Then Elena joined me in laughing, in between the tears from the pain of the window on her trapped legs. We both knew that we were doomed. Sure enough, we soon heard the elevator, and then Mrs. Tutwiler showed up with half a dozen teachers. At that point, we were no longer laughing," but at that point, Novotny certainly was.

"Carty, that is a wonderful story. So what happened to you?"

"Dad had to rush down to SPA that Saturday to meet with Mrs. Tutwiler. Mom had long ago given up on these 'Carty Meetings' as she calls them, from when I was at Cross Creek Elementary and things slipped out of control every so often. In those days, though, I really was not at fault. This time, there was no question that I was in deep.

"Since Mr. Rafferty lives in Cuba, he could not come on such short notice, so he convinced Mrs. Tutwiler to allow Dad to stand in for him on Elena's behalf. Suffice to say that we were placed on probation for the remainder of the semester. We also were assigned kitchen duty every Sunday after church and were made to tutor other freshmen who were having difficulty with studies. Actually, we kind of enjoyed the latter assignment.

"Although suspicion had fallen on Sandy, Elena and I refused to implicate her. She really did not know what we had planned, so it would have been unfair for her to suffer."

"So how did the softball team do without you two in the championship game?"

"Oh, well, Mrs. Tutwiler does not like to see the faculty and students being scared out of their wits watching a body falling four stories to an apparent death. Mrs. Tutwiler does not like students violating rules of any kind. And Mrs. Tutwiler especially does not like students trespassing in the faculty residences. But what Mrs. Tutwiler likes the least are the Sarasota High Sailors.

"She told us that not only were we to play in the championship game, but she also ordered us to win. Elena and I were so scared, we both had our best games of the year, and we smacked the Sailors 10-2. But the performance did not earn us any leniency; that's for sure. I shudder to think what might have happened if we had lost."

"A toast to your victory, Carty," Novotny said, tipping his glass in her direction. "Now what kind of favor can I do for you?"

"You know that the leader of the criminal gang that attacked Sally Canfield's escaped and has never been identified."

"Yes, Carty, The Cuban, the so-called 'Mr. Smith.' Some believe that he might have perished in the swamp and become food for the critters there, but the sheriff and most others believe that he did get away."

"Mr. Novotny, I can confirm that he did get away, because a month ago I saw him in Havana. I was visiting Elena during summer vacation, and I noticed him at a coffee shop near the University of Havana.

"I set up a surveillance operation to see if I could track him to his home, but that didn't work out. Mostly, I failed because I took a very conservative approach. Elena does not have skills necessary for tailing someone, so I could not put her at risk. And my knowledge is in wilderness tracking, not following someone in a city."

"That sounds very prudent of you, Carty. I know your reputation. If you say you saw this man, then I know that you truly believe he was the one – but I have to ask, how certain are you?"

"In the swamp, that man was closer to me than you are right now. I could feel his muscular arms and smell his cigar breath.

"I once tripped while hunting and fell flat on the ground, where I ended up looking into the eyes of a water moccasin coiled up less than one foot from my nose. Mr. Novotny, I'd rather face those reptilian eyes again than have my cheek up against The Cuban's. I'm very good at recognizing people, and there is no question in my mind that he was the man I saw in Havana."

"Very well, Carty, but why does this bring you to see me?"

"Had he been in a swamp, I would not have hesitated following him, but on the city streets of Havana, I was entirely outside my area of expertise. In fact, he did what I call a 'double-back' that would have caught me flat footed had I attempted to tail him. I'm here because I want to ask you to teach Elena and me how to tail someone in a city."

"What makes you think that I could teach you those skills, Carty?"

"Mr. Novotny, most everyone in town knows you were OSS in the War. In fact, a few minutes ago, I noticed the photograph of you with William Donovan[16] in your hall. Dad has a photo of him in our house."

"Hale hasn't said anything to you?"

"Oh, not Hale. He clams up whenever anyone brings up the subject."

Novotny was pleased to hear that. He had really taken to the Wending family, and Hale in particular. He believed that Hale knew how to keep a confidence and liked getting this confirmation from Carty. He decided to probe before discussing Carty's request further.

"I haven't seen much of Hale since he met Lucille. He seems to be quite taken with her. I hope that his involvement with her doesn't sidetrack him from college."

"Oh, Hale likes her a lot, but that is not what is taking up all of his time. Mack Stein, one of The Crew, took a job writing for *The Gazette*, and Hale does a lot of background research for him in his spare time. Hale has no intention of letting a 'fluffy young thing,' as he describes her, interfere with his career ambitions – I can assure you of that. Besides, Lucille has her sights set on Tuskegee when she graduates."

"What does Lucille think of being called a 'fluffy young thing,' Carty?"

"Ha, she usually rolls her eyes, but sometimes she conks him one and says, 'Watch yourself, Ironhead.'"

"When I arrived in Winter Free after the War, Carty, I did not advertise my experience with the OSS, but as I was retired, and as the OSS was closing up shop, I did not take elaborate precautions either. That was a sloppy oversight on my part, because I am returning to Washington to join the CIA, the Central Intelligence Agency.

"After the country floundered a few years without a serious intelligence operation, the CIA started up in '47, and with the Russians getting nastier, it is being ramped up. They are calling a number of us old OSS types back to impart our experience to the new recruits.

"My position will be administrative, not covert, so I am not required to maintain secrecy. It is just good practice. Can I count on you to keep this information to yourself, Carty?"

"Of course, Mr. Novotny. No one knows that you are headed to the CIA?"

"Only a very few. In Winter Free, people know that I'm moving to Washington – the moving van company and the post office, for example – but I've kept the reason close to the vest. As I said, it is not really crucial, but I'd prefer to keep the reason confidential, if you don't mind."

There was no reason for Novotny to confide in Carty, but he was impressed with her and thought that in a few years, she might be someone he could use. Novotny learned to plan years ahead. Now was a good time to give her a test to learn if she could keep a confidence.

"Carty, I could help you with your request, but I'm not sure that having you two tracking this fellow is a good idea. Your parents are not likely to appreciate my encouragement."

"Truthfully, Mr. Novotny, Mom doesn't know anything about it. She would go cuckoo if she knew.

"However, Dad sent me over here. He has confidence that I could handle it if I learned your principles, since I took to his teaching about wilderness tracking so well. He is agreeable that I can try to track The Cuban to his home, provided that I avoid any confrontation. He trusts my judgment to keep Elena out of harm's way, and he got Mr. Rafferty's approval.

"Sheriff Elsmore and Sally tried to find The Cuban during their honeymoon. The sheriff spotted him at the same café where I saw him, but they were no more successful than we were in tracking him down. The sheriff is leery about going through the local police force, because he is afraid that it might result in someone tipping The Cuban off. Apparently, the sheriff had an unpleasant experience along these lines on another matter a few years ago.

"I'm going to Havana to stay with the Raffertys when I take a six-week Spanish immersion course during next summer vacation. Dad is letting me out of my commitment to work at his limerock mine during that time, and I think he wants me to have something more to do than Spanish homework. He is a firm believer in the 'idle hands being the devil's workshop' concept.

"I had to give up daily archery practice while I'm at Sarasota Prep – you can imagine what Mrs. Tutwiler would think with me firing arrows in the courtyard – and Dad is convinced that the 'Spud' saga occurred because I did not know what to do with my free time.

"Elena will be spending Christmas vacation with us next month. We could start then. Is that too close to your moving date?"

"Not at all, Carty, and it'll give me some time to prepare an instruction course for you and Elena." Novotny flipped through a calendar. "When are you available?"

"Shall we say bright and early on Saturday, the thirteenth?"

"That sounds good to me, Carty."

"How early? Six? Seven?"

"Seven is fine, Carty. We'll begin with breakfast. I'll start with general discussion as we eat. Be prepared for quite a bit of desk work at first. It'll be several days before we go into Winter Free and practice what you learned.

"Bring several changes of clothes – jeans, dresses, skirts, blouses, shoes, socks, hats, both casual and dressy. Some should be loose fitting and some snug. Bring a variety of colors. Borrow some of your Mom's clothes too, preferably older styles she no longer wears, if she won't miss them. I'll supply the rest."

"It's really nice of you to help us, Mr. Novotny. Hale has been so complimentary of you and what you have meant to the Wending family that I knew you would."

"I hope that my help proves useful, Carty, but finding one man in a large city may require more than I can teach you."

"I know that we may not be successful, but we saw him twice near the university and so did the Elsmores. I believe that he will return there. Since I'll be taking my class on campus, there is a good chance that we may see him there again.

"I have to be going, Mr. Novotny. My cousin is waiting for me at Sally's.

"I am free during the day tomorrow. If you think that I could be of assistance, I'd be happy to help you with your packing."

"That's very nice of you to offer, Carty, but I'm almost done. Homer gave me a seemingly unlimited supply of boxes from his store, so packing went smoothly. I'll see you two girls next month."

# CHAPTER 16

## *Circus Circus*

*What I dream of is an art of balance.*
HENRI MATISSE

**NOVEMBER 1952**

When Elena showed up for her third year of training with The Flying Wallendas[17], she impressed them with her progress. Karl Wallenda thought back to that first day two years earlier when he discovered her latent talent. "If I had not known better," he thought to himself, "I would have thought she was a long lost relative, as good as her natural abilities are."

## NOVEMBER 1950

*SARASOTA* Preparatory Academy had always taken the entire Thanksgiving week off, rather than only the Thursday-Friday. Since SPA was a boarding school with students from dozens of states and countries, many lived too far away to make the trip back home with only a four-day weekend.

Despite the week long break, however, SPA's dorms remained open to accommodate a good number of the foreign students as well as a few American teens whose self-centered parents were too busy to retrieve them. Fortunately, the Ringling Bros. and Barnum & Bailey Circus wintered in Sarasota, and SPA had long-standing arrangements for those students to work with and learn from the circus performers during Thanksgiving week.

The Anderssons invited Elena to spend her first Thanksgiving break with them. However, she opted to take advantage of SPA Circus Week.

Students had opportunities to watch performers training and practicing new acts. It was not all play, however, as the visiting students were expected to work during their stay – such as feeding the animals and cleaning their cages and helping with repair work on equipment and torn costumes.

A few students who displayed talent were sometimes allowed to apprentice with the performers at introductory levels. Elena had no interest in animal training, but she had been fascinated with the Wallendas, the high-wire performing family.

Like her brother Roberto, Elena possessed exceptional athletic skills. Karl Wallenda, the family patriarch, spotted her natural ability when Elena came to SPA Circus Week that freshman year.

He had strung a wire three feet from the floor of the indoor training building to show the students how difficult it is to balance on a strand of steel cable. First, he walked out on to the wire as easily as walking on a sidewalk while explaining techniques used to stay steady. He did not bother with a balancing pole.

After the brief lesson, the students slipped on moccasin-like shoes, and he invited them to try to walk the fifty-foot length. This challenge was always a source of good-natured amusement for the Wallendas and for the students, who seldom travelled as many as three steps before dropping off of the wire, often in a clumsy heap.

As usual, that day everyone toppled off – often on to their backsides – to the laughter of their classmates. When Elena approached the wire, her friends sensed that she might exceed the three typical steps, because she displayed uncanny balance every time gymnastics were part of physical education classes.

They were right. To Karl's surprise, Elena walked the entire length, slowly and tentatively at first, but then with more confidence and slightly more speed as she passed the half-way point. When she reached the far side, Karl motioned her back, to the applause of the other students and a few of the circus performers who had been enjoying the clumsy falls of the students earlier.

"You were *wunderbar*, Elena," Karl complimented when she made the return trip flawlessly and at speed double her first effort. "You have natural ability that is rare but necessary to perform on the wire. We can teach technique and hone skills, but we cannot teach balance, and we cannot teach fearlessness. Those you must be born with.

"I'd like to see how you do up there," he said to her, pointing to the high-wire about seventy feet above. "Would you like to give that a try?"

"Would I?!" the exhilarated girl answered, to the gasps and nervous giggling of her classmates.

"Okay, tuck your sweater into your trousers and tie your hair back so everything is as sleek as you can make it."

Karl led her up the pole until they reached the small takeoff platform. This would be the real test to see if she would be given the chance at a full week of training. Most people looking down from seventy feet above, even with the safety net strung below, would be sufficiently intimidated to back out.

Not Elena. Karl walked out on to the wire about twenty-five feet from the platform and motioned for her to come toward him, which she did without hesitation. When she reached him, he spoke with her for nearly a minute, ending with Elena nodding her head.

He squatted and reached out about knee high, cupping his hands. Elena stepped into the cup with her left foot and grasped him by the shoulders. Then she placed her right foot on to his left thigh and, as he maneuvered her around, lifted her left foot out of his hands and on to his right thigh. He spoke with her momentarily and got next the nod he sought.

With strong hands, he gripped her calves and lifted her upward. Elena stepped on to his shoulders and spread her arms straight up.

From down below, not a sound was heard. Elena held the position as Karl walked back to the platform, where she dismounted as gracefully as she had climbed up.

Wild cheers broke out from her classmates and teachers as she waved and grinned while climbing down the pole. When the congratulatory mob scene showed signs of tapering off, Mrs. Tutwiler led the students to the next part of the tour. Elena, however, remained to speak with Karl at his request.

"Outside of my family, many of whom inherit the ability, I have never seen anyone take to the wire so naturally. Have you ever done anything like this before, Elena?"

"I have a confession, Mr. Wallenda. One of my brothers, Roberto, and I strung a thick rope between two trees back home in Havana. It spans a small stream at our summer cottage. We've walked our rope for so many years that it has become second nature. At first it swayed too much, but then Roberto anchored the center with a post. We call it rope walking.

"As good as I may be, Roberto is better. I've ended up in the water many more times than he has, as we try to outdo each other's tricks.

"The funny thing is that none of our other brothers or sisters can walk it. They fall off after a few steps like the other girls on your wire today. Roberto and I have a lot in common that differs from our siblings. It is as if we are twins. However, he is about three years younger."

"Elena, I would like you to work with me this week if you would find that interesting. Perhaps more importantly for you, I will teach you some things that your brother will not be aware of. By the end of the week, he won't be your match, and you can dunk him at will.

"Oh, that sounds wonderful, Mr. Wallenda. I can't wait to spring it on him."

"At the week's end, next Sunday, the circus puts on an abbreviated show for families of the students. If we find students who show some aptitude, some of us incorporate them into the acts. For example, Mary Tighue, who is an SPA sophomore, was part of the lion taming act last year. She has no fear of the animals – only respect – and that is the key. I'd expect that a couple of the girls with equestrian experience will ride the horses and elephants. And we always get several to don clown costumes."

"We could develop a small part for you if you are interested. In a couple of years, you could be the student star of this show, but you'll need more than one week to do anything special. I have always wanted a student representative, but until now, none has ever showed your ability."

Karl introduced Elena to the other members of his family and told them that they would be training a new member of the troupe. "Elena is an SPA student, and if we train her well enough, maybe we can convince her to run away to the circus."

Karl's laugh was hearty enough to convince Elena that he was not serious, but for a fleeting moment, his joke inspired a romantic impulse. "Poor Father would have a heart attack," she thought to herself, "if he thought about me running away to join a circus."

For the next week, Elena worked harder and with more intensity than she had ever before dedicated herself.

"Repetition, repetition, repetition is necessary to achieve success, Elena. You must teach your muscles to respond exactly as you want them to at all times. They must perform naturally and automatically, because you cannot concentrate on everything at once. The only way to achieve that is to practice again and again."

Elena had good muscle tone and had always excelled at sports, so strength was not an issue. But back in her SPA dorm room on Saturday night after the first day of training, it seemed that every muscle ached. Her calves, quads, and feet especially found little relief despite a long soaking in a hot bubble bath. With most of the students away, she was grateful for the uninterrupted time in the tub.

"What did I get myself into?" she moaned, only partly in jest. "It is going to be tough un-kinking myself tomorrow morning."

But she gamely hung on all day Sunday after chapel. Whether Karl did not know that she was suffering or did not care, he pushed her beyond what she thought possible. She did notice that the repetition seemed to be helping. She noted that she was able to twirl ribbons from batons in large slow loops while barely paying attention to the wire she balanced on.

The aches on Sunday night did not appear to be quite as severe as she melted into another bubble bath.

By Monday night, her muscles were barely complaining, and her mind was concentrating solely on what she had learned. She was looking forward to three more years of this expert training.

## NOVEMBER 1952

"I practiced at home on our rope again all summer, Mr. Wallenda. Roberto won't go near me when I'm on it, because he knows that I will dump him into the creek. He tried everything that first summer, but your training put me too far ahead. I have relented slightly and taught him some of your techniques, but not enough to let him catch up."

One of the women took her measurements. "You are still growing, Elena – I'll get to work letting out your costume for you. In the meantime, you can wear one of mine."

"Elena," Karl advised, "You can be ready for a real act at the wrap-up performance this year if we really put an effort at it. Are you willing?"

"I can't wait, Mr. Wallenda."

Elena was progressing rapidly, and Karl wanted Elena to stay late each evening for additional work, but she had no way to return to the school after the SPA bus left. When Mrs. Tutwiler learned about Karl's request, she told Elena to stay. Alternative transportation would be provided. That evening, Elena was surprised to discover that Mrs. Tutwiler herself provided the ride in her personal car.

Elena had been a thorn in the side of Mrs. Tutwiler almost from the first week at SPA. Frequently Elena found a way to bend the rules – often for no more reason than wanting the challenge or seeking the excitement that the risk of being caught entailed.

Sometimes she slipped beyond bending, and sometimes she managed to co-opt another girl, occasionally Carty, into a scheme. Elena was a born leader, but she seemed devoted to directing that talent in the wrong direction. That was what infuriated Mrs. Tutwiler the most.

Mrs. Tutwiler admired Elena's spirit, though, and strove to reach this girl who had so much to offer. Reprimands and punishments had little effect. Praise was likewise largely ignored. The headmistress welcomed the opportunity that the car rides would provide to be with Elena outside of the structured school setting.

On the road from practice on the first Saturday night, Mrs. Tutwiler said, "I noticed you on that high-wire this afternoon, Elena. That is quite an improvement over your first and second years. The Wallendas are working you hard. I hope that it is not too much for you."

"Oh, no, Mrs. Tutwiler. They don't ask me to do anything that they do not do themselves. Anyway, if they let me slack off, then I would have to work all the harder to make it up. I really want to do a good job at the show next Sunday. I don't want to let Sarasota Prep down."

"That's it," Mrs. Tutwiler thought to herself. "Loyalty is the key to this girl. She will dedicate herself to protecting those she attaches herself to: her family, her school, her country. I've got to harness her devotion. I'll turn her into a model student yet.

"Elena, we are planning to involve students in the administration of the school rules after the Christmas break. The concept is to set up a student court or a tribunal to deal with minor transgressions." Mrs. Tutwiler was making this up as she spoke.

"We teachers have enough to do, keeping students' minds on their studies. It would be better if we could be relieved of routine disciplinary issues.

"Of course, the student administrators would necessarily be juniors and seniors. I would like to appoint you as one of the two juniors to serve. It will take some of your free time, but you are a good student, so I know that you are capable of taking on the added responsibility without your grades suffering."

It was as though Mrs. Tutwiler had spoken to her in a foreign language. Elena was not certain that she heard correctly. She paused at length before replying.

"You want *me* to be some sort of dispenser of discipline for rule-breakers? I don't understand. In all honesty, I don't seem to be the right person for that kind of job, Mrs. Tutwiler."

"Nonsense, Elena. Look at the discipline you applied to yourself to work on the high-wire. That is what I'm talking about: a dedicated and motivated person.

"Of course, we have to set the parameters yet, and we need to involve you girls in that process as well. We can start working on it as soon as classes resume. What do you say?"

"May I think about it, Mrs. Tutwiler?"

"Certainly. We will have a meeting with the girls who are selected next week. We have a lot of work to do. I'd like the group to be meeting regularly when the next term starts in January."

The next day, Mrs. Tutwiler placed two long distance phone calls.

*"SUNDAY* at 1PM," the program read, "Ringling Bros. and Barnum & Bailey Circus and Sarasota Preparatory Academy present a private showing of talent and excitement."

A total of fourteen SPA students were listed in the program as "assistant performers." Senior Mary Tighue was highlighted as a student lion tamer, and Elena Rafferty as a student high-wire performer. Several others were included as student clowns, riders, and tumblers.

The crowd of several hundred spectators, mostly friends and relatives of SPA students, grew restless as the time drew near. At precisely 1PM, the master of ceremonies strode to the center of the building. This being a training facility, it had only one ring for performances.

"Ladies and gentlemen," he began, as expected. "Welcome to the Ringling Bros. and Barnum & Bailey Circus and Sarasota Preparatory

Academy Special Performance of 1952. Students have worked diligently during the past week to give you a great show today. Let's hear it for them and for their instructors."

The first act involved acrobats who performed on the floor initially. Some of them jumped on to and off of rapidly circling horses at first and then elephants afterward. SPA students were relegated to riding the animals and waving. Afterward, trapeze artists swung though the air in a series of awe inspiring moves that did not include any SPA students but which were appreciated by the audience nevertheless.

When that ended, a tiny Henry J car rolled on to the ring and clowns began exiting the sub-compact vehicle. One by one they emerged, seemingly without end, until twenty-four clowns circled the ring, engaging in all sorts of high jinks that would have made The Three Stooges proud. Among the clowns were four students dressed in SPA school colors of silver and gold. Even their bulbous noses were bright gold.

Next, a large steel apparatus was wheeled into the ring and was quickly assembled into a cage for lions. Small cages on wheels, with lions inside, were connected to the main cage. When the gates were opened, the lions, having performed hundreds of times, knew what was expected of them. They moved into the main cage with regal bearing.

After the introduction of the lion tamer and Mary Tighue, they entered the cage, each with a whip and chair. The lions cowered on their perches. These were the older cats, those who had performed for years and who were inclined to behave well.

One took half-hearted swipes at Mary's whip and chair from time to time, but the others pounced on to and from the small stands and stood up on back legs as she directed. The trainer stood at the entrance, ready to take over if anything went wrong. However, he had trained her as well as he had the animals, so she performed the basic tasks with them perfectly.

The Wallendas were next. The announcer cautioned the audience to remain quiet during the performance, as any sudden noise might disrupt the precise balance required for the tricky performance. In reality, a locomotive could have roared though the building, and it would not have bothered these performers. The announcement was intended to heighten the anxiety of those in the audience.

The Wallendas put on an abbreviated but remarkable show on the high wire, including the famous pyramid that stacked seven family members with the woman on top seated on a chair. In fact, performing in this practice environment was almost routine for the family members, who often worked without a net during the actual circus.

When they finished, the announcer boomed out, "Ladies and gentlemen, Ringling Bros. and Barnum & Bailey Circus and Sarasota Preparatory Academy are pleased to present from Havana, Cuba, Miss Elena Rafferty, our student performer."

Elena appeared at the center of the ring, waving a hand to the audience as she walked to the center pole. She wore a shimmering silver outfit with bright gold piping, much like an abbreviated, one-piece swimsuit. Her tights were skin colored, her hair pulled into a tight bun.

The orchestra accompanied her ascent as she climbed the pole. To build excitement, she combined starts and stops punctuated with waves, the way she had rehearsed with Karl.

When she reached the platform, she bowed deeply, took hold of a long balancing pole, and stepped on to the wire. With grace and balance, she walked forward carefully as the orchestra drummer trilled continuously. The SPA contingent was spellbound. Most would have been afraid to simply climb the pole, let alone walk out into space on no more than a thin steel cable.

Elena picked up speed after she reached the half-way point where she had briefly paused. Then she almost sprinted to the far platform. When she reached the other side, she bowed to the wildly applauding crowd.

Next, she walked back and stopped at the center. After a moment, she swung a leg around to reverse direction. At this point she appeared to lose her balance, causing the audience to gasp in unison. She took a few moments to right herself and returned to the platform. Actually, she was in complete control. The shaky turn was planned showmanship.

For the finale, Karl Wallenda came out to the center of the wire and lifted Elena to his shoulders, where she stood motionless in a pose not unlike the Statue of Liberty.

A short time later, she returned to the ground in triumph and joined the entire troupe in the ring for final bows. Friends, family, and students rushed the floor to congratulate all the school performers as the professionals departed to enthusiastic applause.

Elena was shocked to see her parents, two of her sisters, and Roberto approach.

Rushing to embrace them, she asked, "What are you doing here? I didn't know you were coming!"

Hugging her, Margarite said, "Mrs. Tutwiler called us when she saw how well your practices were going. She told us we should not miss the performance. We decided a surprise was better so that you didn't have any extra pressure knowing we were in the audience. You had us all holding our breath."

"No wonder you keep dumping me into the stream," Roberto said in awe. "That was amazing."

The Crew waited patiently to the side until Elena had greeted all of her family. Then Carty said, "Mrs. Tutwiler called us too. Why didn't you tell me you were so good at this? I knew you trained every year, but I had no idea you could do that."

"I see you brought The Crew along," Elena said, "but not your cousin, Grant."

"No, we dropped the Meiers at the airport on the way here. It's too bad. Grant would like meeting you."

Blake blurted out, "Gee, you're kind of beautiful in that costume, Elena." Then, having surprised himself by saying it, he blushed. Carty, Hale, and Mack looked at one another and rolled their eyes at one more of Blake's faux pas involving a girl – embarrassing things he always seemed to come up with that they had dubbed "Blake-dumbs."

Elena had been tempted to laugh but, sensing his discomfort, answered gently instead, "Why, thank you, Blake. It is a bit risqué, but it has to fit tightly so that I don't snag on anything or catch an unexpected breeze. It would not take much to lose my balance."

She pulled two pins from her hair and let it fall free. "See, even my hair was tight.

"I was actually not at risk up there because of the safety net," she continued, changing the subject and diffusing any discomfort for Blake that might have lingered. "Would everyone like to see it?"

Without waiting for an answer, she took Blake's hand and led him and the others to the net, where she explained its effectiveness. "I fell twice during training, and one time I took Karl Wallenda with me. I was scared to death, not because of falling, but because I was afraid that he might boot me out of training."

"Instead, he quietly explained what I had done wrong and showed me how to avoid doing it again. He is an amazing teacher. I have learned as much from him about the art of teaching as I learned about the high-wire."

Indeed, Elena had learned how to make Blake forget his silly comment and become comfortable with her – even though, especially in costume, she was definitely a girl. Within minutes, Blake was laughing and enjoying being with Elena, talking about safety nets and anything else that came to mind, and amazingly to the rest of The Crew, not saying anything stupid.

Carty watched them and shook her head ever so slightly. "I was beginning to think Blake would never get over his shyness with girls. Thank heaven for Elena."

# CHAPTER 17

## *"Professor" Sally*

*Believe in yourself! Have faith in your abilities! Without a humble but reason-*
*able confidence in your own powers you cannot be successful or happy.*

NORMAN VINCENT PEALE

**DECEMBER 1952**

Sally watched her hands tremble. The event was still a month away,
and already she was experiencing stage fright.

"I don't know if I can do this, James. I've never spoken before a group
before. What if I faint or forget what I'm planning to say?"

"You read *The Legend of Montooth* to The Crew a few years ago in
this very same room. You weren't nervous then, were you?"

"No, but then the audience was afraid of me. I wasn't afraid of them.

I was a 'witch' and had the upper hand. Now I am Sally Canfield Elsmore, mere wife of Sheriff James Elsmore, and the audience will be there judging how well I perform."

"Wow, where do I start, Sally? First, no one is coming to judge you. They are coming to learn from you.

"Second, you are not a 'mere' anything. You are the most important person in my life, and you are the most notable person in Winter Free. Everyone in the county knows who you are. I'm the sheriff, and fewer people know me than you."

"Sure they know me, James. I'm the scary 'witch' who apparently turned into a 'princess' or at least a good witch. No one knows what to think, but they are so curious that they put my life under constant scrutiny. It is as though I am some kind of movie star. I never sought this fame, and I'm so often afraid that I will make a wrong move and embarrass you and ruin your career."

"Sally, you told me that your entire life has been under scrutiny. Whenever you went to town, you played the witch, and you had no difficulty in that role. Just think of this event as a new role that you can perform just as well."

Sally looked blankly at James for several seconds and then beamed. "James, I love you. You are the smartest man in the world. Why didn't I think of that? If I could play a witch when I wasn't one, surely I can play a learned lecturer when I am not one of those either."

Sally jumped up from her chair, kissed him, and sauntered away whistling happily, leaving James to muse, "If only all problems could be so easily solved."

*SALLY* truly did continue drawing attention as she had in prior times. Then, though, she appeared in public only a few times yearly. Now she was out and about almost daily. Her notoriety, her position as the sheriff's wife, and a growing status in the town's social structure kept her in the public eye.

Lilly Andersson introduced her to philanthropic endeavors, encouraging Sally to take over some of the groups that Lilly had founded or helped grow. "I'm getting too old, Sally," Lilly explained, "to keep up the pace with all of these worthy groups. I really need you to back me up and to begin to take over."

Sally took to her guidance well. She shepherded the most recent March of Dimes campaign for contributions to nearly double its previous Winter Free record. She harnessed the local Explorer Scouts, Boy Scouts, and Girl Scouts in a door-to-door drive for contributions.

Nearly all the polio research in the country was being funded by the March of Dimes, and its mission appealed to youngsters and their parents since the paralyzing disease attacked primarily the young. Almost every school in the country had at least one serious case of polio, and most had several.

Deaths and paralysis were all too common. The specter of living one's life entombed in an iron lung machine hung over every youngster.

The important purpose of the collection efforts, supplemented with the promise of a wrap-up party at the Canfield house for the scouts and their families, generated a one hundred percent participation of Winter Free's scouts.

The rumors of the Canfield witches would never completely dissipate, but Sally found that she could mold the community's curiosity to good advantage. Residents sought opportunities to see her and her famed house.

The nationwide collection drive for the March of Dimes took place each January, which struck Floridians as odd. It could be chilly in the Sunshine State that time of year, but it had to be bone-numbing cold in the North for campaigners to knock on doors seeking contributions there. Maybe that was the idea: sympathy for the volunteers in miserable conditions.

Sally stood in front of the bookshelves for a moment and removed a maroon-colored, leather bound volume from a shelf several inches above head high. The ribbon marking the last entry that had been read was still positioned at the end of *The Legend of Montooth*.

Sally recalled the day nearly three years earlier when she finished reading that fable to The Crew, moments before the malevolent "Mr. Smith" and his gang launched the attack.

The ribbon's placement did not date to that time, however, but to a more recent event last year. Because of the publicity that the attack generated, especially involving the two criminals whom the real Montooth was believed to have eaten, the fable became famous. So much curiosity developed that Sally was persuaded to publish *The Legend of Montooth* as a small Christmas book the previous year.

Sally had authored an introduction to the story in which she explained that the original Montooth was a real alligator and that his descendant played a key, though inadvertent, part in foiling the designs of the criminal gang. Because her introduction mentioned that *The Legend of Montooth* was one of many such stories captured in the Canfield lore, widespread interest developed concerning the others.

Thus, Sally was to highlight the festivities capping off the March of Dimes event with a public reading of one of the other fables. She paged through the book deliberately, searching for the ideal entry, though she knew the contents as well as those in any other book in the vast family library.

"These fables of Morgan Canfield's are more than interesting stories. Now which one will it be?" she wondered, as she skimmed through the book.

Morgan Canfield was the patriarch of the American branch of the Canfields who had moved the large family to the swamps of Spanish Florida in the early Eighteenth Century. He led them from Salem, Massachusetts around 1690 to escape witch hunters who were targeting his wife.

Morgan subsequently made fortunes in shipping in Boston and banking in New York City before more rumors of witchcraft emerged and chased the family from both cities.

Finally, in frustration, he led his family into Spanish Florida. A total of over twenty Canfields, including children, took up residence between Morose Swamp and Duck Lake. Morgan decreed that the rumors of witchcraft that chased them to this isolated place would henceforth be used to keep people away.

Most but not all of the fables in the book had been authored by Morgan. It was never clear to Sally to what extent the fables involved actual events. Certainly, Montooth was real, and Duck Lake was an expansive haven for mallards, but how much of his story really happened?

In recent times, Sally's grandmother re-wrote the stories in more modern English so that they would be more easily understood. Like the originals which sadly she had discarded, the updated tales were written in a flowing, almost artistic cursive, and her grandmother had obviously embellished them for easy reading.

Sally leafed deeply into the book. "Hmm, *Montooth and The Black Ibis* is one of my favorites," she whispered to herself, "or how about *Dragonflies and Flutterbies*? No, they won't do for the Scouts." She continued to page onward until well past the half-way mark.

Then she stopped and stared at a title page with an ink smudge. With a little imagination, the smear looked almost like an arrow pointing to the title, as though her grandmother had wanted Sally to notice this fable, *The Legend of Montooth and the Dillos.*

Sally recalled that her grandmother had read about the dillos to her when she was a young girl. At one time or another Sally had heard all of the fables that Morgan had written. Sally remembered the moral of the story very well but began reading to refresh her memory of how the tale unfolded.

# The Legend of Montooth
## and the Dillos

# CHAPTER A

## Coyote Strike

The young dillo ambled aimlessly through the underbrush. He should have been digging for grubs, acorns, and other good food, but he had no appetite today. His name was Willit, and he was not a happy fellow.

He lost his best friend, Aron, yesterday and the reason was becoming a much too frequent event. That morning had started well enough. Actually, initial signs suggested that a delightful day was developing.

The early hours were warm and sunny. The light rain that fell the night before made the soil softer, so digging for large, juicy grubs became easy. The fat white ones were the best, and wet soil seemed to puff them up, but Willit knew that was probably his imagination.

Aron and Willit were young, but old enough to be on

their own. They still saw their families from time to time, but they were of the age where they were thinking of starting their own families. That was not on their minds that morning, though. The appeal of tasty grubs and worms ranked well above the lure of girlfriends that fateful day.

Not that these young dillos lacked attractiveness for the young ladies in the village. Tan in color, sleek and smooth in skin with nary a wrinkle or a blemish except for a little dirt from digging deep, Willit and Aron were among the handsomest of all the young fellows.

Their aerodynamic bodies of over two feet in length enabled the fleet dillos to run with a speed faster than most of the animals in the swamp. It was this speed that helped dillos evade predators who craved tender dillo meat. But the dillos' poor eyesight put them at risk, because enemies sometimes pounced on them before the dillos could use their speed to escape.

Willit and Aron ambled along, feasting on the yummy treats. The effort was not easy. First they had to locate an area that promised good hunting, and that was always the most difficult task. All the digging in the world would be for naught if the soil contained no grubs. But Willit and Aron had a particular knack for discovering the best land, especially after an evening rain.

Today was no exception. They chose Clover Hammock, a slightly elevated expanse of land that rose from the surrounding swamp. The high, drier ground had attracted loggers many years earlier. When they left with the trees, rich, warm sunlight streamed through the missing canopy into the large meadow. Tall grasses flourished, providing a habitat for many animals different than the creatures living in the surrounding swamp.

Willit and Aron realized the advantages that the hammock afforded them after a good rain. Their favorite grubs preferred soft, moist soil, but they also liked soil slightly warmed by the beaming sun. The surrounding swamp kept the soil damp, and the Florida sun kept it warm. The conditions were perfect.

Like human fishermen, dillos preferred to keep their favorite places to themselves. Willit and Aron always tried to slip away so no one could discover their secret location. As usual, however, they were followed by Obnock, the village's most ambitious dillo and leader of the Dillo Council. Long ago, Obnock had learned that he would find the best digging ground by following Willit and Aron instead of searching for himself.

What Obnock lacked in a strong work ethic, he compensated with ambition and glibness. He had a knack for giving the right compliment at the right time to the right dillo, and he spoke with an authoritative tone no matter how ignorant he was of the subject at hand. His affable but insincere smile melted the hearts of female dillos both young and old.

He was always alert for gathering the latest gossip to glean an advantage. He saved his criticisms to achieve the greatest benefit for himself while purporting always to be looking out for the good of the village.

When a consensus on an issue developed, Obnock was the first to give strong voice in its support, always striving to give the impression that he had developed the idea. In this way he eventually maneuvered himself to the top position on the Council.

Few dillos were sufficiently perceptive to see his shifty methods. Willit and Aron were among the few.

"Have you noticed Obnock dogging us again, Willit? What a leech."

"How could I miss him? He's always following."

"Just once I'd like to see him do something on his own," Aron complained. "Oh, great. Here he comes."

"At least try to be nice, Aron."

"Hello, fellows," Obnock greeted them with a smarmy smile. "What a surprise to see you here. This is one of my favorite places after a good rain. Are you doing well?"

Willit breathed deeply and replied politely. "Yes, Obnock. I don't remember seeing you out here before, though."

"I do believe that you are right about that. We must have come at different times, but we both know this really good place. Great minds must think alike, don't you agree?"

Though Aron's biting reply went unsaid, the look on his

face let Obnock know what Aron thought of his question. An evil darkness came over Obnock's countenance that was unconnected with the small amount of shade from the few bordering cypress trees.

Before matters could deteriorate further, Willit changed the subject.

"I was thinking of heading over toward the west. There are overhanging oaks there, and it'll be a bit cooler in the shade. Care to join me, fellows?"

"No," Aron answered, "I'm going to try my luck in the tall grass to the south."

"Looks like it will be just the two of us then, Willit," Obnock offered. "I'll join you."

Aron gave Willit a look that suggested, "Don't blame me. You made the offer."

The three moved off in the two directions and enjoyed several hours of good food. Willit was grateful that Obnock concentrated on eating instead of talking. If Obnock had continued to spout stupidities, even Willit's enormous store of tact might have been depleted.

The sun angled low in the late afternoon. Branches, tree trunks, and Spanish moss contributed oddly shaped shadows to the hammock. Obnock paused and rose to stretch. In the distance, he saw Aron at the edge of a small clearing. He was about to resume eating when he noticed what appeared to be a shadow moving though the tall grass that bordered Aron's clearing.

Curious, Obnock kept watching. The large gray smudge moved steadily closer to Aron. Then a brisk breeze swayed the grass just enough for Obnock's poor vision to make out that the darkness was not a shadow, but rather a coyote. Clearly, the coyote was stalking Aron, slowly, cautiously, and with deadly intent. Obnock was about to yell a warning, but the memory of Aron's earlier facial expression came to mind.

Willit had his head down and was unaware of what was developing. Obnock kept quiet and watched with fascination as the coyote crept closer. Suddenly, the coyote sprung from the grass and snatched Aron with a mouthful of sharp, pointed teeth. Aron had no chance of escape, and barely made a whimper as the coyote strutted away with Aron's limp body crushed in its jaws.

"What was that noise?" Willit called out.

"I don't know," Obnock lied. "It sounded like it came from over there," he added, pointing in the general direction of the coyote attack. "Let's take a look. Maybe Aron is in trouble," he continued, feigning concern.

By the time they located the site, the coyote and Aron were long gone. From the marks on the ground, it was clear what had occurred.

Willit was devastated. "A coyote," he said. "There is no doubt from the tracks. Aron was always careful, but he must have lost concentration this one time. I should have insisted that he stay with us. It's my fault," he lamented.

Obnock put a paw on Willit's shoulder and consoled him. "It was no one's fault. These things happen. We lost Milder and Janey earlier this year. We cannot be on the alert all the time. Luck plays a big part."

Insincerity almost dripped from Obnock's mouth, but Willit was too distraught to notice.

# CHAPTER B

## *Carekeepers*

For weeks, Willit sat quietly in his den. He seldom ventured out except to eat a small amount that was barely enough to stay alive. The few times he left, his heart ached more because he had to pass Aron's empty den on his way.

Life in the remainder of the dillo village gradually resumed its normal pace until another coyote attack occurred. This time the dillo saw the predator just in time to make a hasty escape, though. Obnock was quick to exploit any event for personal gain, this one included.

"As I tried to explain to Aron and Willit on the fateful day, it is always better to stick together. True, if we stay alert, we are able to use our speed to get away – but it is too easy to become distracted, and when that occurs, we are too vulnerable.

"That particular day," he boasted untruthfully, "I took Willit and Aron to a spot I know that is full of grubs on warm days after a rain. I warned them about the coyote that frequents the place and said that we should move as a group of three. You know how Aron was, though – always the loner. He insisted in wandering off on his own. What a sad loss.

"This recent attack on another lone dillo, coming so soon after we lost Aron, failed. However, the danger is increasing. It brings to mind an idea that I have been developing. We should have a law that requires dillos to travel in small groups. More importantly, we should assign a village Carekeeper to be part of each group. The Carekeeper would be on the alert to assure the safety of the group."

Obnock offered to head up a village agency to make the assignments. Since it would be a full-time job for Obnock, the village would have to issue a decree for each dillo to pay him six grubs per week. Many in the village agreed that the plan had merit and decided to vote on it the next day.

Bento visited Willit that evening. "Hello, Cousin," he greeted a still somber Willit. "Have you heard of Obnock's plan?"

"No, Bento – what is he up to now?"

When Bento finished explaining what Obnock had in mind, Willit was appalled. "Do you mean Obnock will get the authority to tell us whom we have to associate with – whether we want to or not?" he asked. "And then we have to pay him as well?"

"Hmm, I guess so, Willit. When you put it that way, it doesn't sound quite so good."

Snapping out of his weeks' long lethargy, he replied, "It's not good. For thousands of years we have managed quite well without forced associations.

"True, an occasional tragedy occurs. I'll never forget my friend Aron. But safety is not worth losing our freedom to go where we want to go when we want to go, join anyone we want to, or wander off by ourselves.

"And I certainly do not need Obnock to organize my life for me or to assign a 'keeper' to me."

At the village meeting the next day, Obnock presented his plan. Willit was the only one to object.

Responding to Willit's challenge, Obnock insisted, "This is not a village mandate. Individual dillos will be allowed to organize their own groups. I will not be in charge of determining who is in the group. I will have the power to merely assign a Carekeeper to each group, and each group would pay only for its own Carekeeper.

"If an individual dillo did not want to join a group, he is free to stay independent."

"If I chose not to join a group, would I still have to be assigned a Carekeeper?" Willit asked.

"Of course. It is the only way to stay completely safe. We cannot allow you to evade the requirement and put yourself at risk."

"But if I understand your system," Willit objected, "I would have to pay the entire salary of a Carekeeper plus pay you. That makes staying alone economically impossible."

"Perhaps, Willit, but it is for your own good."

"I do not believe that allowing you to assign a Carekeeper to me is for my own good.

"Let me propose another solution," Willit continued. "During these past several weeks since the coyote grabbed Aron, I have been thinking about a different solution, one that would not require a reduction in our freedoms as you propose."

Turning to the assembly, he said, "Let's delay the Council vote on Obnock's plan until I can present my plan as an alternative."

Although most in the village had originally supported Obnock's plan, Willit's numerous objections and questions produced a good effect. A few dillos had changed their minds entirely, and many more had become unsure. The chance to avoid making an immediate decision appealed to most in attendance.

Sensing that the tide had turned away from his position, Obnock appeared outwardly magnanimous, while seething inside. "All right, then, let's meet again the day after the next full moon. We will hear Willit's plan and decide then which plan to adopt. Will that be enough time for you, Willit?"

"Yes. I have the theory worked out. Now I need only to work on the implementation."

"'The theory,'" Obnock repeated with a slightly sarcastic tone. "Of course. You work on implementing 'the theory,' and we will meet again to see what you come up with."

As the crowd dispersed, Bento sidled up to Willit. "Do you really have a different solution, or were you simply trying to delay Obnock?"

"Both. I do have an idea that might be a solution, but I was not motivated to actually do anything about it until I saw what Obnock had in mind. I could use a helper. Care to join me?"

"You can count on me. When do we start?"

"Right now."

Willit sent Bento out to gather supplies and a little food. Willit was not planning to search for any food while he was hard at work on his project.

Later in the evening, long after Bento had gone to sleep, Willit roamed along the edge of Big Lake which humans called Duck Lake due to the enormously large population of mallard ducks.

Willit cut pieces of two-foot tall Florida sawgrass with his teeth. He buried the blades under mounds of whitish-gray limerock mud at the water's edge. Further from the shore, the mud became darker and easier to work as he buried the sawgrass blades. Nevertheless, it was tricky avoiding the sharp saw-like teeth of the tough grass.

With the darkening skies hindering his poor eyesight, he did not notice a duck until almost stepping on him. The duck was on its back, breathing heavily but not otherwise moving.

"Are you all right?" Willit asked.

The duck moaned softly, and in a barely audible voice replied, "My legs are caught in weeds under the water, and I've been struggling all day to get loose. Right now, I'm exhausted and resting. I'm really clumsy, and I'm always getting into predicaments like this. I was about ready to give up."

"Let's see if I can help. My name is Willit, by the way."

"I'm Millard, and I appreciate your help."

Willit dived below the water. It was too dark to see anything, but with his paws he could feel the tangled weeds clinging to Millard's feet. He used his teeth to chew through several of the weeds and then surfaced to breathe. A dillo can hold its breath for several minutes, so Willit had made good progress.

"I'll have you out in no time. It'll take more diving and chewing, but it should not be a problem."

"I hate to bring up another issue at this point, but there is one other problem," Millard said. "Unless I am mistaken," he continued, pointing to the west, "that grass is swaying because of a fox. It appears to be closing on us."

"Then I better get to work fast," Willit said as he dived below the surface again. Willit forced himself to stay under until his lungs were about to burst. He managed to free one of Millard's legs and part of the other when he had to surface.

He came up sputtering and gasping for air. He also came up staring into the malevolent eyes of a large, bushy-tailed fox not two feet away.

"Aha, Mr. Fox," Willit said cheerfully, to the surprise of both Millard and the fox, "It is good to see you. If you can excuse me for another moment, I have one more thing to do, and then I'll join you." Willit correctly assessed that the surprise of his nonchalant behavior would delay the fox's attack.

As Willit dived into the water again, Millard and the fox examined each other as prey and hunter. The fox said, "What was that all about, and who is he? Doesn't he know that I'm here to eat him as well as you?"

"Oh, you know those dillos. Always a sense of humor." Millard searched for anything to say to continue the conversation, because he felt Willit chewing through the last of the weeds on his leg.

"Once, when I was a little duckling, a dillo ran into our village yelling about a fox in the vicinity."

"He was giving you a warning about an attack?" the smug fox asked.

Millard felt his remaining leg gain its freedom. "Oh no – he was warning us to hold our noses because of the stinky smell that foxes have."

"What?!" the enraged fox yelled, momentarily stunned

at Millard's brashness. As the fox recovered from his anger and prepared to charge, Millard flapped his wings and took off. Willit came out of the lake clinging to Millard's leg, just beyond the fox's snapping teeth.

As Millard flew low to the water, Willit yelled up to him. "A little farther and swoop down. I'll drop off. I'm a better swimmer than a fox."

"Thank you for the help," Millard replied, as he dropped slightly above the lake surface and allowed Willit to release and splash to a landing.

# CHAPTER C

## *Meeting Montooth*

Willit slept late the next morning, exhausted from the evening's ordeal. Bento's knock on the door brought him around. He saw by the high sun that he was running late.

Bento dropped a tasty night crawler on the floor of the den. Willit gobbled it up and thanked Bento.

"Here are the palm fronds you asked me to gather," Bento said.

"Perfect. Now I want you to strip their edges into long slats. They will be very strong and perfect for our needs. I'm heading back to the lake to collect more sawgrass."

At the water's edge, Willit resumed cutting the tall blades. When he finished and began collecting the piles of grass, he felt uneasy, a prickly sixth sense alerting him that he was being watched. "Has the fox returned?" he wondered.

He darted his eyes to the sides while imperceptibly pivoting his head to the right. Nothing unusual appeared to be there. He swiveled his head to the left, still slowly enough to keep from alerting anyone watching. He saw the two large eyes staring at him from barely above the water's surface.

They belonged to an alligator, and, despite dillo speed, Willit knew that an alligator could outrun him in a short distance sprint. Willit tried the same trick he played on the fox in the hope of buying enough time to think of a way to escape. "Oh, hello, Mr. Gator. What a pleasure to see you."

The gator did not look confused as Willit expected. Instead, he laughed with his mouth wide open. "My," Willit thought, "That is one big mouth! And those teeth – yikes. Wait a minute – one of those front teeth is extra big. Oh, no, this has to be the famous Montooth. I'm really doomed."

Montooth stopped laughing and said, "My brother Millard told me how you tricked the fox into delaying his attack with your cheerful, unconcerned greeting. And I thought it was the fox who was supposed to be so clever."

The gator's friendly tone of voice gave Willit hope. "You're Montooth, aren't you?"

"At your service – and you are Willit, right?"

"Yes, yes, Willit it is, and it's not nice to eat someone whose name you know," he added hopefully.

"Eat you? Of course I'm not going to eat you. You saved

my brother's life. It would not be very generous of me to eat you after that."

"You keep saying that Millard is your brother – but Millard is a mallard duck, not a gator."

"Oh, it's a long story. Maybe I'll tell it to you some day. Anyway, he is my brother, and I'm not going to eat you.

"I've noticed you here before. What keeps bringing you back to this spot? It's a bit off the typical range for dillos, isn't it?"

"Yes, it is. A coyote ate my best friend, and I have an idea that might keep the other dillos safe. I've been cutting and burying this sawgrass in mud to harden it, and in three days, I'll dig it up and carry it to my den to work with it."

"That looks like a big load for one little dillo. Could you use some help?"

"Hmm, if you would let me strap the sawgrass on your back, you could carry it to my den in one or two trips. Otherwise, I'd have to spend many days making numerous trips."

"Consider it done. I'll meet you here in three days."

True to his word, Montooth returned and lumbered out of the water when he saw Willit arrive.

"My, you surely are big," Willit remarked, a momentary spark of doubt entering his consciousness. He wondered if this was a good idea.

Willit dug into a mound and felt the sawgrass blades. He announced that they had hardened just the way he had hoped – a cross between leather and stone.

It must have been a comical sight for the birds and small animals who witnessed the procession, but it was not funny to Bento. He had just finished stripping the last of the palm fronds into strong strings when he came out of the den to stretch in the warm sun.

There he watched as Willit walked a few steps in front of the largest alligator he had ever seen – indeed the largest animal of any kind that he had ever seen. Moreover, the trailing alligator was piled high with sawgrass that made him appear almost twice as big.

Momentarily awed into silence by the sight, Bento soon recovered and shouted a warning to Willit. "There's a gator behind you! Run!"

Instead, Willit smiled, waved, and continued walking toward him at a leisurely pace. Despite Willit's unconcerned demeanor, Bento backed toward the den, keeping a wary eye on the enormous alligator acting as a pack mule.

By the time the travelling party of two stopped at the entrance to the den, Bento had moved as far back into the protected area as possible.

"Hello, Bento. There is no reason to be afraid. This is my friend, Montooth."

Bento motioned Willit forward and whispered into his ear, "Are you crazy? Any gator is bad news, but you bring home Montooth. He's the scourge of the swamp and lake, and we'd probably be eaten already if he weren't too big to get his monster mouth into your den. How you survived the long walk with him is beyond me, but I seriously suggest that you hide out in here with me until he leaves."

"You have nothing to worry about. Montooth is my friend. It seems that I saved his brother from a fox, and he is so grateful that he has offered to help with our project. Come on out and I'll introduce you."

"If it's all the same to you, Willit, I think I'll stay inside. I can't recall saving anyone from a fox lately, so your new friend may not take as kindly to me."

"Nonsense. I'll ask him. Stay put until I get back."

"'Stay put?' What do you think I'm going to do – go out and perform the Dance of the Seven Veils for that behemoth?"

After briefly consulting with Montooth, Willit returned. "He says he won't eat you. He says he is not even hungry – he had a couple of big fish and a turtle already today. Look at his big smile. Isn't he cute?"

"Uh, seeing all of those teeth in his smile isn't helping me come around to your way of thinking. Why don't I just yell to him if I need to communicate?"

Willit threw his front paws into the air in exasperation. "That's it," he said. "We can't work together if you want to spend the time hidden away in the den. Montooth will not hurt me or you. He gave me his word. So come out to meet him. Now."

Bento eased forward reluctantly, and at Willit's insistence, put out a paw to shake. Montooth took hold of Bento's paw and shook it aggressively. "It's good to meet you, Bento. Your cousin has been singing your praises. I'm sure we will work together really well."

Bento agreed that Montooth appeared friendly – at least right now. But he wondered what might happen if Montooth did not get a good solid meal the next time they met. He thought to himself, "Maybe I will ask about his breakfast each day to know whether to be concerned or not – and make it a point to stay away from his mouth regardless."

# CHAPTER D

## *Early Experiments*

They began working on Willit's idea that afternoon. Their first job was to expand the size of Willit's den so that Montooth could come inside to work. Dillos have strong, long digging claws as do gators, so that was accomplished in less than a day.

Willit explained that the actual production line involved three tasks: initially, unload the sawgrass blades from Montooth's back; secondly, cut the blades using Montooth's extra large tooth; and thirdly, Montooth had to make his big tooth available.

"Are you telling me," Bento asked, "that either you or I have to reach our paws into the big guy's mouth and use his tooth to cut the sawgrass blades?"

"Yes. That is the easiest job, because you can sit down

while doing it. The other job of unloading and stacking involves plenty of lifting and hauling. I'll be happy to take on the hard job if you'd like to do the cutting."

Bento took a sideways glance at the two rows of large sharp teeth surrounding Montooth's big tongue and hastily replied, "No, no, Willit. You're the brains of this outfit. I can't expect you to do the heavy work. I'll unload, haul, and stack. You reach into his mouth and do the cutting."

Montooth winked at Willit and chuckled to himself.

Bento unloaded the blades and took them to Willit, who cut them into the right lengths. Montooth's big tooth proved to be perfect for the job. Bento sorted the cut blades into five different sizes and stacked them neatly into piles. By the end of the day, Willit announced that he had enough of a supply for his experimental device.

They all slept soundly that night, with Bento staking out a position on the side away from Montooth and Willit positioned in between. When they awoke, Montooth announced that he was going to do a little fishing so that he would not get too hungry later on.

"No sense in getting tempted working near such delicacies as dillos," he said. Willit rolled his eyes as Bento rolled his insides.

"He's just kidding, Bento," Willit said, as Montooth slither-waddled toward Big Lake.

"I know that, I know that," Bento answered nervously,

all the while keeping a wary eye on the unfed gator heading toward the lake.

By late morning, Willit was ready to begin in earnest. "Okay, Bento, this may prick a little bit – a little like stepping on a thorny branch."

As much as Bento was nervous around Montooth, he did not mind a little pain if it would help Willit. "Cut when ready," he answered bravely.

Using a sharp edge from a sawgrass blade, Willit made two small incisions behind Bento's armpits. Then he inserted one end of a sawgrass blade into each cut, stretching the blade across Bento's back. He used strings that Bento had stripped from the palm branches as stitches to fasten the ends of the blades to Bento's skin.

When he finished, he repeated the process, slightly overlapping the first blade with the second, about half an inch down Bento's back. He followed that with a third blade, slightly overlapping the second. Next, he continued adding blades all the way along Bento's back until his patient was fully covered from neck to tail.

Finally, he sewed smaller blades in circles around each leg and mounded a cap on Bento's head.

"Good," Willit announced. "How does that feel?"

"Cumbersome, if you want to know the truth, but, except for the cap, it's not nearly as heavy as I thought it might be. Let me walk around."

Bento walked a bit clumsily at first, but soon he got the hang of it. Then he scurried into a swift waddle as the other two watched.

"You are faster than a turtle, but you definitely have lost speed," Willit assessed. "Besides the added weight, your legs are too bound up.

"Also, the cap must be too heavy, because you appear to have trouble keeping your head from sagging. I need to think about that. Let's get you out of this, and we'll gather back here the day after tomorrow."

Dismantling the apparatus was much faster than sewing it. When Montooth dabbed aloe from a nearby plant on Bento's slit skin, it felt so good that Bento forgot to be afraid.

# CHAPTER E

## *Obnock's Opportunity*

That evening, Willit visited Obnock and explained that he was inventing a way to prevent coyotes and other hunters from eating dillos. "I believe that I will be able to outfit a dillo with enough protective material to ward off most predators."

"You are certain that this will work, Willit?"

"I am eighty percent through with testing. I see no reason why it will not be successful, though there is always a chance that something unforeseen may arise.

"Also, there will be a cost. I need to be paid so that I can concentrate on this work instead of spending my time hunting and digging for food. Do you think that the Council will approve that?"

"You can count on me to insure that they do, Willit. Nothing is more important to our community, and no one would begrudge you for benefitting from your efforts. Leave it in my hands. We have a Council meeting tomorrow morning. I'll talk with you afterward."

Obnock knew that his Carekeeper idea was not going well in the community after Willit presented so many objections, so he was looking for a way to save face.

At the Council meeting that night, he began, "As you know," he told the Council, "I have had serious reservations about the Carekeeper idea," ignoring the fact that he had introduced and campaigned for it. "That is why I recommended that we defer decision on the Carekeeper concept until Willit and I could further examine an alternative idea that we came up with."

Only a few of the Council members realized that Obnock's speech lacked basic honesty, while a solid majority was impressed as always, oblivious to his deceit.

"We are almost ready to present our idea," he continued. "I have put Willit in charge of finishing up. If we are successful, we will need to be compensated for our work, of course. I assume that there would be no objection to that."

The Council agreed that the Obnock-Willit team should be compensated, with the amount being dependent on the quality and value of the result.

Obnock decided to pay Willit a visit to see for himself what Willit was doing. As he neared the den, he heard talking from inside. He recognized the voices of Willit and Bento, but the third voice did not sound like any he had ever heard. Each word ended in a hiss, much like the sound from a snake's mouth, but huskier.

"I wonder who that could be. Probably an outsider who is telling Willit what to do. No matter. I'll find out who it is and learn about this operation myself."

With that said, Obnock entered the den without knocking, which startled the three partners who were hard at work. Startling a dillo is not a risky move. Dillos tend to jump straight up in the air when surprised, and that is a relatively harmless result for bystanders.

Startling an alligator, however, especially a twenty-footer, is like pinching a lion's nose. It is a good way to lose a hand, an arm, or an entire head. When the three heard Obnock say, "So how does the work go?" the dillos indeed jumped straight up – so high they bumped their heads on the den's ceiling.

Montooth, on the other hand, swung around and instinctively snapped his enormous jaw in the direction of the unexpected sound. Then it was Obnock's turn to jump straight up – minus the tips of two fingers.

Obnock twisted completely around in mid-air so that when he came back to earth, he was pointed toward the exit. He shot out the door and was saved only because Montooth recognized that he was a dillo and did not pursue him. Obnock did not stop running until he reached the village.

For the first time, he looked at his aching hand and was appalled to see that he was missing parts of two fingers. Suddenly, he lost all curiosity in the Obnock-Willit project's methods and vowed to let Willit continue alone with development.

"Who was that?" Bento asked.

"I did not get a good look, but it was definitely a dillo," Montooth said, licking his lips. "I've never had dillo fingers before. You guys have a yummy, sweet taste."

That statement had Bento backing away from Montooth once again. Willit shook his head as Montooth began chuckling.

Willit had solved many of the problems of his first design. Instead of two small slits at each end of the sawgrass blade, he made long slits from right to left over Bento's entire back. By sewing the entire blade to Bento's back instead of merely the two ends of the blade, Willit was able to strengthen the connection to Bento's skin. This stronger anchoring also enabled Willit to use longer blades that hung over Bento's sides, covering his legs without restricting his movement.

"These slits are quite a bit longer than the small cuts in the first version. Do they hurt?" Willit asked.

"Only a little sting. It's not bad, and it does not last long when Montooth adds the aloe."

Near the front of Bento's back, he sewed an extra wide

blade to protrude forward. Thus, Bento had a covering without the heavy weight on his head.

"This way, we don't need to cover your head, legs, and tail with heavy blades," Willit explained. "You can roll yourself into a ball and pull your head, legs, and tail under the protection."

After Bento scurried around in a test walk, he announced that he was pleased with the changes. He tried rolling into a ball, and that worked as well.

"The first version was too heavy and too restrictive. This upgrade is much better. I can move around much quicker – not nearly as fast as I ran without the protection, but way faster than I could with the heavy version."

"Okay, Bento, you know how it's done. It is your turn to try it out on me."

# CHAPTER F

## Feather

"Now comes the ultimate test, Bento. We are going to have you climb into Montooth's mouth while wearing the armor. We'll see if you can withstand crushing."

Bento stared in disbelief. "You can't be serious. Montooth could crush a boulder with those jaws. I'm not getting into his mouth no matter how much I want to help."

"I'm just kidding, Bento. This is a test for me. It is my idea. I'll take the chances."

With that said, Willit, wearing armor, climbed into Montooth's mouth, and the big gator began crushing. Suddenly, Willit cried out, "Stop! Yikes, stop!"

Montooth opened his mouth, and Willit climbed out unsteadily. "Oh, that really hurt. Your jaws are too strong, Montooth. This isn't going to work after all."

Willit stretched and rubbed his back gingerly.

"I'm so sorry, Willit," Montooth said with remorse. "I do not know my own strength. Please forgive me." He looked so despondent that Willit felt worse for him.

Willit patted Montooth in consolation, who responded, "I can't believe that I almost crushed you. How could I be so stupid?"

Willit continued to rub Montooth's back until the big gator rolled over and allowed Willit to rub his belly. Soon Montooth was no longer upset. Instead, he began to calm down.

"He's purring," Bento said.

"No, I'm not," Montooth replied.

Bento joined Willit rubbing Montooth's belly. "Yep, you're purring."

"Don't be ridiculous. Alligators do not purr."

"I can feel you purring," Bento insisted. "Ha, alligators purr," he stated loudly.

Bento was chuckling as other animals stopped to watch.

Embarrassed, Montooth denied it again. "We do not purr. Stop saying that. Keep your voice down. Everyone is listening. Shh."

Suddenly, Montooth flipped over, rushed into the water, and swam away.

"Oh, great, Bento," Willit complained. "You chased him off. That was not nice."

"Not nice? I rubbed his belly the same way you did."

"You know what I mean. You embarrassed him. I hope he comes back. He has been a real friend."

The next day Montooth did return. He showed no signs of holding any grudges, the big smile once again prominent on his face.

"I have solved our problem, fellows. We can retry the crush test."

"I don't think so, Montooth. Willit is too sore from yesterday's try, and I'm not climbing into your mouth. You might not be over the purring incident."

"Not my mouth, Bento.

"Come on in, Feather."

A much smaller version of Montooth slither-sashayed into the den. Otherwise, she looked much the same as he, except she lacked the large misplaced front tooth. She smiled brightly at Montooth.

"May I present my good friend, Feather. Isn't she elegant?"

Feather beamed at the compliment and somehow managed a pink blush on green cheeks. Neither Bento nor Willit associated the word "elegant" or the name "Feather" with the leathery, knobby, moss-covered, green creature before them, but they both greeted Feather effusively.

"You can see that Feather is smaller than I am," Montooth explained. "She has offered to help us with the experiment. If you climb into her mouth, she will give you a good test without so much risk."

"I am so happy to help Montooth," Feather rasped. "He is so good to me. I barely have to stalk a meal with him around. And so handsome, too," she added, as she nudged his shoulder with her snout.

Those comments produced Montooth's trademark smile, but Bento was unimpressed, especially at her mention of food. His mind raced. He pulled Montooth aside and whispered. "Okay, Montooth, you know that she isn't supposed to eat me, and I know that she isn't supposed to eat me, but does she know that she isn't supposed to eat me?"

"You are such a funny guy, Bento," Montooth laughed. "Feather promises to clench down slowly so that you can call out at anytime and stop her. Isn't that true, Feather?"

"Whatever you say, big guy. You have nothing to worry about, Bento. Just be careful to climb in without snagging on my teeth. They are rather sharp."

"Uh, you did eat today, didn't you, Feather?" Bento thought to ask just before he climbed on to Feather's tongue.

"Of course," she answered. "Don't make me giggle, or I might clamp down too hard by accident."

"Oh, great," Bento sighed.

When he was positioned in a ball, Feather began closing her mouth. She applied stronger and stronger pressure, but Bento noted nothing more than if he were carrying a heavy load. After one final grunt, Feather opened her mouth.

"That's as hard as I can clench with slow squeezing. Do you want me to try a snapping motion? That would be a tougher test."

"What do you think, Bento?" Willit asked. "Want to give snapping a try?"

Bento was feeling more confident. "Go ahead. I'll risk it. The protection seems to be working well."

He centered himself on her tongue again. On Willit's signal, she clamped down hard at about three-quarter strength.

The three held their collective breath. "No problem," came the call echoing from inside. "Let's go with full strength this time, Feather."

Once again, Feather clamped down hard in a quick snap, this time with full force. Once again, the call came, this time more confident than ever. "I hardly felt it. This is great."

"Come on out, Bento. I want to examine you."

Willit checked every blade. They were all totally intact. There was no damage despite Feather's strong efforts.

"I'm ready for a tougher test," Bento stated confidently. "Let's do it before I get scared again."

Bento rolled into a ball this time, perched precariously on Feather's sharp teeth. She clamped down hard, but at the reduced strength.

Willit examined Bento's back and saw no structural damage. There were only superficial scratches from her teeth in the design of Feather's jaw line.

"Once more into the breach," Bento exclaimed bravely as he reentered her mouth. "Fire when ready!"

This time, Feather clamped down with full force, her teeth in the middle of Bento's back. They heard him grunt, and they held their breaths. Bento struggled out a little unsteadily when Feather opened her mouth.

"I felt that," he groaned, "but it wasn't too bad. How does it look?"

They all gathered to look at his back. Slight indentations from teeth marks ringed the hardened sawgrass blades, but none of the teeth had penetrated. Bento said that he was not feeling any pain. The experiment was a success.

"Perfect. I'll let Obnock know that we are ready to present our solution to the coyote problem – one that avoids any need for Carekeepers."

*"YES,"* Sally spoke quietly to herself, "This will be perfect."

The decision made, she marked the story with the ribbon and returned the fable volume to the bookcase.

# CHAPTER 18

## Urban Trackers

*Good teaching is one-fourth preparation and three-fourths theater.*
GAIL GODWIN

**DECEMBER 1952**

Elena was so enthusiastic about their training that Carty was having second thoughts about involving her. Tracking in the wilds required steady nerves and a calm attitude. Carty suspected that the same requirements applied to urban tracking. Elena was displaying neither.

On the one hand, Carty was pleased that Elena met the expectations of keeping the matters to herself. Her friend showed no tendency to confide in any of the other girls about the project to track The Cuban. Had Elena failed Carty in this respect, she would have cut Elena out of the mission in a moment, despite their close friendship.

In the confines of their dorm room, on the other hand, Elena could not contain herself.

"This will be the most exciting thing I've ever done, Carty, and the most worthwhile," Elena gushed, pacing to and fro. "How can I be so lucky? Thank you, thank you, for having confidence in me. I cannot wait to tail this evil man to his hideout so we can nab him."

"Elena, we are not going to nab anyone. We are going to find out where The Cuban lives and, at most, find out his name for Sheriff Elsmore. That's it. We're not going to get anywhere near the guy. We'll be unarmed, and he probably won't be. Anyway, he is strong enough that he could probably snap both of our necks bare handed.

"I promised Dad that we would err on the side of caution when we go back to Cuba – no contact and nothing close enough to be grabbed." Unusually irritated, she added a sharp, "Got it?" Then she immediately apologized.

Elena instantly became serious. "Carty, don't let my Latin enthusiasm mislead you. On the outside, I'm excited and electrified. Inside, I am as cool, calm, and deadly serious as you. I know exactly what we could be getting ourselves into if we got carried away. By 'nab,' I didn't mean to physically grab him. I meant it figuratively. You'll see a different Elena when Mr. Novotny trains us. Trust me."

Elena could be goofy sometimes and often displayed questionable judgment, but on those rare occasions when Elena demonstrated that quiet, serious tone, Carty had learned to trust her.

*TRAINING* time with Novotny had arrived. The early morning sky to the east brightened as Carty drove her mom's DeSoto. As a newly licensed driver, Carty drove well under the speed limit, unsure of herself, not wanting to risk damaging the car.

A slight fog misted the farm fields along the route. Elena was so excited that she literally bounced in the passenger's seat.

"Mr. Novotny is so nice to help us, Carty. I can't believe that we are going to be trained by a real spy."

Novotny was waiting for them at the front door as they arrived.

"Good morning, girls. Come on in. You can put your bundles on the bench in the kitchen."

To Elena he said, "You must be Elena. My, Carty told me that you resembled each other, but I did not expect anything this close. If you dressed alike and had matching hair styles, nine out of ten people would say you were twins."

"It is nice to meet you, Mr. Novotny. Carty has told me so much about you; I seem to know you already." Elena thrust out her hand and shook Novotny's with a firm, confident grip, unlike the weak, unpleasant grasp of too many girls and women that he usually met.

"I've got link sausages and Belgian waffles almost ready. I became particularly fond of the waffles while I was in Europe. I prefer Vermont maple syrup to the powdered sugar and jam that the Belgians favor, though. Lead the way, Carty."

Novotny was pleased at the look on Carty's face that took in the change in the living room. A good urban tracker needed to recognize change.

"I see that you noticed the improvement, Carty. Most of my boxed items are on their way to my townhouse in Georgetown. That's where I'll be living in Washington. The large pieces of furniture will stay here.

"I'll be sailing my boat from Tampa Harbor up to Chesapeake Bay with the few remaining items. I found a nice marina to store it, so I'll be able to sail it from there if I ever get some time off."

Carty held the plates while Novotny placed the food on them. Elena poured coffee for Novotny and herself and milk for Carty.

"It's not the strong Cuban coffee you are probably used to, Elena."

"Oh, that's okay, Mr. Novotny. I've become used to the weak dishwater they serve as coffee in the SPA cafeteria. This has to be better than that." Her failed attempt to hide the slight grimace following her first sip suggested otherwise, however.

"Before we get started, tell me how your family is faring with Batista's coup."

Novotny had already heard Carty's version, but he always sought corroboration in areas he deemed important. The Cuban political situation was historically important for the U.S. Government, and Novotny expected that his new duties would include what happened in Havana.

"My father is unique among the bankers in Cuba, Mr. Novotny. He stays entirely away from political involvement.

"That has been bank policy from the day that my grandfather started Banco Rafferty. He was a New York banker who fought with Teddy Roosevelt's Rough Riders. After the Spanish American War, he stayed in Cuba and founded the bank. His beliefs still guide the bank's operation, especially the principle that if a bank needed Government help, its finances were not worth backing."

"Off the record, does he approve of Batista's administration?"

"Off the record, Mr. Novotny, Papa would prefer a government that operated as yours does in the United States, regardless of who happened to be in power at any given time."

Polite but noncommittal, Novotny noted. He realized that Elena had no intention of surrendering her father's trust. Though he had hoped to use her to augment his information about Cuba, he admired both her judgment and loyalty. She was going to be as worthy a student as Carty.

*"CARTY*, when you are tracking in the wilds, the most important things are to avoid being seen or scented by your prey; you follow the tracks and the disturbed environment. However, you have to remove that concept from your thinking for urban tracking. You cannot avoid being seen tracking in a city, or you will lose your prey. On concrete sidewalks, a man in an urban environment leaves no tracks for you to follow, so you must remain close.

"Because you have to keep him in view, that means that he may see you. The most important part of trailing him is to minimize the damage when you are seen. The way to do that is to make your target believe that he is not seeing what he is seeing, i.e., misdirection.

"Taking on a tail in Havana – you two are already starting out with three strikes against you, which gives you only two more outs in the inning. Do you have any idea what one strike is?"

Elena spoke first. "We are both blond, which is unusual in Cuba, and we look alike, so we will stand out."

"Good, Elena. That is right on the mark. Anything else?"

It was Carty's turn. "We are considerably taller than most women in Havana. In fact, we are taller than many men."

"Right again. You two are going to be good pupils. Okay, what is strike three?"

The girls looked at each other blankly and shrugged.

Novotny smiled at their naïveté. "You two are way too pretty. I've seen the double takes that you create when you walk by men and boys in Winter Free, Carty. Since you two are nearly twins, I suspect that you have the same effect, Elena."

The girls blushed at the compliment and glanced at each other before giggling nervously.

"No need to be so modest. The question is, what do we do about these three issues. That is where I come in. I'll go through the clothes you brought while we eat." He continued talking as he sorted through the garments.

"Your height is the most difficult problem. We can't make you shorter than you are. We can limit the problem, but not eliminate it. We start with shoes, most logically. You will not wear any raised shoes like high heels. In fact, you need to wear shoes with as little heel as possible.

"Actually, we might be able to use your height to advantage in one way. Hold that thought for later.

"Leave your penny loafers with me when you leave. I'll replace the heels with a flatter version.

"Moccasins will be ideal, and even slippers might work if the rain stays away. These Keds are good," he said, as he found the tennis shoes while rummaging through the bundles.

"Less obvious help will come from your clothes. When you wear loose dresses and long skirts, you have the opportunity to crouch or slouch slightly without making it apparent to your target.

"The pedal pushers that you are wearing were a good choice for a foundation garment. You'll be layering a number of articles with the snugger items underneath. You will seldom have an opportunity to change clothes during an operation. You may have to discard one layer quickly so that you take on a new persona without delay.

"It's good that you are both acclimated to hot temperatures. Multiple layers of clothes will not be comfortable in Havana's climate. I doubt that northern girls could handle it very well.

"Carty, your broad shoulders and slender build give you a versatility advantage over Elena. We can make you into a boy or a man, if necessary, which will help with your height. Elena, your more developed figure keeps you as a girl, I'm afraid."

The girls laughed, and Carty said, "I see you noticed the one area where we are not twins, Mr. Novotny." If Novotny had not been such a professional, it would have been his turn to redden. Instead, he continued without pause.

"It's good that you are not obsessed about your physical characteristics. When you are in disguise, you need to act the part you are playing. You first have to convince yourself who you are seeking to be before you can convince the target."

He continued discussing some of the methods that he would be teaching the girls as they finished their breakfast. While the girls cleaned up the kitchen, Novotny organized their clothes into several piles. He handed one bundle to Elena. "Take these into my den through that door to the right. Put them on one layer over the next in the order I set out. Give me a call when you are done, and I'll come in for a final touch."

As Elena left, Carty asked Novotny about his time in the OSS. "Where did you spend most of your time, Mr. Novotny? Is that something you can tell me? The photos on your wall seem to place you all over Europe and North Africa."

"That is true, Carty. I was in fourteen different countries during the War. When I look back, I'm amazed myself that I was able to travel so extensively under the noses of the Nazis. Ironically, I had the most trouble in Allied territory whenever I crossed lines. The Army knew that I was a spy, but they never seemed entirely convinced that I was on our side."

"Didn't that make you feel bad, sir?"

"On the contrary, Carty. It always made me more confident that I was doing a good job. If our side would have had no reservations, I would have been worried that I was not performing well enough for the bad guys."

"Were you always successful in your missions?"

"I cannot divulge much, but I can tell you in general that I failed almost as often as I succeeded. – a better batting average than a Major Leaguer, but with stakes a lot more critical. Often our missions had little chance of success but had a big payback if we pulled them off, so they were almost always worth the gamble. On occasion, though, we were sent on wild goose chases.

"We field guys had to learn how to separate daydreams from realistic goals. One misguided project I was asked to take on was so dumb I refused. It got me in hot water and almost sidelined me until Col. Donovan heard about it and backed me up. Its silliness makes it one of the few stories I feel able to reveal.

"The OSS in Rome thought they had found their one informant in the Vatican, an Italian named Virgilio Scattolini[18], who claimed to know everything about that little city state. In fact, he provided information to anyone willing to pay, and he usually made up most of what he reported. To keep the money flowing, he kept revealing increasingly outlandish developments from phantom contacts.

"The ironic part of spying on the Vatican was the obsession with trying to get information that was of almost no strategic or tactical value. Intelligence services on both sides had an oversized view of the importance of the Vatican's information.

"The Pope didn't care about troop strength or fortifications or fuel supplies or aircraft numbers or other critical military information. He was interested in Catholic refugees displaced by battles and bombing, damaged churches and schools, and persecution of religious personnel behind the Soviet and German lines.

"Nevertheless, every intelligence service spent inordinate resources trying to penetrate the Vatican's inner circle.

"By 1945, we had pushed the Germans into northern Italy and taken most of the country including Rome, so Vatican City was no longer surrounded or threatened by the Axis powers. Scattolini reported to gullible OSS personnel that the Vatican was planning to build an airstrip in the Vatican gardens. He never came up with a valid reason why the Vatican would want or need it, but the OSS chief in Rome believed that he had discovered an important strategic secret.

"You have to understand that Vatican City is a tiny one square mile in size, right in the middle of Rome. Its limited space is almost fully built-up with churches and office buildings. At most, the strip would have been a hundred yards long, built on the side of a hill, and tucked next to St. Peter's Basilica, the highest building in Rome. The prospect of planes landing and taking off in such a location was absurd on its face.

"When I was told to plan a surreptitious entry into the Vatican to copy the plans, I refused. In the first place, no one would be so stupid to build it. More importantly, the functionality of such a short airstrip would be nil, and it would create no possible problem for our War effort if it were completed. No fixed wing aircraft could land or take off from such a strip. There was no way I was willing to risk anyone under my authority in such an operation.

"When FDR heard that I short-circuited the ridiculous plan, he sent me a congratulatory letter. It concluded with, 'If one of your guys had been caught sneaking around the Vatican, it could have cost me half the Catholic vote.' Of course, he did not live long enough for the next election."

"What happened to Scattolini? Was he arrested?"

"Ha, ha. No, amazingly, he hung on for the remainder of the year, still peddling his fantasies to anyone willing to pay. As the war ran down, he was eventually sent packing, but he probably had a nice stash to see himself into retirement."

A shout from the den indicated that Elena had completed dressing. Novotny left Carty in the kitchen and joined Elena. About fifteen minutes later, the doorbell rang, and Novotny called out to Carty, "Could you answer the door, Carty? We are not quite done here."

Carty hustled through the house to the front door and greeted a woman about mid-fifties in age. She had thick brown hair that flowed aimlessly about her shoulders. Deep wrinkles in a dark olive complexion creviced her face.

Her gray polka-dotted cotton dress on a faded green background hung listlessly, almost to the floor. The long sleeves hid all but the age spots speckling the backs of her hands. She carried a paper shopping bag with the contents obscured under a threadbare towel.

"Hello, may I help you?" Carty greeted pleasantly.

The woman stared at the floor through thick eyeglasses and shook her head gently. She pulled the screen door open and stepped into the house. The heavy paper shopping bag in her right hand hunched her forward with a slight list to starboard. The woman used it as a shield to edge past Carty.

Carty was startled by the woman's uninvited entry but did not want to appear rude. "If you'd care to wait here, Ma'am," she said urgently, "I'll get Mr. Novotny for you. May I say who is calling?"

The woman did not answer and shuffled past Carty toward the back of the house. In desperation, Carty called out loudly, "Mr. Novotny, there is someone to see you."

Hearing no reply, Carty could do nothing but follow the woman as she proceeded into the kitchen. Carty was relieved to see Novotny seated at the table and more than a little curious when the woman stood before him and nodded.

After a few quiet moments, the woman began laughing with glee more than familiar to Carty. Novotny beamed a big smile.

"Elena, it's you!" Looking to the two conspirators, she continued, "How did you do this? I had no idea. Turn around. I want a better look."

"Where did you get that dress? It isn't one we brought. It isn't one I would allow in my closet. It isn't even one Mom would allow in our house!"

"Believe it or not, girls," Novotny interjected, "It is one that I wore on a foray into Poland in 1943."

Carty examined Elena more closely. She saw that the hair was a wig and that make-up created age spots on her hands. Elena's wrinkles fascinated Carty. Irish genes from Elena's grandfather's family coursed through her. Normally, her light complexion sprinkled with a small number of freckles was as smooth as marshmallow, not grooved and pitted.

Carty drew her fingers over Elena's cheek, noting that the ridges were real, not a visual trick of shading.

"How did you do that, Mr. Novotny?"

"It's my own mixture. It starts with rubber cement that I groove into crow's feet, pock marks, and deep wrinkles around the mouth. Various combinations of normal women's make-up mixed with cigar ash gray the color."

"Is it hard to remove?"

"'Remove,' Carty? It can't be removed. It's permanent."

"What? Permanent?" Elena gasped, only to be greeted with laughter from both Novotny and Carty. A relieved Elena said, "Please don't do that to me again, Mr. Novotny."

"Seriously, Elena. I know that it is you, but I would not have guessed it if I had seen you on the street."

Elena's smile at the comment brought a wide-eyed gulp from Carty. Elena's formerly bright white teeth were a drab yellowish gray. "Wow, I hope Mr. Novotny didn't make those permanent," Carty added.

Novotny said, "We're not ready to display you and Elena outside. I only wanted you both to see what we can do with a little time, makeup, and effort. You can see how easy it is to transform yourself. However, you need to learn techniques to capitalize on the changes.

"For one thing, we did not have time to work on Elena's voice. That is why she did not speak to you at the front door. We will be spending our class time expanding on more sophisticated techniques for the next week.

"So," gesturing the girls to the table, he said, "Let's get started."

Carty stepped briskly into her seat while Elena shuffled listlessly toward her chair, settling down with an audible sigh as she sat. That brought an admiring smile from Carty.

Novotny said, "You can relax now, Elena, and be yourself."

"Oh, no, sir. I seem to recall someone saying that we had to convince ourselves of a new persona before we will be able to convince our target."

"So I did Elena, so I did." Impressed, Novotny thought to himself that this project might be easier to accomplish than he had expected.

**THIRTEEN** days later, the day after Christmas, they were ready for field work. They headed into Winter Free to track a real person – their friend, Mack Stein.

Mack had taken some criticism for an obituary he wrote for Hale's uncle, Eugene, a War hero and minister at First Methodist. *The Gazette* had never included the obituaries of Winter Free's black residents until Mack convinced Geiger to allow him to write about the city's most decorated WWII medal winner.

Most residents were so interested in Eugene Wending's exploits during the War that it served as a good pioneer piece for the paper to expand coverage for the black community and raised less controversy than Geiger had anticipated.

Novotny complimented Geiger on the article during one of their frequent dinners at Bell Mill Chop House, the best restaurant in Winter Free.

The restaurant was located on one of the few hills in otherwise mostly flat Florida terrain. Producing flour in small, local mills became uneconomical around the turn of the century, so the Bell family converted their grist mill into a restaurant.

As later generations of Bells took over, the family continued improving the facilities and the menu. They retained the grinding stone from the original business, and it dominated the entry. Though no longer grinding grain, it still functioned for display purposes, powered by the waterwheel on a fast flowing, spring-fed creek – rare for Florida.

**WHEN** Novotny had arrived in Winter Free a few years after the War, Geiger expressed an interest in writing an article about his exploits in the OSS, but Novotny demurred. "I'd rather that you highlighted others, Mr. Geiger," he had said. "The OSS operated under the radar, and even though it is being closed down, one never knows if it might need to be resurrected in the future. I would appreciate it if you would not print an article."

"I understand what you are saying, Mr. Novotny, but it's not easy to walk away from a good story."

"Well, Mr. Geiger, we're not talking about the Lindbergh Kidnapping or the Bonnie and Clyde kind of story here."

Geiger laughed, "Yeah, you're right. Why don't I run a small 'Welcome to Winter Free' article about a retired lawyer from New York?"

"In that case, please call me Vosmik and accept a dinner invitation on me. Where is the best restaurant in town?"

"Bell Mill for sure, and I'm hungry right now. What do you say I close up early, and we can drive out there together? By the way, Vosmik, I am Knode, and if I had known you were throwing around bribes," he laughed, "We could have solved this issue a lot quicker."

"You didn't look like someone who might be susceptible to that kind of inducement, Knode," Novtony countered with a smile.

"Actually, you're right. If you had tried that, you would have been plastered all over the first page."

From that point forward, Novotny and Geiger were the best of friends.

*ABOUT* the time Novotny was readying his training plan for the girls, he met Geiger for another dinner. When Geiger happened to mention his surprise that The Gazette received few complaints about the obituary Mack wrote, it gave Novotny an idea.

Later, one particularly threatening, unsigned letter was delivered to the paper's office. It warned Mack to watch his back for writing the obituary. It implied that there were many places in town where anyone could lurk, ready to spring out when Mack walked by.

Geiger told Mack that such warnings were an occupational hazard for newsmen, and that such letters seldom resulted in anything more than the author wasting a three cent postage stamp mailing it.

Given Mack's inexperience and history of fleeing Nazis as a child, though, he became more alert going about his business. He looked for people sitting in cars for no apparent reason, for strangers dressed differently than the usual locals, and for anyone looking his way for more than a moment.

In short, he was vigilant, which was just the way Novotny and Geiger intended. And that is why they joined forces to draft the phony letter threatening Mack. Novotny needed someone for the girls to tail, and since Mack knew them, he was ideally suited as a difficult assignment. Of course, Novotny did not tell Geiger the precise purpose for the girls' training. Novotny was committed to the "need to know" principle, and Geiger needed to know that the girls were in training and nothing more.

For two days, the girls stalked Mack in various disguises. Elena was so bold at one time that, as an older woman, she asked him to hold her bag of groceries while she retrieved a dime from her purse for a phone call. While he waited, she pretended to ask for a taxi to pick her up and complained loudly when the supposed dispatcher told her that it would be an hour's wait.

Then she had alarmed Mack by telling him he would have to hold the bags for that hour until her taxi arrived. Before he could think of a reason to explain why he could not stay that long, Carty showed up in disguise and offered to stay with her "sister" for the hour instead.

Over the two days, between the pair, they had brushed against him in one disguise or another, and had spoken to him seven times, without his realizing who they were.

Finally, it came time for the graduation ceremony at Novotny's school. He invited The Crew and Elena to his house to meet his immigrant Latvian "aunts" who were visiting from Pennsylvania.

Since Blake's Crosley was small, he borrowed his dad's Hudson and picked up the boys. "Carty and Elena told me that they will join us a little later. They have to do some shopping with Mrs. Andersson," Blake explained.

"Since Carty wasn't making the trip with us, I picked up a 3 Musketeers candy bar just like the old days, Hale." Handing it to him, he said, "You have the honors."

"Ever since you joined The Crew, Mack, we had to drop an old tradition." Peeling the wrapper off of the 3 Musketeers, Hale pointed to the two creases in the top of the candy bar. "When we were only three in The Crew, we could break the 3 Musketeers into three tidy pieces to share. Now that we are four, we cannot do that anymore.

"When we were little kids, 3 Musketeers came in vanilla, chocolate, and strawberry sections, so the indentations were designed to separate the flavors. Then I guess they decided that the chocolate was so popular that they made the entire candy bar that flavor. But they kept the indentations, so kids could still share. "

Hale used the creases to break the candy bar into three equal parts and passed them around.

"I never could figure out why the Mars Company did that. It seems to me that they would sell more candy bars if they got rid of those creases, so kids couldn't share so easily."

"They probably don't want to throw out the molds with the indentations."

"Whatever the reason, keep it to yourself, or they might do away with the creases."

"Now that there are four of us in The Crew, maybe we should move on to Chuckles. We'd have an extra one of those, though."

When they drove along Novotny's drive, they noticed two elderly women through the front window of his house. "Those must be Mr. Novotny's aunts," Blake said.

After brief introductions to his aunts, Agata and Lidia, everyone sat at Novotny's kitchen table where he served fried chicken, mashed potatoes, corn on the cob, and lemonade.

"You know I can no eatink corn, Vosmik," Agata (Elena in disguise) cackled in her best Central European accent, handing the corncob back to him.

"No teets, you know," she continued by way of explanation for the boys, her big smile revealing several gaps in the "teets" in her mouth.

Lidia (Carty) could not maintain composure and began giggling with her face buried in her hands.

The boys thought Lidia was laughing about Agata's missing teeth, not realizing that Elena's humor had set off the giggling spell. They were on the verge of catching the laughter virus themselves and were avoiding eye contact with one another and doing everything else that they could think of to avoid being so impolite.

But Elena continued to push. "Lost one toot to a beeg salami long time back from now. You know da leetle peppery corns in salami. One of dem got me large time."

Shoving a fist deeply into her mouth, she pointed at an apparently missing molar, "Snapped dis beeg toot in two. Dat really hurt beeg, but you sure don't have knowed it listening to Vosmik and Lidia. Dey dought it was very funniest ting since da Irish potato blight."

Turning to Blake, she added, "Still havink a couple of toot roots saved, dough, Sonny. You like to feel dem?"

A shocked Blake responded, "Uh, no, Ma'am. That's not really necessary."

At that point, Vosmik joined Carty, both of whose faces turned bright red as they tried to stifle laughing. There was no stopping it, however, and then the boys joined in as ever so gently as they could, but for different reasons.

"Looks like all bodies tink my misink teets are funny. Vell, I don't be tinkink so." With that said, Elena got up and stomped away from the table in a huff.

By the time she was out of earshot, tears were streaming from everyone's eyes. No one said anything, and they tried to eat, but just as they managed to get food into their mouths, one would break into laughter and tears and cause the entire table to erupt once again.

After several long minutes, a semblance of decorum settled in, and they were able to resume eating. Hale was the first to speak, offering an apology to Mr. Novotny for their behavior and for causing Agata to leave the table. Just as Novtony finished saying that there was no need to apologize, Lidia piped up.

"Not to worryink. Agata get over missink teets fastly. Only don't say anytink about her mustache. She is many more touchy about havink shave it off every day."

That set the table off on another laughing outburst with Lidia leading the way. Agata hollered from the adjoining room. "So you tinkink my moustache is humor? Hmmph! Wait when you seeink Lidia's bald head."

With the boys looking on in shock at Lidia, she began removing her wig. When she had it off, though, her head was not bald, and there was no mistaking Carty's blond hair. The boys realized that they had been had when Elena returned still dressed as Agata but without her wig and the make-up.

Novotny announced, "Boys, you see the first graduates of the Novotny School of Disguise. They did a great job, don't you think?"

More laughter, awe, and amazement ensued. All were on display as the boys took turns looking closely at Carty's make-up and tracing it with fingers.

As they resumed eating, he filled them in on the purpose for the girls' training. "Normally, I would not be telling you this, but Carty told me that you were previously aware of her intention to track down "Mr. Smith" this coming summer. Please keep this to yourselves for their safety."

He apologized to Mack for the threatening letter ruse that was intended to put him on the alert and make him a better test for the girls as they tried out different disguises in town.

"Frankly, Mr. Novotny, it is a relief. I have been living in dread of running into the lady who would make me help with her bag of purchases again."

# CHAPTER 19

## *The March of Dimes Gala*

*Fear is the tax that conscience pays to guilt.*
GEORGE SEWELL

**JANUARY 1953**

The large great room in the Canfield Mansion was still festooned with some Christmas decorations. Normally, Sally put Christmas things away on January 7, the day after The Feast of the Magi, but as the crowd was coming later in the month, she decided to retain the tree, holly, and a few other decorations.

James had borrowed seventy folding chairs from the St. Mark's Church community room to supplement the chairs in the house. It was a tight squeeze, but they were arranged in neatly arched rows facing the fireplace that already roared with a great fire needed to warm the high ceilinged room on the unusually chilly evening.

Some old timers in Winter Free were warning that the area might experience a rare frost in the early morning hours, something that had not occurred in over thirty years. More than one local insisted that a global cooling was underway.

Although Castillo and Easter were normally scheduled to work at the Andersson place on this day of the week, Lilly sent them to Sally's to help with the food and the crowd.

**WHEN** Castillo pulled his 1938 Studebaker pick-up truck to the front of Sally's house, he was surprised to see Easter at the door to greet him. Castillo had loaded up food and other supplies at Homer's and was delivering them to the house before expecting to return to Lilly's estate to get Easter.

He kissed Easter and gave her an affectionate hug. "How did you get here, Easter? I was supposed to pick you up after dropping these supplies off."

"I wanted to get an early start, Castillo, so I walked through the swamp. Miss Lilly gave me directions."

"You did what?!" Castillo screamed. He grabbed her by the shoulders and put his face inches from hers and yelled. "I told you never to go near the swamp, did I not? Why did you disobey me? What got into you?"

Easter was shocked into speechlessness. Never in the almost three years they had been together did Castillo ever raise his voice to her. He was as gentle a man as she had ever met. She could not believe what was happening.

He grasped her shoulders and shook her, not violently, but forcefully, and repeated the question, "Why did you disobey me?"

Easter could not answer. Instead she burst into tears.

When Castillo saw Easter so distressed, he regained control of himself and was immediately remorseful at what he was doing to her. That's when he noticed Sally watching them from inside the house, and he was embarrassed as well.

"Come," he said gently, "I want to talk with you." With an arm draped affectionately around her waist, he led the sobbing woman down the step and into the garden where Sally could not hear.

Castillo shuddered as they walked away from the house. He could not banish the memory of the mammoth alligator dragging him into what should have been a watery grave, save for the bulletproof vest that had protected him. He was sorry for frightening Easter, but she shocked him so unexpectedly announcing that she had traipsed though Morose Swamp that he lost control.

"Easter, please forgive me. I do not know what came over me. You do not deserve anyone yelling at you, me least of all. Dearest, you can never go through the swamp. It is a treacherous place. There are dangers you cannot imagine lurking there. I could not live with myself if something happened to you.

"Will you promise me that you will never go through the swamp again for any reason? That's the only thing I have ever asked of you."

Still sobbing from the fright, Easter fought to speak. "I did not know that you feared the swamp so much, Castillo. I was only trying to help Sra. Elsmore by coming early. The long way around the forest is too far by foot, and you had the truck.

"I saw nothing to fear, but I promise you that I will stay away from the swamp from now on."

Castillo was smiling now, and after a few more minutes, both regained their composure. "Let's get to work, Easter. We have a big party to prepare for." They walked arm in arm back to the house, neither of them noticing Sally's discreet observation.

*SALLY'S* newly renovated kitchen was being put to the test. The abrupt cold snap required a quick change in the menu in both food and drinks.

Instead of ham on the original menu, Easter prepared two enormous batches of chili with two levels of seasoning. Castillo sampled a spicy version first and said, as he wiped tears from his eyes, "Whew, this hot version will take the chill off the guests."

"'Hot version,' Castillo?" Easter asked, "You took that sample from the mild kettle."

That revelation brought a rueful laugh from Castillo and initiated a considerable adjustment to moderate both batches, but she had plenty of time before the guests arrived.

In the meantime, Castillo prepared a spicy grog and a buttered rum while Sally pitched in to brew the coffee and hot chocolate.

As arranged, Aunt Lilly arrived early with Carty as her driver. Lilly, the previous March of Dimes coordinator, continued to play a prominent role, and she would join James and Sally greeting guests as they arrived. Carty had volunteered to help on the serving line to keep things running efficiently.

Carty's parents were at the Florida Roadbuilders' Convention in Miami Beach, the first time that they had been away together since starting the limerock mining business years ago. Carty was staying with Aunt Lilly for the weekend.

Castillo took their coats to the master bedroom to place on the bed. There he saw a large ruby on black velvet resting on the dresser. Normally, Sally kept the ruby in the drawer, but she had left it out inadvertently. He approached it almost in awe. He did not touch it, but tilted his head from side to side mere inches from the red beauty. Then he snapped himself back to life and returned to his kitchen duties.

Lilly and Sally both wore red in keeping with the decorations in the house. Lilly's floor length velvet had full length sleeves with a high collar and white lace cuffs.

Sally, as was her custom, wore form-fitting, shimmering satin with a sufficiently scooped neck to display one of the many Canfield necklaces, this time a garnet and jade array. Sally had intended to wear a favorite emerald piece, but, to her surprise, it was not in the jewelry drawer. "Another time when I left it at the bank," she chided herself.

She wore her hair up for a change and held it in place with a tiara of light green jade. She noticed for the first time that the red dress fit ever so snugly, though the effects of her pregnancy were not showing yet.

She chuckled to herself that even with the small amount of green, she did look sufficiently "witchy" in bright red to be the talk of Winter Free for the next week.

Guests began arriving at 6:30, and they were grateful for the warm drinks. Guest after guest headed for positions near the large fireplace to warm themselves after being greeted at the door.

Though Sally and James had put in indoor plumbing the previous autumn, the outhouse was still functional. James greeted the male visitors with the good-natured announcement that since the indoor restrooms were not sufficient to handle a crowd of this size, the men in attendance were assigned to the outhouse for their needs, not a particularly pleasant prospect in the cold temperature outside.

"Brrr," Harrison Wending, Hale's father, said, "We're living in Florida to stay warm. We do not deserve this."

"Oh, hush," his wife admonished, "Be grateful to the Lord that it isn't snowing."

Only Mack, who had spent most of his life in the cold climates of several European countries, seemed unperturbed by the sudden drop in temperature.

By seven, the hosts closed down the receiving line, leaving James to handle any stragglers, and announced that the serving line was open.

Blake and Hale, both Explorer scouts, gravitated to Carty as she was finishing with her serving line duty. Mack was not a scout, but he was in attendance as a reporter for *The Gazette*.

"I see that Dolder is here. What a mooch. Just because his younger brother is a Boy Scout, Dolder decides that he is invited too," Blake complained. "He doesn't seem to be enjoying himself, though. He is sweating like a pig."

That brought enough of a giggle from Carty to get the others' attention. "Okay, Carty, what's going on?" Hale asked.

"Oh, nothing," she whispered, "except when I heard Haywood bragging to his brother that he was going for the hot version of the chili, I slipped a little extra of Easter's special chili powder on to my serving spoon when he came though the line. I mixed it into his serving and watched as he forced himself to eat it in front of his brother. He has been drinking water nonstop ever since."

"And you kept that secret from us, Carty? No fair."

"Sorry, guys, there was no way I could get to you while I had serving duty.

"Look I'll join you guys a little later. Save me a seat. But right now I have to help Easter and Castillo clean up."

"Do not worry about the clean-up, Srta. Carty," Easter said. "We take care of it. You join your friends out front. *Gracias* for all the help you gave us."

Carty removed her serving apron to reveal her version of the red dress of the evening. It was a simple A-frame of warm cotton with three-quarter length sleeves, and sufficiently non-form fitting to put Blake at ease. He became flustered whenever he saw Carty dressed in anything that suggested "girl" rather than "good buddy," though he now seemed to accept Elena in a female role.

The Crew found four seats together and settled down to listen to Sally. All of them remembered the first time they heard her in this room nearly three years before. They had been terrified when they entered this house of a rumored witch that day, but they departed that evening relieved.

Sally walked to the small podium in front of the fireplace. Her book of Canfield fables perched already open with the marking ribbon positioned at *The Legend of Montooth and the Dillos*. She began with an enormous, bright smile. She acknowledged Lilly Andersson's work in previous years and invited well-deserved applause. Then she thanked all the scouts for going door-to-door seeking donations as well as the parents for supporting the scouts' efforts.

"Two years ago there were over 20,000 cases of polio in the United States, and every indication is that the year just past will be much worse. We have had over a dozen youngsters here in Winter Free struck with polio in the last three years.

"Fortunately, there are several test programs under way as I speak. Dr. Jonas Salk is testing a vaccine using a dead polio virus, and Dr. Albert Sabin is testing a live virus. Other trials are taking place as well.

"Polio is a scourge that can be defeated, and the work that all of you did last week for the March of Dimes and the work that others around the country did will play an important part in furthering the research needed to protect our young from this horrible disease.

"I know that many of you enjoyed reading the book that I published, *The Legend of Montooth*. I thought that you might be interested in another story that includes Montooth, and so I have selected *The Legend of Montooth and the Dillos*."

She stepped closer to the podium to better read her grandmother's flowing, cursive writing.

The audience listened attentively as Sally read through the story. She used so many different voices for the various characters, including a particularly haughty tone when Obnock spoke, that the reading seemed like a professional radio show. When she reached the point where Willit and

Bento were to make their presentation of the invention, she paused.

"That last chapter was a long one. Let's take a short intermission while I get something to drink to rejuvenate my voice. Please help your-selves to any of the left-overs."

Carty and the boys could not help but chuckle when they saw that Haywood was the first to jump up and race the women to the restroom.

After about fifteen minutes, James approached the podium and called everyone back. Sally resumed where she had left off.

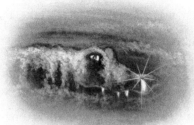

# CHAPTER G

## *The Big Show*

The exciting day came almost a week later. Obnock delayed the presentation in order to build on the anticipation of what he called the Obnock-Willit Innovation.

That morning of the presentation, Willit made a final examination of Bento's back. "There is something strange going on," he remarked to Bento. "You appear to be growing some bone along the edges and over the top of the sawgrass blades. The blades appear to be fusing into your body. Do you feel any discomfort?"

"No. In fact, it is beginning to feel like part of my body instead of an attachment. Maybe there is something in the mud that you used that allows the blades to both harden and grow into my back."

"Whatever the cause, we don't have time to do anything about it now. The test is in a few hours."

**OBNOCK** spoke to the conference about an hour before Willit and Bento were scheduled to arrive. He told the dillos of his hard work and the difficulties that he faced while coming up with a design that would protect them. He gave Willit the briefest mention and ignored Bento's participation entirely.

By the time Willit and Bento arrived, most at the conference believed that Obnock had generously included them as his mere assistants. It was only because Montooth and Feather had arrived early and hidden in the weeds to avoid frightening the assembled dillos that Willit later learned about Obnock's duplicity.

"I see that our friends have arrived with our invention," Obnock announced to great applause as he pointed to the arrivals. "Let us hear the presentation I have arranged for them to make."

Willit and Bento strode to the front of the group. "I'm not much of a public speaker," Willit began, "so I will limit my talking. The best way for me to explain it is to demonstrate it rather than to talk about it."

"We have developed a protection device that you see on Bento and me. It will protect us from many dangers, and it can protect all of you too."

At that point, he motioned toward the weeds and called out, "Please come forward."

Responding, Montooth and Feather emerged from their position in the tall weeds. The dillos gasped in horror as the green monster and his smaller friend moved forward to where Willit and Bento stood. The crowd shrank back, ready to sprint away at the slightest quick move from either gator. Obnock unconsciously rubbed the ends of his shortened fingers as he stared.

Feather came closer and slowly opened her mouth. Bento climbed in and rolled into a ball. Willit held his hand high as if signaling the start of a race. No one in the crowd was breathing.

Suddenly, Willit brought down his arm in a signal, but not nearly as hard or fast as Feather clamped her jaws on to Bento in response.

Dillos gasped, groaned, and cried. Obnock, who had moved to the rear of the crowd was readying for a quick escape.

Then Feather opened up, and Bento unrolled, emerging unscathed. He wore a big smile on his face and reached his arms above in triumph.

Cheers erupted, partly in relief and partly in amazement. Willit and Bento walked back and forth shaking the paws of everyone who offered. Willit had trouble keeping up with the questions as they came so fast. Bento was walking around, allowing anyone to touch his back.

"You can see the way Bento moves that the protection

slows him down, but he no longer needs to run away. His armor is strong enough to withstand a normal gator's bite. If you do not want to get the armor, you can still be a dillo. But if you do want the armor, you will become an 'armadillo.'"

Smoothly, Obnock eased to the front of the crowd. A natural performer, he allowed the enthusiasm to continue until it ebbed naturally. Then he raised his hands and motioned everyone back.

"You see," he said, placing himself into position to claim the glory. "We have been working hard, and the work has paid off. Our plan is to authorize Willit to go into immediate production of the armor. I doubt that there will be many who do not choose to become armadillos."

Montooth and Feather shrank back into the grass, unnoticed in the excitement. Feather sensed a sadness around Montooth. "What is wrong, Montooth? You should be happy for your friends."

"Oh, I am happy for them. It is that Obnock who has me worried. He reminds me so much of someone I knew as a child – a duck named Drack. I hope that Willit always stays alert when Obnock is around."

The two slid into the warm water of Big Lake and swam silently away.

# CHAPTER H

## Discovered

As Willit and Bento went into production, Obnock took over scheduling. They were happy to be able to concentrate on outfitting the armor on each dillo rather than worrying about who would be first or second or third or last. Obnock took on his task with relish.

Of course, he chose himself to be first. "You need to get me out of the way first so that I can concentrate on scheduling the entire village," he rationalized, ignoring that he could just as easily concentrate while going last.

Unbeknownst to Willit and Bento, Obnock arranged for the remainder of the village to line up in the order of who would be most politically beneficial to him or who offered him the biggest side payment.

At the end of the first week, Willit, Bento, and Obnock

munched on grubs that had been brought in payment. Willit's fingers ached from all of the sewing. Bento was in charge of stringing palm branches as well as of cutting, curing, and hauling new sawgrass, so he could not pitch in on the sewing.

Montooth had told them how Obnock was trying to take credit for Willit's invention, but Willit had suggested that Montooth misunderstood Obnock's intentions.

"Obnock has always been friendly, Montooth. He can be a little cloying at times, but everyone seems to like him, so I'm sure he means well. In any event, we don't seem to be having any difficulty getting customers since he took over."

Of course, Willit did not realize that his invention was such a success and in such great demand that keeping customers away was the current problem. And he had no idea that Obnock was misusing his position both on the Council and in the armoring operation.

"Public service is truly taxing," Obnock suggested to an assistant, with far more truth than he intended. "It's tough doing the people's work. I don't know how I keep up," he remarked.

"Mostly by sitting on your rear," Bento thought, but kept to himself.

"Fellows," Willit announced. "I am going to have to expand. There is no way Bento and I can keep up cutting new supplies and sewing them on to the customers' backs. We are not even five percent through the village yet. We need help."

The next day, Bento contacted all of the armadillos who had already been outfitted so he could solicit trainees. Six were eager to go to work. Four proved to be good at sewing, and two worked out well as sawgrass cutters. Production ramped up.

Shortly afterward, one of Bento's new helpers happened to make an offhanded remark about giving Obnock an "extra payment" to move up to the front of the line when getting armored. Bento was shocked and asked another new worker about it. He got the same answer.

That afternoon before closing, he called a meeting of the entire company, except for Obnock who was away on Council business.

This time Willit could not deny what he learned. Every new employee who had previously been outfitted with armor stated that Obnock required an extra payment. What was worse, each thought Obnock had been operating under Willit's instructions.

The next day Willit had planned to tell Obnock that they could get along without him now that they had enough workers. However, Obnock beat him to it. "I would really like to continue helping you, Willit," Obnock had said, "but I have assisted you in getting off the ground, and now I must devote my efforts to Council business which requires increasing amounts of my time. Public service is my calling."

Thus, the unpleasant details of bribery remained unspoken. What Willit did not know was that one of his questioned workers had mentioned the company meeting to his brother who was a Council ally of Obnock's. Obnock had learned that Willit found out about the bribes, so he avoided a confrontation.

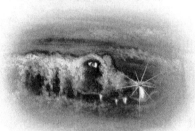

# CHAPTER I

## *Placing Political Pressure*

The summer passed quickly, nearly unnoticed by Willit and Bento who were working almost nonstop.

Because of increased production, Willit was able to reduce prices in the autumn, but, by winter, he had to increase prices back up to the original level. Production costs were rising. The sawgrass that was easy to harvest was gone by December. As the daylight hours diminished, they were working harder in more difficult conditions and with more workers to gather the same quantity from less accessible areas.

Then in the spring, the first armadillo was born to two parents who had been outfitted with Willit's armor. The baby was born with armor already on her body. She would not require retrofitting like her parents.

Willit might have been disappointed that he would get no repeat business if babies were being born already armored, but he was not. He had enough business to last quite a long time, and he was happy that future generations would be protected no matter what.

When everything seemed to be going so well, however, Obnock returned. Entering the large den, he remarked, "My, my, you have really become successful. Look at these facilities. Look at all these workers. Look at these fine offices.

"I believe that the complaints the Council is hearing are totally unfounded – I want you to know that. But I have to investigate. That is my job. I know you understand that as well."

Willit and Bento looked at each other and shrugged. "Complaints? I'm not aware that we have failed to produce anything but good work," Willit said.

"You see, we are off to a bad start already, fellows. There are no complaints about the quality of the work here. Everyone knows that if you want to get dillo armor, this is the place. Why, you even take in dillos from other communities, we hear."

"Well, just a few. What we do mostly is teach dillos from other communities to use our techniques. Then we set them up and sell our materials to them."

"There you go. Everyone praises your work."

"So what are the complaints, Obnock?"

"These are the things that we hear, Willit – not things that I necessarily believe. Please understand that. No one is a bigger supporter of your work than I.

"There are complaints that you are becoming greedy and that you do not accept customers in a fair way. Well, there it is. I'm not saying that any of this is true, mind you. I'm just repeating some of the complaints that we are hearing."

Bento reacted angrily. "'Greedy?' Not 'fair?' I'll show you greedy and not fair. I'll show you the door," grabbing Obnock by the arm and attempting to escort him out. Willit stepped in the way.

"Okay, Bento, calm down. Let's hear what Obnock has to say."

Turning to Obnock, he continued. "Can you give us some details? We truly do not know what you are talking about."

Obnock straightened himself with a huff and explained. "A dillo by the name of Diptipper alerted us that he applied to be armored but that you turned him down."

"I do not see how that can be true. I have never turned anyone down. I do not involve myself with scheduling. My only concern is to do the best armoring possible for the greatest number of dillos."

"When I say 'you,' Willit, I do not mean you personally. I mean someone in your organization. It's your organization, though, so you are responsible for anything that anyone in it does."

"Of course I am, but I seriously doubt that anyone in my organization would turn down an applicant for armoring. We are here both to serve and to make a profit. Why would we turn customers away?"

"Hold on," Bento interjected. "Diptipper. I knew that name sounded familiar. He came in about ten days ago and tried to push his way to the front of the line. He claimed he had Obnock's permission to receive preferential service. I sent him on his way – to the delight of the dillos already waiting in line, I might add."

"Well, there you have it," Obnock said smugly. "You admit turning away Diptipper after I sent him over here to be taken care of. That makes it easy. I do not need to do any further investigation. You confessed that Diptipper's complaint is valid."

"Wait just a second, Obnock. I admit to telling him he was not entitled to preferential treatment, not to refusing him service."

"Diptipper is my protégé. I am working him in as my second-in-command. He is an important part of the Council's activities. You had no right to reject him when I need him in full operational mode immediately."

"Look," Bento answered sharply, "I did not know the clown was working for you. Anyone could come up and make that claim to get to the front of the line. Besides, who gave you the right to tell us who to serve first?"

"You'd better watch your language, Bento. Diptipper is an important dillo in the village, almost as important as I am. You could get yourself in big trouble with your impertinent attitude."

Willit could see that this situation was getting out of hand, so he offered a solution. "I do not want to take an appointment away from someone else to move Diptipper ahead, but I will be happy to work on him after we close tonight. Send him over just before sundown, and I'll handle him myself. There won't be an extra charge."

Obnock shot a satisfied smirk to Bento and replied. "Actually, that brings up the second complaint."

"You have another protégé that you want us to work in?"

"No, no. Nothing like that. You see, there are several dillos who are not able to pay your prices, and it is not fair for them to be left out. Indolan and Slugy both have complained that you refused service because they could not afford your fees."

"Obnock, those two are well known as the laziest dillos in the village. If they cannot pay," Bento added, "It is their fault, not ours."

"I'll not stand for you slandering our fellow dillos, Bento. You had better be careful. In any event, the Council believes that you should provide for the unfortunate without charge, or at least you should offer them a discounted price."

Again, Bento jumped into the conversation. "What? Have you lost your mind? Why should we cater to them? It is not our fault that they are too lazy to be able to pay us."

"That is just the attitude that proves that the complaints are valid. You two are really asking for trouble. When I have to report to the Council, I'd hate to be in your shoes."

"What could we do to help the situation?" Willit asked.

"Why don't we set up a program to help the unfortunate? For every fifty of your regular customers, you agree to take care of one unfortunate dillo without charge. I could bring up that plan to the Council in two days."

"We'll be there, Obnock."

After Obnock left, Willit turned to a fuming Bento. "I know what you are thinking, but we have no choice. Obnock will have the whole Council down on us if we don't agree in some way to comply."

Bento was in no mood to agree. "He is just looking for votes from his friends, the dumbest and laziest in the village. I for one will not help him. I quit."

"Stick with me a little longer, Bento – please. I've been working on something that may help us on all fronts. I was going to tell you about it when I was sure, but I'll move it up under the circumstances. Hear me out."

"Okay, you're my cousin – but more importantly, you're my best friend. I'll listen, but it had better be good."

"After we changed out your armor for the second version, I noticed that it seemed to be stronger than the armor on everyone else. That puzzled me for quite a while, so I experimented whenever I had a few minutes to spare. I think that I know the reason.

"Those first few sawgrass blades that I cut almost a year ago were buried in whitish-gray limerock mud that was difficult to dig in. Later that day and from then on, we buried the blades in soft dark mud that made for easier digging. It seemed to make sense.

"However, I am convinced that your armor is stronger because it developed from the limerock-cured blades instead of the mud-cured blades."

"Recently I tried an experiment with Feather. My original armor was the mud-cured variety. I rolled up inside of her mouth, and she slowly began crushing. She barely got to fifty percent when my armor began giving way and she had to stop. You see, the mud-cured armor does not form hard like the limerock-cured blades.

"To prove my theory, I had you replace my armor with limerock-cured blades last month."

"I remember. You said that your early version was too tight."

"I made up that story because I did not want you to know what I was up to in case I was wrong. You didn't notice anything unusual because the blades look the same when they are implanted. It is only later that the change takes place. Sure enough, within a few days, boney growth appeared on my new blades. Take a look."

Bento examined Willit's back for several minutes.

"You are right, Willit. You are reacting to these blades the way I have to mine."

"And guess what? Feather tried again, and my new armor held up perfectly – just like yours."

Willit continued his explanation. "Remember when we ran the demonstration with you and Feather? Your limerock-cured blades were already re-forming with a strong, natural material. Your back had become strong enough to withstand the pressure from an alligator's mouth – except for Montooth's, of course.

"Mud-cured blades are only partly protective. They are good against a fox and a coyote, but a large bear and even a medium-sized gator are too strong for it.

"I've kept my discovery secret. If the Council meeting goes the way I hope it will, I plan to reveal it.

"Let's see how the Council meeting goes before you quit. The Council will have to put it up to a Village-wide Vote if even one dillo demands it, and I will demand it. Then we'll see if Obnock can get his way. Are you with me?"

"I'll be at your side for the Council meeting, Willit, and I'll be keeping my fingers crossed for you, but I do not share your confidence."

# CHAPTER J

## *Fateful Decision*

Meetings before the Council seldom attracted large crowds, but this one had drawn nearly every dillo in the village.

The sounds from the attendees reminded Bento of buzzing bees as dillos whispered among themselves while the Council began assembling. A number of other swamp animals huddled on the periphery, curious about the evening's activity and wondering what the dillos were planning.

A few raccoons meandered about separately. At one time, the entire raccoon community had banded together cohesively, but nowadays they went about independently. They had no interest in dillos as a rule, but raccoons liked to lurk around groups of animals in the hope that a baby might venture away from the protection of the elders.

A skunk family took care to take a position downwind. Skunks were sensitive to the effect that they had on other animals, and they had no desire to disrupt the meeting.

Oscar, an ancient owl and the oldest bird in the swamp, perched high above the action on a branch next to Penny, a green parrot. Normally, a parrot, like any small bird, would be terrified of an owl, but Oscar and Penny had developed a friendly relationship over the years. Penny admired Oscar's sage advice and commentary, and Oscar valued Penny's ability to translate human speech to the animals.

Obnock motioned for silence as he began the meeting. "As you are aware, we are here to discuss the complaints against Willit and Bento. They have already admitted to refusing service to an important Council representative, so we do not need to go into that. The more serious complaint involves their greed.

"The Council has established that some dillos cannot afford to make standard payments to Willit-Bento, and that Willit-Bento has refused to help them," Obnock charged. "By the way, it is not compassionate to refer to these dillos as 'poor.' The better term is 'Worthy.' Let us not forget that."

High in the treetops, Oscar remarked to Penny, "Have you noticed that Obnock no longer refers to the armoring operation as 'Obnock-Willit?' Now it is 'Willit-Bento.' That is not a good sign."

Obnock detailed the heart-rending cases of Indolan and Slugy. He described their hard life and dire circumstances. He explained that Willit-Bento had insisted on receiving payment before proceeding with the procedure on the two unfortunate Worthies.

Obnock continued to pull on the heartstrings of the crowd, citing every sympathetic ruse available. Meanwhile, Willit and Bento grew increasingly uncomfortable, particularly as many in the audience glared at them.

Obnock then called for the Council to vote. The proposition required Willit-Bento, as a matter of law, to provide armoring for a ninety percent discount from the normal price to any dillo designated as Worthy. The Council would have the sole right to determine who would be Worthy.

Obnock then called on Willit and Bento to speak if they chose to contest the charges.

Willit motioned for Bento to remain seated as he walked to the front of the assembly. He looked several of the dillos and armadillos in the eyes before speaking.

"Many of you have already benefitted from my invention. Croxy, you told me yourself that a fox rolled you around for nearly an hour before giving up. Mardol, you saved your unarmored brother from a coyote by getting in the way and allowing him time to escape. You laughed at the coyote's confusion.

"Many of you are already armadillos, and if we maintain our schedule, the remainder should be finished within a year. Do any of you believe that you are not better off because of what Bento and I created? Would you want to go back to your unarmored days?

"There are ways to improve upon what you have, but you cannot take from us what does not belong to you and expect us to continue developing enhancements. Where is the incentive?

"We create value for the community, and then the Council decides that we should be punished for doing so. Does the community really believe that we will continue working under that kind of direction?

"The Council may desire to help out those deemed Worthy in the hopes of gathering favor and votes from those individuals, but there is no valid reason to steal from us to make it happen. If the Council wants to subsidize Worthy dillos, then the Council should ask all of the dillos to contribute – not single out Willit-Bento to suffer the loss.

"Accordingly, I call for a Village-wide Vote on the grounds that this is too important a decision to leave to the Council alone."

A shocked murmur rippled through the assembly. The call for a Village-wide Vote was a serious demand, but one that could not be denied under village rules.

Obnock took over. "All right, everyone calm down. The Council will confer and review the call for the Village-wide Vote." A short time later, Obnock returned and called for order.

"Willit has called for a vote on the matter of requiring Willit-Bento to provide a ninety percent discount to Worthies designated by the Council. As you can see, Diptipper is passing out the ballots that the Council has quickly prepared. Mark 'Yes' if you believe in requiring the discount. Mark 'No' if you support Willit's position that Willit-Bento does not have an obligation to provide the discount."

As the ballots were passed forward and counted, Oscar remarked to Penny. "I do not believe that this will go Willit's way. It is too easy to make yourself feel good by requiring others to give aid while paying little or nothing yourself."

Bento was still shaking his head and arguing with Willit. "Why didn't you tell them about the improved armor you discovered? It might have influenced the vote in our favor."

Willit reminded Bento of his earlier pronouncement. "You were the one who said you were quitting. If the vote goes the wrong way, you can still quit. They may be able to force us to give discounts for our work. They cannot force us to do the work.

"Besides, dillos should make a decision because it is the correct decision, not because we hold out the possibility of an improved version of armor. If they do not understand that principle, I have no interest in continuing either."

Shortly afterward, the ballots revealed overwhelming

support for granting the subsidies. However, several ballots contained notes suggesting smaller discounts ranging from thirty to eighty percent.

The Council agreed to reexamine the level of discount, but declared that Willit-Bento would henceforth be required to provide discounts to any Council-designated Worthy.

Willit and Bento walked dejectedly back to the den while most of the other dillos slinked off to their homes, feeling embarrassed but not quite sure why.

Penny complimented Oscar, "As usual, you analyzed that correctly. How do you think that Willit and Bento will react if the Council compromises with a lower discount?"

"I've known them for many years, Penny, and I am almost certain of what they will do. It would not matter to them if the discount were lowered to one percent. They will believe that they are being cheated. I doubt that either will be around tomorrow when some of the Worthies show up to demand their procedures."

Oscar was correct in this assessment as well. Willit and Bento went back to the den, packed up, and left the village forever.

After word of Willit and Bento abandoning the village spread to the Council the next day, Obnock took over the armoring operation on behalf of the village by employing the former workers. Eventually, all the dillos became armadillos, but with the old, unimproved armor. All descendants were born with the weaker armor as well.

Willit and Bento eventually relocated in a distant meadow on the south side of Duck Lake. They found mates on whose backs they installed the strong version of armor. Later, their offspring developed the stronger armor naturally. To this day, only a very few armadillos, all descendants of the Willit and Bento families, have strong armor that withstands even the largest swamp animals such as bears, panthers, and gators.

Conversely, all other armadillos have the weaker version of armor, sufficient to fend off smaller predators, but not rigid enough to withstand the bites of larger animals or the wheels of a heavily laden wagon.

# CHAPTER 20

## *Wrap Up*

*Fate rules the affairs of mankind with no recognizable order.*

SENECA

**JANUARY 1953**

After the applause died down, many of the guests approached Sally, suggesting that she publish this new fable the following Christmas as her second children's book.

During Sally's post-intermission reading, Dolder left for the restroom twice, still not going to the outhouse. The Crew had difficulty stifling giggles each time that he left. The second time, Castillo nearly bumped into Dolder rushing to return to his seat.

"Oh, sorry," Dolder said, "The chili really upset my stomach, and I did not have time to go outside."

"I understand," Castillo replied with a chuckle. "Even Easter's ice cream can be *muy caliente* sometimes."

But Sally's homemade raspberry ice cream with chocolate sauce that was served at the conclusion of her reading was suitably cold and enjoyed by all who had eaten the chili earlier and still remembered it both physically and mentally.

Castillo busied himself retrieving coats for the satisfied crowd as the guests began to dwindle away and head for home. Carty was one of the earlier to leave, as she was chauffeuring Aunt Lilly who no longer handled late hours well. From The Crew, only Mack stayed late as he wanted to obtain a few final quotes from the hostess.

"That might be a better fable than the original *Montooth*, Mrs. Elsmore," Mack complimented, "but for me personally, nothing will ever match that first story you read to us. I shall never forget how it played out in our lives."

"Sometimes, Mack, I wake at night. I'm not startled or afraid. I just wake and lie in bed thinking of how my life changed because of the simple act of allowing the four of you into my house. God was looking out for all of us that day, but for me the most."

"About the reading this evening, Mrs. Elsmore, do you actually believe that there are some armadillos that have super armor as described in the story?"

"Mack, I've learned never to ignore the meanings of the stories in Canfield lore. I've seen enough flattened armadillos along the highways to know that the regular armor is not adequate to protect them from automobiles.

"But is there a strain of armadillos strong enough to stand up to a one-ton auto? I don't know, but when Morgan Canfield felt strongly enough about something to write about it, I have never found him to be wrong."

"As to the moral of the story, do you believe that governments will attempt to steal patented products as a means of catering to voters?"

"George Washington said, 'Few men have virtue to withstand the highest bidder,' Mack. Let us hope that our political people have the moral fiber to avoid trying to buy votes, and that the people have the sense to recognize a voter bribe for what it is."

After Mack left, Sally went to the kitchen where Castillo and Easter were finishing the clean-up.

"My, you two have done a wonderful job of putting everything back into order already. That was a big crowd, and you could not have performed better. Thank you so much for everything."

Sally motioned Castillo aside and slipped a tightly folded twenty dollar bill into his hand.

"Oh, no, Sra. Elsmore. That is not necessary. You and Sra. Andersson pay us well, and we are happy to help with special events like this."

"Nonsense, Castillo, you have put in extra time and effort. Take the money and buy your wife a nice present. She is a good woman and deserves to be treated well."

"As you put it that way, *Señora*, I cannot say no. There is no finer woman I could have found, it is true. *Gracias*."

"Tomorrow is your regular day here, so you can finish cleaning then. Get some rest. Good night."

James had left at the end of her reading to attend to a problem at the county jail. Sally did not expect him back until the early morning hours. She surveyed the big room. Except for the folding chairs stacked against the walls and a little additional clean-up, the house was back to normal. She walked into her bedroom and rolled the large ruby in her hand before putting it away.

# CHAPTER 21

## *More Lore*

*Call it a clan, call it a network, call it a tribe, call it a family.*
*Whatever you call it, whoever you are, you need one.*

JANE HOWARD

**JANUARY 1953**

The morning following Sally's reading of *The Legend of Montooth and the Dillos*, she picked up the book of family legends to return it to its place on the bookshelf. As she reached above her head and slid the book back, she noticed that it seemed to catch on something. She jostled it about and tried again. Try as she did, she could not move the book fully back into its slot.

Sally pulled a chair over and stood on it. She saw the problem. Another book, positioned oddly behind all the others, had fallen in a way that prevented the fable volume from sliding all the way back.

She reached in and pulled the book from its jamming position, slid the fable book into place, and stepped down from the chair.

Sally thought that she knew every book in the vast library, but she did not recognize this one. She opened randomly to the middle of the book and said, "Grandmother worked on this one too. I'd recognize her handwriting anywhere. I wonder why she never showed this book to me."

Sally found out the answer to the question when she sat down and read the first page.

*Sally,*

*If you are reading this, then you have found the Extended Family History. This book chronicles key events in the lives of all the Canfields who have lived in our Morose Swamp house at one time but who decided, for whatever reason, to move away.*

*I never told you about the extended family. I was afraid that you might, as a young woman living alone, seek some of the family out before you were capable of handling finances on your own. The Morgan Canfield treasure is substantial, and I am concerned that if you get too close to other family members while you are still very young, one of them might attempt to take it away from you.*

Canfields have always been honest, honorable people, but black sheep can run in every family. A sneaky cousin caused the loss of the family castle in Scotland.

A wily nephew by marriage mutinied aboard a British warship and turned pirate. That situation proved providential, however, as his plunder became a major part of the vast family fortune when, on behalf of the Crown, Morgan tracked his errant relative to North Carolina. That story is chronicled in this book as _The Ocracoke Oracle_.

I pray that you are a mature woman by the time you discover this book, for then I would be confident that you would not allow others to take advantage of you.

That being said, I believe that you will enjoy the rich and colorful history of all of the Canfields who came and left. My personal favorite involves Elisabeth Canfield in a wild saga I have named, _The Ryland Ruby_. I recommend that you read it first.

The Ryland Ruby

# CHAPTER I

## *Ryland Arrives in Burma*[19]

Bappa knocked on the door and entered carrying a tray with a cup and saucer, a steaming teapot, a bowl of sugar, and a plate with three crispy sweet pastries.

"Professor, I have your tea."

Prof. Ronald Ryland wiped his brow from the stifling Burmese heat and looked up into the breeze from the ceiling fan. Hotel fans were powered by a small water wheel, turned by the slow-moving stream that passed below the building. It was one of the few structures in Rangoon, Burma offering such automated comfort in the mid-Eighteen Hundreds.

"Yes, yes, of course, Bappa. Bring it over. Thank you."

When the British Museum directors sent Ryland to Burma in 1852, his father hired Bappa, a Nepalese Ghurka, to serve as Ronald's guide, guard, and man servant. Ghurkas enjoyed a reputation for dedicated loyalty and fierce devotion to duty, and Bappa deserved that standing.

Ryland was a three-year army veteran and capable of taking care of himself, but he welcomed the administrative assistance and the additional security. Burma was a land wracked with internal dissention as well as resistance to recent and growing British presence, if not control.

In the mountainous terrain of distant Nepal, over forty years before, determined but under-provisioned Ghurkas had fought the British Army to an unlikely stalemate. Eventually, the British came to a compromise with the Nepalese and absorbed Nepal as a semi-autonomous protectorate rather than a colony. Since that time, Ghurkas served loyally in the British Army in nearly every war. They earned respect if not awe throughout the British Empire for their tenaciousness.

Ronald's father, Sir Reginald Ryland, wanted his son to follow the family footsteps into law and government. Although Ronald opted for the more scholarly career of archeology instead, Reginald's fatherly instincts remained strong.

Bappa preceded Ryland's arrival in Rangoon by a month and had arranged Ryland's requirements in that time. Bappa quickly became more than Ryland's companion, assistant, and bodyguard. An unwavering trust developed between the two men.

"Shall I pour, Professor?"

"No need to bother, Bappa. Just leave it on the table. I'll attend to it shortly. Thank you."

Ryland relied on Bappa implicitly. However, Ryland could not shake the belief that Bappa was the saddest man on the planet. Ryland often avoided Bappa because the gloomy mood became infectious and disrupted Ryland's generally positive outlook.

The other individual who darkened Ryland's mood was Capt. Fisk Carothers of the Royal Navy, a disagreeable blowhard of more brute strength than brains, but a man with dogged tenacity.

Ryland had earned Carothers' enmity a few days after arriving in Burma. Walking near his hotel, Ryland came upon Carothers whipping a Burmese boy of no more than ten years. The boy was curled up on the ground and barely moving when Ryland grabbed Carothers' arm on the backswing and wrenched the whip from him.

"Maybe you'd like to see what that feels like," Ryland shouted, with the whip held over Carothers' head.

"You'd better cease interfering with official Government business," Carothers countered. "Hand back that whip, or you'll get some of it too." With that said, he lunged for the whip.

Ryland pivoted away from the rush and landed a balled fist on Carothers' chin. With his other hand, he pitched the whip into the river. The snap to Carother's neck rivaled the sound of the crack of Ryland's knuckles, and Carothers rolled into a fetal position. He was too groggy to continue the physical confrontation but, as his men secured Ryland, managed to croak out a threat of taking Ryland to jail.

"I do not believe that your superiors will support the senseless beating of a child," Ryland countered. By that time, many in the gathering crowd murmured agreement, including Elisabeth Canfield, daughter of the pastor of St. Andrew's Anglican Church.

Before Carothers and his men could decide on their next move, the boy took the opportunity to run. "You see, you fool, that little thief escaped due to your meddling."

Ryland held his ground and glared at Carothers while the marines noted the menacing and growing crowd with trepidation. Then the young Englishwoman spoke forcefully.

"Capt. Carothers, why don't you go tend to that bruise on your chin before Mr. Ryland tries again?"

Carothers touched his hat to her with a snarl on his face, barked an order to his men, and pushed his way through the locals.

"My, my, Mr. Ryland, that was quite a manly display for a mere university scholar," she said playfully, taking a hold of his swollen hand for a better look. "Let's get you inside to patch that up."

Ryland looked at her for the first time and saw her

pleasant features. She was barely five feet tall and slender. An unnecessary corset squeezed her waist tightly beneath a calico dress. Widely spaced violet eyes sparkled with fun. Her nose turned up gently, and her wide cheekbones glistened with perspiration from the hot, humid climate. Long brown hair so dark it was nearly black was piled partially inside of a wide-brimmed bonnet.

"You have me at a disadvantage, Ma'am. You seem to know who I am, but I am sorry to say that I do not know who you are."

"Miss Elisabeth Canfield, sir," she said, adding a small curtsy. "You may call me Lis – everyone does. My father is Rev. Ezra Canfield, pastor of St. Andrew's. The British community here is not large, and word gets around quickly. Everyone knew you were coming to Rangoon weeks before you arrived."

With a slightly accusatory tone, she added, "I expected to see you in church yesterday."

"Oh, yes, uh, well, I should have been there, but I only arrived on Saturday, and I'm still trying to get organized."

"Hmm," she replied skeptically, "Well, let's go in to meet Father and tend to your hand."

As they entered the small house at the rear of the adjacent church, Ryland encountered Lis' father. Physically, the churchman appeared an unlikely parent to the diminutive Lis.

The Rev. Ezra Canfield was an imposing figure; his extraordinary six and a half foot height plus two inches of wild, thick white hair was accentuated with both long neck and nose. He was half a foot taller than Ryland, who himself stood out among the smallish Burmese.

If it were not for the sunny demeanor expressed with a cherubic smile and crinkled eyes, Rev. Canfield would seem more capable of frightening parishioners away from the church than welcoming them.

"Hello, Father," Lis said. "I would like you to meet Mr. Ronald Ryland."

"It is a pleasure to meet you, Rev. Canfield. Your daughter helped me out of a potential scrape."

"Mr. Ryland had an encounter with Fisk Carothers and needs to have his hand tended to. If you men can acquaint yourselves, I will get something for your hand, Mr. Ryland."

As she departed, Rev. Canfield called after her, "Please ask Mya to bring us something to drink, Lis."

Lis left the room as Rev. Canfield directed Ryland to a chair in the parlor. "We have been looking forward to your arrival, Mr. Ryland. It is not often we get a learned man in these extended outposts of the Empire. I'm afraid that Carothers is a far more common type."

Ryland took a few moments to notice the tidy room highlighted by a long shelf stocked with books mostly of a religious nature. Rev. Canfield allowed Ryland a few moments of reflection before speaking.

"Lis manages the house for the most part, Mr. Ryland, with assistance from our local maid and cook, Mya, who lives with us. My wife, Elizabeth, may she rest in peace, passed away less than a year after Lis' birth. It is a shame that Lis did not know her mother. Their resemblance is uncanny, and Lis displays many of the same mannerisms. I marvel how that is possible.

"Elizabeth and I called our daughter 'Lis' to avoid confusion with their similar names.

"Tell me – what was the nature of your quarrel with Capt. Carothers, Mr. Ryland?"

"It was nothing, really," Ryland replied, glancing at his scraped hand.

"'Nothing' is not an accurate description," Lis interrupted as she reentered the room. "Carothers was mistreating a native again, this time a young boy. Mr. Ryland gave Carothers a well-deserved whipping." She described the run in with effusive detail, to Ryland's embarrassment.

"Good for you, Mr. Ryland. I am a religious man, but occasional conflict can be both warranted and instructive. Even Jesus displayed righteous anger when he chased the money changers from the temple.

"Be forewarned, however. Carothers is unlikely to forgive you such a public humiliation. You would be wise to avoid him whenever possible."

"Yes, sir. I have neither reason nor inclination to meet Carothers again."

Lis dabbed a foul smelling liquid on to the scraped skin on Ryland's hand, causing him to flinch. She smiled gently in response and chastised him playfully. "Surely the big, strong pugilist isn't afraid of a little sting."

He held his hand steady and smiled back. "I think that I can take it, Nurse Canfield. Carry on."

"So, tell us a bit about your assignment, Mr. Ryland," the churchman asked as Mya presented tall glasses.

Ryland looked over the cloudy liquid dubiously but said nothing.

Rev. Canfield noticed Ryland's expression and laughed. "My initial reaction as well, Mr. Ryland, but it is actually quite good. Mya claims to be unable to tell me what is in her specialty, but I suspect that if she did inform me, I would refuse to drink it. So I remain oblivious as I enjoy it.

"In these far flung, forgotten places, I have learned to 'do as the Romans do' in minor matters."

Ryland sipped tentatively, and the appreciative smile on his face signaled his agreement with Rev. Canfield's assessment of the drink.

"As you may know, sir, the King's Library wing of the British Museum is planning for the public opening in five years. The museum has sent several of us around the world to gather historical documents that will make the library preeminent in the world. I am afraid that my task here is not going as well as I had hoped.

"Important documents are in the Buddhist monasteries, and if I cannot convince monks to relinquish some, the South Asian Section of the library will be a disappointment."

"I do hope that you achieve success, Mr. Ryland, but it is good to see that you show no tendency to enlist the Navy to come to your aid. Simply because we have achieved military success here is no reason to exploit these people."

"That is the museum's attitude as well, sir. Some in the government had proposed putting the Army and Navy in charge of these expeditions with us scholars operating as mere advisors to evaluate the finds. Fortunately, more reasoned heads prevailed, and the military was specifically kept out of the effort. To be honest, I would rather return a failure than return with documents wrested from these people by force."

Mya, with a smile in her mind but no expression on her face, filled their glasses with more clouds.

"Mr. Ryland," Lis interjected, "Next Sunday, after the *eleven o'clock Service*," she emphasized with raised brow, "we are hosting a small luncheon for recent arrivals to Rangoon. The invitations are going out tomorrow, but as you are here today, we'll extend yours directly."

Lis ignored her father's confused expression as Ryland accepted. "It would be an honor, Miss Canfield and Rev.

Canfield. I'll be looking forward to it."

Later, as the door closed behind Ryland, Lis stared her father down. "Now don't you start on me, Father. I know we did not have a luncheon planned, but we do now, and I do not have time to discuss it with you. I have work to do.

"Mya," she called, rushing away, "I need your help. We have a luncheon to plan."

Ezra could not hold back a wide smile, though Lis did not see it as she rushed out looking for Mya. He believed that it was more than time for his daughter to show interest in a man, and this one demonstrated a lot more promise than the pantywaist suitors and coarse roughnecks that Lis had thankfully been ignoring the past few years.

"Elizabeth," he murmured gently, looking upward, "I believe that you would have liked this one."

During the next month, Lis and Ryland found excuse following excuse to be together as though they were young school mates too shy to be on a "real date."

Whenever Ryland failed with another monastery, he returned to Rangoon in a depressed mood. However, Lis was always his first call upon returning, and she improved his demeanor in minutes.

Eventually, Ezra decided it was time for some parental discussion. He knocked on the door to his daughter's bedroom. "May I come in, Lis?"

"Of course, Father. What is it?"

Taking a chair, he began, "We need to talk. I truly wish your mother were here for this discussion, but I believe that I have done reasonably well by you all these years so you'll have to settle for me.

"You really do not need to have so many accidental meetings with your Mr. Ryland, you know. You are twenty-one, plenty old enough to know what you want, and I have taken you to such far flung places that you are more capable of taking care of yourself than many of the men back in England are.

"Not that it matters, I suppose, but I approve wholeheartedly of Ronald."

"'Not that it matters?' Of course it matters to me what you think of a man I might marry. If you said that he was unacceptable, do you think for a minute that I would not send him packing?"

"Then you are becoming that serious?"

"Hmm, I am, and I believe he is, but given all these problems he is having with the monasteries, he has difficulty thinking of anything else – well, he thinks of me a little, but I'd say that I am definitely in second place."

"Don't be too sure about that, Lis. I see how he looks at you after each of his unsuccessful forays into the interior."

That brought a flush to her face and a laugh to Ezra.

"I'm not laughing at you, dear. You reminded me so much of your mother just then. I'd forgotten how I'd look for little ways to embarrass her to get that same reaction. I loved her so much." Tears welled up in his eyes, and a drop fell to his lap.

"We will see how much the heart grows fonder soon, Father. It seems that Ronald has received an invitation to visit a monastery in Monywa up north. I may not see him for a long time, because he is actually going to reside in the monastery for quite a while. What if he decides to become a monk while he is there?"

Ezra could not stop another laugh, and this one was deep and forceful.

THE British Museum completed construction of the King's Library in 1827, but it was to be opened to the public for the first time in 1857. The museum sought to acquire writings of important historical note in celebration of the expanded library facilities. The museum sponsored a small army of scholars – Ryland among them – and dispatched them to the far reaches of the Empire and beyond on collection missions.

Ryland was capable of differentiating valuable documents from the mundane, not at all easy given the mixture of Oriental languages he encountered. Appropriately, he was fluent in several and sufficiently knowledgeable in many others, including a few so ancient, only the written form remained.

In a short time since arriving in Rangoon, Ryland had

accumulated enough Burmese materials to make his voyage a modest success, but he knew that the finest documents had eluded him.

Eventually, his smooth, easy-going demeanor and caring personality led him to a discovery that could have made his name famous. Only a series of barely related incidents of bad luck kept that from happening.

Ryland knew from research that Buddhist monasteries were the prime repository of ancient documents in Burma. While he was able to gather a hodgepodge of lesser papers from other sources such as shops and private individuals, he needed to access the monasteries to reach the full expectations of the museum.

Unfortunately, he was frustrated at every attempt. Not only was he unable to convince monks at monasteries to relinquish important papers, but he could not even gain entrance beyond the public areas. No monk was willing to meet with him, let alone hear his pleas.

Then, just before he was about to give up seeking assistance in the religious buildings, a monk struck up a random conversation with him near the marketplace. Ryland understood the behavior to be exceptional and was more than leery when the monk suggested a visit to the monastery at distant Monywa, part of northwestern Burma that was near to much of the unrest between King Pagan Min and the British.

Ryland considered the possibility that the monk was a fraud and one of the rebels. He wondered if the approach was a trick to kidnap him for ransom. He had not heard of that occurring in Burma, but it was a risk that he considered. In the end, however, he judged the monk to be sincere.

Though partially cloistered and usually uninterested in political turmoil, the temple's monks were well aware that the British had defeated the Burmese in a number of skirmishes that began twenty-five years earlier and continued to the present. They were generally unimpressed with the European invaders who knew little or nothing of Burma or its people and showed little interest learning.

Unimpressed, that is, except for Ryland, who displayed not only knowledge of their religion, language, and culture, but unlike many of his countrymen, showed respect for all three.

After much deliberation, Ryland did travel to Monywa where he spent over a month in the monastery. There he learned much of Buddhist behavior, during which time he survived on the near starvation diet common to the monks. By the time he was ready to leave, he had lost weight but had gained their trust that his cause was not to loot but to spread knowledge of the Burmese culture to the Western world.

The monks gave Ryland several remarkable pre-Fourteenth Century scrolls when he departed the temple. The museum had authorized him to pay for important finds; however, to offer remuneration to the monks for their gift would be an affront. Later, though, Ryland allocated an appropriate sum from his museum funds as a donation.

Leaving the monastery, Ryland re-joined Bappa and their Burmese guide who had been camped on the exterior grounds for the duration. As they were readying to leave, Ryland saw a detachment of British marines under the command of Fisk Carothers approaching.

# CHAPTER II

## *Mindon Min*

"Ryland, what are you doing here?" Carothers more commanded than asked.

"I could ask you the same," Ryland countered, lacing the shoes that Bappa kept for him while he was inside the monastery.

"It's my business to keep these savages at bay wherever trouble erupts. And lately, you, Ryland, seem to be around whenever that happens. You appear to be unusually friendly with the rabble."

"If you mean the Buddhist monks in this monastery, I'd hardly call them 'rabble.' I find many of them to be among the more learned men I have ever come across. You would do well to give them your respect. A little understanding on your part, and you wouldn't need to worry about controlling anything."

"I'll not need you to tell me my business, Ryland. Now answer my question. What are you doing here?"

"You very well know why I'm here. The museum sent me to collect manuscripts and other cultural writings of historical note. What better place to seek them than a house of learning? I spent several weeks in this monastery living with these pious men and earned their trust as well as this gift of immeasurable historical importance."

With the last comment, Ryland motioned the saddle bags toward Carothers and immediately regretted it. He did not want Carothers getting into the documents.

"Is that so, Ryland? Why don't we take a look and let me judge how valuable they are?"

"You've no right to interfere, Carothers."

"I've every right. I'm the law here, and I want to see what you are smuggling from these traitorous monks."

Ryland glanced toward Bappa in a way to signal him to stand down. As fierce a fighter that Bappa was, he was no match for Carothers backed up by several armed marines.

Noticing the look, Carothers challenged, "What, Ryland – you think that one Ghurka with a knife, partnered with a simple native guide, can help you? And Little Miss Muffet isn't here to protect you this time either, so hand over those bags. I want to see what is in them."

Bristling at the slight to Lis, Ryland handed the bags to Carothers. "Be careful. The museum would not take kindly to any damage, and I would not hesitate to inform them and your superiors if you so much as smudge or wrinkle a document."

Carothers heeded that warning and removed the documents from the saddle bags carefully. He leafed gently through the scrolls and other papers with an expression pretending to understand what he was reading but in reality comprehending nothing of the Burmese script on the pages.

He was about to hand the papers back to Ryland when he came to the last page. Though he could not read it, he was enough of a military man to recognize a map.

He stared at it intently and demanded, "What is this, Ryland?"

Ryland anticipated the question from when Carothers first accosted him, so he was ready with a plausible reply. "This is a map of a chain of monasteries stretching from Rangoon well into China.

"It records an event similar to the establishment of the string of Catholic missions that the Franciscans placed in California in North America. This Buddhist chain predated those in California by about six hundred years."

"Perhaps," Carothers stated skeptically, "but perhaps it is something subversive. I believe that we will take possession of these for a few days until we can verify that they are as benign as you say."

"That's not possible, Carothers. Those are museum property, and I demand that you return them to me immediately."

Carothers was about to reject Ryland's protest as he took his eyes from the papers, but as he looked up from the documents for the first time in several minutes, he was shocked to see that he, his men, Bappa, the guide, and Ryland were surrounded by several hundred red-robed monks. He could not imagine how they had assembled so quietly during his discussions with Ryland.

Carothers and his men were armed, and he understood that the monks were supposed to be pacifists. However, he and his few marines lacked sufficient fire power to overcome the sheer numbers, and he could never explain slaughtering hundreds of religious men to the colonel.

Ryland sensed that the tide had turned and spoke confidently to Carothers. "Perhaps you had better hand those back to me and leave, Carothers, before something happens that we all will regret."

Carothers hesitated only briefly. As soon as he handed the saddle bags to Ryland, the monks began dispersing.

"Mount up, men. Ryland, you win again, but your luck cannot hold forever. I believe that these monks are involved in the insurrections we have been facing, and if you know what is good for yourself, you'll be avoiding them."

As they rode away, Ryland was approached by the monk who had given the scrolls to him. They spoke briefly, and then Ryland called over to Bappa and their guide. The monk gave directions to them to take a different route back to the city so that they would not run into a possibly waiting Carothers.

Taking the circuitous route with his two companions, Ryland could not help but recall the story of the Magi taking a different route to avoid Herod's men nearly two thousand years earlier. Like the Magi, Ryland and his men successfully avoided confrontation on the return trip.

WHEN Ryland had arrived at the monastery nearly a month earlier, he had hoped to gain sufficient trust with the holy men to convince them to release some of the historical documents in their possession. He knew that they had no interest in worldly possessions and would not be willing to sell anything to him.

However, he sought to convince the monks that the British Museum would be a safe and worthy repository for a sampling of Burmese history. With wars and political turmoil endemic to Southeast Asia, sending some of the ancient documents to England would be prudent.

Not in his wildest dreams had he expected the reception that greeted his arrival. He was met outside the monastery gates and assured that Bappa and the guide would be provisioned outside of the monastery walls for as long as Ryland was within.

He was escorted into the main courtyard where he was greeted by the oldest and most learned man in the monastery. Then he was invited to stay as long as he desired to study any and all documents. Moreover, Ryland was assigned a younger monk, Nu, to assist when he ran across anything too obscure to understand.

"I cannot thank you sufficiently for your hospitality these many weeks," he expressed sincerely to Nu when he had finished and was ready to return to Rangoon.

The monk nodded to Ryland and signaled to two other monks nearby. "We have organized several papers that you will recognize from your studies. We are giving these to you to send to your museum. We take you at your word that they will be preserved for generations so that the world will know Burma."

They approached and handed saddle bags to Ryland. At a nod from Nu, Ryland looked inside at neatly organized papers. When these many items arrived at the museum, Ryland's assignment would be viewed as a major success by his superiors in London and enhance an already sterling reputation.

Finally, Nu took Ryland's arm and walked him away from all of the others. He reached into his robe, retrieved a one-page document, and handed it to Ryland.

He spoke softly, "Conceal this map with the other documents. The map will take you to a ruby mine in the far northeast of Burma, just short of the China border. There you will find a vast cache of rubies including the largest ruby ever mined, nearly as large as a young boy's clenched fist – about 50 carats. It is of enormous monetary value."

Ryland was confused. This monk was the last person he would expect to be talking about the monetary value of anything, let alone a gemstone. "I do not understand. Do you want me to remove the ruby from your country and send it to the Museum?"

"It is Mindon Min who asks me to send you on this quest. He is the brother of King Pagan Min who is in rebellion against the British. Mindon Min does not want war. He wishes to frustrate his brother's lust for war by denying Pagan the gems he needs to fund the insurgency.

"Mindon wishes you to acquire all of the rubies, especially the 50 carat gem, and keep them out of Pagan's hands. Mindon will not oppose his own brother publicly by taking the rubies himself or by employing other Burmese to do it on his behalf. The only way he can, at this time, slow Pagan's war effort is to ask a foreigner – you, Mr. Ryland – to keep the rubies out of Pagan's hands.

"Mindon Min is granting the 50 carat ruby, henceforth called the Ryland Ruby in your honor, to you to keep for yourself as your reward for this responsibility. He wants your word, however, that you will not sell the Ryland Ruby as long as King Pagan is alive. Nor does he want you to give the Ryland Ruby to the British Museum, because he does not want the publicity that could accompany the acquisition of such an outstanding gem.

"Mindon Min wants to stop Pagan's war, but does not want his brother to know that he is involved in the disappearance of the jewels."

For several seconds, Ryland stood speechless in thought.

The monk continued, "I know you well, Mr. Ryland. You are wrestling with the moral dilemma that you are obliged to give the Ryland Ruby to the museum. Do not be so troubled. Your charter from the museum is to gather documents of historical importance, not gems. Moreover, your personal time is yours alone.

"I know that you have taken no holiday since you arrived in Burma, so you are free to embark on this adventure using your free time. Moreover, with the documents we have given you, your quest for the museum is now complete."

"What of the remaining rubies, Nu? What does Mindon Min wish me to do with them?"

"Those you are to bring to the monastery, where we will bury them beneath our feet. Only when the fighting is over will we bring them out to present to the kingdom."

"What of King Pagan? Will he not prevent me from getting the jewels? Does he have guards at the mine?

"Ah, you do analyze well, Mr. Ryland. The mine had been closed and forgotten for apparently many centuries and was only recently re-discovered by a poor farmer who reported it to the nearby monastery. Mindon Min eventually learned of it through the monastery chain.

"There is a caretaker, Aye, on site, sent there by the monastery. The writing on the back of the map instructs Aye to turn over all of the stones to you on Mindon Min's authority. The message is in code.

"Unfortunately, King Pagan recently learned of the stones. One of Mindon Min's previously most trusted aides sought favor with King Pagan and revealed the existence and location of the secret mine. That traitorous revelation has brought matters to a head.

"Fortunately, Pagan took time organizing his expedition, and his men left only two days ago. They will be travelling overland because they are slowing to conscript more soldiers as they proceed.

"Your map includes a faster route primarily by river. If you leave promptly, you will be at least a week ahead of Pagan's men. By the time that you land your boats, march overland to the mine, and return to the river, you should be on your way south before Pagan's men arrive.

"Do not delay. Pagan's men are led by Htay Maung. He is not a pleasant man and will not treat you kindly if he discovers that you are attempting to secure the rubies. Indeed, he is so volatile that he may kill you just for being British even if he does not know the purpose of your quest.

"Maung has left the bulk of his men encamped northeast of the Chindwin River where it merges into the Irrawaddy across from Myingyan, so he is working with a troop small enough to travel quickly."

"I can read a map, Nu, and know my way around remote areas somewhat, but I am not an expert in the wilds of Burma. I do not know how to provision a project like this. Your cause is noble, but it is truly beyond my capability."

"Your Ghurka is capable in ways you are weak, and I will provide you with a guide. They will provision the expedition and hire Tibetan porters in Rangoon to carry supplies. Bappa's saddle bags have already been loaded with enough silver to handle those situations.

"Keep the purpose of the quest from the porters, and if you can evade Htay Maung on your return trip, you should make it back safely.

"It would have been better for you to have begun this journey weeks ago, but we had to be certain that you were the right man."

"But why am I the right man?"

"Your clash with Capt. Carothers over the beating of the young boy brought you to Mindon Min's attention. Reports about your attitude against using force to steal documents enhanced your reputation."

In all the time he had been in-country, Ryland could recall mentioning that attitude aloud only to Rev. Canfield. "It must be Mya, the Canfields' servant girl, who reported my comments to Mindon Min," he reasoned to himself.

"Those incidents earned you the invitation to our monastery here at Monywa. Your time in the monastery has given Mindon Min confidence in you. Are you the man he can believe in, Mr. Ryland?"

Ryland looked intently into the eyes of this monk. "I will do my best, but I have one question of you, Nu. Are you Mindon Min?"

The monk smiled enigmatically. "It does appear that you are indeed the man whom Mindon Min can believe in."

Mindon Min's confidence in Ryland's Ghurka was well placed. When Ryland explained that they had less than two days to organize the trek, Bappa's disposition brightened measurably. He smiled for the first time in Ryland's memory and charged into the tasks at hand.

# CHAPTER III

## *The Quest*

The muggy morning hung heavy with a steady, warm drizzle, nothing unusual for the coast, even in the beginning of the dry season. The weather did not matter in any event. They needed to be ready to embark no later than seven the following morning regardless.

Ryland arrived on the dock well before sunrise, expecting to be the first there for loading operations. Instead he was pleased to see Bappa supervising a dozen porters who were busy moving cargo to the longboats. He also saw that Nyunt, Mindon Min's promised guide for the expedition, was already on the dock checking the manifests against the supplies being carried aboard the four boats.

Ryland was pleased to see that Bappa and Nyunt were

313

meshing smoothly in the loading phase. That boded well for the trip.

On the other hand, he was surprised looking at the dock stacked with enough provisions for perhaps two months. He hoped that they would be travelling for no more than three or four weeks, but he did not want to break the remarkable improvement in Bappa's mood by questioning him. Besides, he realized that Lis and her father had something to do with the expanded supplies.

RYLAND'S conversation with Lis over tea the previous afternoon had not gone well. In part, it was his own fault for the unintentionally condescending attitude he kept expressing.

Exasperated, she challenged, "Are you telling me that I cannot go with you because, as a woman, I am incapable of handling the journey? I'll have you know that I probably have more time in the field than you do. I rode elephants in India and camels in Egypt before I could read. I can fire a Minié rifle as well as most of Carothers' recruits and probably almost as well as your Ghurka."

"Look, Lis, please don't misunderstand me," Ryland backtracked. "I would love to have you join the expedition," he fibbed, "but your father would kill me if I even suggested it."

"Nonsense. Before Father became a priest, he was a captain in the British Army. Father has taken me to the most primitive places on earth since Mother died and he got his calling to serve God. Because his missionary zeal took us to dangerous places, he has always made certain that I was capable of handling myself in every situation."

With her last comments, Ryland saw his salvation. "Really, Lis, if your father gave his approval, I would have no problem with your joining us."

Confident that calling her bluff would end the conversation, he inquired, "Shall we ask him?" He fully expected that Rev. Canfield's answer would be a resounding "no," and, though Ryland was a brave man, he was happy to be able to transfer Lis' wrath to her father on this issue.

Lis surprised him by agreeing to the challenge, and then she raised the ante by insisting that they go immediately.

Entering Rev. Canfield's library, Ryland began by apologizing for the intrusion, given the frivolity of the issue.

"Father, Ronald will never get to the point at this rate. We are here because I told him that I wanted to go with him on his expedition to the north, and he insisted that you would not allow it."

"I see, Lis. Tell me, Ronald, do you have concerns about her accompanying you?"

A bit taken aback that Rev. Canfield had not immediately put his foot down, Ryland stammered an answer. He had to be careful about what he said. He had promised Mindon Min that he would keep the quest for the lost ruby mine secret. Moreover, he did not want to worry the Canfields about Pagan Min's parallel excursion.

"It will be rough going through areas few people travel, and there may be unfriendly insurgents to contend with as well. I do not mean to demean Lis, but given her diminutive size, she does not look physically up to such a trek. Moreover, I believe that you of all people would agree that an expedition involving over a dozen men is no place for one unattached lady."

He could see that his comments gained him no points with Lis, who by this time was glaring at him relentlessly.

With growing uneasiness at the resulting silence, Ryland was shocked when the two Canfields began snickering, which soon evolved to uproarious laughter. He was becoming upset at being the apparent butt of a joke that he did not understand, and only his upbringing and respect for the priest kept him from an angry response.

When Lis gave him an unexpected embrace in front of her father, and then Rev. Canfield rose to place a strong hand on his shoulder, Ryland had the momentary feeling that he had lost control of the situation. Indeed he had.

Rev. Canfield began, "Ronald, we have been having fun at your expense. Please forgive us. Let us sit while we explain."

Whatever the result, Ryland thought momentarily, it seemed well worth Lis' warm embrace. His heart beat faster from that pleasant encounter than from the apprehension of what was to come.

Rev. Canfield continued, "Evidently, it did not occur to you that mounting a major expedition with great excitement and commotion would generate curiosity among the natives and activate rumors through the Burmese grapevine.

"By keeping the purpose of your expedition secret, did you not understand that you were drawing even more interest to yourself? Do you not believe that Pagan Min probably will hear of your trip and want to know what you have in mind?"

The name Pagan Min shocked Ryland to full alert.

"I see by your reaction that you did not expect to hear me mention that name. Mindon Min has been a secret visitor to this house on several occasions this past year or so. Several years ago, he managed to place his daughter, Mya, here as his spy. What better place to listen to the invaders' innermost thoughts than the safe confines of a religious environment?

"Eventually, Mya came to believe in our good intentions, and she encouraged him to make his presence known."

Lis continued. "When Mindon Min realized that you had not considered the need for a plausible story to justify your trip to the mine, he contacted us with a solution."

"You know about the mine?" Ryland gasped.

"Yes, yes, long forgotten mine, rubies including one exceptionally big one that he now calls the Ryland Ruby, trying to keep them away from Pagan, etc, etc. We know as much as you do, and we know one more thing. We know what your cover story will be for the expedition."

With a sly smile, Lis began, "Father has been here in Rangoon for three years serving the English community and the natives who are taking to Christianity. Many of our Burmese converts have implored Father to extend his ministry into the interior of the country. The time has come for him to do so.

"Yesterday, Father wrote to his assistant, Rev. Cherrystone, summoning him back from India. Rev. Cherrystone has been here on temporary assignment on a number of occasions, so he is capable of assuming duties upon arrival. Since Father is leaving for an extended trip, Rev. Cherrystone will be taking over temporarily."

"Lis, sometimes you confuse me beyond all reason. Pray tell, what are you talking about? What does this have to do with my expedition? Where is your father going?" Immediately upon asking the last question, he began to fear that he knew the answer.

"Perhaps I can put the situation into better order," Rev. Canfield replied, as Lis smiled widely and lightly swayed in her chair, reveling in delighted mirth.

"Lis, one of our Burmese parishioners by the name of Khine, and I will accompany you on your trek. Rather, you will accompany us, given that the publicly expressed purpose of the trip is an expedition into the north to set up an Anglican mission for the people there. While that is the excuse for your expedition, it is not untrue. We will actually be setting up the mission."

"Had you been at Holy Communion yesterday, Ronald," Lis interjected with a miffed tone of voice, "you would have heard Father make the announcement from the pulpit. You really do need to be more regular in your attendance, Ronald," she gently reprimanded, "There is so much you can learn." With that last statement, she swayed slightly more.

Ryland's mind raced, dealing with the complexity he would have shepherding a clergyman and his daughter in seldom travelled, primitive country. He began voicing objections.

"We are leaving tomorrow. How could you be ready so soon? I haven't planned for provisions for three additional people. I do not know if I can find enough supplies with only one day notice.

"My purpose for the trip is to secure the gemstones and return them to Mindon Min as soon as possible. As much as your goals are important and laudable, I cannot take additional time for you to set up a missionary post."

"All valid points, Ronald," Rev. Canfield answered. "Let's examine them in order. We are, in fact, ready to go." He pointed to a far corner of the library where Ronald saw a trunk. "All packed up as of this morning. We had a head start because of Mindon Min's visit last night.

"In addition, he notified your man servant of the plan, so Bappa went ahead and secured the additional provisions.

"Keep in mind that we will not be accompanying you for the entire journey. We will travel with you by boat from here in Rangoon, past the small village of Amarapura, then on past Myitkyina. Depending on how far north we are able to sail after that, we will have anywhere from thirty-five to eighty miles by foot to the mission site. After we drop out, you will have another thirty miles to the mine according to Mindon Min's information.

"Pick us up on the return trip. By that time, we will have built Khine a shelter and a chapel, and he will be ready to take over the mission on his own."

"No offense, Reverend, but I cannot simply drop you and Lis off in the wilderness in the middle of an uprising while I continue on northward."

"Please understand that we are not babes in the woods, Ronald. Lis, why don't you take our two friends, the Walkers, out to the hill behind the rectory and show him?"

Ryland moaned to himself at the thought that two more people were to be involved. Lis went to the bookcase and removed two oversized tomes. She reached through a small hinged door in the back of the shelves and withdrew two well-shined revolvers.

"These are Walkers, the newest six shooter from Sam Colt, the American arms manufacturer. Colt opened a factory in London last year when Father was at Canterbury for consultations.

"Colt's general manager in London served under Father in the Army in the South Pacific decades ago, and he has never forgotten how Father saved his life during a Dutch ambush. Father was among the invited guests, and he was given the Walkers to commemorate the factory's opening.

Ryland was a bit disconcerted by the ease and familiarity that Lis displayed handling the weapons.

The Walkers shined with polished silver plating, and both were engraved with the name "Ezra Canfield:" one with the appellation "Capt.," and the other "Rev."

Lis handed Rev. Walker, as she called it, to Ryland and told him to load up. She began loading bullets into Capt. Walker while Ryland tried to keep up with her loading speed.

"Ready, let's go," she announced abruptly, heading briskly toward the back door.

Ryland was pleased to see Lis carry the gun pointed down and that she kept her finger off the trigger. He did the same following her to the hill behind the rectory.

"Don't be misled by the fancy plating and engraving. These are remarkably accurate handguns, and they fire fast. Watch me first so you can see how it is done."

Ryland bristled at the slight until he realized that Lis was gently chiding him and smiling through it.

"About twenty-five yards out by the hill is a big tree. We'll fire six shots in quick succession."

"That shouldn't be difficult. It's a thick trunk."

"Not the trunk, Silly, the small dead branch on the ground to the left of the trunk."

Ryland looked at the slight piece of wood and then back to her with an attitude that suggested that she had gone mad. Before he could say anything, she leaned her left shoulder for support against the side of the building and began firing with her right hand.

Bang, momentary pause; bang, momentary pause; bang. That continued for six shots. Each one caused the dead branch to jump into the air, break apart, or slide away. Six for six. That was the equivalent of putting six shots into the heart of a silhouette target at rapid speed.

Ryland realized for the first time that this was a special woman, much more than just a pleasing companion who made his heart race.

"Your turn."

"I don't believe that I can match that," he answered humbly.

He stood steady but did not brace himself as Lis had. Bang, miss, pause; bang, miss pause; bang, a small piece of bark taking airborne, pause. The next three shots hit the branch more solidly, but none with the full force of Lis' shots.

"My apologies, Lis, you really do know what you are doing. To say I'm impressed is an understatement."

"When I lie down on the ground and brace my elbows, I get the most accuracy, but I did not want to get my dress dirty. Anyway, it's always good to brace some part of yourself if you have the opportunity. Standing unanchored as you did invites a bit of unnoticed swaying."

"Tell me, Lis, how did you learn this?"

"I mentioned that Father was an Army officer before he became a missionary priest. He expected to travel to some of the most remote Colonies, and he wanted me to learn to protect myself. We have practiced on three continents in all types of weather. He relented only when I became a better shot than he was."

# CHAPTER IV

## *On The River*

Rev. Canfield and Lis walked down to the dock the next morning. Bappa had picked up their trunk the previous evening.

Their arrival drew a small crowd of curiosity seekers who were out and about that early. Ryland soon saw what the commotion was all about. Lis showed up wearing trousers under her beige skirt. No one, Ryland included, had ever seen a woman in trousers. With the pants layered under an abbreviated-length skirt, the ensemble was even more extraordinary.

She greeted Ryland with, "I say, Ronald, you'd think that the world was coming to the end just because of my trousers. Wait until I show up without the skirt."

"You wouldn't!"

She laughed, "You're right. That I wouldn't do, but if I did, it would probably make *The London Times* under the headline, 'Preacher's Daughter Shocks Rangoon – Wears Trousers in Public.'"

Ryland laughed. "Well, I'm not so certain that *The Times* would run such an unserious headline, but there are no reporters around anyway."

"As soon as we finish loading the fresh fruit and vegetables, we'll be off."

Rev. Canfield was in conversation with several members of the parish who had come to send him off.

Ryland spoke with Lis. "Our long boats have sails which should make travel up the Irrawaddy River a lot faster. Bappa tells me that Nyunt is an expert on the river. He will avoid most of the stronger currents as we head upriver and take the fullest advantage of them on the way home.

"The river current is not too strong with the limited rain for the last few months, so it should not have a major effect either way. We'll get a little benefit from it on the way home. If we can stay with wind power, we are hoping for sixty miles per long day initially and then eighty with the current on the return trip. We have ample manpower for rowing, if necessary.

"The hard part starts when we travel by foot. Then we'll be walking miles every day." Looking at her sturdy men's shoes approvingly, he said, "Are you sure you will be up to that?"

"Ronald, you are getting awfully close to getting me angry again. Father and I are no less capable of keeping up than anyone else on the expedition – except maybe for Bappa, who is extra human."

"You know that I am not implying that you are weak, Lis, or that your father's age may hold him back. I only want to warn you of the problems ahead."

"Understood and accepted. Now, shall I board? Which one?"

"Take the second boat. That is mine. Nyunt will captain Boat One, as he is leading us into the best parts of the river. Your father and Khine will be in the third boat. Bappa will be in that boat to keep an eye out for anything unexpected approaching from behind.

"The porters are distributed three to a boat. Nyunt gave them lessons on using the sails and then assigned the best sailors one to a boat. That way we will have two capable men on each boat. He had planned to teach your father how to navigate the boat, but it turned out that Khine had experience on the river."

As she clambered aboard Ryland's boat, she found a spot near the front that she made comfortable by rearranging some of the softer storage packs. Ryland was disappointed, fleetingly, that she did not settle in the back near his position, but he shook off that thought quickly, knowing that this trip's dangers required his full attention.

The boat pilots arranged a combination sound and hand gesture system of codes to communicate while on the water. One short blast on a horn meant to slow, two to stop. Three signaled danger. One short and one long meant land the boats port side, and one short and two long instructed a starboard landing.

There were hand and arm motions for more detailed maneuvers, such as massing four abreast, moving into a vee formation, or tightening the single file line. They carried megaphones for close communication.

The trip north was largely uneventful for the first four days. They had the opportunity to view the varied wildlife in and along the river. Large rhinos grazed in the shallow waters near the shoreline.

The highlight was the sighting of a full grown tiger and her cub feasting on a deer carcass at the water's edge. The bright orange stripes shone in the low sun against dark green foliage. Nyunt signaled for a slowing and eased the line of boats as close as possible without annoying the pair.

Saltwater crocodiles roamed the southern reaches of the Irrawaddy, where the water was a brackish mix of muddy fresh water and salty backflow from the Bay of Bengal. Larger crocs were known to snatch unobservant rice workers and to attack small boats on rare occasions. These craft were large enough to make that risk unlikely, but prudence dictated avoiding the reptiles when possible.

After two more days, the fleet had sailed far enough north that crocodiles were no longer cause for excessive anxiety, but still a possible encounter. Bappa had been thinking that his precautions for such an eventuality turned out to be unnecessary. That was when Nyunt sounded three short blasts on his horn to attract everyone's attention.

He followed that with arm gestures mimicking the motion of a croc's jaws and pointed to the right rear of his boat, indicating that he was safely beyond the creature. The trailing vessels were not close enough for anyone to sight the croc until Lis shouted the alarm.

The croc appeared to be on the high side of the size range, not quite as long as the vessels. It had sufficient mass to swamp a boat, if so inclined. Supplies would be lost, and, more importantly, some or all of the party aboard would likely be tossed into the water. At least one would become the reptile's dinner – and that was assuming that the croc had no friends nearby as yet unsighted.

Ryland tried sailing away from the croc, but the change in direction seemed to energize and anger the creature. Lis and Ryland both drew Walkers that sparkled in the sunlight. Neither planned to shoot except as a last resort, mostly because they would need many shots to amply penetrate the croc's tough hide. Moreover, a wounded creature might be spurred into doing the most damage.

Then they heard a distant horn from Bappa, bringing up

the rear but closing. He signaled for them to slow to allow him to catch up. Ryland successfully fought the urge to run for it, knowing that Bappa was right; the croc could match the boat's speed.

As Bappa's boat came abreast, he kept the croc between his boat and Ryland's, drawing the reptile's attention by banging the sides of his vessel's hull. As the croc turned his eyes to Bappa, the Ghurka reached down and grasped the remains of the deer that they had eaten the previous night. He dropped it into the water with enough of a splash to capture the croc's attention.

Bappa then signaled for Ryland to break to starboard while maintaining his previously quick pace. Khine had already swung Boat Three to port and managed to stay well away from the action that had erupted like a small explosion in the water as the croc went after the deer carcass.

As they resumed, Lis made her way aft to be with Ryland. The encounter encouraged her to give up the solitude that she had seemed to desire.

"Did you get a good look at that crocodile, Ronald? He did not look normal."

"Not really. I was too engrossed in maneuvering the boat. From what I did see, he looked like any other croc – just somewhat larger than normal. What did you notice?'

"A tooth, an enormous tooth in the right front of his lower jaw. I know what croc teeth are like, but this one tooth was three times the length it should have been. And he smiled at me so as to suggest that he did not plan to hurt me. I'm going to call him 'Bigtooth.'"

"Ha ha, 'Bigtooth' he is, but let's hope that we don't see enough of him on this trip to determine the real purpose of that smile."

Ryland's thoughts went to Bappa's preparations and to the way he quietly and calmly dealt with the situation. It had not occurred to Ryland that Bappa was storing meat aboard his vessel, and he wondered how Bappa handled the smell of meat in this heat and humidity.

That was when the realization hit that Bappa was happy only when he faced overwhelming difficulties and discomfort. In the quiet months of their lives in Rangoon, Bappa had seemed the saddest man in existence. When faced with the tremendous complexity of putting this project together in an unrealistically short time, Bappa's mood brightened perceptively.

Ryland wondered how Bappa would fare when the trip was over and Ryland returned to England. At that point, for the first time, Ryland realized that Lis would be staying with her father in Rangoon when he left.

"Omigosh," he spoke aloud.

"What is it?" a startled Lis spoke up, "Is Bigtooth back?"

"No, no, nothing like that. I was just thinking of loose ends that need tending."

"Loose ends," he though ruefully to himself, "Lis would definitely not like to think of herself as a 'loose end.'" He was so lost in thought the remainder of the day that Lis wondered if she should have retained her seat in the bow.

BAPPA was well prepared. Twice more he saw large crocs closer to the boats than he liked, so he flung bloody pieces of meat as far as he could. The travelers watched in awe as the reptiles tore through the offerings like machines on high speed.

Each night before dark, they landed the boats, set up tents, and ate the day's only hot meal, well prepared by Nyunt who could turn whatever Bappa caught or shot into a tasty feast.

Boar and deer made the menu most often, but smaller animals occasionally found the spit. Ryland remarked to Rev. Canfield that the food seemed better on this primitive expedition than the food he ate back in Rangoon.

"Don't you remember your times in the army, Ronald? I never ate such delicious food as when the cooks were able to get a good fire going while we were not being harassed by adversaries. There is something about eating well cooked meat outdoors when you are tired that improves the taste."

"Now that you mention it, sir, I do recall with fondness some of those meals under similar circumstances. As long as Bappa can continue to provide for us whenever we land,

I believe that we may remember the food as the most momentous part of this trip."

That belief turned out not remotely prescient.

They slept early and well each night and left before sunrise each day. Two porters served as night guards on a rotating basis. Guards from the previous night always were set up below deck on the boats to sleep during the following day.

Only Bappa seemed never to sleep. Ryland had always found him awake, regardless of the time of day or night. If Ryland got up mid-night to relieve himself, Bappa was awake talking with a guard. When Ryland was preoccupied and up late, he would see Bappa roaming the outskirts of the camp. When Ryland woke early, there was Bappa tending to the morning coffee, smiling and cheerful.

They passed the big bend in the river just south of Amarapura two days ahead of schedule. The men had taken to sailing quickly, and the winds stayed favorable. Ryland was feeling increasingly confident about the success of the trip. He was kicking himself for thinking that way because overconfidence had never worked well for him.

A few days later, well past Amarapura, they polled the boats to shore for a night camp. They were getting close to where the boats would no longer be useful, due to the rapidly shallowing water. The tropical south was giving way to drier, cooler, and more pleasant highlands.

While enjoying another good meal, they heard thunder rolling and saw subdued flashes among the clouds in the distant north. Nyunt remarked, "That is a good sign. Rain this time of year is unexpected. Every inch of rain is another forty to fifty miles of river travel for us."

Within an hour, their wish appeared to have come true. They could smell the moist air coming from the west in the winds that shook their tents. The camp was too far south to get the rain, but every indication was that the north was under a deluge.

As they climbed into the boats the next morning, everyone could discern that the river had risen overnight. Moreover, the currents had picked up considerably.

Passing Myitkyina, they were still in comfortably deep water with no sign of shallow water ahead. "Actually," Ryland explained to Rev. Canfield and Lis, "There has been more rain than necessary to help us. Nyunt tells me that we could keep going almost to the China border, but if we go too far, we would pass our best trail for the trek to your mission site and the mine.

"Tomorrow we will reach where the river jogs before its final northward run to China. We will put ashore there to take advantage of the easternmost location. The mine is a four-day march northeast from there, and your mission site is on the way, about two days from the river."

On schedule the next day, they secured the boats for

the return trip and left one porter to stand guard as they began the walking phase. Almost immediately they discovered that the beneficial rains that helped to fill the Irrawaddy for their boats had also swelled every stream and depression on their land route.

On more than one occasion, they had to ford deep, muddy water. When the short porters and Lis were in the water, they were sometimes up to their shoulders. By the time they reached the first campsite, Lis' white shirt was stained nearly the same tan as the rest of her attire. Fortunately, a nearby spring bubbled clear, cool water for cleaning and cooking.

They reached the mission site one day late and lost another helping the three soaked and tired missionaries set up their base camp. A small number of Burmese locals arrived to satisfy their curiosity and then pitched in to help.

As the explorers prepared to leave for the mine, Ryland took Rev. Canfield aside. "Our goal is to reach the mine in two days, take another day at most to secure the rubies, and return here to pick you up for the return to Rangoon.

"That puts us back here in five days if everything goes well. Do you still believe that this will give you enough time to settle Khine here?"

"That will be more time than we need to establish the

bare minimum, and that is more than we hoped for. Khine is already interacting well with the locals. We will put the extra time to good use, adding living quarters for Khine in the rear of a chapel.

# CHAPTER V

## *The Ruby Mine*

Ryland was no stranger to rough terrain and arduous conditions, but the land route to the mission site was worse than the first leg from the river. Even without the hazardous flooding, the route would have been a challenge. The obscure trail was overgrown from minimal use. Nyunt did most of the cutting as they walked forward.

They lost one porter fording a rushing torrent that would have been a placid stream under usual climate conditions. Bappa jumped into the raging water and made a gallant attempt at saving the man. Bappa was able to save himself only by the fortuitous arrival of a floating tree that carried him through the rapids to a slower flowing eddy which eased him into a calm pool. Sadly, the porter had disappeared beneath the surface and never reemerged.

Once they resumed travel, Bappa took up the rear as usual, and he seemed especially agitated. Ryland asked if he had worries of being followed, but Bappa acknowledged only that it was essential to remain alert at all times.

Despite the hardships and tragedy, they arrived at the mine, such as it was, nearly on schedule but too late to leave the same day. About a mile from the mine, Bappa had organized half of the porters into defensive positions in anticipation of the unknown while the others pitched camp. The porters were not to be made aware of the existence of the mine, so they had to remain short of the goal.

MANY months earlier, Mindon Min had sent three men to question the mine's discoverer and to ascertain the validity of the claim of untold riches. One was the traitor who later went to Pagan Min. Nyunt was another, and Aye, who stayed on as caretaker, the third. Besides the recluse farmer who had since passed away, those three were the only men who could have found the mine.

This area of Burma in the dry and higher elevations should have been relatively barren. However, the mine was in a deep valley whose choking vegetation hid the mine entrance better than what any camouflage expert could arrange.

Ryland, Bappa, and Nyunt continued on toward the mine until Nyunt put up a hand in a stopping signal. "We are here," he shouted.

Nevertheless, no one came to greet them. Nyunt shouted for Aye, and hearing no reply, they began to worry that Pagan may have arrived first after all, though that seemed impossible given the speedy mode of travel Ryland's expedition took. Nyunt gave a louder yell.

Moments later, a sleepy Aye struggled out of the foliage, arms stretching wide as he tried to awaken from an afternoon nap. The group broke into relieved laughter at the sight that said all was well.

Nyunt and Aye spoke quietly at length, and then Nyunt introduced Aye to Ryland and Bappa. Nyunt asked for Ryland's map.

A short time later, Nyunt returned. "I have explained to Aye that we are to give you the rubies, Prof. Ryland, and Aye has decoded Mindon Min's message written on the back of your map. I have explained the traitorous actions of our former colleague and the likelihood that Pagan Min will be arriving shortly. Aye has agreed to accompany us on the return trip for his own safety."

Aye stood barely fifty-two inches, made worse by stooped shoulders punished by too many years of hard labor in the Burmese rice fields. Ryland could not help but wonder if Aye could make the arduous journey. Lis looked like a locomotive compared with this broken down hand-car of a man, and Ryland had been skeptical of her stamina.

"A pleasure to make your acquaintance, Aye. I take it

we are in the area of the mine?"

"Yes, sir. Follow me and I will take you to it." Aye led them on a narrow path through about 300 yards of thick ferns and brambles choked with tenacious flowering vines. Well up in the canopy, families of monkeys chattered and dropped nuts and small sticks on to the humans. Whenever the monkeys succeeded with a direct hit, they shrieked in a version of laughter.

Aye suggested to the troop's members that they do their best to ignore the mischievous, annoying monkeys. "When they suspect that they are bothering me, it emboldens them."

A few hundred feet later, they arrived at a solid wall of granite rock. Aye pulled long, low lying branches to the side, and Nyunt led the others to a narrow split in the rock. As they peered into the cleft, they could see that it appeared to stop after no more than fifteen feet.

Nyunt motioned Ryland forward. As he squeezed into the narrow passage and reached the dead end, he saw another fissure to his left. He made the turn and, after no more than another fifty feet, found that he had entered a grotto about the size of a small church. Only after his eyes adjusted to the dim light did he notice the small candle burning in the far corner.

The others had followed closely so that all four men were within the large room. No one spoke as the newcomers were awed and the prior visitors waited to allow them the experience.

Aye broke the silence. "It is inspiring, is it not? Beyond this room are a number of tunnels, all natural. None were dug. Follow me."

Aye led them across the room where he used the candle to light torches for each of them to hold. He led them into the left most tunnel of four.

"The other three tunnels die out after a few hundred yards each, and they are bare granite. Only in this left tunnel did we find anything of interest.

After 500 feet – about the length of a city block in London, Ryland noted to himself – Aye pointed to a wooden trunk. The wood appeared to be fragile, but Aye said that it was still sturdy despite its obvious age.

Ryland saw what they had come to acquire stacked high on top of the chest: a large platter mounded with gleaming red rubies of various sizes ranging from three quarters to three full carats by his estimate. Truly these were remarkable gems, and the quantity was difficult to believe.

As he approached and reached out to pick one up, he spotted the Ryland Ruby surrounded in the center by hundreds of smaller stones. The large gem shone brighter than the others and better captured the flickering light of the burning torches. Its red appeared deeper, but the size made it stand out. Described to him as a child's fist or an oversized golf ball, he thought it much larger. Regardless, this was a valuable gem.

Aye again broke the silence. "I have examined all of the caves and tunnels. Only this cave is different. Look over here."

He took the men to the left rear of the cave.

"Notice the difference in the color of the rock. Everywhere else, the walls, floor, and ceiling are dark gray to black. In this small area here, this softer rock takes on a white hue. Look closely and you can see where workers have pried rubies from the rock. Notice the holes pockmarking the walls.

"Unfortunately, the vein dies out rather quickly. You can see where they hacked away at the wall to try to find more, without success.

"Thus, what you see may be the entire production of the ancient mine. At least it is the final production.

"Over here you can see the remnants of the cutting and polishing operation. Apparently, the mine did not ship uncut or unpolished stones. It appears to have been staffed by expert gem cutters. The polishing apparatus is still mostly intact, and the polished stones were abandoned with everything else. Very odd."

Ryland knew enough of geology to realize that the white ruby-bearing rock was limestone, a mineral formed by the crushing of sea-shelled animals over eons. He guessed that a small bay of ocean water once sent a finger into the granite where ancient sea creatures lived, prospered, and died, only to be crushed into stone that somehow became infused with minerals that became rubies.

"Did you find any clue to what occurred in this mine, Aye? Someone went to quite a bit of effort to mine these gems. It seems odd that they would go to the trouble of polishing them and then just walk away and leave them in a pile."

"There are documents in the trunk, but I cannot read them. This cave is cool and dry, which has preserved the wood of the trunk and the papers inside. Would you care to examine them?"

"Of course. Lead the way."

Aye took them back to the trunk and removed the platter of rubies from the top. That allowed him to lift open the top of the trunk.

Ryland peered in. Despite the dim light, he saw one scroll atop a flaking leather pouch.

"The pouch contains another five scrolls, Prof. Ryland. When I realized that I could not read them, I left the remainder intact to better preserve them."

"A good decision, Aye. The more they are handled, the more they may be damaged."

Lifting one out, he immediately recognized ancient Hebrew writing. He scooped up the remaining scrolls and announced, "We have to know what happened here, and the best way is to read these. I would like to stay an extra day and get an idea of what we have in these documents."

Nyunt protested. "Respectfully, Prof. Ryland, I cannot allow that. Htay Maung is not far behind. We probably gained enough of a lead on him because of the fortuitous rains, but there is still risk. The longer we delay, the greater the chance that we will meet him on the return trip to the boats."

Ryland knew that Nyunt was right, but his researcher mentality would not let him give up so easily. "All right, but it is too late to start back this late in the afternoon. We cannot leave until tomorrow in any event. I'll use the remaining daylight to examine the papers, and then we will leave early in the morning."

They poured the rubies into a knapsack and carefully carried the scrolls outside where Ryland began pouring over them. He wrote notes in his notebook as fast as he could. The first scroll merely discussed how the mine had been discovered, so that information was of limited historical interest.

The second scroll that he chose provided information describing the mining operation, and it detailed their unsuccessful search for a vein of rubies aside from the one that yielded the cache of gems now in Ryland's possession. It included an accounting of the first and second shipments that had been sent to Solomon previously.

It was the third scroll that shocked Ryland. The scroll was an elaborate map drawn in colored inks. Though he marveled at the beauty of the designs, Ryland had difficulty understanding what the map represented at first. Only when he began reading the accompanying fourth scroll did the map begin to make sense. Soon he came to the realization that he was holding a master map of King Solomon's mines. "Incredulous," he whispered to himself, "This cannot be."

But as he continued reading and referring back to the map, he knew that he had stumbled on to papers that were more valuable in the scientific and historical field where he resided than all of the rubies now in Bappa's backpack. The map included sites, among others, of gold and diamond mines in east-central Africa, copper mines in Jordan, sapphire locations near Soomjam, India, an emerald mine farther north from there, and the ruby mine where they now rested.

Rumors and legends existed about King Solomon's mines, and there were references in the Old Testament of Israel's wealth around the time of his reign, but here was solid evidence even showing the locations of over a dozen mines, including the annual production rates. Each mine processed its gems or metals into finished product on site rather than shipping raw ore to King Solomon.

The fifth scroll suggested that Solomon, as he was getting older, expected political chaos after his death. He had given the order to shut down all of his mines.

Solomon believed, incorrectly it turned out – perhaps

his reputed wisdom was overrated – that rival successors would not go to war against each other if the value of the kingdom's wealth were reduced. Accordingly, he sent out a small cadre of trusted men to close each location and abandon all remaining valuables in place. That explained the pile of deserted rubies and opened the possibility of locating similar caches of gems and valuables at the other sites.

It was left unsaid, but Ryland reasoned that mine workers in all those locations would have to have been killed to preserve the secrets – a rather grisly thought. He hoped that he could return someday to search for a mass grave to probe that theory.

Ryland wanted so badly to continue reading, but darkness had settled on the campsite and attempting to read by burning torches was not practical. Besides, he needed sleep to be ready to leave early. Reluctantly, he packed the unread sixth scroll with the five he had examined.

# CHAPTER VI

## *Captured*

In the morning, Bappa took point instead of the usual rear guard position. He now knew the way, and the danger, henceforth, was more likely from the front. With the restrictive vegetation already cut away from the trail on their trip to the mine, they more than doubled their speed on the way back to the mission.

They neared the mission as the sun was setting. Bappa signaled them to stop.

"Please remain, Professor. I am uneasy, but I do not know why. Set up a defensive position and wait for my return."

After twenty minutes, they heard rustling in the tangled vegetation. As the noise came from several directions, they knew Bappa was not the cause. Suddenly a white flag flapped in front of them, and a man ventured forward.

"Gentlemen," the intruder greeted as he approached, accompanied by two poorly dressed soldiers. The leader was of average height for a Burmese, but broader around the shoulders and neck. He had a more angular chin and cheekbones than the more rounded faces of most locals, suggesting that he had at least one ancestor of a different ethnic group. He showed not the slightest inclination to smile.

After signaling with his hand, he began speaking in passable English. "You are surrounded by ten of my men, as you will see when they come forward. Please set down your weapons and we will take you to join your colleagues."

The soldiers indeed began appearing from the dark green foliage. Ryland took the Walker from its holster, put it on to the ground, and stepped back. Aye and Nyunt dropped their long-guns gently and allowed the weapons to be gathered by the closest soldiers.

"You, sir, must be Prof. Ronald Ryland. I am Col. Htay Maung. You led us on quite a fast-paced chase. When I learned of your expedition, I did not for one minute believe the story of the Anglican mission, though I am impressed that you went to the trouble to create one.

"Unfortunately for you, Nyunt's mere presence on the loading dock explained the real purpose of your trip. When we heard of it, we switched from a land expedition to boats. Your fleet had already passed well north of our position by that time, however, so it was quite a race for us to catch up.

I had to give up most of my men for speed since we found only two suitable boats to commandeer.

"I know that you came for the rubies, and if you give them to me, there is no reason for me to keep you prisoner." Ryland knew that Maung's last statement could be taken two ways, and one of them was not pleasant.

"What have you done with the people at the mission?" Ryland demanded.

"They caused us no trouble, so they have suffered no harm. They insist that they do not know why you ventured deeper into the jungle, however, which does try my patience. I suggest strongly that you do not continue down that obstructionist trail.

"When we get to your mission, we will search your belongings for the rubies. If you do not have them, you will have one opportunity to tell us where they are or we will begin executing your colleagues one per hour. Surely, you do not want that."

"Why do you believe that we are here for gems? I am a professor of ancient texts, not gems. You must be aware of that. You seem to know quite a bit about me. You should know that, at least."

That statement drew a grunt from Maung, who prodded them along at a faster pace.

At the doorway of the newly built chapel, they were literally thrown through, piling on to the floor in a heap of humanity. As the door slammed shut, Ryland greeted his fellow captives, "Hello, Reverend, Miss Canfield, Khine."

While stumbling into the room, he had noticed Maung's guard posted inside, and he wanted to establish a formal relationship with the others, especially Lis. Maung would gain leverage if he learned of any close relationship.

Maung would expect chivalrous behavior from an Englishman under any circumstances, but even more so if affection or friendship existed. It would be impossible for Ryland to hold out if Maung truly threatened Lis.

"What happened?" Ryland asked.

Rev. Canfield answered, "We had just finished the window shutter as the last item of the chapel. Of course we did not bring isinglass on this trip, but we wanted to get the framing set up for a later delivery. We finished yesterday.

"That's when the soldiers rushed in and took us forcibly. We were overwhelmed. Khine had no time to get his rifle, and the porters scattered northward, probably on their way to Tibet.

"The leader of our captors, a Col. Maung, insists that we are involved with stealing some diamonds or emeralds. He does not want to believe that we are here simply to start our mission and that we are not involved in what you were doing further north."

Rev. Canfield was being careful in the way he spoke, pretending that he had no prior knowledge of Col. Maung, and, as a mere churchman, misstating the types of gems in question as if he had no understanding of worldly jewels whatever their type.

He had perceived early on that Maung's guards understood English, though none of them spoke while on duty inside the chapel which now served as a prison. As long as they spoke openly, the guard showed no reaction. Only if they tried to whisper did the guard approach with a threatening gesture.

"They have treated us as well as we could expect, but I do hope that they allow us to continue with our work soon."

A few hours later, the door flew open, and Maung marched in accompanied by Zaw, the traitor, Mindon Min's former aide.

Zaw approached Aye first. "Where are the rubies? We have searched all of your belongings and have searched the mine. They are nowhere to be found."

Aye responded bitterly, "This is how you treat your former friend. I do not have your rubies. They were moved from the mine and taken to the fort in Myitkyina weeks ago."

"Then what part do you and Nyunt play in this charade?"

Ryland interjected some doubt. "Surely you know that my task in Burma is to acquire important documents for my museum in England. When I learned that several historically significant papers were found in a cave in this area, I proposed to Rev. Canfield that we pool resources.

"No doubt you have found the scrolls in my backpack. To my museum, those are the real treasures of this trip, not the gems you are apparently seeking. I do hope that you have not damaged the papers."

"We have examined the scrolls, but do not understand the language. Nevertheless, we fail to see the value mere papers can have when compared with gems."

Ryland offered, "The museum sent me to collect papers, not gems. Is it not obvious that the museum values papers such as these more than gems? Different people with different organizations have different goals."

"No matter. My forces are in control in Myitkyina as of three days ago. I will travel there to see for myself if the rubies are in the fort.

"If I find that Aye has lied, I will return to cut out his tongue. Then I will begin cutting off parts of all of your bodies until nothing remains but a pile of parts. Now, one final time. Is there any other statement that you might want to make before I leave?"

They remained silent while Aye and Zaw glared at each other.

Through the door they heard Maung barking orders. It was clear that he was leaving the bulk of his men and taking only six. That left a formidable force of about eight or nine, Ryland estimated.

Ryland remembered that Lis had holstered her Colt beneath her skirt and wondered if Maung had bothered to search her.

That evening the guard changed, but the captives continued to speak carefully in fear that the new guard also knew English. As darkness settled in, Ryland stretched, feigning sleepiness, and said, "Sometimes I wonder what happened to an old friend of ours from London, Rev. Walker. He was always a big help to me in times of doubt."

Lis offered, "I understand your feelings, Prof. Ryland. I have the same feelings about Rev. Walker. He was a comfort. I still feel close to him even in this small room." Dropping her right hand near her hip in a way that masked it from the guard, she pointed with her index finger.

The darkness hid Ryland's pleased look from the guard. He sought confirmation of what he thought had to be too good to be true. "I recall that his brother, Capt. Walker, was lost a short time ago."

"I am so sorry to hear that, Prof. Ryland. I am certainly happy that we have not lost Rev. Walker, at least, but why don't you come nearer, and we can pray for the captain before we go to sleep?"

Ryland rose and walked to her side and sat down so that Lis' body hid the area between them. They said a few prayers and then reflected quietly.

Although Lis had shown that she was a better marksman than Ryland, that was aiming at an inanimate target.

Shooting a man would be more difficult, and she realized that. She preferred to allow Ryland to handle the Colt.

About an hour later, the guard's attention wandered, and ever so slowly, Ryland slid his hand under the hem of her skirt.

As he continued slowly moving his hand along the side of her leg, she heard his breathing deepen and knew its cause was not from potential danger of the guard. Because of the darkness, Lis made no attempt to hide her smile at his discomfort.

Eventually he reached the bottom of the holster. He inched up further until he was able to grasp the grip of the gun.

He eased the Colt from her holster, and slid it slowly from under her skirt. He managed to stuff it into the back of his trousers, hidden under his shirt, without alerting the guard.

Among the other captives, only Rev. Canfield knew what had transpired between the pair. He got up and walked quietly toward the guard, focusing the man's attention. He made a motion that he needed to go outside to urinate, which initiated a well-known ritual.

The guard knocked on the door and said something in Burmese to alert the guard on the outside, who unlocked the door and moved away from it so that Rev. Canfield could leave without getting within arm's length. The outside guard left his post and escorted Rev. Canfield to a nearby tree.

By the time that the inside guard shut the door, Ryland had closed to about ten feet. He knelt about waist level and aimed the gun between the guard's legs. When the guard turned, Ryland growled in passable Burmese, "If you ever want to have children, I suggest that you drop that musket and stay as quiet as a mouse."

The last thing Ryland wanted to do at that point was to pull the trigger, as that would bring soldiers from every direction. He needed the man's cooperation and hoped that where he was aiming provided the greatest chance. It did.

The guard's eyes bugged and his mind raced. He could not imagine where the gun had come from, but there was no denying its gleaming horror even in the darkened room. He froze in place.

By this time, the others were alert. Nyunt sprinted to the guard and took the musket from his rigid hand. Ryland stripped off the guard's outer garment and placed it over his own. Aye sat the guard on the floor far from the door while Lis secured and gagged him with deftly tied knots.

Ryland waited next to the door for Rev. Canfield's return with the outside guard. He intended to surprise the man, and with Rev. Canfield's help, subdue and more importantly silence him before he could sound an alarm. He held his head down so as to prevent the guard from seeing his lighter skin in the moonlight.

After three minutes at most, a knock sounded on the

door. As it opened, Ryland saw that the plan was going awry. The guard was behind Rev. Canfield where Ryland could not get to him. When Rev. Canfield saw Ryland in the guard's uniform he smiled brightly and reached his hand to the Walker. He gently pushed the gun downward so as to avoid having it in play, and shook his head.

Then he put an index finger vertically to his lips and stepped to the side. Behind him, Bappa's bright smile gleamed though the darkness.

"Where is the guard?" Ryland whispered. Rev. Canfield pointed sadly to the ground next to the building where a bloodied body lay.

"Bappa knew that someone would have to make a midnight run like mine, and he was ready. The poor man knew not what hit him, or rather, cut him. We dragged him back here."

# CHAPTER VII

## *Escape*

"Gentlemen, I suggest that we go inside to determine our plan," Bappa said, as if the dead man were no more than an inconvenient gnat he had squashed.

Inside, Bappa quieted the immediate turmoil with a raised hand.

"Let Bappa speak," Ryland proposed.

Cognizant of the guard's presence, but not acknowledging it, Bappa began, "This is the optimum time to escape. The guards have already changed for the night, so we should have at least a seven hour head start before anyone notices. The colonel has left, and his command structure is weak. There will be initial confusion working to our advantage.

"They will expect us to go southwest for the boats and will track after us that way." To unhappy murmuring, he said, "That is why we will go south overland instead. By the time that they realize their error, we will have added another two days to our lead.

"Take whatever you can carry. Unfortunately, we cannot rescue our supplies and weapons because the risk of discovery is too great. You have five minutes.

Bappa went back outside, propped the body of the guard on his make-shift stool and secured the back of the dead man's uniform to a loose nail on the building. A distant observer, on a night run similar to Rev. Canfield's, would not notice anything unusual if he glanced toward the chapel.

Ryland opened the door, and everyone followed out. Bappa said, "Once we slip beyond hearing of these men, I will lead you on a very fast pace. Be very careful not to trip. I do not relish having to carry anyone who sustains a broken leg or ankle."

To everyone's surprise and relief, he did not lead them south as he had outlined for the trussed-up guard's benefit. Instead, they charged southwest toward the boats at a jogging pace over the tangled trail. Fortunately, nearly two dozen people had trampled the path into a relatively smooth lane over the past few days.

Bappa pushed them hard all night and all the next day so that by evening they were unable to take an additional step. No matter – he intended for them to rest at that time as he wanted to approach the boats in daylight. He was unsure if Maung had left guards on the shore.

IN the meantime, Bappa was confident that his ruse had sent the trailing soldiers in the wrong direction, and in that, he was correct. For nearly six hours before the rescue, Bappa had trampled a careless trail south from the camp. He had kicked up dirt and leaves, broken branches haphazardly, and scattered cut vines for mile after mile.

When he had reached a shallow creek about twelve feet wide, he strapped his shoes on to his feet backwards and returned to the mission, giving the impression that several people had trekked south; none had returned; and when escapees entered the creek, they had kept to the water in one undetectable direction or the other.

The soldiers caught a break of sorts when one woke early and was kind enough to bring a cup of hot tea to his friend who was propped up in front of the chapel. Within moments of discovering the grisly remains, the good Samaritan had the entire camp up and alert.

The guard tied up in the chapel, who did understand English, confirmed what Bappa had intended him to hear; the escape route was overland to the south.

The faster the soldiers rushed along Bappa's fake escape trail, the further away their prey moved. A clever guide might have realized the deception, but to these relatively inexperienced men, Bappa's trail appeared genuine.

When the soldiers arrived at the creek, half of the men went upstream and the other half went downstream, searching for the place where the escapees emerged from the water. By the end of the first day, having failed to find the point of egress, both groups realized that they were out of earshot for the musket signal if the other group found the new trail.

The downstream party eventually turned around and headed back up. The upstream group with less senior leadership continued to move away until they tired and then they rested in place. The two did not rendezvous until late the next day. Neither fared well later when Pagan Min received their reports.

NEAR the end of the trail to the beached boats, Ryland joined Bappa while the others rested. They approached the shore from two sides slowly and stealthily. Both spotted the soldier resting under a tree, giving scant attention to his duties.

They did not see another soldier, and Bappa knew that made no sense. One guard could not be on duty twenty-four hours a day. He had to sleep sometime. Surely, there had to be one or probably two additional soldiers in the area.

He signaled Ryland to stay under cover while he examined the site more thoroughly. After a lengthy search, Bappa concluded that Maung had apparently assigned only one soldier, though he had trouble accepting the fact.

Bappa signaled Ryland that there was only one man and that he would take care of him. Ryland signaled back for Bappa to wait. He wanted to talk to the man and was concerned that Bappa might kill him before they had a chance to interrogate him.

Ryland eased through the heavy foliage efficiently until he stood behind the tree where the soldier sat resting his back. He could see the soldier's musket standing against the tree, in no position for the man to react quickly.

Ryland swiftly stepped around the tree, and pointing the Walker at the man's head, said in Burmese, "If you want to live, stay quiet and listen. Do you understand?" The man's eyes grew large, and he nodded vigorously. Ryland noted that the man's name on the uniform read "Thant."

Calmly, Ryland asked, "Where are the other soldiers, Thant? Surely you were not assigned here by yourself."

"There were two others, but they ran off almost as soon as Col. Maung departed. Both have family in this region, and they took advantage of that good fortune to leave."

In the meantime, Bappa had joined the pair. He removed the musket from within the man's reach and placed it into one of the boats. When he returned, he directed the man to stand and proceeded to search him. The man had no other weapons. Bappa departed to gather the rest of the group.

Ryland continued his interrogation in a conversational tone. "Do other soldiers have a problem with Col. Maung?"

The man looked fearful and glanced to each side as if expecting to see the Colonel monitoring his answer.

"You have no reason to fear us if you answer truthfully. We have no love for Maung."

"Col. Maung is a hard man. It is not possible ever to do well by him. Punishments are common, and most of us have been impressed into the colonel's army from our farms and families. He often forgets to pay us. I could not leave with the others because my family lives south of Rangoon."

"And Pagan Min. How do you view him?"

"It is not the place of a poor peasant to have an opinion of the king. The king is the king."

"Is he a good king?" Ryland persisted.

Reluctantly, with a facial expression as if experiencing a tooth being pulled, Thant would answer only, "It is hard for the farms to pay the king's taxes, but he is the king, and I believe that he must know what is best."

Sensing this line of questioning would produce no more information, Ryland took another tack. Because the porters left during the early fighting, Ryland recognized the value of another man on board.

"If you lend us a hand, we will take you as far as Rangoon from where you can join your family by river or overland travel. I expect you to work for your passage, however. Is that acceptable?"

Thant bowed his head and was speechless. He had quietly resigned himself to his execution by the Englishman. Not only was the Englishman not going to kill him, but he was going to help him get back to his family. What he had done to deserve such good fortune, Thant could not imagine.

When the others returned, Bappa had already assigned positions in the boats. Nyunt would again pilot the lead boat, with Rev. Canfield, Thant, and Khine aboard. Rev. Canfield insisted that Khine, for his safety, abandon the mission for now and return to Rangoon.

Ryland would pilot Boat Two with Bappa, Lis, and Aye aboard. If Maung caught up to them, Bappa wanted the best sharpshooters on the rear boat. He debated about switching Aye for Thant, but he was not as confident as Ryland that Thant was reliable.

Bappa was already teaching Aye how to pilot the boat in the expectation that the other three might be needed to fire their weapons.

As they loaded the boats, Bappa reminded Ryland that he still carried the rubies. "Yes, I know, Bappa. I am only sorry that the scrolls had to be abandoned. If there had been any way to get them, I would have attempted it, but we could not risk rousing Maung's soldiers."

Bappa smiled an impish grin and took off his backpack. "Do you mean these scrolls, Professor?" he asked.

Ryland sucked in breaths to avoid being light-headed. "How, when, where..."

Bappa chuckled. "While I searched Maung's camp for weaknesses, I discovered that the scrolls were left unguarded. They had no value to Maung, and he left them under minimal security with their food and other supplies. I thought that you might like me to acquire them."

"Bappa, you rogue. You kept this secret from me. This may be the happiest day of my life. The rubies have the monetary value, but it is the scrolls that I treasure."

Before they climbed aboard, Bappa, Nyunt, and Ryland chopped holes in their abandoned vessel and Maung's remaining boats. Then they pushed the damaged vessels into the river and watched them sink. Those boats might be repairable to Maung's soldiers once they realized the ruse that Bappa had perpetrated, but they would have lost too much time.

Ryland announced, "We will not camp at night. We will sleep in shifts on board and eat on board. We will make landfall every six hours or so for necessary functions and to retain our land legs.

"When we near Myingyan, I will divert my boat northwest on the Chindwin River to the monastery at Monywa. Nyunt's boat will continue south on the Irrawaddy to Rangoon. South of Myingyan you should be safe from Maung and Pagan as you will be nearing occupied British territory at that point."

Left unsaid were the dangers in disputed lands around Monywa.

Ryland entrusted the scrolls and the Ryland Ruby to Rev. Canfield.

"Be sure to put the scrolls on the first boat to leave Rangoon for London, Rev. Canfield. The museum will not be expecting anything of that significance, so I have added a brief note to hold them safely for my arrival, which brings up an additional point." They stood in additional private discussion for another ten minutes until Bappa suggested strongly that it was time to go.

They made fast time for the first twenty-four hours. The winds, though slight, had shifted direction in their favor, and Nyunt proved ever as capable catching the downstream currents as he had avoiding them while sailing upstream. They sailed past Myitkyina while Maung was in the fort. It was their last piece of good fortune for quite a while.

FORTUNATELY for Maung, his men had the foresight to send a soldier to him with a report of the escape. The messenger pulled his small canoe-like, commandeered boat into the dock at Myitkyina but only caught up to Maung about the time that Maung was in the fort verifying that the rubies were not there.

Maung immediately swung into action. He returned with his men to his boat and began sailing north as fast as the wind would take him and his seven men against the strong current. He intended to head off Ryland. Maung did not realize that the two Ryland Expedition boats had preceded his man and were already hours downstream. Maung was moving away from Ryland.

Disaster struck Ryland's party a few hours later. A welcomed wind gust came from behind to thrust Boat Two's sail full, propelling the vessel an extra two mph. Unfortunately, moments later the same gust caught up to Boat One where the effect of the full sail cracked the mast below the halfway mark. Only Nyunt's quick actions kept the boat from capsizing as most of the sail and mast pitched into the water.

By the time the boats were able to land, the sail and mast were lost. "There is no telling what happened," Nyunt explained after examining the damage. "There was probably a fragile spot in the wood that was never noticed, and it weakened over the trip to break at a very bad time."

They ate while they considered options.

One boat was inadequate for eight people, so to continue doubled up was not possible.

Several volunteered to attempt to continue by foot so that the key people could use the remaining boat. That was rejected. The route was too long for such a small group, and they could not carry adequate supplies without porters who were trained to carry heavy packs. More importantly, Ryland did not want to break up his small party in case they met Maung again.

They considered returning to retrieve a mast from one of the scuttled boats, but that risked running into Maung's soldiers who had probably realized Bappa's ruse by this time.

Moreover, that led them to worry about the soldiers repairing the sunken boats. With the big lead, two boats, and Nyunt's guidance, they had little worry. With one damaged boat, however, that dynamic changed. It might be possible for the soldiers to repair the boats and give adequate chase to Ryland's weakened convoy.

They decided on a final option. They used an axe to fell a suitably sized teak tree and shaped it into a replacement mast. Nyunt did not have the look of a pleased man.

"Teak is not a good wood for a mast. The best woods are from trees like pines because they are softer and will give a little in the wind. Teak is so hard that it won't bend. I am afraid that we risk another breakage problem if we get a big wind. Besides, teak will add a lot more weight to the boat and slow us down."

"Is there an alternative?" Ryland asked.

"Unfortunately, no. I've seen no soft wood trees in the area tall and straight enough for a mast. We will have to go with the teak and pray for modest, regular wind."

In the meantime, each man had removed every piece of unnecessary clothing, and Lis re-formed and sewed each piece of cloth into a makeshift sail. Eventually, she gave up her skirt to the cause, earning a chuckle from Ryland, who, despite the dangerous situation, saw her joke of wearing trousers without a skirt come true.

"Don't even think of saying anything," she challenged when he grinned at her.

"Not a word," he replied in a conciliatory tone but retaining the playful grin.

"By the way, what were you doing with a needle on a trip like this?" he had asked.

"No woman goes on an overnight trip without her sewing kit," she told him.

Despite the dark that had descended during the repairs, they decided to launch right away. Into the black night they pushed off, wondering if Lis' handiwork would hold up to the rigors of steady wind.

After a few uneventful hours on the water, Lis asked Ryland, "What do you think about Nyunt's rebuilt boat?"

"We seem to be travelling at about three-quarter speed. The teak has not proven to be a problem yet, and your sail is holding up, but cotton clothes do not harness the wind as well as a canvas sail. A lot of the wind that canvas would capture goes through the cotton. Under the circumstances, though, I am more than pleased."

# CHAPTER VIII

## *The Chase Begins*

When Maung arrived at the sunken boats, he knew that Ryland was well ahead by this time. "We have lost two days going the wrong way," he lamented. "Throw everything overboard except weapons, ammunition, and the canned meats," Maung commanded, as they set off. "We'll need speed to catch them."

Maung was berating himself for leaving his poorest soldiers to guard the boats. He had gained grudging respect for the professor and expected that those guards had been little more than an inconvenience to this man who escaped from a locked and guarded building.

With no woman aboard, Maung dispensed with the niceties of regular landings. The men relieved themselves over the sides of the boat. A diet of canned meat soon be-

368

came as monotonous as the rhythmic slapping of water on the sides of the boat, but onward they pushed.

Several days north of Amarapura, Maung hailed a fishing boat and offered some of his canned meat in return for information. He learned that two boats had sailed past the village less than forty-eight hours earlier. An Englishwoman was aboard one of the boats.

Energized by the information, Maung re-launched his boats and resumed the chase.

As the sun was rising the next morning, Ryland's sprits were moving in the same direction. They would soon be coming up on Myingyan. The Chindwin River, flowing from the northwest, merged into the Irrawaddy there. He calculated that the confluence, augmented by storm-fed waters, could be as much as three miles wide. They planned to make the turn near the south side to avoid being seen by Maung's soldiers.

"Why so glum, Bappa? It looks as though we will make it."

"I am not so certain, Professor. I've been watching those dark spots behind us get larger and larger. It was difficult to see in the twilight, but it is clearer now. There are two boats, and they are not normal river traffic."

Ryland signaled Nyunt's boat to come abreast so that they could talk. "Rev. Canfield, there are two boats behind us, so when we reach Myingyan, we will not stop. Continue on to Rangoon. We will go northwest in our boat as planned, and hopefully they will follow us."

Ryland put his boat directly behind Nyunt's to pro-vide protective cover for it in case the trailing boats were Maung's and the soldiers came close enough to fire on them. For most of the remainder of the day, Maung's boats crept closer and closer. Nyunt's and Ryland's boats reached Myingyan with a lead of less than half of a mile.

The two boats split as planned. Ryland slowed as he turned up the Chindwin, and he kept watch for the two boats. Only when he saw that both chasers turned to follow him did he relax.

"Your father is safe, Lis. They turned to follow us." No sooner had he spoken than a shot rang out from behind. "Take cover," he commanded, but it was too late for Aye, who was hit in the back and knocked into the water.

Lis scrambled for the Minié, the British Army rifle that they had confiscated from Maung's boats, and took a prone position in the rear deck. A reasonably accurate weapon to 600 yards, her weapon would be fired from less than that. Any reluctance to shoot another human was lost when she saw Aye topple into the river. Her first shot hit a soldier rid-ing in the lead boat, and that caused Maung's other men to take cover and stop firing.

"I told you it is more accurate to fire from a prone posi-tion," she remarked to Ryland, who appeared shocked at her sharpshooting. It was one thing to shoot at tree branches, but quite another to shoot at a fellow human – especially one who was shooting back.

Lis reloaded and took aim a second time. With this shot, she took out the helmsman in the boat next to Maung's. The man fell over the tiller, and the boat lurched to port. The two remaining men aboard stayed under cover until the vessel had drifted out of her range. The swift current from the Chindwin pouring into the Irrawaddy at that point sent the boat beaching into the far shore before they were able to resume control.

Maung was not deterred, however, and he continued pursuit. No longer having to match the slower speed of Rev. Canfield's damaged boat, Ryland was able to maintain his small lead up the Chindwin until the rapids became too shallow for navigation. At that point, they took to shore.

Maung and his men landed several minutes later and chased after Bappa, Lis, and Ryland. Lis was a marksman, and she had proven her stamina on this trip, but Ryland knew that her foot speed was no match for Maung and his soldiers.

"Bappa, you and Lis must get the rubies to the monastery. I will stay here and delay Maung as long as I can." Lis was about to argue, but this time Ryland had a different look.

"Yes, Ronald," she said, as she kissed his cheek.

While Bappa and Lis continued toward Monywa, Ryland took up a defensive position along the trail and waited for Maung.

Lis showed that she was not in the least intimidated by actual combat conditions. Bappa was as good as four normal men. There was no reason that the three of them could not best Maung and his three sailing comrades.

However, Ryland reasoned that Maung, as he sailed past Myingyan, would have signaled for his men to join him in the hunt. Three shooters could not stop an army. His plan was to slow its pace to allow Bappa and Lis time to get to Monywa where he hoped Mindon Min would give them refuge and that Maung would respect the sanctuary of the monastery.

With his eyes concentrating on the trail, he was startled when he heard volleys of shots ring out. They were close, but too far to be directed at him. Then he heard artillery. When curiosity overcame fear, he crept back along the trail to see what was happening. After less than a mile, he was confronted by a British marine.

"Halt," the marine ordered. Ryland recognized him as one of the marines who had been with Fisk Carothers on earlier occasions.

Ryland stopped on command, set his rifle on the ground, and put his hands up. Two more marines arrived. One picked up the rifle, and the other took Rev. Walker from Ryland's holster.

"What is happening?" he asked, but he was told to be quiet.

The barrage continued in the distance for another twenty minutes, and then an eerie silence settled over the woods. The three marines marched Ryland forward until they reached a tented area that appeared to be a head-quarters. As they neared one of the tents, Carothers came out and saw Ryland.

"What is this?" he demanded of the marine in charge.

"Sir, we found this man on the trail ahead of the route that Maung's army was taking. He appears to be a scout for Maung."

"What do you have to say for yourself, Ryland?" Caroth-ers demanded.

"That is ridiculous. I am no friend of Maung's. In fact, just the opposite. Maung had already captured me once, and I was trying get away from him."

A marine handed the Minié to Carothers. "He had this rifle in his possession when we nabbed him, sir. You can smell gunpowder; it has been fired recently."

"This is a British Army rifle – probably stolen by Maung from India or British Burma. How do you explain having it?"

"I took it from one of Maung's men when we escaped from him."

"So you admit that this Minié was in Maung's posses-sion. The more that you say, Ryland, the deeper the water gets for you. Speak no more.

"We have been watching Maung's small army for

weeks. A short time ago, they left the area and headed out at a fast pace. We had the good fortune to be in perfect position to ambush them. Maung himself may have escaped, but your benefactor cannot help you now."

"Look, Carothers, I have nothing to do with Maung. It is mere coincidence that I was near to where your battle took place.

"When we get back to Rangoon, there will be plenty of people who will vouch for me."

"Ryland, you are not going to Rangoon or anywhere else. You are a spy, and you will be hanged at sunrise. I don't have time to banter with you. We are still chasing down remnants of your friend's army.

"Corporal, place this man under guard. He will be executed tomorrow morning."

Ryland's protest was met with a rifle stock to the side of his head. He went to the ground in a daze. By the time he regained most of his senses, he found himself tied tightly to a center post in a large tent. An armed guard stood at the entrance. Ryland's Minié and his Walker were next to the guard and well out of reach.

Ryland was having difficulty understanding the turn of events. The blow to his head had residual effects. As he shook his head for clarity, he called out, "Marine, can I have some water?"

The young marine ducked his head into the tent and

replied, "I'm under orders not to approach you, sir, while I am alone. The captain does not want to risk your escape. When my shift ends at six, and there is another guard, I will give you something to drink then."

A few minutes after six, as promised, the young man brought a bucket of water and a ladle that he brought to Ryland's mouth. Ryland eagerly sucked in the cool water.

"I am sorry that you are being executed, sir. You seem a fine sort. If you held out any hope of escape, though, you can despair now. I see that my replacement is a Ghurka. No one escapes a Ghurka."

With that said, Bappa ducked into the tent dressed in a British Navy uniform. He said to the young man, "That will be enough water, Marine. We do not want to pamper the traitor. Be on your way."

As soon as the marine cleared the area, Bappa returned to his guard post outside the tent. As no one was near, he could speak freely through the flap.

"I delivered the rubies to Nu at the monastery, but it was not possible to secure sanctuary there for Miss Canfield. No matter what the circumstances, no woman may enter the monastery.

"However, Nu guided her to the river and obtained a small boat for her. I understand that it is quite a bit smaller than our boats, but we should be able to squeeze three on to it. Miss Canfield is sailing down the Chindwin, and she will wait for us sufficiently west of here to be away from the battles."

"How did you know where I was, Bappa?"

"The monks seem to know everything that goes on in their territory. The people have great respect for them and pass on whatever they learn."

"Carothers believes that I work for Maung. I'm to be executed at sunrise."

"We had learned that you were captured, but we did not know what Carothers planned. No matter, as soon as it gets dark, we will leave. Your replacement guard, who provided my uniform, will not be found until daylight regardless."

"I do not want unnecessary harm to come to British marines. You didn't kill him, did you, Bappa? "

"Reluctantly not, Professor. Your sensitivities do make my work more difficult, but I try to serve you as directed."

Ryland could not hold back a short chuckle.

As soon as Bappa deemed it dark enough, he swept into the tent and within seconds had cut Ryland's ropes.

Ryland grabbed Lis' Walker but abandoned the Minié. The latter was, after all, Army property.

Bappa led the way to the river to the area where he expected Lis to be waiting. As they approached the shore, Ryland seemed to hold his breath for minutes on end. There was no sign of her or a boat. He was about to ask Bappa what he recommended when he recognized a voice no more than five yards ahead.

"You gentlemen have no manners, keeping a lady waiting for so long." Ryland rushed through the ferns, brush, and branches that were both naturally growing and strategically arranged to hide the boat and occupant.

He grabbed Lis in his arms and swung her around as much as the entangling vegetation would allow. "Sir," she laughed, "Unhand me, sir. I cannot believe that you are so presumptuous."

He swung her around again. "I could do this for hours, Lis," he said with elation, "but we best be going. I have a death sentence on my head, and I fear that I will be executed before I have a chance to exonerate myself."

Within minutes, they were on their way down the Chindwin, and before sunrise the next day, they were well on their way, travelling on swift currents to Rangoon on the main river. With Carothers engrossed in finishing off Maung's army, he had no time to worry about Ryland – for now.

# CHAPTER IX

## *A Respite*

On the day they reached Rangoon it was nearly noon and few people were on the docks. As haggard as they looked, they attracted little attention. With Lis wearing her hair under her hat, no one noticed that she was a woman. Ryland took Lis to the rectory while Bappa stayed in the area to find out if word of Ryland's troubles had reached the city.

Rev. Canfield and Lis embraced in the doorway as Ryland looked on. "Please," the priest said, "Come in and eat something while we talk."

"Mya," he called loudly, "something to eat and drink."

"Not for me, Father, until I get cleaned up. I have not been so filthy since you entered me in the greased pig chase against the boys on that farm in Athens."

"You won, as I remember."

"Oh, yes, and no Greek boy would talk with me for the remainder of our stay. It was worth it, though. I still have the ribbon."

She left them as they ate bread and meat and drank the mystery cloud. Rev. Canfield reported success. No one had followed his boat south of Myingyan.

He found a commercial vessel, the Glen Surrey, on the day it was leaving for England, so the scrolls were on their way.

He handed Ryland a white handkerchief. "Here is your ruby, Ronald. What a beautiful stone. It glistens like fire."

Ryland gazed at it. "This was not the main purpose of the adventure. Saving the smaller rubies from Pagan Min was far more important. But it does dazzle, doesn't it?"

"Tell me about what happened to you after we split away."

Ryland detailed his capture and ended the narrative, discussing the remarkable camouflage that Lis had used to hide the boat.

Rev. Canfield added, "The Canfields have been capable at stealth, camouflage, and disguise dating back to the Templars of Crusading heritage. That is why we kept the Scottish castle and lands from the English for so many generations. We were too much trouble for them. It was only the traitorous actions of a worthless cousin that finally did us in and caused the clan to scatter from Scotland to Ireland, England, and America.

"In fact, that latter location gives me an idea. In American Colonial times, a relative, Morgan Canfield, owned one of the largest American shipping lines. He later sold that venture and took his extended family to what is now Florida of the United States.

"However, his family has maintained its connection with shipping on a silent investment basis so that many of the American ships that ply these waters in south Asia are Canfield financed.

"There is a ship docked in Rangoon until Thursday. It is the Cape Cod, owned by a syndicate largely made up of the American Canfields. I know that you had planned to return to England now that you have completed your duty for the museum, but perhaps you should consider going to America.

"Until this situation with Carothers calms down, England will not be any safer for you than Burma. If he presses the point, you will face trial. Already, he has sent word to apprehend you if you show up in Rangoon. You will probably be exonerated, but there is risk and expense.

"I'm sure that I can make discrete arrangements with the captain. He knows that I am related to the owners, and I intervened to help one of his officers who ran afoul of the local authorities. He owes me a favor."

"America? But Rev. Canfield, you and I spoke about my taking Lis with me to London. I do not want to lose her."

"Taking me where?" Lis asked, as she entered the room in lady-like attire, looking as fragile as Ryland knew she was not. "Don't you think that such a discussion was a bit inappropriate? Unmarried ladies do not travel with men on ocean voyages."

"Oh, yes, of course, Lis. We were to be married first. Then we would go to England."

"Married first, then to England? Hmm, you discussed this with Father, but it has not occurred to you to mention it to me? Or is it to be a secret marriage that only men know about?"

Rev. Canfield could see it was time to take his leave and did so with scant notice from the other two, though Ryland did look momentarily and futilely for help.

"No, Lis, I was going to tell you..."

"*Tell* me that we would be married. How nice of you to let me know."

"No, not tell you, ask you. In the midst of all the troubles with Maung, I asked your father if he would consent if I asked and if you agreed to a proposal of marriage. I was so pleased that he said he would welcome me into the family that I forgot – not forgot, got distracted.

"Since then, there has never been a suitable time for me to propose. Honestly, there really hasn't been, has there?"

"No, of course not," Lis stated emotionlessly.

"'No of course not,' what?" Ryland asked in a confused tone.

"No, of course there has not been a suitable time for you to ask for my hand in marriage." As she ambled slowly through the sentence, her smile grew with each word until she was grinning from ear to ear.

"You are not angry with me, Lis?"

"How could I be angry with my hero? You are just too much fun to play with. I hope that you never catch on."

"But wait, that was before. Now your father is suggesting that I go to America until someone can get Carothers under control. Your father thinks that London may be too dangerous for me now."

"America it is, then. What an adventure that will be. Father has taken me around the world, but never to the Americas. Now it is your turn to lead, and there we shall go.

"Give me a hug, and then we will tell Father."

# CHAPTER X

## *The Fast Wedding*

Because of the primitive posting to Rangoon, Rev. Canfield had received delegated authority from the bishop to waive the necessity for publishing the banns before a marriage ceremony. Thus, he was able to officiate at the wedding for his daughter and Ryland the next day without the usual waiting period.

With the rushing about and excitement of the parishioners gathering on such short notice, Lis really did not feel the full implications of her decision. That would come soon.

On the morning after the wedding, the day they were scheduled to leave for Savannah aboard the Cape Cod, Lis awoke early and looked at the man sleeping soundly next to her.

"I know that he is a good, capable, and brave man," she

told herself. "Nevertheless, I am about to leave the home of the only man I really ever knew for a man I hardly know."

She slipped from their bed in the rectory and padded to the kitchen for a small breakfast. Mya had the stove already working.

"You look apprehensive, Miss Lis. Was everything all right last night?" she added with a sly smile.

With a meaningful look, Lis replied, "Oh, yes, Mya. Everything was perfect. It is just that for the first time, I fully understand the enormous change my life will be taking. It is more than a little frightening."

"My sister was married last year, and she says it was the best thing that ever happened to her, but her friend cries every night about her marriage. From my understanding, the difference is the man. If you have chosen a good husband, your life will be full. You have nothing to fear. You have chosen the best man you could have found."

"Thank you, Mya. I believe so."

After Lis ate, she left to see her father. He was not in his room as she expected. She went to the library and was surprised to find him in deep conversation with Ryland.

"Good morning, gentlemen. I trust that this is not some secret 'passing of the daughter to the husband' rite."

"Ha, ha, not at all, Lis," Ryland greeted, as he embraced his new wife.

"I was arranging with your father to have all of the documents that I have collected to be sent to the museum on the next available ship. Even if I cannot accompany them to London, it is important that they are included in the museum's holdings.

"In addition, your father has written a letter of introduction to your family in Florida for us and has drawn a map from Tampa to the family estate. We should have no trouble getting from Savannah to Tampa by stage coach, but we'll need to buy a horse and wagon for the trip into the interior and get some directions as we approach the estate.

"He has promised to stay abreast of my situation with Carothers and the Government and keep us informed. We can stay with your family in Florida until I am exonerated."

"There is one problem, however," Rev. Canfield added.

"Lis, I've never mentioned why the family left Massachusetts and relocated in Florida. In the last years of the 1600s, the family patriarch, Morgan, took the family away because his wife, Lauren, was accused of being a witch. Rumors of witchcraft followed the family to Boston and New York so that Morgan eventually departed for Spanish Florida.

"Once in Florida, the family maintained an isolated life which they promoted by encouraging the witch rumors. I am afraid that when you arrive in the nearby village of Winter Free and ask for the Canfields, locals may act in an unfriendly way. I am certain that you and Ronald are capable enough to handle anything that may come your way, but I want you to be forewarned."

"Witchcraft? Father, that is ridiculous. Will they think that I am a witch?"

"From what the family has written to me over the years, I expect that if you say that you are a Canfield when you arrive in the area, you are doomed to everyone acting oddly at best or angrily at worst. My suggestion is to emphasize your new Ryland name and avoid mentioning that you are related to the Canfields."

"In any event, the Cape Cod leaves this afternoon. I suggest that it is time to pack."

Ryland raced back to his hotel and settled his account. Bappa had already packed Ryland's wardrobe, books, and papers into a trunk.

Ryland went looking for Bappa. "Have you decided, Bappa?" he asked. "Lis and I would very much like you to accompany us to America."

"It is a difficult decision, Professor. On the one hand, Florida has warlike native tribes, ferocious storms, and deadly creatures like alligators, bears, panthers, and venomous snakes, so there are many positives to consider. On the other hand, I have heard that America is civilizing quickly."

That description drew a smile to Ryland's lips as Bappa continued. "I believe that I am better suited for distant parts of the British Empire like Burma. Besides, Carothers will likely return soon, and I can do a better job of disrupting his vendetta from here in Rangoon if he attempts to pursue you. You have my deepest thanks and sincerest best wishes for a safe journey and full life, but I shall stay."

Ryland had to hold back a tear as he shook Bappa's hand. "I will take your trunk to the vessel, Professor. You should go now and pick up your new wife."

# CHAPTER XI

## *In Florida*

The trip to Florida was uneventful for the enraptured couple. They enjoyed excellent weather to Savannah, and the bumpy coach ride to Tampa, while difficult on their backs, passed without incident.

Aside from an odd look or two, Winter Free residents did not display a bad attitude toward the Rylands who were seeking the Canfield place. Following Rev. Canfield's advice seemed to work out well.

Back in Rangoon, Carothers had arrived three days after the Cape Cod sailed, and he attempted to dispatch an English man o' war in pursuit. However, the captain was a friend of Rev. Canfield's and accepted the priest's explanation of Ryland's actions. He told Carothers that the ship needed repairs and would not be sea worthy for a week, too late to give chase.

The then-current Canfield patriarch in Florida, David, greeted them with hospitality and offered the estate's facilities without charge, provided that they contributed with the farm chores. That they did for nearly two years until Lis was clearly too far along in her first pregnancy to do more than sewing and housework.

About that time, an important letter arrived at the Canfield Mansion.

*Dear Ronald,*

*I have good things to report and one negative piece of news. The bad news is that the Glen Surrey sank with loss of nearly all hands and cargo sailing past the Cape of Good Hope off the South African coast. It has taken this long for the news to get to Rangoon.*

*You will recall that the Glen Surrey was the ship that I entrusted to take your scrolls to the museum. I am truly sorry for both men and documents.*

*On the other hand, shortly after you left for America, the Marines defeated Pagan Min and formally annexed lower Burma into India. Not long after, Mindon Min and his brother, Kanaung, overthrew King Pagan. The British Foreign Office seems to be content to allow them to rule in the north. Mindon Min's guide Nyunt, it turns out, was actually his brother, Kanaung.*

*Mindon Min has announced that he will be moving Burma's*

capitol to Mandalay which he is creating a few kilometres from Amarapura. I'm certain that you remember Amarapura from our race up the Irrawaddy. The royal pair seems to be industrious, forward looking, and benevolent. In any event, peace prevails in this area.

Carothers has been reassigned to Singapore and is no longer a problem for you.

The best news is that which comes from London. It is safe for you to return, thanks in large part to the efforts of Bappa, who is now back in England. He is doing quite well, importing teak and other exotic woods from this area. Apparently, he has quite a following among prominent architects who are influential with Government Ministers.

The museum recently wrote, seeking my assistance in locating you. Now that your name has been cleared, they wish you to resume your prior position. Of course, I would not divulge your location without permission, but I assure you that there is no longer any danger.

Ronald, I have included an accompanying note for Elisabeth. Please pass it on to her. I truly do miss her and look forward to the letters she sends so regularly about your soon to be growing family.

Yours in Christ,

Rev. Ezra M. Canfield

**Somewhat later, Lis wrote to her father and, as she usually did, penned a copy of it to keep for herself.**

*Dearest Father,*

*Ronald, young Ezra Ronald, and I have been in excellent health since I last wrote, and I hope that this letter finds you the same. Though we have not found the "Fountain of Youth" here in Florida as yet, the climate seems to work in our favor in that way – save the extremely hot and rainy summer months that remind me of Rangoon.*

*Ezra Ronald is walking, and he enjoys the out of doors so much that we have to keep an eye on him every moment for fear that he will wander off into the swamp and be eaten by the huge alligator that roams the area.*

*Ronald has successfully corresponded with the museum about a letter of recommendation, as he is determined for us to stay in America. We have just recently learned that he will be taking a position with The Smithsonian Institution in Washington, D.C. as a result of a highly complimentary letter that the British Museum wrote on his behalf.*

*The museum was delighted at the quality and quantity of the documents that Ronald had acquired. In fact there were so many that the museum offered to lend some of them to the Smithsonian on a long-term basis.*

*Only tomorrow we will be leaving our wonderful*

extended Canfield family at the edge of Morose Swamp in Florida. Ronald is presenting the Ryland Ruby, and I am giving the Rev. Walker to the family as our tokens of gratitude for the gracious hospitality and refuge they have shown us.

Dear Father, I must rush off to ready our things for the trip. I will write with more detail after we arrive in Washington. I hope that I will be able to once again become accustomed to a colder climate after all these years in tropical Rangoon and Florida.

Perhaps you could be assigned to Washington at some time, though I know you prefer less civilized postings. It would be lovely for you to see your second grandchild who is due in two months.

My deepest love,
Your daughter, Lis

# CHAPTER 22

## *James and Burma*

*In all...tons...of supplies were ferried to China over the Hump, but at a cost: more than 600 planes and 1,000 lives were lost in the airlift.*

ROBIN A. PALMER

**JANUARY 1953**

Sally closed the book and placed it in her lap for a few moments. She thought to a night nearly twenty years earlier. Cora Hostetter had come to her aid to nurse Sally's grandmother.

Her grandmother had been bitten by a coral snake, and the venom had pushed her into a deep coma. Cora had asked for a gun to kill a small animal. Sally had given her an old revolver.

They chose a goat, and Cora put the revolver to the animal's head and pulled the trigger. Then she removed the heart and other internal organs which she applied to the snake bite wound to draw out the snake's venom. Sally and her grandmother credited Cora's action with saving her grandmother's life, though Cora was never certain that her remedy actually helped.

"Could it be?" Sally wondered. She put the book back on the shelf and pulled open a drawer in a small table. She removed the badly tarnished revolver that Cora had used that night and examined it closely. Sure enough, barely observable but definitely there: "Rev. Ezra Canfield." She had never before noticed the engraving in the badly stained metal.

Sally verified that the gun was unloaded and went to a cupboard to retrieve a can of silver polish. She poured a large dab on to a cloth rag, and began rubbing it on to the gun vigorously. One hundred years of tarnish is not removed easily, but with sufficient effort, it does come off. It took Sally most of the remainder of the day, but by the time James came home, Sally was holding the silver-plated Rev. Walker in its shiniest form.

When James saw Sally asleep in the chair with the silver gun in her hand, he entered the room slowly to avoid startling her and carefully took the gun into his own hand. Sally awakened and stretched.

"You aren't upset with me, I hope," James said with a smile as he kissed her.

"Hmm?" she murmured, until he pointed at the gun he was holding.

"Oh, the gun? Of course not. I do have an interesting story to tell you, though, but I'll save it for your day off."

*THE* next morning, after James had left for work, Sally opened the drawer that held her jewelry. She had slept poorly as her mind raced with curiosity about the Ryland Ruby.

The removable felt bottom of the drawer allowed her to remove an entire jewelry display intact. She slid the felt out of the drawer carefully and placed it with all of the gems and precious metals on the top of her dresser.

Though the number of valuable gems was extensive, it was but a fraction of the others she kept at Ensign Bank.

Most of the treasures before her were gems set in necklaces, rings, and bracelets. There were diamonds, emeralds, and sapphires at the top end of the value scale and numerous lesser but beautiful gems like garnets, opals, and amber to set off the higher-priced stones. Sometimes the intricate gold, silver, and platinum settings were more valuable than the gems they grasped.

Only one gem was unset, the large red star ruby that at times took on an implied bluish tint. Sally had handled the ruby many times over the years from as far back as she could remember into her young childhood. Its size, greater than a golf ball, but not that of a baseball, dwarfed all the other jewels in the Canfield collection. That distinction alone had appealed to her as a young child.

But it was the deep red color and the impression of a six-pointed star when certain light struck it that drew Sally to the stone. Although Sally frequently rotated her jewelry between her house and the bank, she always kept the ruby at home. She never displayed it publicly, and because it was too large to put into a setting, she never wore it. But she always kept it close.

Her grandmother had always referred to it as the Ryland Ruby. Until Sally read the story about Ronald Ryland and Elisabeth Canfield Ryland the previous night, she had not known where the name originated. Now she was even more fascinated about her favorite gem and about those relatives.

As she returned all of the jewelry to the drawer except for the Ryland Ruby, she was momentarily confused. "That's odd. I seem to be missing my rose diamond ring."

She searched the floor and reached into the back of the drawer, both efforts meeting without success. Eventually she decided that the ring must have been included with the last rotation of jewels she took to Ensign Bank. "I'm only thirty. How can I be losing my memory already?" she chided herself.

That evening Sally said to James, "I want to show you something. I know that you are not interested about jewelry as I am, but I believe that you will be impressed with the ruby I am going to show you."

She led him into their bedroom and pointed to the Ryland Ruby resting alone on black felt. Light from a nearly full moon streamed through the window and struck the gem so perfectly that the "star" glistened subtly from beneath the red surface.

"My, that is a beauty." He picked it up and tested its weight. "Where did it come from? I've never seen it before."

"It's called the Ryland Ruby. I've always had it in my jewelry drawer and only rarely take it out to hold. It is too big to wear, but I have kept it close at hand since I was a little girl. From what I read in one of Grandmother's family histories yesterday, it has an historical significance.

As she handed him the book, she said, "I'd like you to read about it tonight because my curiosity has really been roused, and I need your help."

*JAMES* had the next day off, so they had plenty of time over breakfast of French toast, sausage, fresh squeezed orange juice, and coffee to discuss the story about Ronald Ryland and his adventure in Burma a hundred years earlier.

"Those relatives of yours are impressive. Can you imagine an Englishwoman wearing pants in the 1850s? That may have taken more guts than facing Pagan Min's men.

"But I am fascinated with the part they played in Burma's history. When Mindon Min took over from his brother Pagan, he convinced the Brits to tread lightly on the northern part of Burma.

"He ushered in the longest peaceful period in the country's history and generated the most productive economic age. Mining and forestry boomed, and he got the Brits to cooperate instead of dominate."

"Wait a minute," Sally interrupted, "You can't tell me that Winter Free schools taught you about Burma of all places. How can you know anything about it? Grandmother gave me intensive training in geography, but I'm not certain that I could find Burma on a map without some time and effort."

"I admit that Burma may be rather obscure in the line-up of prominent countries, but I had a special interest in it. Though I was in the Shore Patrol in the War, I wanted to be a pilot. Every time I applied, though, my application got sidetracked.

"In 1943, Col. Robert Scott's <u>God is My Co-pilot</u> was published. It was one of the first morale-boosting books in a war that was not yet going well for us. I couldn't put the book down. It chronicled the exploits of the Flying Tigers in Burma, China, and India."

"Actually," Sally said, pointing to the bookcase, "We have that book in our history section. I remember reading it myself years ago, but what does that have to do with Mindon Min? He was around a hundred years earlier."

James got up and went to the bookcase. He returned with Scott's book and remarked, "This will be my next read. It'll do me good to refresh my memory about the exploits of those guys."

"Okay, good, but stay on point, kind sir. You were explaining how you know so much about Mindon Min."

"I tend to become fixated on a subject when it gets a hold of me. When I read Scott's book about the Flying Tigers flying the Hump over the Himalayas to keep the Chinese supplied during the War, it just sparked my fancy.

"I remember Scott explaining that we had only a handful of fighters in operation, but the maintenance guys repainted the nose cones with a different color after each mission. The Japanese were tricked into thinking we had an escort force many times greater than the small number of planes that were actually in service. If Japanese pilots had known how limited we were, they could have wiped out the airbase with one heavy attack, but they were intimidated by the apparent size of our force.

"Anyway, I pestered the local librarians for everything they had about Burma, so I learned a lot about the country's history. I don't recall anything about rubies or anyone named Ryland, but there was a lot about

Mindon Min's reign and the assistance of his good brother, Kanaung.

"If I remember the maps correctly, in the early days of the War, Japan controlled much of the territory where Ronald and Lis found King Solomon's ruby mine.

"So, Sally, what help do you need? You aren't suggesting a vacation trip to Burma, are you?"

"Oh, no, nothing like that. According to Grandmother's book, Ronald and Lis lived here on the estate for a few years and then moved to Washington where he went to work at the Smithsonian some years before the Civil War. I want you to find out if I have any surviving relatives living now who descended from them."

# CHAPTER 23

## *State Department*

*I know that you believe that you understood what you think I said, but I am not
sure you realize that what you heard is not what I meant.*

ROBERT MCCLOSKEY, U.S. STATE DEPARTMENT

**JANUARY 1953**

Flagstead Toth knocked at the open door where his boss, Walker Malcolm Pettigrew IV, sat behind a massive cherry desk. Plump, with a ruddy complexion, and bald before his time, Pettigrew provided a cherubic impression that defied his actual character.

A wag in the Justice Department with whom Pettigrew liaised combined Pettigrew's personality and initials to create the nickname "Wimp," known to nearly everyone who worked with Wimp, but not to Wimp himself.

Wimp earned his undergraduate degree from Princeton and barely squeezed out a law degree from Yale in 1936. He fit well inside the U.S. State Department.

His pedestrian intellect and supercilious personality, despite impressive family fortune and contacts, kept him from developing a successful career in the legal firm that had hired him out of Yale. He recognized quickly that he disliked work that required performance and results. Within a year, he was seeking a different career.

War had broken out in Europe in 1939, and events seemed to be drawing the country ever closer to joining in. Wimp had no desire to be called if his country became involved. He found the ideal situation at State – a potential career that would require minimal actual results and one likely to keep him out of the military should war come.

He used his Ivy League contacts to secure a position and soon found that he had made the ideal choice. It allowed him to move though the politics of Foggy Bottom[20] culture and the evening social scene, spouting haughty commentary on any and all issues without ever being held accountable for his blather.

Sounding far more intelligent than he was, especially to like-minded colleagues, he had advanced to a senior position by the time that Flagstead Toth came to his attention in 1951.

Wimp was the perfect mentor for Toth, who was an attorney, a cynical critic of traditional American life, and former principal of Cross Creek Elementary School in central Florida three years before arriving at State.

Toth, unlike Wimp, did not lack intelligence. After leaving his position in Florida, Toth rushed through law studies, also at Yale, with little strain, and went to work at the State Department upon passing the Virginia Bar. Wimp encountered Toth during a training session for then recent hires.

In the early stages of WWII, ostensibly neutral Sweden acquiesced to the German Wehrmacht and permitted Germany to transport its soldiers on Swedish trains to facilitate attacking neighboring Norway. By the end of the War, even the Swedes were embarrassed by the actions of their government.

In a mock diplomatic training session for new hires, Toth put up an energetic moral-equivalence defense of Sweden's shameful behavior. During the exchange, Wimp recognized Toth's potential and assisted in Toth's rapid rise through the bureaucracy.

Though Wimp lacked smarts, he did possess a good judgment for people. He disliked most people; actually, he disliked all people, but he knew how to use people whom he could tolerate. Toth was at the top of that roster.

"*YES*, sir – you asked me to come over."

"Toth. Yes, of course. Come in. Join me with a cup of coffee at the conference table."

Toth knew the office well. Unlike many of the ordinary government offices with plain steel furniture and limited wall decorations, Wimp reigned from a well-appointed room with no expense spared.

He framed his long dark cherry desk with an enormously large, mixed blue Persian rug. The walls displayed numerous artifacts from each of the countries where Wimp had been posted over the years. Wimp found that the machetes from The Philippines and shrunken heads from Borneo made a forceful impression on those he sought to intimidate.

While Wimp was always on the lookout for ways to manipulate the system and tap taxpayer money for his decorative whims, he paid for most of his office décor from his own inherited fortune. Wimp's elaborate offices had always served him well, giving the impression that his position was more important than it was, thus becoming self-fulfilling.

Toth had been to many of these meetings which usually involved Wimp giving him a new assignment. He knew his fast-moving career hinged on his willingness to wholeheartedly support Wimp's direction. Fortunately, this was not difficult because Wimp and Toth generally thought alike, and the assignments were usually enjoyable. That day's direction, however, would involve distasteful tasks.

He set a cup on the table for Wimp, double cream and triple sugar as usual. Toth preferred his with cream but always drank it black in public to encourage the strong image he sought to portray. If there was one thing important to Toth, it was image.

"Flagstead," Wimp began, alerting Toth that something unpleasant would follow. On the rare occasions when Wimp used Toth's first name, the subsequent words were seldom agreeable.

"We have had a directive from upstairs resulting from Congressional pressure. It is a waste of time, but fortunately, it isn't one of their batty issues to embarrass us with our friends abroad this time."

"Some senators, especially Brath of Florida, expressed the belief that we are too inbred here at State, 'too Ivy League' they say. I don't know what they expect. Can you imagine turning over our foreign policy to Ohio State, Michigan, and Texas A&M?" The two men chuckled together at that thought.

"Nevertheless, we have to show some compliance, because the Senate holds the purse strings and Brath is the key committee chairman. Our college recruitment people have already agreed to make an effort by selecting a few hires from colleges in the interior. We can ship those recruits to Bolivia or Thailand or somewhere else where they cannot mess things up too badly.

"In addition, we are mollifying Congress with an elaborate plan to channel high school students – juniors and seniors – toward college curricula that will lead them to a career here at State. As these high schoolers advance to college, we will award a limited number of scholarships for non-Ivy League colleges, followed by a master's in diplomacy at Georgetown University so they can get a little polish.

"This high school program is getting State's emphasis, because it will be five or six years before any of those candidates graduate. By that time, we can hope for senators to retire, to be replaced, or to grow so old that they forget about this nonsense.

"Several department heads were asked to volunteer a man to speak to students in high schools around the country. It is a one-month assignment, so it isn't too much of a burden. I felt that it was important for our department to show we were on the team, so I volunteered you as our contribution. You were a school principal years ago, so I knew you were the man for the job.

"I managed to secure Florida as your territory which should be nice this time of year. I hope that you appreciate my fighting for you. Pierpont over at Passports and Visas was angling for Florida for his man, but you know how low P&V ranks. His man will spend February in Minnesota. Heh, heh."

"Yes, sir, Mr. Pettigrew, I'll take Miami over St. Paul any winter day. Thank you."

Toth was thankful for the geography, but he had no interest in the assignment. He had run with near frantic haste from Cross Creek Elementary as soon as his contract expired. He could not tolerate children when he was a principal, and he had suffered through the two most embarrassing moments in his life because of the worst of them, Carty Andersson, a chronic troublemaker in his opinion.

His thoughts raced back to the worst day of his life. "She brought that enormous snake to school, to my school. Apparently, she thought she was Ramar of the Jungle[21]. With that horrible reptile clamped on to my neck" – involuntarily his hand reached for the small scar – "I had cried publicly in front of an entire class of noisy, smelly, riotous brats while suffering the humiliation of relying on her to pull that serpent off of me."

He never forgot the meeting with her father later that day either. Though Michael Andersson said all the right words about punishing her, Toth was convinced that he was laughing beneath the exterior. That was the second most embarrassing episode in Toth's life. If he had retained any illusions of continuing as principal a second year, they dissipated into nothing on that day.

He saw no reason why he would feel better about students now. What a lousy assignment.

"It sounds interesting, Mr. Pettigrew," he lied. "When do I start and where do I go?"

"Mrs. Barnett is coordinating with the senators' offices to work up a schedule for everyone. Yours should be ready by next Monday."

*AFTER* a week in high schools in and around Miami and Palm Beach, Toth worked his way to the center of the state where he returned to Winter Free for the first time since June of 1948. As he drove past Cross Creek Elementary, he visibly shuddered at the memory of sitting on the floor of a classroom, sobbing, as the little Andersson horror coaxed the snake from his neck.

He arrived at Winter Free High around noon and had lunch with the faculty in the school cafeteria. The teachers were dutifully attentive, he had to admit, given his lofty position as a State Department official. Toth employed his most haughty tone of voice to insure that they understood his visit was quite a magnanimous gesture by Washington.

Speaking later to the two junior classes proved singularly uneventful, and Toth could not wait to end the day and be on his way. A black boy, Hale Wending, whom he remembered from Cross Creek Elementary, actually had intelligent things to say, but he could not imagine coming back to State suggesting a scholarship for a black boy.

Toth would be surprised later in the month when Wimp would tell him that State needed blacks for work at embassies in emerging Africa and asked him if he had encountered any such worthy prospects during his travels.

"Indeed, I did," he would answer. "I knew as soon as I met this young man that he was an ideal candidate. I had planned to suggest him to you when you were less busy," he would lie.

Toth hated the question and answer session part of the presentation. When he gave his prepared remarks about State Department operations and career opportunities, he knew that he was maintaining a high level of sophistication for the rubes. When they spoke, however, inevitably to ask inane questions, he felt that he was listening to chattering in a zoo. A student in the second junior class proved slightly interesting, however.

"Haywood Dolder, sir," the boy had begun. "Does the State Department make policy for dealing with foreign countries, or does it follow the lead of the president? And when a new president is elected with new ideas, how does the State Department handle that, especially if the new president's ideas contradict years of established policy that you have worked hard at achieving?"

Toth had not realized that Dolder's father had coached him. Sen. Brath had confided in Denton Dolder, a generous campaign contributor, of the purpose of the State Department's visit, and Denton took advantage of the chance for Haywood to shine.

Toth was not about to be on any public record for answering truthfully. State's bureaucrats really believed that they knew better than any president, of course. Sometimes the president happened to stumble on to the correct policies that State sought, earning complete support from the bureaucracy. More often, the president was off in an unworthy direction that required State to thwart the initiatives as quietly but as forcefully as possible.

"The President and the Secretary of State set the tone," he answered with insincere humility. "We civil servants exist to carry out their dictates. It is a difficult job, but it is an important job."

As the class broke up and the students filed out, Toth motioned Dolder over. "Good questions, young man. I really had to give you the party line, so to speak. But off the record, we career officers at State actually set the policy. If necessary, we have to teach the president. By the time a president is ready to leave office, he has usually learned a lot and has come around to the correct policy.

"You said your name is Dolder. I know that name from my year at Cross Creek. You had some altercations with a girl there a few times, I seem to recall – a Catherine Andersson?"

"Yes, sir. Carty. She doesn't go to Winter Free High. She's at some hoity toity academy in Sarasota. Thinks she's too good for us."

His criticisms and tone of voice were musical to Toth.

"Didn't she have something to do with an attack on someone's house a few years after I left?" he queried.

"That's right. Everybody thinks she was a big hero, but in my opinion, those criminals were so dumb that anyone could have fought them off. In fact, she was so incompetent that she let the ringleader get away."

Toth gave his contact card to Dolder. "Let's stay in touch, young man. You seem to have what it takes. If you decide to follow a college plan suited for State, my department has a limited number of scholarships for clever students. I might be able to steer one your way."

# CHAPTER 24

## *Moncada*

*It is amidst great perils we see brave hearts.*

JEAN FRANCOIS REGNARD

**FEBRUARY 1953**

Meyer Lansky, Cruz, Batista, and two generals, one from the Army and one who headed the Air Force, examined the cards that had been dealt them. Lansky's winnings so far, not surprisingly, were up as were Batista's, though not as much. Cruz and the generals were diplomatic enough to avoid taking Batista's money even in this low stakes, "friendly" game.

Batista would not hold a grudge if he were beaten by a professional gambler like Lansky, but the others needed to be careful. In fact, Batista was a weak player, bluffing so often it became predictable. He should have lost his table stakes by this hour, but the three deferential players often folded their winning hands to allow Batista to win.

It did not always work. One time Cruz discarded a pair of kings to weaken his hand only to draw a pair of aces in return, but that was an exception.

Lansky expressed his worry. "It's in the nature of us casino owners to keep close to the ground. We love the rich losers, but the middle market losers pay a lot of the bills, so we listen to them. They are not happy with your coup last year. Maybe we should have tried stealing the election like we do in Chicago and Philly."

Batista did not want to hear of this. "Gentlemen, the people love me. They know that the coup was necessary for the good of Cuba. There may be a few radicals and malcontents. There always are. But I have the support of the people, do you not agree?"

A momentary silence hung heavily and painfully. Cruz had been waiting for this opening.

"No one denies that the people love you, Fulgencio," he lied. "That is not the issue. The problem is that the people have no enthusiasm. Then there are radicals who will not keep quiet and noisy politicians in the United States complaining that the American Government should stop supporting us.

"What we need is a cause, a reason for the people to realize that, without you, they will be inviting chaos. I have an idea that will bring them more energetically to our side while ridding us of many of the radicals and shoring up our American support."

Lansky and the generals were relieved that Cruz had diffused an embarrassing moment. That bought Cruz a sympathetic audience.

"As you know, I have been working with the radical elements at the university for about two years. The first year, I tried to convince Eduardo Chibás of the Ortodoxo Party to see the value of joining your cause, Fulgencio, but it became apparent that he was too head-strong to control. Unfortunately, he was the de facto leader of the strongest opposition, so he had to be dealt with to enable my second choice to move up among the disparate groups.

"That was when I had to arrange his 'suicide' during that famous radio broadcast. It is a good thing that we did not have this new fangled television back then. It was a lot easier to shoot him on a radio show and claim that, "My suicide is the only way to convince the people of the importance of our cause."

The authenticity of Cruz's mimicry of Chibás' well known voice startled Batista and the generals. One asked incredulously what the others were thinking, "Chibás did not really commit suicide? You gave the speech in his voice and then killed him?"

"Not the entire speech, only after he finished. We moved him off-mic, and I mimicked his voice for the critical sentence.

"It was necessary to move my man to the top. I believe that we can influence the new man in ways that the volatile Chibás would not allow."

"But how did you pull it off? Surely there were others in the radio station who would have seen what happened."

"Of course, but plenty of pesos gained the initial quiet that I needed. There were three others in attendance – the radio announcer, the engineer, and one of Chibás' assistants. I had arranged a limited number for 'security' reasons."

"But how could you be sure that they would not talk later?"

"I could not be sure. That is why the assistant was killed by a hit-and-run driver two days later, the engineer had a fatal 'heart attack' the following weekend, and the announcer went for an unexpected ride to my hacienda in the Sierra Maestra and never returned."

Lansky spoke with a note of admiration in his voice, "You bumped off all of the witnesses to a murder that everyone believes is a suicide. Marvelous. Where were you when I was setting up shop in Vegas, Cruz? I could have used a man like you."

Since Chibás' death, the more radical elements in Cuba were leaderless, and no one had emerged to fill the vacuum. Cruz was suggesting that he could develop a leader who would secretly be under his subtle guidance.

Batista asked the obvious questions. "One, why would we want to create such a leader – even one under our control – instead of leaving the quivering mass of opposition floundering? And two, who is this man?"

"Fulgencio, if we do not work to guide events, a leader will eventually emerge to fill the vacuum anyway. It is better that we have influence and knowledge. And let me be candid. I will not be able to fully control the selected person. My goal is to earn his respect and get him to rely on my advice.

"In the meantime, you have taken enough of my money with your poker prowess. How about we take in some of Lansky's entertainment? What's playing tonight, Meyer?"

"In the main room we have a mariachi band from Mexico. Quite popular and energetic."

"How about something quieter?

"Well, we have Sara Ann Dan, the American actress, in the lounge, but I don't think she is what you are looking for. Her acting career has tanked. She thought that she might be a good enough singer to start a new career. She thought wrong.

"I signed her for a one month gig as a favor to Sinatra who is appearing in one of our Vegas spots, but I'm not renewing her. She can't draw anyone to her shows."

Cruz recalled reading about Sara Ann Dan in the Tampa paper after the fire he started at the Standard Oil station. She was endorsing some wacky organization, Society Against Greed and Excess (SAGE), that was promoting the idea that Standard Oil was blowing up its own stations for profit. He remembered thinking at the time that she had just the bimbo mentality that he could properly mold.

"Actually, I would like to hear her, Meyer. When does she come on?"

Lansky looked at his watch and said she would be on stage in about fifteen minutes.

"We won't have any difficulty finding a table. I can assure you of that."

Lansky was not adverse to ejecting patrons from a desirable table if he needed it, but he preferred to avoid hassling the paying customers. In this instance almost all of the tables would be available.

The generals and Batista begged off and called it a night as Lansky and Cruz made their way to the lounge. As they sat at a front row table and waited for their Scotch, Cruz asked, "Meyer, have you noticed any American newspaper reporters with a gambling problem?"

"A problem? No, Cruz," Lansky chuckled ruefully. "Most of them come in, drink, and lose. No problem."

"I understand, Meyer," Cruz chuckled. "No problem from your perspective, but I mean from theirs. Are there any having trouble controlling the gambling urge?"

Lansky thought for a few moments and said, "A couple, actually three. There's Johnson from *The Chicago Tribune* – he actually knows what he is doing at the tables, but he drinks too much and then he loses badly.

"Ken Oldermann from the *New York Post* and Mike Maxton from *The Miami Herald* don't drink too much. They are just losers. They don't know the odds and make wild plays. Maxton knows enough to stop when he is tapped out, at least. Oldermann is into us for almost a grand."

"In that case, I need to be introduced to Oldermann, Meyer. Can you arrange that?"

As Lansky nodded an assent, the band leader took the stage and made a brief introduction. Sara Ann Dan entered from the left in an extremely low cut, shimmering red gown so tight she had to take small steps to move across the stage. Even Cruz, who seldom paid much attention to the opposite sex, took notice when she bent forward in an elaborate bow to the smattering of polite applause from the sparse crowd.

She alternated slow, sultry songs such as "You Don't Love Me" with upbeat "Rum and Coca Cola" and "Swinging on a Star." At the end of the evening, when she finished her version of "After You've Gone," the applause was enthusiastic, if not voluminous.

"She's really not bad, Meyer. The audience seemed to enjoy the show."

"I know, Cruz, but she isn't drawing them in."

"Can you introduce me to her?"

Lansky was surprised at his request. Cruz had never indicated any interest in women, and Lansky was actually happy to hear the request. "Sure, Cruz. Let's go backstage."

Lansky's security man knocked on her dressing room door and announced, "Mr. Lansky and another gentleman to see you, Miss Dan."

"I'm as decent as I get. Send them in, Miguel."

After introductions, Cruz complimented her on the show and asked how she enjoyed the work. Despite his previous apparent disinterest in women, Cruz displayed a smoothness Lansky had not seen.

"I do enjoy singing, Mr. Cruz, but I am afraid that our mutual friend, Mr. Lansky, does not seem to believe that my new career is going anywhere. To tell you the truth, he may have a point. It has been three weeks, and my audience is no larger now than when I started."

"Nonsense, that crowd was as enthusiastic as any I've seen at Meyer's casino. It won't take much longer, I'll bet on it."

Sara Ann Dan found herself strangely attracted to this rather plain if not borderline ugly man. The combination of compliments, money, and connections did have a way of turning a lady's head.

The next night, Cruz was once again seated in the front row. This time many more patrons occupied the room – not a full house, but definitely an improvement. Sara Ann Dan varied her program slightly, but when she ended with "After You've Gone" once again, it brought applause from standing enthusiasts and boisterous cheering in both English and Spanish.

Cruz had arranged for flowers to be waiting in her dressing room when she returned. He delayed quite a while before going backstage to make certain that she read the card and wondered if he would visit. He wanted her to want him to come. "Mr. Cruz," Miguel announced as he knocked gently.

"Send that delightful man in, Miguel. He is my lucky charm."

By the next day, Sara Ann Dan was spending the first of many days with Cruz on his vast tobacco plantation. She proved herself capable on a horse which both surprised and pleased him. "I appeared in enough westerns in the early years of my acting career to make riding second nature," she informed him.

*ON* the day after his first encounter with her, Cruz had arranged with Lansky to give a half-off discount for drinks to Air Force officers at her show that night. Then he asked Batista to publicize the arrangement with his men.

The following day the offer was extended to the Navy, the day after to the Army, and finally to the police – each night, a larger pool of potential patrons. On the second to last day of Sara Ann Dan's engagement with the casino, Lansky invited Oldermann, the reporter with the *New York Post*, to be his guest at the front table for an "entertainment scoop," as Cruz suggested.

With the three of them at the table, Oldermann was suitably impressed by the enthusiastic crowd and Sara Ann Dan's reasonably talented voice and revealing costuming. In the interview in her dressing room afterward, she charmed him easily. After all, she was an actress. His dispatch to New York extolling her performance was picked up via AP by most of the Havana papers, contributing to the sold-out show on what was to be her last night. Cruz's publicity strategy had succeeded where previously modest talent had not.

Lansky renewed Sara Ann Dan's contract for a year, and Cruz found himself with an appreciative lady friend and a reporter pal, both of whom would prove helpful in years to come.

## JUNE 1953

*THE* three men sat together in the café, expecting it to be the final time there. As usual, the other customers were few during late morning hours, allowing for easy discussion that was interrupted only when the waiter took their orders and delivered the bread and coffee.

Cruz could see the tension in the brothers' body language and strained voices. This was normal in seasoned fighters, so he expected it with the inexperienced pair.

"Thank you for what you have done for us," Fidel began.

"Do not thank me. It is you who are risking everything for your country. I am a mere helper who is too old to provide any other assistance but finance and experience." Unknown to the pair, Cruz was in perfect physical condition and would have been the finest fighter in their force had he joined.

"As you know," Cruz continued, "I am nervous about your choice of Moncada Barracks as your objective," Cruz told them with feigned sincerity. "It can be defended effectively, especially if the soldiers are well led and inspired."

No matter what target the Castros had selected, Cruz would have given them the same caution. The warning was about establishing his reputation with them, not about suggesting a different target.

"We do not believe that the soldiers will fight. They might even come over to our side. This will be a victory, Sr. Cruz. You can count on that."

"Fidel, Raúl, I want you to know that I am hoping that you are right, but if things do not go well, you can count on me to do whatever I can to help you."

# CHAPTER 25

## *Tracking*

*To dare is to lose one's footing momentarily. Not to dare is to lose oneself.*
SOREN KIERKEGAARD

**JUNE 1953**

Elena was nearly as jittery as the Castro brothers as she and Carty watched the two young men greet and shake hands with The Cuban when he arrived at their outdoor table at the café. Cruz was dressed in light colors as usual: an off-white suit, checked yellow tie, and white and brown saddle shoes. He again wore a white Panama, but probably a different one as its band matched the new tie.

Unlike the girls' protracted stake-out the previous summer, this one was achieving success early, on the third day.

"Any idea who those young guys are, Elena?"

"No, I don't recognize either one of them. Shall we get to work?"

They retreated to a nearby restroom on the university campus. Elena quickly changed into her "old-woman" clothes and gray wig while Carty applied the aging techniques to Elena's face the way Novotny had taught her. A brown wooden cane finished the look.

Carty piled her blond hair inside a short black wig, darkened her own face slightly with make-up, and changed into her chauffer's outfit.

Elena shuffled to the café while Carty took a circuitous route to the Rafferty's car that they had parked on Avenida Bonita in anticipation of The Cuban returning there.

At the café, Elena selected a table as far away as she could from the group while close enough that she might pick up snippets of conversation. Carlos approached and took her order as she took out knitting needles and began adding to the beginnings of an unidentifiable piece of light pink clothing, perhaps seemingly for a new granddaughter.

Upon her arrival, Cruz instinctively lowered his voice, but the Castros continued as if she had no interest in them. She could not make out complete sentences, but she heard a number of words that caught her interest.

She continued knitting and was developing a serviceable little sock by the time she finished her coffee and bread. It was good that she actually knew how to knit, because Cruz occasionally glanced her way to verify that her effort was genuine.

When she sensed that they were about to finish, she rushed to pay her bill first and shuffled away from the café toward Calle J. Once around the corner and out of sight, she picked up her pace, though not enough to be out of character. Novotny warned them, "Never assume that you are free to drop your disguise because your quarry cannot see you. There is always the risk of being in view of an accomplice."

When Elena reached the car on Avenida Bonita, she sat in the back seat.

"Everything go all right?"

"As far as I'm aware. You are right about The Cuban. He is like a bird. He was always looking from side to side as if a hawk were circling him. I saw him check out my knitting a couple of times. He did not seem nervous, so I think we are okay. Like your hat, 'Jeeves.'"

Carty chuckled. She had changed into a man's jacket, slacks, and a chauffer's cap. Seated behind the steering wheel of the large American car, it appeared that Carty was a young man driving the older Elena.

As soon as Elena got in, she removed the old woman's dress to reveal a chic white blouse and black skirt. She traded her gray wig for a slick black one with the curl forward under her ears.

She worked bright red lipstick boldly around her lips and used a large amount of rouge for her face. She darkened her eyelashes and eyebrows and added a hint of crow's feet around her eyes.

"You look quite stylish, Miss Crawford," Carty remarked, looking into the rearview mirror. Made up that extreme, Elena did in fact resemble the actress, Joan Crawford, in her early forties.

About fifteen minutes later, Carty saw The Cuban in the side view mirror and said, "Here comes White Suit." She started the engine and pulled into the street well ahead of him. She expected that The Cuban would follow the same path as the last time she spotted him. She was encouraged when she noticed his parked car, the same one that he had used before.

Carty continued driving, passing the first intersection where she found a parking spot. She wanted The Cuban's car to go by so that they could follow.

Elena got out, carrying a large hatbox, and stood inside the doorway of the closest shop. As The Cuban's car approached, Elena left the shop doorway and returned to the car. She tossed the hatbox on to the seat as if she had just acquired a new hat and climbed in. They knew that The Cuban was too observant and suspicious for "Joan Crawford" to have been sitting in the car under a blazing hot sun as he passed by.

Carty, a confident driver by this time, pulled into the street two cars behind The Cuban. The four car caravan fought its way through bumper to bumper traffic until the city streets opened up to an extra lane headed south. Gradually, the intervening cars had turned off, and the girls' car was immediately behind The Cuban's – not where they wanted to be positioned.

For over an hour, the two cars drove on, with Carty lagging well behind and trying, as Novotny had taught them, to ease behind an intervening car whenever possible. Carty said, "This is not good. Traffic is too light. No matter how well we are disguised personally, we can't hide this car forever. He is going to figure out something is not right if this keeps on much longer. I figured that he would have led us to his home before now. I wonder how far away he lives."

Shortly afterward, The Cuban's car pulled into an Esso gas station.

Carty passed by without hesitation. She drove another mile and pulled into a Texaco station, mostly to give The Cuban a chance to catch up. "Fill it, please," she told the elderly attendant. Elena took advantage of the stop to place their other clothes in the trunk, and then went to the restroom.

Carty paid the attendant and waited. With her eyes trained on the highway to make certain she would notice when The Cuban's car passed by, she failed to notice when his car drove up to the pump behind hers. Suddenly a strong hand grabbed her left arm though the open window. "All right, Amigo, why are you following me?" Her strong arm muscles kept him from realizing she was a girl.

Carty was struggling for an answer, but she was afraid to risk speaking because, even if she could pass herself off as male, he would surely recognize her American accent. Just then Elena appeared and said, "Hello, *Señor*, may I be of assistance?" doing a good job acting as old as her forty-something appearance.

Turning his attention to her, Cruz let Carty's arm loose. "Actually, yes. I want to know why you are following me."

"Following you?" Taking a long look at his car parked behind theirs, she added with an offended tone, "*Señor*, it appears that you are following me. And I cannot say that I appreciate it."

"Don't give me that. If you are buying a woman's hat, you don't purchase it in a hardware store."

Until that moment, it had not registered that, hours earlier in the city, she had stood in the doorway of a hardware store while they waited for him to pass. This man noticed everything.

As Cruz walked around the car and approached her, the menacing look in his face told Elena all she needed to know. She looked back at the building to see if any help might come from that location. She saw only the elderly attendant.

Suddenly, a huge crash of metal and glass erupted behind Cruz's Packard. Steam gushed like a geyser from the engine of an old, dilapidated truck that had smashed into the sturdy Packard. Most of the damage was to the front end of the truck, but the trunk of Cruz's car suffered too.

Two disheveled locals reeking from alcohol emerged from the truck. They wore baggy, tattered trousers and sweat-stained shirts. They apologized profusely for the accident in their inebriated way. The older man bled from his forehead. Elazar and Cruz confronted them with expletives and demands.

"Insurance? No, *Señor*. I am sorry. I have no insurance," the young driver said with sadness as he wrung the brim of his dirty cap, appearing as if he expected a throttling at any moment.

Carty was having difficulty understanding their slurred Spanish, but she was happy for the diversion.

By this time, a crowd was gathering. The attendant examined the damage, wondering if he had a chance at the repair work. Drivers of two other cars, attracted by the steam pouring from the damaged radiator, pulled in to see what the excitement was all about. Two teenage boys appeared from a nearby house, along with their pair of wildly yapping dogs.

Disgusted, The Cuban motioned to Elazar to get back into the car. He wanted to see this through, at least with the satisfaction of pounding the two drunks if he could not get monetary restitution. But the crowd precluded his taking more aggressive action. Besides, he had more important things on his mind, and he did not want to be distracted at this critical time.

With a frustrated look at the smashed-in trunk, he growled, "Let's get out of here, Elazar."

With one last look at Elena, he growled out a warning. "*Señora*, I had better never see you again."

"That would suit me more than you," Elena responded, with more bravado than she felt.

As they pulled away, the drunk driver staggered up to Elena and pleaded with her to stay for a few minutes while his friend spoke with the attendant. In the meantime, the crowd began to disperse.

After a few minutes, the driver stumbled out of the station, opened the front door of Elena's car, and sat on the front passenger seat. The other drunk entered the car and sat on one of the back seats.

Carty and Elena stared at them and then at each other in disbelief.

"You can't ride with us," Elena insisted. "Please get out."

"But *Señora*, we have no transport. Our truck, she is destroyed. Look, you can see the damage. I have sold it to the attendant for twenty-five pesos." Reaching his hand toward her, he offered, "Here are five pesos for you to pay for our ride."

"I do not want your money, *Señor*. You cannot ride with us. Now I have to insist that you get out."

Elena looked at Carty for support, but only got a confused smile. This infuriated Elena more, especially when Carty added, "I think that we should give them a ride, Elena. After all, they did help us out of a bad situation."

"They didn't help us out of anything, Carty. They crashed their truck, and they smell like they bathed in a distillery. They can't ride with us, and that is final." The last point she emphasized with crossed arms and a vigorous stomp of her foot that sent Carty and the two men into a fit of laughter.

Seeing that reaction, Elena exploded into a torrent of those Spanish words that Carty did not know. Carty put out her hand in a conciliatory manner as the younger man said in unaccented English, "Miss Andersson, maybe you should tell Miss Rafferty why you want to give us a ride."

Elena did a double take as she heard her name and the change in language. "How did you know my name and Carty's name? Who are you?"

No longer slurring his words, he replied with a slight bow, "Jacob Cole, at your service, and my amigo here with the bloody head and big smile is Vosmik Novotny."

"Mr. Novotny!" she squealed, "What are you doing here? Were you following us? Where did you get that wreck of a truck? Carty, did you know they were following us? Are you injured badly, sir? Why didn't you tell me?"

The pulsating stream of questions, fired off like a machine gun burst, generated more laughter all around.

Carty went first. "No, I had no idea, Elena. I only recognized Mr. Novotny from his smile when Mr. Cole started to plead with you. He sure had you going."

Novotny wiped the fake blood from his forehead. "Three parts corn syrup, the rest red dye and a dash of chocolate syrup for a more realistic color." He introduced his companion, Jacob Cole, part of the CIA staff in the embassy in Havana.

"We had you under surveillance each time you arrived at the university campus, and we tailed you when you followed your "Mr. Smith.""

"Wait," Carty interjected. "You've been following us? I thought you taught us enough so that would not be necessary. Yikes, I thought you taught us enough that we would notice being followed."

"You have done very well, girls, but Jacob's people are professionals. That short course I gave you is something that they have been doing over their entire careers. Carty, would you expect me to be your equal in a swamp after a short course from your dad?"

"No. Now that you put it that way, I can see that we were in way over our heads on this.

"But why are you here, Mr. Novotny? Not that I'm complaining, you understand, just that I'm curious," Carty asked.

"Before you visited me with your request for training, your dad called me to talk it over. He figured that with training, you could learn to track in an urban situation somewhat as well as in the wilds. However, he understands that there is no substitute for experience, and yours was certain to be limited no matter how much effort we put into it.

"He also knows that the human prey is far more deadly than any other creature that might turn against the hunter. He told me that this character, The Cuban, is no one to trifle with.

"We decided to allow you some leeway if your training went well, but only if I kept you under our silent guidance at all times.

"Today, we knew you might be in trouble when Elena pretended to buy the hat in the hardware store, but traffic was too congested to stop you from following. Every time we got close, another car got in our way.

Once you got on the main road, our old truck could not keep up."

"If you had been our professional operatives, Jacob and I might have allowed The Cuban to take you so we could have followed him to his quarters. However, that is risky, and it would be well beyond what your father and I agreed we would allow. That is why we stormed in to break up the confrontation.

"Why don't we head back to town as we discuss this further? I really did sell the old truck to the attendant, and we really do need a ride."

Elena snatched the five pesos Novotny still held in his hand and placed it into her small purse. "Five pesos it is, Mr. Novotny. Let's get going." This time she joined in on the laughter.

"I'm sorry we botched things," Carty said in a disappointed voice as they drove back toward Havana.

"Not at all, Carty. Except for the hardware store, you two did well. We snapped some photos of him and got a license plate number. We also have a general idea of where he is headed – at least we know the direction is toward the Sierra Maestra. I'd say your elusive "Mr. Smith" is well on the way to being identified. We will follow up without the involvement of the police to reduce the chance of him being tipped off.

"All in all, I'd say you girls did a superb job."

"And," Carty said, "I still have time to make my afternoon class."


*AFTER* Carty dropped them off near the center of Havana, the men retrieved their Dodge and drove back toward Cole's office.

"I'm curious, Vosmik. It would have been easier and safer to have Miss Andersson simply point out The Cuban to us and let us track him down. Why did you allow them to get so involved?"

"You're right about that, Jacob, but I wanted to see them in action. They really did do well. I assume that you noticed how steady both were when The Cuban was confronting them. They stayed in character and showed no panic.

"You cannot pinpoint new agents too soon. I envision Elena as a possible contact for your office in the future. Carty...I don't know what to make of her yet, but I'll be keeping an eye on her during her college years."

*CRUZ* was both unnerved and angry about the encounter with the woman and her chauffer but he did not have time to brood about it. He was back at the café a few days later on absolute alert but not expecting that they would be so stupid to try a second time.

He spooned two heaps of sugar into his thick, black coffee, and stirred and gulped the entire liquid in one motion. The law school graduate and his brother listened intently.

"Clearly, this man Batista has no interest in the people of Cuba, but he is not going to give up power without a shove – and a hard shove at that. I have watched you two brothers for some time now. You can win the hearts of the people with the right support and guidance. Batista's coup has decided things for me. The question is, whether the coup decided things for you." They were already aching for a fight, but a goad from Cruz could not hurt his cause.

Fidel spoke first as was normal. "You may know that Fulgencio is a family friend. Indeed, he gave my wife and me a $1,000 wedding gift four years ago. What you must know is that the Revolution is more important to us than any individual, however. Is that not true, Raúl?"

Fidel's brother nodded in agreement. "We are single minded on this, Sr. Cruz. We will fight to the death to bring fairness and equality to everyone in Cuba. Help us to achieve our goals. We need funds. We need weapons. We need ammunition."

"I understand your enthusiasm, but it is not your deaths that I want to see. It is not sufficient to launch uncoordinated or under-manned assaults. Batista will not sit idly by while you attack."

Raúl continued, "You do not have the faith in our people that we have, Sr. Cruz. When the people learn of our attack, they will rise up in a nationwide revolution and retake the country from Batista."

Cruz was pleased to hear this rambling nonsense from his protégés. Extreme confidence with no basis in fact played right into his plan.

"I will help you. You are the only hope that we have at this difficult time, but I must remind you that I do not share your confidence. There is as much chance that you will fail as succeed.

"How many men can you put in the field? I will need to supply you with enough rifles and ammunition for each of them."

"Can you outfit 150 men?" Fidel asked.

"If you can gather that size of a force," Cruz replied, "I can see that you get what you need. Get to work on recruitment, and let's meet here again in three weeks to go over final details.

Cruz was surprised at the boast of 150 men. He had not expected that the Castro brothers were capable of getting that much support for an attack on a well-defended position. The size of the force played into his plan, though. The larger the force for Batista to defeat, the better Cruz liked it.

*CRUZ* reiterated his plan to Batista as they finished their coffee in the presidential office. Batista was showing weakness and needed encouragement.

"Fulgencio, the Castro brothers' force will be large enough to make your victory look like an important achievement. If a mere dozen men attacked, that would not attract the attention we are seeking. The idea is to show that resistance is futile.

"Moreover, the larger the force, the better. It concentrates more of your potential enemies in one place and makes it easy to put all of them out of commission in one blow. The Castros will be leading their supporters into a trap."

"You are certain that we will have no difficulty stopping them, Cruz?"

"I will let you know exactly when the attack will come, how many insurgents to expect, and where it will be. You will have no difficulty setting up an ambush. Just be certain that you are ready to alert the newspapers of your victory and make certain that you don't allow reporters to interview the rebels. Control the news; that is the key."

"I want you to know, Cruz, that I am really hesitant about arming these rebels with firearms. Why not just give them knives and pitchforks?"

"Fulgencio, we have gone over this before. They need to have the confidence that a rifle or gun gives an inexperienced 'warrior.' Otherwise, the Castros will not be able to field enough men to make an impression. Restrict them to knives and farm implements, and most of the men will lose faith and walk away.

"It is important for you to defeat a force that appears well armed, but remember that their weapons do not need to be the most modern. Just be certain that the guns are in workable condition to maintain the fiction that I am their trusted advisor and supplier."

"Very well, Cruz, I will arrange for 150 rifles to be delivered to your hacienda."

"And a machine gun, Fulgencio. I must have a machine gun."

"I really do not like the idea of arming the rebels with a machine gun, Cruz. Is that really necessary?"

"We have discussed this," Cruz answered patiently, while suppressing frustration. "It must look good and be able to fire initially, but it's fine if it fails after a while."

As it turned out, Batista delivered the weapons for the rebels to Cruz's hacienda. The firearms included limited range .22 caliber rifles, a 1903 Springfield, several 1898 Krag-Jorgensen rifles that belonged in a museum, and shotguns that were essentially useless for the long range that was needed. The handguns were modern and in generally good condition but of little value for assaulting a fortified position manned by soldiers with modern rifles and artillery.

Batista even came through with a .45 caliber machine gun that had a history of jamming.

# CHAPTER 26

## *Another Jewel Theft*

*Thieves respect property. They merely wish the property to become their property that they may more perfectly respect it.*

G. K. CHESTERTON

**JUNE 1953**

The burglar ran along the narrow path, racing away from the Canfield Mansion in a southwesterly direction. The path led through a densely wooded forest to Hostetter Cutoff near the old Hostetter farmhouse. His heart raced more from the excitement of his latest theft than from the exertion of the fast pace. He rolled the ring in his fingers as he ran, smug in his thoughts – so self-satisfied that he failed to notice another man watching from a distance as he left the cleared land behind the house and entered the forest.

The other man did not know what had occurred or that the furtive figure had been inside the house, but he was struck by the oddity of the thief's demeanor. As the thief disappeared into the deepening foliage, the man was tempted to follow, but the separation was great so he discarded that thought.

Deep into the Canfield Forest, about fifty yards before reaching the cutoff, the thief darted to the left at the edge of a small meadow. With trees protecting his back, he examined the clearing ahead to assure himself that no spying eyes invaded his privacy. Satisfied, he retrieved a small gardening shovel from under a palmetto, alert for any nasty critter that might lurk nearby.

He scraped away a thin layer of dead grass and leaves and dug into the soft, sandy soil. With only his second shovelful, he hit a metal surface. After removing an additional amount of dirt, he pulled the steel strongbox from its shallow hole. He took a key from the watch pocket of his Wranglers and opened the box. Then he took the ring from another pocket. He was always careful to keep the metal key separated from the jewelry. Scratches could diminish the value, he had read, and value was what the effort was all about.

The bright sun shining into the clearing drew out the facets of bottomless green in the polished stone. He liked emeralds as well as any gem, but he appreciated them for their monetary value, not their dazzling beauty. He had only a general idea of this ring's worth, but he was determined to accumulate a large stockpile of jewelry before he concerned himself with value or trying to sell the pieces.

The 3.8 carat stone of medium deep green was nearly perfect, without any inclusions observable to the naked eye, and clear from every angle of its elaborate marquise cut. The five diamond cluster nest of three quarter carat stones was a mere fraction of the emerald's value, irrespective of its remarkable history.

The emerald had been pulled from Colombia's Muzo mine in 1621 by native Indians working under severe conditions of the Conquistadores. It was brought to the attention of the governor, who sent it to King Philip IV's queen to be set into her crown. However, the pirate, John Carpenter, waylaid and sunk the Spanish treasure ship, diverting its cargo to his village on Ocracoke Island, North Carolina.

The thief smiled as he examined the accumulated hoard. The topaz and diamond necklace was by far the most elaborate handiwork of the collection. However, he correctly judged the new acquisition to be the most valuable. Though he was by no means an expert, he had devoted brief library time to learning what he could.

The bracelets and earrings from earlier forays were clearly of lesser worth. He had been careful starting out, always going after one small item at a time to see if Sally became suspicious and alerted her husband. Her lack of alarm encouraged him to gradually ratchet up the quality of the items taken.

"I certainly know how to keep adding to the hoard," the thief muttered, humming contentedly as he looked at the contents of the box before adding the ring. "It is merely a matter of knowing when to stop."

He returned the box to the hole and covered it with dirt and camouflage. The shovel went back under the plant, and he continued on his way.

"Time for a little celebration," he told himself. "I think I can afford some burgers and a Dr. Pepper from Krystal[22]."

He crossed Hostetter Cutoff and got into his car, letting out a sigh of satisfaction when the car started without difficulty. Even at slow speed, he seemed to risk losing the car's fenders as it bounced into and out of countless chuckholes in the old dirt road. "You'd think the sheriff would have enough influence to get this road fixed," he complained to no one.

As he neared the end of Hostetter Cutoff, he spotted an armadillo ambling across the asphalt surface of Mocking Bird Road. "Ha," he barked, "This will be fun."

He gunned the engine and down shifted a complaining transmission into second gear. The car lurched forward, kicking up dust in a swirl of clouds behind the spinning tires as he fish-tailed on to the paved road.

The startled armadillo reacted typically when he saw the noisy vehicle approaching. He used all four legs to spring straight up in a useless vertical leap instinctive to the animal. Had the car been fully up to speed, the armadillo would have leapt directly into the car's undercarriage and been killed.

But by jumping early, the armadillo actually landed back on the road just as the still-accelerating car reached his position. The car could easily clear over him. Unfortunately, the good luck did not hold.

The driver, a capable motorist, had aimed the car's front tire directly at the armadillo. The car bumped upward twice as both the front and rear right tires crushed the armadillo and flattened the animal into the road. The double hit at least assured that it did not suffer, not that such a silver lining was of any concern to the driver.

"Stupid armadillo," he laughed. "The dumb things think that they are invincible, but I show them how untrue that is every time I get the chance. Ha, ha."

He continued on Mocking Bird Road and headed for town, secure in the knowledge that he could continue adding to his gem collection at will. His plan was nearing its climax.

"She is so rich and has so much jewelry – she'll never miss anything as long as I take one item at a time, spaced out over several weeks. She plays right into my hands by rotating jewelry between the house and the Ensign Bank vault. She can't keep track of what is where."

He was correct in his expectation that she had so much jewelry and rotated it so frequently that she lost track. He believed he could go on for years before she became suspicious. However, he had no intentions of waiting very much longer before cashing in.

All he needed was an outlet. He first considered a "fence," a dealer who would be willing to take the gems at a discount. He had learned that fences paid very low prices for stolen goods that the authorities were looking for, but the Canfield gems were especially attractive loot in that they had not been reported as stolen.

However, he gave up on the idea of scouring the seedy parts of Tampa for a fence to unload all of the gems at once. It was appealing to make a one-shot killing, but he deemed it too risky. The fence could always be an undercover cop or someone who might try to take advantage of him by grabbing the loot without paying.

"Criminals have no morals," he had thought on more than one occasion, failing to include himself in that category.

No, the plan was to drive to Miami and visit every pawn shop there and in surrounding counties over a two- or three-day period. He would offer no more than a few pieces in each shop to avoid suspicion. He figured Florida's east coast would be far enough away from Winter Free that no one who knew Sally would ever show up in a social event wearing something he had stolen from her and pawned.

In the meantime, he tried out his plan by selling only a small brooch or bracelet from time to time. Besides giving him the confidence that his plan was viable, he was able to generate a little cash flow as well.

# CHAPTER 27

## Up and Down

*Our real blessings often appear to us in the shape of pains, losses and disappoint-*
*ments, but let us have patience and we soon shall see them in their proper figures.*
JOSEPH ADDISON

**JULY 1953**

Michael raced into the house, not caring that the screen door slammed
noisily behind him. "Bay, Carty, where are you? Have you heard?"

They stopped shucking peas and looked up at him with mild surprise. He seldom displayed emotion so boisterously. Bay asked, "What is
going on, Michael?"

"The armistice. The UN – well, really, Ike – announced that we
would be signing an armistice with the North Koreans. It was just on

television. I saw it at Ted's Barber Shop. Can you imagine a television in a place of business? Maybe we should get one of those gadgets for the house.

"Anyway, the Korean War is over! It probably means that our reserve unit won't be called up after all. What a relief. Good grief. I might even vote for a Republican next time if Ike runs again."

After WWII, Michael had stayed in the Reserves, and as the Korean War dragged on, it looked more and more like his Rangers were going to be called to active duty.

"I never knew you were as worried as I about your going back into combat, Michael," Bay said.

"Combat? No, I wasn't worried about that, though I am not the young man I once was. I was worried about having to leave the limerock business for you and Carty to run while I was gone. It might have meant taking Carty out of school for the duration."

That shook Carty. "Wow, Dad. I had no idea. Would you really turn it over to us? Would you have taken me out of school?"

"Yes, ladies. What else could we have done? Business is booming, and we couldn't just shut down. Mom could handle the finances all right. She does most of that now anyway. I'd need you out in the field, Carty. We just do not have adequate back up. Sure, the guys know how to run the equipment, process and load the limerock, and handle routine issues. But what about scheduling, sales, hiring the right workers, reacting to emergencies?"

"But, Dad, I'm just a kid. That is way over my head."

"War is war, Carty. You'd have to figure it out day by day. I've been working you into every facet of the business whenever you are home. You could have done it. But we do not need to worry about it now. The War is over."

Bay and Carty gave each other a meaningful look, but neither one was sure about bringing up the issue now when Michael was so happy. However, Bay decided to charge forward.

"Michael, please take a seat. We ladies need to have a serious discussion with you."

"This sounds interesting. Are you pregnant, Bay?" he asked hopefully.

"Pregnant? I'm thirty-seven years old!"

"Darn, it would be nice with a new little person around here."

"Well, not from this wife. Maybe from some other one."

"I don't think that I am allowed more than one. Anyway, if you are not pregnant, what is this all about?"

Carty always enjoyed their banter. Her dad, who was always serious with everyone else, often turned into a silly kid around Bay. Carty sometimes wondered what more went on behind closed doors.

"Carty is not sure that she wants to be groomed to take over the mine when you decide to retire. I can't say it any clearer than that."

Michael looked as if he had been hit with a shovel. He remained speechless as he looked at the two of them, with sadness etched on his face. The mine was almost the second child that they never had.

"I see," he managed to say after a long pause.

"Gee, Dad, I like the mine, and I like the work. I really do. I just don't know if it is what I want to do with my life. It might be. I just don't know yet. That doesn't mean I don't want to go to Purdue and become an engineer. I do want to follow in your footsteps that far for sure. It's just that I'd like to keep options open awhile. Can you understand?

"I'll even continue learning about the mine just in case that is where I end up. Is that okay with you? I don't want you to be disappointed in me."

When Carty said that, Michael realized the agony she had to have been going through, trying to find a way to bring up the subject.

"Disappointed in you? Carty, don't you ever think that. I'm disappointed that you are not grabbing hold of the mine, but I am not disappointed in you. You are the best. You do crazy things sometimes, but that simply breaks up the monotony of doing everything else so right."

"I told you it wouldn't be so awful, Carty," Bay added. "He's really not too bad a guy." The three of them embraced for a few moments.

"Do you have any ideas of what you might like to do instead, Carty?"

"Mostly I'd like to wait awhile before committing to any solid direction. Is that okay?"

"Yes, Carty. I would like to ask that you talk it over with me when you do have a good idea. Is that fair?"

"Sure, Dad. In the meantime, there is one thing about what we are running into on the eastern side of the mine that I'd like to talk over with you. Could I take a break from the peas to discuss it with Dad, Mom?"

"Of course, Carty. You two go talk mining. Supper is at 6:30 tonight. We are running late."

Michael and Carty sat on the porch swing and started it moving. The gentle evening breeze felt pleasant. "After Bombshell Number 1," he asked, "What more do you have for me that your mother cannot hear?"

"You know me too well, Dad."

"Not entirely. I know the mine too well. There is nothing unusual occurring on the east side."

"Hee, hee. That is true. Actually, the reason I wanted to talk is that I do have an idea what I might like to do, and I don't believe that Mom would like it. I might like to ask Mr. Novotny if he would have a place for me in his organization after I finish at Purdue."

"The CIA? Have you discussed it with him?"

"Not really, but he seemed to think I did a good job in Cuba tailing Cruz. Now that Jacob Cole has identified our "Mr. Smith" as Cruz Cruz, Mr. Novotny passed out a lot of praise to Elena and me. I would like to find out if he would encourage me along that direction. I don't know if the CIA would have an interest in engineers, though."

"Actually, they have needs for all disciplines. I really do want you for the mine, but now that you mention it, you would be very good in Novotny's field. Do you know how to reach him to ask his opinion?"

"He gave me his address in Washington. With your permission, I'll write him a brief letter."

"It seems that I should think about developing an alternative as my successor, Carty."

He put his arm around her shoulders and pulled her close as they continued swinging.

Looking from the open window, Bay said under her breath, "The CIA. I wonder when they will get around to telling me about that."

# CHAPTER 28

## *Ernesto*

*Everything I do, I feel is genius. Whether it is or it isn't.*

RUFUS WAINWRIGHT

**JULY 1953**

Ernesto's motorcycle was showing signs of wear, but the motor still ran smoothly. The months' long trip with his friend, Alberto, included many rough roads in Argentina and Chile, but those were like paved highways compared to the roads in the Peruvian highlands. The oft repaired tires were almost more patch than tire.

Low on funds, the two young graduates of the medical school at Argentina's University of Buenos Aires combined their medical knowledge with guile and personality to scrounge free room, board, and transportation with little difficulty in the primitive mountain villages. Despite their degrees, neither had developed interest in pursuing a calling in the healing profession; instead, they rather preferred the free-spirited life of vagabonds.

In Cuzco, they happened on a doctor that Alberto had met at a conference some years earlier. He lent them his Land Rover to make the trip to the famous Inca ruins at Machu Picchu. After a day of sight-seeing, they came upon a soccer game on the outskirts of the ruins. Joining in, they displayed enough talent to attract the attention of a local innkeeper who also played. He graciously provided a free room at his inn as it was not full at the time.

However, after two days he had to ask them to leave because a busload of American tourists was arriving, and they had reservations.

"Americans, bah," Ernesto complained to his friend. "Who do they think they are? They fly in, take up all the rooms, eat all the food, and fly back with no care about the inconvenience they cause others. What arrogance."

Alberto knew that Ernesto often displayed strong opinions, though not always entirely logically. He seldom took issue with Ernesto, as it usually generated anger and resentment for days. However, these comments caught Alberto so off-guard that he responded without considering the likely result.

"We have no complaint, Ernesto. The tourists have reservations, and they are paying for the rooms. We were living free. I do not see what difference it makes where they came from. Would you feel better if they were Brazilians?"

That met with a scowl and a biting comment. "Alberto, it is clear that you do not understand how the Americans act. I visited an uncle in Miami years ago. Do you think that his American friends would give me proper respect? No. Would they listen to my ideas? No. They ignored me. Me, Ernesto Guevara. One day I will be famous, and the Americans will respect me then. I guarantee it."

Alberto mentally braced himself for several days of the silent treatment, and in that he was not proved wrong. Ernesto held to his opinions, and woe be to anyone who thought differently.

# CHAPTER 29

## Betrayed

*A true friend stabs you in the front.*

OSCAR WILDE

**JULY 26 1953**

As Cruz planned, the Castros' attack on the Moncada Barracks was a complete failure. That the 150 men turned out to be only 135 was not the biggest problem. It was everything else. The rag tag 135 had no military transport, and set out for the fortified barracks in a caravan of civilian cars from two-tone sedans to wood-sided station wagons.

The procession looked more like an outtake from a Mack Sennett Keystone Cops[23] routine than a smoothly run military operation.

On the 26th of July[24], about ten miles short of the barracks, the caravan, with Fidel in a '51 Oldsmobile 88 convertible second in line, stopped for him to give a final briefing. Tension competed with excitement. Spirits were high. Every man, including Fidel Castro, expected a decisive victory, achieved in rapid time, with minimal effort. Such was the inexperience and naiveté of untrained militia.

Fidel led the largest force of about ninety with the goal of taking the barracks building and radio station. The smaller contingent was targeting the other buildings. In the meantime, a couple dozen additional men launched a small diversionary attack several miles away in Bayamo to confuse anyone who might be asked to send reinforcements to Moncada.

The diversion turned out to be of no value, however, as reinforcements had arrived in Moncada two days earlier, already with full knowledge of the impending attack.

As the offensive force was about to resume moving toward Moncada, Castro told his driver, "I'll drive the rest of the way. Keep your weapon at the ready."

The main caravan snaked along the narrow winding road, with both sides hemmed in by dense vegetation. Castro was pleased to see a shallow ditch running parallel to the road. With less than a mile to go, Castro let out a yell and jerked the wheel abruptly to the right and into the ditch to disable the car.

However, he had not anticipated the frightened reaction of his inexperienced forces. Two men panicked at the sight of the car crash and fired toward an imaginary danger forward of Castro's position. A third and a fourth man joined in, spooked by the noise from the first weapons fired. None of the shots were aimed at an actual target, and none had a purpose.

Suddenly, though, the undisciplined firing brought a withering amount of accurate return fire from near the front of the barracks and from the dense foliage on both sides of the caravan where Batista's soldiers had set up their ambush. Castro's men returned fire in a confused manner, unable to see the defenders in well-concealed and fortified locations.

The battle ensued with no hope for the rebels, who were out-gunned, out-positioned, and without effective leadership. The machine gun saw no action as the soldiers picked off the rebels manning it in the first volleys.

In the meantime, the other two smaller forces were rapidly wiped out before their attacks began in earnest. A few of the captured rebels were executed on the spot by lower level soldiers until officers got control and placed the captured men under arrest.

While the bulk of the main force was picked apart by pre-positioned soldiers, Castro and a small number of men sought safety in the surrounding forest.

That proved a lost cause for most, because Batista's soldiers waited in key locations to round up the stragglers.

Raúl Castro was captured early, but Fidel managed to elude Batista's men for several weeks as he made his way into the mountains of the Sierra Maestra. He probably could have evaded capture indefinitely, but for men in the area who worked for Cruz and reported Castro's presence to him. Cruz had put together a team years earlier to steal from tobacco plantations, and the group remained in operation even after Cruz left the cigar business.

A simple follow-up phone call from Cruz to Batista sealed Castro's fate. "Have your soldiers report to the location I identified, Fulgencio. He is located in the valley where a peasant farmer is hiding him in a barn. Approach quietly from four sides, and when he sees that he is surrounded, he will surrender peacefully. He is not suicidal."

Ironically, Castro always believed that the untimely weapons discharge of his jittery men gave the soldiers in the barracks too much warning, and that mistake resulted in the rout. It never occurred to Castro that he had run into an ambush, one arranged by his friend and mentor, Cruz Cruz.

In the aftermath, Batista took the opportunity to rid himself of most of the outspoken opposition to his rule, including many who had not been involved in the Moncada operation. The dead for the most part included few of the actual leaders, but the trials took care of incarcerating them.

Sentences ranged from fifteen years for Fidel Castro down to seven months for lesser players. Nineteen of the actual rebels were acquitted in reasonably fair trials. However, many of Batista's political rivals were imprisoned, more than a few of whom had no knowledge of the attack.

*THREE* days prior to the failure at Moncada, Cruz had counseled the Castros. "Amigos, you must be aware that early events in revolutions frequently end in failure, and the leaders are often killed. Then others rally to take the flag to victory, but those replacements are seldom worthy of the sacrifice of the vanguard.

"I do not want you to be among those early contributors who are lost to the cause. You are too important, too valuable, too rare. You must listen to what I am telling you."

Cruz encouraged them to hold back and allow the others to push forward into the battle. "Only if you see that the operation will be a success should you move forward. If things do not turn out as planned, you must seize the opportunity to save yourselves."

"But the men need our leadership, Sr. Cruz. How can we send them into battle without our direction?"

"They will have your direction. They will be following your plan. Lead them right up to the front lines and then create an unexpected diversion to delay your personal involvement. Allow them to move on ahead. I suggest that you lose control of your vehicle and drive it off the road. Tell your men to continue on from there so that the critical timing of the action is not compromised, and let them know that you will follow.

"If things are going well when you arrive, join in. If things are out of control, take to the hills and escape."

Cruz knew that things would not go well for the Castros, but he hoped that they would survive and be captured. If they survived with his advice, he was certain to have their enduring gratitude.

*AFTER* Fidel Castro's trial and conviction, Cruz arranged for Castro's confinement to be in a facility as comfortable and as large as a hotel room. Cruz sent Castro a message, "It is the least that I can do for a true patriot."

It was the willingness of Batista to give the rebels generous treatment that taught Castro a lesson he remembered well when he ultimately gained power six years later: never be gentle with political opponents.

*BATISTA* reveled in the victory. Cuban newspapers ran photos of Batista awarding medals to his victorious soldiers, of captured weapons, and of destroyed rebel vehicles that gave an impression more of a poor used car lot than the result of a military battle. Cruz took advantage of Batista's good feelings to convince him to allow trials instead of summary judgment.

"It will show the world and especially the United States that you are a fair-minded and compassionate man. The important rebels will be put away for a long time, and we can use the trials to jail many of the opposition politicians who were not involved.

"Your position is now solidified. Some who might have opposed you will now know that it is futile. Others who did oppose you are in prison. You ran an excellent operation, Fulgencio."

Cruz wanted to keep the Castros out of the way but available in case he needed them. A long prison sentence was ideal. He could maneuver a release if it would be beneficial, but for now he had helped to strengthen Batista's position and had solidified his standing with both sides.

Cruz was beginning to believe that he had little to worry about from Florida, which gave him pause. "Whenever, I get a contented feeling, that is when things go awry," he lamented. As usual, he was correct.

# CHAPTER 30

## *Extradition*

*Any sufficiently advanced bureaucracy is indistinguishable from molasses.*

UNKNOWN

**SEPTEMBER 1953**

Flagstead Toth stretched in his office chair. It was almost four, and he wanted to get an early start on the weekend. He had an exquisite meal in mind for tonight, and he wanted to impress colleagues from Defense and Treasury whom he had invited, including two with their wives. It never hurt to cultivate friends in other agencies who might be helpful.

Toth was a master chef, and an invitation to his Capitol Hill townhouse was a desirable social occasion despite the deteriorating condition of the neighborhood. Toth took a contrarian point of view on real estate.

When others bought, he sold; when other sold, he bought. In the late Forties, Capitol Hill was in the early stages of a long downward spiral.

Toth knew that the trend was headed in the wrong direction and that it would take decades to reverse, but he anticipated that it would turn around. More importantly, he was attracted to the undeniable convenience of the area and knew that it would only be a matter of time before others agreed. He could walk to work on nice days, and a bus was a short hop when the weather was foul. Farmers brought fresh produce to historic Eastern Market where he could stock up weekly.

"Let the fools relocate to the suburbs and spend their time on the road," he thought. He preferred to arrive at home early and prepare culinary feasts.

He had found a long, narrow, three-story townhouse for sale on East Capitol Street near 2$^{nd}$ Street SE, with a view of the Capitol and the Supreme Court Building. The owner, the head of a family of four, feared the declining condition of Washington's school system and was anxious to move to a new housing development in Virginia. Toth, with no children to worry about, would have been willing to pay more than they sought for the prime location and delightful architecture, but he was more than happy to take the discounted price.

Outside, the unpainted gray granite stood out nicely against the neighboring browns and red brick that abutted his place. An unusual feature for the area was an easement from 2$^{nd}$ Street that led to a garage behind the house. He appreciated not having to park in the street where auto thefts were becoming commonplace.

Bright sunlight shining through beveled glass windows in front of the house dispersed hundreds of rainbows on to beige carpet and cream walls of the living room. As the sun moved into afternoon, the rainbows traveled the room, changing shape depending on angles. Nearing sunset, they extended in elongated, multicolored spears.

Despite the age of the house – built in 1884 – it had been modernized in recent years and was contemporary by standards of the time. Electrical, heating, and plumbing were all brought up to code in a major overhaul in 1946 when the owner returned from the War.

That owner did not update the kitchen at the time, however, which Toth did not mind. Toth doubted that it would have been done to his satisfaction anyway. He dipped deeply into his savings and turned the kitchen into a gourmet's workshop.

In his office, Toth's mind wandered to the three Chateaubriands – one per two persons – that he was already preparing. His secret was to marinate the meat for twenty-four hours in a cheap white – not red – wine and spices instead of rushing it to the oven.

His wine selections were legendary. He was as well read on them as anyone else in Washington. He travelled to Europe annually where he purchased excellent wines by the case, nearly always from French vineyards. That night he would serve a 1949 Chateau Petrus, a wine from Bordeaux, and the most expensive in his cellar.

He chuckled at the thought that his guests were oblivious to his use of inexpensive California wines for cooking. There was no reason to waste the good French wines preparing food. Those were for drinking and for ostentatious display of labels.

He was so anxious to get started in his kitchen that his mouth was watering, but he decided on reviewing the last file before heading home so that he would have a fresh start on Monday. He read with little interest the final file that he needed to review, labeled "Burglary/Kidnap Suspect."

Suddenly, he sat up straight. It contained the details of the attack on the Canfield residence in 1950, including the conviction of Clemens Hostetter and the escape of one of the culprits.

Through efforts of "embassy staff" in Havana – Toth knew that this euphemism meant the CIA – a man by the name of Cruz Cruz had been identified as the elusive "Mr. Smith," the leader of the operation. He had been recognized in Havana by none other than the snake-brat from Cross Creek Elementary, Catherine Andersson.

The Criminal Division of the Office of International Affairs (OIA) in the Justice Department was one of Toth's least favorite. When fugitives and suspects in crimes committed in the U.S. fled to foreign countries, that office was in charge of seeking extradition from foreign governments. The legal documentation was prepared by attorneys then sent to Toth's group at the State Department, the Office of the Legal Advisor's Law Enforcement and Intelligence, for delivery to the foreign government.

Though such matters seemed simple enough tasks, complications often set in. Routine extraditions might take a few months, but many extended to two years. Really complicated requests often took four years or more; indeed, some extradition requests in Toth's file were still open past the twenty-year point.

Extraditing a fugitive from a foreign land was a thankless task and hard work and more often than not, it caused bad feelings with the foreign country. No matter how difficult the hurdles surmounted, there was seldom any praise. "How hard could it be to ask for a criminal?" was the prevailing thought.

The officer had to be mindful of every nuance of the treaty that dealt with seeking the foreign fugitive. One little technical error, one small typographical mistake, and a bureaucrat overseas would often reject the request. Some of the major countries with repetitive requests, such as Canada and England, were easier. The language and legal traditions were similar to those in the U.S., and the officers were familiar with the treaty provisions.

Problems more frequently arose when dealing with a different language and when the foreign country had a different legal system, such as countries which had developed under Spanish colonial authority. Countries with a strained diplomatic relationship created especially complex difficulties.

When an individual, indicted for a crime in the U.S., fled to a foreign country, OIA prepared the elaborate documentary requirements petitioning the foreign government to turn the individual over to the U.S. authorities for trial. Usually, this occurred with little fanfare or controversy. Sometimes, however, the matter became ticklish.

For example, the foreign government may not have a treaty with the U.S. setting out the protocol, usually because the foreign government was not on friendly terms.

Sometimes, violating a law in the U.S. was not considered breaking a law in the foreign country. For example, evading taxes in the U.S. was a criminal act, but tax evasion under Swiss law was not criminal, but merely a civil violation. Thus, the Swiss refused to honor extradition requests for tax violators.

Often, a foreign country wanted its citizens returned who had fallen out of political favor, not because of any crime in the normal sense, but due to public criticism of the political situation there. In instances when the U.S. refused, the foreign government often used the denial to resist cooperating in returning criminal suspects that the U.S. sought.

If controversy and publicity surrounded the targeted individual, some governments took advantage of the situation to try extracting unrelated benefits from the U.S.

Then there was always the possibility that Uncle Sam's target was politically active or a friend of the foreign country's president or other prominent people. Toth's office always had to consider these and other potential pitfalls when presenting a request for extradition.

This request to extract Cruz Cruz from Cuba, seen as routine by one of Toth's underlings, had already gone forward three weeks earlier when, according to the file, it ran into an unexpected hurdle.

Immersed in the file, Toth suddenly noted how quiet it had become. He looked up and realized that he was alone on the floor and glanced at the clock. The time had flown by without notice. It was already nearly six, and he would be late with dinner. "That Andersson brat is still harassing me," he growled, as he rushed out of his office.

# CHAPTER 31

## *Caught*

*The best laid plans of mice and men often go awry.*
JOHN STEINBECK, *OF MICE AND MEN*

**NOVEMBER 1953**

The thief stared at the enormous red ruby. He had seen it before, of course, every time he had ventured into this room – every time he had picked out a piece of jewelry to steal. At first, he was mildly curious about the value of such a large gem, but he was too careful to take it. "No, she'd miss that one," he muttered the first night.

He stuck to his plan to move slowly and steadily, selling no more than a few small pieces for necessary funding. When he accumulated a fortune, and only then, he would dispose of everything for cash – tax free cash. The last thing he wanted was for Sally to realize that she had lost so many pieces of jewelry. Losing the ruby would probably cause her to take a thorough inventory.

As usual, he had entered the house through the unique window in the back. From appearances, both inside and out, the window looked like those elsewhere in the house – much too small for an adult to climb through. However, this window was one of the emergency escape areas that had been built into the house as a safety measure more than a hundred years before, and the thief was well aware of it.

A mechanism expanded an opening in the wall to double the size of the small window opening. During the attack on the house two years earlier, Cruz Cruz had exited the house by squeezing through the expanded window opening when he left to stalk Carty in Morose Swamp.

The thief's resolve to resist the ruby weakened on each visit to the jewelry drawer. Maybe it was the large size of the gem; maybe it was the rich red color; maybe it was the haunting six-pointed star embedded within. Whatever the attraction, he was increasingly tempted to take the ruby every time he saw it, despite the risk.

He lifted a gold necklace from the drawer. The bright metal offset the subdued green of the delicately carved jade animal figure charms that marched in single file as if in a parade.

He picked up the Ryland Ruby for the first time. He had never before even touched it, as if by doing so he might have been tempted to add it to his collection. It did, in fact, act like a magnet. He did not want to take it, but each time he reached to set it down, he hesitated and clung to it. It was a cold stone, but in his mind, it felt warm – even hot – to his touch.

In the midst of his indecision, he heard the unmistakable sound of the antique Pierce Arrow engine approaching the house. Panic gripped him. He was not expecting them back so soon. They left barely twenty minutes earlier. That had never happened before.

Quickly, without thinking, he slipped the ruby into one pocket and the jade necklace into the other and raced out of the bedroom, past the large fireplace in the great room, and into the back utility room where he reached for the window. He expanded the opening and climbed out, closing it from the outside when he left. He turned to his right and ran for the path through the forest.

A man caught a glimpse of the thief climbing from the window and running from the back of the house – the same man who had witnessed someone running from the house once before. This time the thief was closer, so he followed the suspicious man. The trailing man did not know that the other was a thief, but that was a good guess.

The curious man sprinted on to the narrow path through the woods. Though he was not in the condition of his youth, he steadily gained on the slower thief without giving himself away. After about a quarter of a mile, he saw the thief stop about a hundred yards ahead, so he slowed and took cover to avoid being spotted.

*IN* the meantime, James stopped the Pierce Arrow in front of the house and opened the passenger door for Sally. "I'm sorry, James," she said. "This is the first time I've been sick since I became pregnant again. I hope you are not disappointed at missing the opening night of the movie and the party afterward."

"Not at all, Sally. Besides, seeing 'How to Marry a Millionaire' seems redundant since I already married one. Can I get you anything once we get you settled?"

"Oh, maybe some tea, James. I feel tired and just want to change into something comfortable and rest."

Sally went into the bedroom and reclined on their bed while James went to the kitchen to brew the tea. Her eyelids drooped closed, and she nearly fell asleep. "No," she told herself, "If I fall asleep dressed, I'll sleep all night and wrinkle my dress."

She forced herself up and went into the bathroom to change into her favorite gold silk pajamas which boosted her spirits. Then she took her earrings to her jewelry drawer. As she reached out, her hand stopped short. The Ryland Ruby was not on the black velvet where she had put it earlier in the evening. Normally, she kept it inside the drawer, but she had been running late for the movie premier and left it on the dresser.

Sally stared at the velvet where the small depression was still evident. She checked the floor to see if it had rolled off; it was more oval than round, but it could roll. That failing, she opened the drawer to be certain that she had not put the ruby back inside.

"It's not in the drawer, not that I thought it would be. I know that I placed it on the velvet before we left. I have to face facts. It has been stolen."

Though Sally had been trying to tell herself that she was getting forgetful, she had begun to suspect that someone was stealing from her for the past few weeks. Since Easter and Castillo were the only people with access to the house, they were prime suspects.

Sally truly did not want to believe that they were thieves. They were devoted to each other and seemed dedicated to both her family and Lilly Andersson. She looked forward to even more help from them when the next baby was born.

She dreaded telling James about the thefts. Unfortunately, with the missing ruby, there was no question that someone was stealing from her. She did not return to bed as the adrenalin from the discovery had banished her illness.

She put on a matching robe and padded into the kitchen as James was pouring the tea into cups. "You can lie down, Sally. I'll bring it in."

"No, I feel better already. We can drink it here."

They sat at the small table for two. James watched her absently stir six spoonfuls of honey into the cup before adding lemon.

She grimaced at her first sip. "Ugh, that is way too sweet. What kind of honey do we have?"

"It is your honey from your bees in your beehive, dearest, the same honey we always use. When you mix in six spoonfuls instead of your usual one, that is what happens. Are you worried about the baby?"

"Hmm? Oh, no, James. Our baby will be fine. I just have a lot to think about, and I am a little distracted."

"A little? Would you like to tell me what the problem is?"

"I need to sort things out first. How about dumping this out and pouring a new cup for me?"


THE trailing man stopped and hid himself behind a wide-trunked oak. He watched from afar as the thief knelt on the edge of the meadow and dug into the sandy earth. In a short time, the thief lifted a metal box and opened it.

Already the thief had decided that it was time to close down his operation. He had taken more than enough, and the loss of the large ruby was certain to be noticed. He was off to Miami tomorrow to begin selling the loot.

He thought about cutting it into smaller parts, but he had researched enough to know he might smash it into worthless bits if it were not done right. He had no interest in keeping it as a souvenir. The ruby would be incriminating evidence if he were ever suspected. He was after the big money, not keepsakes.

He reached into his pocket, retrieved the jade necklace, and dropped it into the box. Then he took the ruby from his other pocket and held it up so that he could examine it sparkling in the setting sun.

The sun had glistened off of something metallic on the item that the thief put into the box, but the hidden man was too far away to identify it. When the thief held the ruby up to the light, however, its size and color were easily identifiable as a gem despite the distance between the men.

"I'll take a hammer and chisel to it," he decided. "If it breaks into smithereens, I'll toss the bits into the lake. If I'm lucky, I'll salvage something from it."

As the thief put the ruby into the box, the man moved from behind the tree and sprinted forward, startling the thief into quick reactions. He turned the key to lock the metal box and tucked it under his arm like a football. Then he began running toward Hostetter Cutoff.

Though the thief was not nearly as fast as the man and was burdened with the heavy box, he had a large lead. After he crossed the cutoff, he threw the box into the back seat of his car, jumped in, and turned the key, nearly flooding the engine in his haste.

He pulled away from the parking spot as the man left the woods and turned on to the cutoff. Even at restricted speed, the car bounced violently on the rutted dirt road as he coaxed the vehicle forward, but the runner was actually gaining by foot.

**CLEM** Hostetter peered out of the window of the farmhouse in bewilderment. He had never seen anyone try to chase a car on foot.

These were odd times, Clem thought, and anxious times as well. With a limited money supply and facing months before his new trial, Clem felt that he had been forced into action, distasteful as that was.

As Clem looked away from the window and buttoned his "Homer's Grocery" shirt, he thought about how unpleasant it had been to apply for a job soon after he had arrived back in Winter Free.

When Homer agreed to take him on as a stock boy – "only because of your mother, as fine a woman as any I've ever met" – Clem did not know whether to be relieved or to cry. "A job," Clem thought. "What is my world coming to?"

Clem hated the work, but he forced himself to do it. He hated starving even more.

**ON** the rutted cutoff, a few hundred feet short of Mocking Bird Road, the careening car bottomed out in a deep hole and lost its muffler and tailpipe.

The resulting racket from the un-muffled motor was deafening as the car slid on to the paved surface with the man running a mere twenty feet behind but beginning to slow as he tired. The runner gradually receded in the rearview mirror as the thief accelerated away at sixty-five mph.

An armadillo appeared in the road ahead. Laughing with relief at his narrow escape and at the armadillo in the road, the thief aimed his front right tire at the animal and added speed. The armadillo tucked into a ball instead of jumping up, a reaction different from the norm. Of course, this rare armadillo was different from the norm in other ways as well.

The tire hit the hard shell of the armadillo, but instead of crushing this animal, the car bounded up and sideways as if hitting a large boulder at high speed. For a moment, the thief seemed to gain control. Then the back tire impacted the hard-shelled armadillo, and that proved sufficient to send the car pin-wheeling end over end along the asphalt and into the drainage ditch paralleling the road.

It came to rest upright against a telephone pole. Smoke drifted from somewhere in the engine. A detached door twirled in the middle of the road. The horn blared from under the partially open hood. The back of the roof was crushed, and not a window remained. Odor from spilled gasoline permeated the atmosphere.

The armadillo uncurled, thankful for the rare extra-hard shell of his family. He shook himself gingerly, satisfied that he had survived unscathed. He looked at the wreckage of glass, steel, and chrome in the distance, shrugged, and ambled, unharmed, across the road and into the reeds.

The runner had stopped chasing, but when he saw the vehicle go airborne, he got a second wind and resumed a fast pace. Upon reaching the wreck, he slid the still-rocking door into the reeds to clear the hazard from the road. Then he yanked the cables from the battery to silence the deafening horn.

He looked inside the car. The thief was curled under the steering column, bleeding from his face and scalp. Fortunately, he looked worse off than he was.

The runner saw that the thief was young, a teenager, but as large as a full-grown adult. "Are you in bad shape? Can you talk?"

The thief moaned an answer that was reasonably articulate. "I hurt all over, but I don't think I broke any bones."

"Okay, I'm going to try to get you out from under there. There is gas everywhere that could ignite, so we don't want to leave you where you are."

The last comment spurred the teenager into action. He struggled to unwrap himself from under the dashboard, and with the man's help, emerged from the cavity. He sat dazed on the seat with his hands on the non-functioning steering wheel.

"Stay there and rest for a moment. If a fire breaks out, we can get you away quickly. Right now it looks safe."

The man walked to the window of a Thirties-era Marmon that pulled to a stop next to the wreck. He said to the elderly couple inside, "The boy, he seems to be all right, but we need the sheriff and an ambulance. Can you call from the new Texaco station about a mile up the road?"

The couple drove off on their assigned task, and the man returned to the wreck.

"You are the Dolder boy," he said. "I remember you from the night of Mrs. Elsmore's reading. You ate some of my wife's extra hot chili."

"And you were working in the kitchen that night, right?" The bump on Dolder's head did not appear to have damaged his memory.

"*Sí*, I am Castillo Zapata."

"I'll be in real trouble when my dad finds out that I wrecked one of the best used cars on his lot. This '50 Bel Air is a classic. It's Chevy's first Bel Air."

"*Señor*, the car is the least of your worries." Retrieving the strongbox of jewels from the floor of the back seat, Castillo continued, "You are facing many years in prison for grand theft and burglary. How much do you have in this strongbox besides the large ruby?"

"It's loaded with gems, gold, and silver. I've been at this for months. This was my last day, and I would have made it if that stupid armadillo hadn't attacked my car."

"How did you get into the house? The sheriff always locks it when they leave."

"When I heard about the shindig for the Boy Scouts at the Canfield Mansion, it gave me an idea. I figured that if I accompanied my brother, I might have an opportunity to search for the escape window mentioned in some of *The Gazette's* articles about the attack three years ago. I hoped to leave it unlocked so I could get into the house at will. It seemed that it would not occur to anyone to lock it later. No one ever had a reason to use it, so they probably wouldn't think to check the lock either.

"The hard part would be getting free rein to wander the house the night of the party, and when the sheriff stated that the indoor restrooms were reserved for ladies only, I was worried. Looking around the house for a restroom was my hole card, but it wouldn't work if I had to use the outhouse in the backyard.

"Fortunately, that dumb Carty solved the problem for me. When I was in line, I goaded her into adding extra hot chili powder to my serving. She thought she was putting one over on me. Ha, she did not account for the cast iron Dolder stomach. I pretended to struggle eating the chili. That gave me the excuse to make several 'emergency runs' for the indoor toilets, when actually I was searching for the escape window.

"I wasn't crazy about going into the witch's house alone later, but I decided that if I entered only when she was gone, I had nothing to worry about.

"Everybody knows she has lots of jewels, because she is always wearing something different and elaborate. *The Gazette* often describes them in sophisticated detail whenever she attends a fancy event. I guessed that she would keep them in the bedroom and knew I'd have easy pickings if I got into the house. It was even easier than I expected; she often left her jewelry in plain sight on her dresser. You'd think a sheriff's wife would be more security conscious.

"Early on, I discovered that you and your wife sometimes worked in the house, though, so I always made sure your truck was not parked nearby before I climbed through the window. If I saw it, I left for a better day. If there is one thing that I am, it is patient.

"Hey, come to think about it, where was your truck today? I didn't see it."

"*Mi esposa* dropped me off this morning. I've been repairing fence on and off for a while. She had to go back to work on the Andersson estate. I had just finished working the fence when I saw you running from the house.

"I'm curious, *Señor*, how do you know what days the house would be empty? Surely you do not hide in your car day after day hoping for the sheriff and Mrs. Elsmore to leave."

"No. That wouldn't make sense. *The Gazette* publishes the schedule of every big social and civic event in town. It's pretty easy to figure out which ones the sheriff and the witch will be attending. In fact, the paper often made it easy for me by printing the guest list.

"I hid out only on days when she and the sheriff were likely to be leaving. It didn't always work, but it did almost every time. The only exceptions were when you and your wife were around. And there was a lull when the baby was born, because she didn't leave the house for a couple of weeks."

For a brief moment, Dolder's diabolical mind reverted to form. Then he brazenly challenged, "You better take off now, Zapata. When the sheriff arrives, I'll say that I saw you running from the house carrying that box. When I gave chase, I lost control of the car and crashed.

"You can hide the box and deny everything, or you can hand over the box with your fingerprints all over it. Mine can be explained because I tried to wrest it away from you. Either way, you lose. Who is the sheriff going to believe, the son of the most prominent businessman in Winter Free or a Mexican who has access to his house?"

"*Señor*," Castillo replied calmly, "He will believe this Mexican. True, my fingerprints are on the box now, but they are not on the jewelry inside of the box. The fingerprints on the jewels inside are those of the son of the prominent Winter Free businessman, not those of the Mexican."

"Oh. Right. I knew that," Dolder replied sheepishly. "I have a better idea, anyway. Why don't we keep this to ourselves and split everything, fifty-fifty?"

"*Señor*, your head – it has been banged around, and you are not thinking clearly. That is the only reason why I am going to be so generous. There is one way out for you. *Mi esposa* and I have a key to the Canfield Mansion to enable us to get inside to clean, even if no one is home. I can return Mrs. Elsmore's jewelry without her knowing it. When the deputy arrives, you can pretend that you were on a pleasant country drive and lost control. I'll forget I ever saw you."

"Why would you do that? How do I know that you are not planning to keep all the loot for yourself?"

"You don't, but it really doesn't matter, does it? Unless you forget you were ever involved in the thefts, you are going to prison. I'm giving you your only chance. I don't know why. You haven't been very friendly."

But he did know why. Easter had given him a second chance, a chance that he did not deserve either. During his recovery, and indeed even as he first settled on to Lilly's property, he would have taken any opportunity to return to the Canfield Mansion for a second try at a part of her treasure.

But gradually, Easter had improved his outlook with kindness and love. Moreover, Lilly, Sally, and James had treated the couple with a respect and fondness that he had never experienced before. His life with Easter, working for the two families, proved more satisfying than any pleasure he could get from cashing in on stolen goods.

"However, you're a kid, and I've always liked kids. I'd hate for you to end up in prison for most of the rest of your life because of one big mistake. Everybody deserves a second chance."

It was a charitable and well-intentioned gesture, but with Dolder, it would prove over the years to have been misplaced.

"Learn from this, *Señor*. Give up this kind of life and don't try anything like it again."

They heard a siren in the distance.

Dolder thought it over, and he couldn't figure a better alternative. He was clearly running out of time.

"Okay. You win. Take the box. I never saw you. You never saw me."

"Here comes help, *Señor*. I'll be going now so they do not see the box and wonder what is inside. *Adios*."

With the box under an arm, Castillo turned and jogged back to Hostetter Cutoff.

**WHEN** Castillo reached the Canfield Mansion, he slipped the box under a rhododendron bush and knocked on the door. James answered.

"*Buenos días, Señor*. I have finished repairing the fence. Easter has not yet returned to pick me up, so I thought this might be a good time to repair the wobbly table leg."

"Of course, Castillo, come in. Actually, it is good that you came. Sally is in the kitchen. She isn't feeling well, and I did not want to leave her alone. However, dispatch just called about a bad accident on Mocking Bird Road. There is a car on the way, but I really should take a look since I am so close. Do you mind keeping her company? I can run you over to Lilly's later when I pick up Jimmy Jr."

"*No problemo, Señor*. I can work on the table and keep an eye on her at the same time."

"I already called Lilly to let her know we were back early, but she told me to take my time about picking up Jimmy. She and Easter are having too much fun with him."

James said his goodbyes to Sally while Castillo went to the tool shed to gather carpentry tools. When he returned, Sally was in her bedroom, so he went outside and retrieved the box of her jewels. He concealed it under the large table in the great room so that he could sneak the gems into her room when he had the chance.

Making certain that Sally's door was still closed tightly, he slipped into the back room to lock the window mechanism. When he finished and turned to leave, he jumped backwards, startled to see Sally staring at him from the doorway.

"May I ask what you are doing, Castillo?" she asked, in the way a mother asks a child about his hand in the cookie jar.

"I have locked this mechanism, Sra. Elsmore."

"And why would you have such an interest in the window, Castillo?"

He had hoped to secure the window and dump the jewelry back into her drawer without her knowledge. She surely would have noticed the abundance of jewelry re-emerging, but she would eventually forget her confusion, especially since everything would have been returned. That plan was no longer going to work.

He decided that the truth would be better than any story he could conjure up on a moment's notice.

"You have been the victim of a series of thefts, *Señora*. The thief has been entering the house from the window that has been unlocked for some time and has been taking jewelry from your bedroom. I discovered this today, and I have locked the window to prevent another try."

"Rather like closing the barn door after the cow has escaped, wouldn't you say, Castillo?"

"Oh, no, *Señora*, much better than that – for I recovered your jewelry as well." Walking toward her and gesturing with his hand, he asked, "Would you care to see?"

Sally gave way and allowed him to lead her into the great room where he pulled out a chair.

"*Por favor, Señora*, have a seat here."

He reached under the table for the box and set it on the table in front of her. "I am not certain, but I believe that all of your missing jewels are inside. I know for certain that your large ruby is in there, because that one I saw the thief put in."

"And who is this mysterious thief?" Sally asked, again with a skeptical tone of voice.

Castillo realized that this explanation was not going well. It was clear that she believed that he was the thief, so he decided to explain more fully but in a way to keep Dolder out of it.

"I understand that it looks like I am the thief, or perhaps that you even suspect that I am covering for Easter. Neither is true. I did discover who the thief is, and I made a deal with him to keep his identity secret – to give him a second chance, in return for what he stole.

"I brought your jewelry back to the house this evening with the intention of returning it to the drawer. None of my fingerprints are on what is inside this box, but the thief's will be on all of them.

"You could tell Sr. Elsmore about this. He knows how to verify what I have said about the fingerprints, but he will put pressure on me to point out the thief, which I will not do. And that would make for unpleasantness and serve no useful purpose, so I ask you to accept the return of your jewelry and allow me to keep the secret."

She thought about that for a short time and nodded her head in acceptance. After all, Castillo did not need to use that window for access. He had a key to the house. Then she asked, "And the reason, Carey, that you wish to give the thief a second chance is that you have been given a second chance yourself?"

"That is not..." He paused and sighed, only then having recognized that she had called him by his previous name, Carey, as in Carey Zeller – and in responding, he had inadvertently acknowledged it to be true.

Resigned, he asked, "How long have you known, Mrs. Elsmore?" He dropped the Spanish accent he used as Castillo and spoke as Carey Zeller.

"For a while, a short time after I saw your reaction when Easter told you that she had walked through the swamp. Your aggressive scolding was so out of character from anything I had seen before that it set me to thinking. Since then I have observed you closely, trying to figure out why you suddenly were giving me an uneasy feeling that I didn't have before. Eventually, I connected your fear of the swamp to that day when you helped to take over my house and Montooth chased you into the pit.

"You look and act quite differently now than that day, but you should remember that I spent nearly thirty years of my own life looking and acting like a different person too. Tell me, how did you escape Montooth?"

He recounted what he could remember and what he surmised. By the time that he had finished his story, he was exhausted, and his shirt was soaked with perspiration. Sally was touched by his description of Easter's ministrations in the little hut in Clewiston.

"So why did you risk coming back to Winter Free?" Sally asked when he finished.

"To steal your treasure, of course – at least some part of it. I figured that if I hung around long enough and gauged the situation carefully, I'd eventually get an opportunity."

Tapping the box lightly with a finger, Sally said, "This seems to have been that opportunity. What happened?"

"Actually, I gave up on the idea some time ago. You, the sheriff, and Miss Andersson took us in with such compassion that I found myself content for the first time since I was a very young child. What could a treasure do for me that I did not already have with Easter?"

"Can you open this box for me?" Sally asked, abruptly changing the subject.

"Of course. I forgot to ask for the key, but I should be able to open it with a bobby pin."

Sally removed one from her hair and handed it to him. It took nearly two minutes, but he worked the simple lock and eventually got it open.

Sally took out the Ryland Ruby, rolled it in her fingers, and placed it on the table. Then she looked at the pile of jewelry remaining in the box and shook her head as she moved the items about. She had forgotten several of the pieces. She placed the box under an arm, picked up the ruby in her other hand, and headed for her bedroom without speaking.

As she walked away, he called to her, "Now what will I do?"

"Why, Castillo," she replied, turning to make eye contact, "Now you will fix that wobbly table. I am rather fond of second chances myself."

# CHAPTER 32

## *The Embassy*

*We do not act rightly because we have virtue or excellence, but we rather have those because we have acted rightly.*

ARISTOTLE

**JANUARY 1954**

The fourth day of January, the Burmese Independence Day, was frigid in Washington DC. The Burmese ambassador to the United States, His Excellency James Barrington, concluded his welcoming remarks. Then he introduced the guests of honor at the dinner: Edward Canfield Ryland, retired curator of the Mediterranean section, Smithsonian Institution; Sally Canfield Elsmore of Winter Free, Florida; and her husband, Sheriff James Elsmore.

Sally took her place at the podium with James and Ryland flanking her.

Stylish in a glimmering black satin sheath with one shoulder bare, she wore a dazzling necklace of alternating diamonds and rubies in four rows that dipped deeply to the top edge of her low neckline. She was there to speak, but she risked diverting the attention of the men in the audience with her elegance. *The Washington Post*'s photographer worked his camera overtime during her talk.

After thanking and acknowledging prominent officials including Ambassador Barrington, U.S. Secretary of State John Foster Dulles, and Secretary of the Smithsonian Institution Leonard Carmichael, Sally explained what had brought them together.

## JANUARY 1953

*"GOOD* news, Sally," James had said as he walked into the house a year prior to the embassy visit. "My friend on the DC police force found a relative of yours living in Alexandria, Virginia. His name is Edward Ryland."

"Gosh, that was quick, James. You have only been on the case for a week. What do you know about him?"

"Well, that is the bad news and also why we were able to learn about him so quickly. It turns out that he has a police blotter a foot long all through the DC area, including Maryland and northern Virginia. Drunk, disorderly, vandalism, petty theft, and shoplifting. It is mere chance that this is one of the few times in years that he is not behind bars."

Sally eyed him icily and challenged, "You had me going with drunk and disorderly, but no relative of mine would waste his time with vandalism or lack the ambition to resort to petty theft and shoplifting. It would have to be big time, or he wouldn't be bothered."

Chuckling, James said, "You know me too well, Sally. I made that up. Actually, he is a prominent enough citizen that my friend didn't have much searching to do. He started with a phone call to the Smithsonian, and that is as far as he had to go."

"It turns out that Edward was the curator of their Mediterranean section for a number of years and still leads expeditions into that part of the world. Apparently, he was too restless behind the desk, so he retired and freelances for them."

"That's better. I can believe that. Did your friend speak with him? Does Edward know about me?"

"No on both questions, but I have the address and phone number here so you can initiate contact." He handed her a piece of paper.

She stared at the number and asked hesitantly, "Do you think that it's too late to call tonight?"

"Too late? It is six o'clock. It's not like you to be so bashful. You're the one who wanted to know."

"You're right, as usual."

Picking up the phone, she dialed the operator. "Bertha, I need you to connect me to a number in Virginia." That call led to the most expensive long distance phone bill yet for the Canfield household.

Edward was 61, a widower for the last twenty years. He had one son of 24 years who was studying archeology in England. When Edward told Sally that two daughters had died during childbirth, her heart missed a beat as she thought about Jimmy Jr.

Edward had followed his grandfather's and father's footsteps into the Smithsonian and hoped that his son, Reggie, would do likewise in a few years.

His grandmother Lis had died in the late Eighteen Nineties, and he had fond but distant memories of her. He had heard the story of the Ryland Ruby from his grandfather and that there had been some Canfield relatives in pre-Civil War Florida. However, he had never sought them out and did not know that any still existed until Sally's call.

He was leading an expedition to Malta in a few weeks that would take him through Atlanta, so they arranged that he would divert to Winter Free on his return for a visit. It was during his time at the Canfield estate that Sally discussed her idea with him that led to the ceremony at the Burmese Embassy in northwest Washington, DC.

## JANUARY 1954

*SALLY* continued speaking at the embassy dinner. "Over one hundred years ago, in 1852, Edward's grandfather, Ronald Ryland, and grandmother, Elisabeth Canfield, a relative of mine, raced into northeast Burma at the behest of Burma's George Washington, Mindon Min. He had sent Ronald on a quest to acquire a fortune in rubies from one of King Solomon's long lost mines. The gems would become the basis of Mindon Min's treasury when he assumed power a few years later.

"The trip resulted in a competition Ronald won against Mindon Min's brother, Pagan Min, who sought the rubies to fund a futile war against the British. As compensation for Ronald's effort, Mindon Min awarded him the largest ruby known to the world at the time, a near perfect stone whose beauty rivaled any gem of any size or color. Mindon Min called it the Ryland Ruby.

"Because of political difficulties with the British colonial administration, Ronald and his new wife, Lis, left Rangoon and departed for America where they sought haven with my ancestors at the Canfield Estate in Florida. They stayed for about two years. Eventually, they departed for Washington where Ronald held a number of positions at the Smithsonian.

"In gratitude for the hospitality the Rylands received from the Canfields, Ronald generously gave them the Ryland Ruby which has been in the family since that time. We have gathered here this evening because I have decided that the Ryland Ruby would be better served being returned to its homeland of Burma.

"For over one hundred years, the gem has been seen only by a few people. Its beauty should be seen by many more. Therefore, I am pleased to announce that the gem will be returning to Burma, but that the Burmese Government has consented to allow it to be placed on display at the Smithsonian for nine months beginning tomorrow."

At that point, James opened an ornate box that he was holding. Sally reached into it and removed the Ryland Ruby resting on a black felt cushion. She handed it to the ambassador to generous applause as camera bulbs flashed like lightning against the shining red stone.

Just before seating for dinner, late arriving Reginald Ryland made the rounds, meeting everyone, including Sally, a relative he did not know he had until recently. He was slightly over six feet tall with sparkling blue eyes and dark wavy hair. The scars on his forehead and squared-off chin suggested an athletic background.

"Sorry," he breathed laboriously, shaking hands, "The snow slowed down our flight from London. We made it to Halifax all right, but we were stalled there for three hours. We weren't able to take off because of the heavy flurries, and I was worried that I would miss the entire ceremony. Fortunately, Mother Nature relented."

When he was introduced to Sally, she remarked how much he resembled paintings of the Canfield patriarch, Morgan.

"And you, my lady," he responded. "You resemble no one, for no one could equal your beauty."

Sally could only laugh. Reggie was showing all the charm that Morgan was reputed to have had.

# CHAPTER 33

## *Stalled*

*Revenge is sweeter than life itself. So think fools.*

JUVENAL

**JANUARY 1954**

"Hello, Dear," James called out as he came through the doorway, disappointed that his little son did not rush up to cling to his leg in greeting. Waving a hello to Michael and Bay Andersson who had arrived moments earlier, he asked, "Where is my little guy?"

"Easter put Jimmy Jr. to bed early. We were at Lilly's most of the day, and he never gets his nap over there. She keeps him too busy. He told her all about staying in the Hay-Adams Hotel when we were in Washington. He loved having room service. Only today he asked why Easter and I

483

don't cover his meals with a large silver dome.

"He definitely needs some siblings so he learns that everyone was not put on earth to serve him, the little dickens."

"Ha! You are the worst at letting him think that, Sally."

"Well, yes, that's true," she admitted. "He makes me laugh. That is why we need more children. I'll be so busy with the younger ones that I won't be able to spoil Jimmy Jr."

"Okay, okay," he chuckled. "You don't see me failing to do my part."

Turning to their guests, he shook Michael's hand and gave Bay a gentle embrace.

"I see that Easter has taken care of your drink needs. I'm sorry to be late. I was signing the final papers to get back my old Hostetter property. Clem's attorney was tenacious. Despite Judge Rock's conscientious attention to the case, Corbane managed to drag out for a year what should have been over in a few months. Oh well, all's well that ends up with the bad guys behind bars.

"Give me a few moments to change into something civilian."

As he left, Sally remarked, "I'm sorry that we couldn't keep Jimmy Jr. up a little longer, but he was dead on his feet. Lilly is amazing with him. Sometimes he speaks very well, but other times the sounds are gibberish to me. It doesn't matter to Lilly; she seems to have no problem understanding anything he says. She is a great substitute grandma."

James returned a few minutes later, looking rugged in black slacks and a red plaid shirt.

"Civvies or not, you still look 'law enforcement,'" Bay said. "I'm glad that I'm on the right side of the law.

"Carty wanted me to ask if there is any news on the Cuban front. It has been almost six months since Novotny's man found out that 'Mr. Smith' is named Cruz Cruz."

"The photos of the real Cruz show an entirely different man than the one whom I met at Rex Seafood in Tampa. Apparently, the guy we interviewed had a fake passport in the Cruz Cruz name. It's too bad that Andy Gilbert is not around to tell us how that happened."

"Do you think that Cruz had anything to do with Gilbert's death?"

Cruz had regarded Andy Gilbert as another of the "loose ends" that needed snipping, and killed Gilbert in the spectacular gas station fire. Gilbert was involved in hiding Cruz's identity from Florida law enforcement, but Cruz feared Gilbert might turn to blackmail.

"It does not add up unless Gilbert was threatening blackmail. Why go to all the trouble to sell the fish business to Gilbert and then bump him off? Once we put Cruz away for the attack on Sally and The Crew, I'll see if I can put together another case for Gilbert's death.

"In any event, the extradition is still bogged down in red tape, and it hasn't moved past the first step. It's usually a simple process to make the request and receive approval from the foreign government following an indictment. The suspect often uses an attorney to delay the process for a year or more, depending on the country involved. Eventually, there's a hearing, and the foreign court orders the suspect to be held for a U.S. Marshal to escort back for trial.

"Everything was moving along smoothly on this case, and then it hit a wall. After Sally and the kids identified Cruz from photos and an undercover movie that our embassy shot, he was indicted in Tampa. The

Justice Department promptly filled out the legal papers and sent them to the State Department, which acted expeditiously.

"The court in Cuba received the papers and was one day from serving them on Cruz when the process stopped. No one at State can get a straight answer. First we heard that a key signature was missing; then weeks later they said it wasn't the signature, but that an entire page was missing. So State got Justice to reissue and sign the missing page. All that took nearly three months.

"Then the Cuban court objected to the Tampa indictment being based on identification solely from photos and a movie. We had to get affidavits from everyone who saw him that day – another two months.

"Cruz should have been served by a legal processor long ago, but this is dragging on interminably, and we cannot get a straight answer from anyone."

*IN* fact, the legal attaché in Havana had delivered the extradition request to his legal counterpart in the Cuban Government, Xavier Romeo, many months earlier. As was customary, Romeo first verified that the name Cruz Cruz was not that of any prominent Government official or the name of any executive of an important commercial or religious organization.

Actually, Cruz was almost his own worst enemy in this regard. He intentionally kept a low profile with Batista so that he could stay out of the public eye. However, so low had he kept his involvement that very few people, least of all a low-level Government attorney by the name of Xavier Romeo, knew about his key advisory relationship.

Thus, Romeo saw no reason to avoid sending the American request to the national police force to serve Cruz with an arrest warrant. Fortunately for Cruz, Romeo turned over the request to a police official, Col. Antonio Lara, who had done many favors for Cruz over the years for which he was generously paid. When the extradition request hit his desk, he immediately called Cruz to explain what he had received.

"Sit on it for one day – you can do that, I'm sure, Colonel. You have something more important to occupy your time, I am certain. You might visit your favorite restaurant on Avenida Tegucigalpa, for example, where you might meet my man, Elazar, whom you have met previously. Elazar might have a valuable envelope with your name on it."

"You are quite correct about that, Sr. Cruz. This document, it appears, arrived in my office very late today. There is no way that I can handle the extradition request until late tomorrow at the earliest, but it would be good if the problem found a solution before that occurred. In the meantime, I probably should go out to eat tonight."

"An excellent idea, Colonel. However, Elazar cannot get to the restaurant for several hours. Perhaps a late dinner would be beneficial."

Cruz hung up and called Elazar into his office. Within minutes, Elazar was on his way to Restaurante Bolívar on Avenida Tegucigalpa, carrying an envelope thick with untraceable cash.

Then Cruz telephoned Batista, who answered in good spirits. "Cruz, hello. My secretary tells me you have an issue that cannot wait. What can I do for you?"

"I have just learned that the American Government has issued an extradition request for me to be taken to Florida. The national police are scheduled to process a warrant and arrest me tomorrow. It's all some crazy mistake, of course, but who knows what enemy or rival in Florida is pursuing some vendetta with bogus evidence? I would not want to rely on the trumped up charges being tossed out. It would be better to avoid it altogether.

"Fulgencio, is there anything that you can do until I can sort this out?"

"Of course, my friend. I agree that it must be an error. I will take care of it. Do not worry."

The next day, Col. Lara called Cruz a second time.

"Colonel, how was dinner last night?"

"Perfect, as usual, and I enjoyed Elazar's company. He has excellent taste in wines."

"Was the arrangement satisfactory as well?"

"Of course, Sr. Cruz. You may also be interested in knowing that I was asked to return your extradition file to a judicial magistrate for review, instead of serving you with the papers. Apparently, there is belief in some quarters – important quarters – that there are serious procedural errors in the documents and that the underlying criminal indictment is flawed as well.

"In any event, the matter is no longer in my hands, and I suspect that it will be some length of time before the confusion can be resolved."

"Thank you, Colonel, for your call. It is a bit of a relief to know that the judicial system is on the alert against overly ambitious foreign prosecutors."

*TOTH* looked over the recent additions to the Cruz file, which had grown to triple the size from when Toth first learned about the case. Since then, progress on the case bogged down – or, more correctly, backed up.

Initially, Toth was irritated that the case was requiring so much time from his department, and he was miffed at the Cubans for slowing the process. Eventually, however, he realized that Carty Andersson was more than a minor player. Additional information reached him about the prominent part that she played in literally tracking down this fellow, Cruz.

"Hmph. Wait until this comes out in the trial. She will be portrayed as a bigger hero than the first time. Moreover, the CIA will try to keep its role from becoming public, so they will pump up her role even more. Of all the people in that little burg of Winter Free that I don't want to see receiving adulation, it is Carty Andersson.

"What difference could it make if this Cruz Cruz is not brought back to trial anyway? He is in Cuba where he cannot cause anyone here in the U.S. any additional difficulty, and he is unlikely to come back on his own now that there is an indictment against him.

"I really don't see why this case should be a high priority. It's only real purpose would be to give that Andersson brat another undeserved pat on the back."

Toth read the latest dispatch from Havana. When a local judge learned that one of the attackers, Clemens Hostetter, was in a Florida prison, he wanted to know why the Florida authorities had not sought corroboration from Hostetter about Cruz's identity. Toth realized that the Florida prosecutor could quickly run photos to Hostetter to have them viewed. If that placated the Havana judge, the process might move along expeditiously – no longer a desirable result in Toth's view.

Toth looked long at that dispatch from his embassy counterpart.

He inhaled his Philip Morris cigarette strongly to brighten the end and placed it against the corner of the dispatch. The document smoldered for a few seconds and then flamed up. He held it with two fingers, twisting it from side to side to engulf as much of the paper as he could before the flame became too hot, forcing him to drop the remnant into the ashtray on his desk.

"That should slow up Andersson's bid for more fame and glory," he mumbled as he maneuvered the remaining flame with his pen. "It'll be months before anyone asks for a status report, and then we can start all over. It's amazing how documents get misplaced in vast Government files. This Cruz fellow has a guardian angel in high places that he does not know about."

Toth saw no reason why the Cruz case could not evolve into an unclosed file for decades.

THE END

# POSTSCRIPT

The closest that Rev. Canfield came to seeing his grandchildren was British Guiana[25] on the north coast of South America. He was excited about the posting at a church much closer to Elisabeth, Ronald, and his grandchildren. Unfortunately, he contracted malaria shortly after arriving and died before visiting the U.S.

After Pagan Min was deposed in Burma, Htay Maung survived by taking the name Maung Lin and changing his appearance. Later, he returned to King Solomon's mine where he discovered an amazing 400 carat ruby that a worker evidently hid before suffering the fate of his coworkers. Maung Lin used the abandoned equipment to cut the stone into three parts – rather clumsily – failing to achieve optimum results.

Nevertheless, he gave the smallest part to Mindon Min to reach an accommodation with his former rival, but secretly sold the middle-size stone in Calcutta. Eventually, Mindon Min learned of his perfidy and paid a large sum to retrieve the Calcutta stone for Burma. Unfortunately, the largest of the three parts has never been found.

In more modern times, Cash Corbane was unsuccessful in obtaining an acquittal for Clem Hostetter in the retrial. Evidence and testimony of too many credible witnesses doomed Hostetter from the start. Judge Lord's decision had been nothing more than a worthless and ill-advised expense for the state's taxpayers.

However, when Cruz realized that his extradition was held up in part by the failure of Florida authorities to seek Clem's identification, he realized that Clem could be more valuable alive than dead. Maldonado visited Clem to explain that a failure to identify Cruz from photos and film was a lifeline that Hostetter would be wise to grasp, and Clem responded positively. In a rare change, Cruz arranged for occasional "care packages" of cigarettes and candy for Clem instead of killing him.

Without the constant fear of being murdered, Clem resumed his role of an ideal inmate. Cash held out hope that Clem would be considered for an early parole.

Cruz and Batista continued to rub each others' backs. Cruz regularly visited Fidel in prison to keep up the young man's hopes and to maintain the mentoring relationship. Castro kept Cruz informed about underground efforts to overthrow Batista, and Cruz kept Batista informed of the opposition's intentions. Batista pledged to keep the Americans at bay, especially since the diplomatic pressure for extradition seemed to be waning.

Elisabeth Lilly Elsmore was born to Sally on July 31, giving the Elsmore children two July birthdays to celebrate.

Elena and Blake carried on an active correspondence over the summer holidays, and they committed to each other's proms in their senior year for the Classes of 1954.

The St. Louis Browns moved to Baltimore and became the Orioles. The Orioles offered Blake a contract after finishing at Winter Free High. After consulting with his father, Hale, Michael, and Coach Normand, Blake decided to accept a baseball scholarship to Purdue instead. The pros could wait.

Hale turned down a dual baseball and track scholarship offered by Purdue, opting instead for the slightly more encompassing State Department scholarship that Flagstead Toth obtained for him. Nevertheless, he intended to engage in both sports at Purdue without the sports scholarship.

Haywood Dolder showed no signs of having learned from the second chance that Castillo gave him. Nevertheless, when Toth came through with a scholarship usable at either the University of Maryland or Indiana University, Dolder decided to follow Toth's lead.

Reginald Ryland completed his studies in England and followed in his father's footsteps at the Smithsonian and in the U.S. Army Reserve. In winter months, both father and son frequently visited the Canfield Estate between assignments.

# ENDNOTES

*1)*  *Weissmuller, Johnny* – German-American swimmer and winner of six medals in the 1924 and 1928 Olympics; he was the most prolific of the actors in the Tarzan movies, appearing in a dozen between 1932 and 1948.

*2)*  *Crosley* – Automobile manufactured in Indiana by Crosley Motors from 1939 to 1952; the small, inexpensive vehicles were noted for their economic fuel mileage, though this was not prized in an era of inexpensive gasoline.

*3)*  *Keystone Combination* – The shortstop and second baseman together; considered the key defensive area on a baseball field because of its central location.

*4)*  *Boston Beaneaters* – Professional baseball team in the National League; later the Doves; eventually the Boston Braves (1912-52), including short stints as the Rustlers and Bees; moved to Milwaukee in 1953 and Atlanta in 1966.

*5)*  *2-way Wrist Radio* – Fictitious communication device used by Chester Gould's comic strip character, police detective Dick Tracy; it functioned much like a modern cell phone at a time when such communication devices were not considered feasible.

*6)*  *Kristallnacht* – A major escalation in Nazi Germany's attacks on its Jewish citizens; on a November night of 1938, roving bands of government-encouraged rioters destroyed and ransacked hundreds of Jewish businesses, synagogues, and homes; the glass-strewn streets from broken store windows provided the name "*Kristallnacht,*" or in English, Crystal Night.

7) ***Florida Cracker*** – Colonial settler in Florida after the Spanish ceded Florida to the British for a twenty-year run in the mid-Eighteenth Century; the term sometimes persists as a description of native, rural Floridians.

8) ***Kansas City Monarchs*** – Charter member and storied baseball franchise of the Negro National League.

9) ***Conrad, Joseph*** – Polish-born, British novelist; noted for effective use of English, his second language.

10) ***Lansky, Meyer*** – Kingpin of the organized crime syndicate that ran Cuba's casinos.

11) ***Boss Tweed*** –Nickname of William M. Tweed (1823-78); head of Tammany Hall, the New York City political organization that kept the Democrats in power through bribery, vote fraud and other corruption.

12) ***Pascual, Camilo*** – Major League pitcher (1954-71); born in Havana, Cuba; noted for an extraordinarily sharp breaking curve.

13) ***Gunsmoke*** – Radio (1952-61) and television (1955-75) Western; longest prime-time, live action drama in U.S. television history.

14) ***Frigidaire*** – The first self-contained refrigerator; company name adopted in 1919 and continued through various owners since; due to the market dominance in the early and mid-Twentieth Century, the trademarked name became synonymous with "refrigerator" in that era.

15) ***Shaker*** – Furniture style embodying sturdy construction with straight lines and almost entirely lacking in non-functional additions; associ-

ated with an American religious group of the same name that reached its zenith in 1840.

16) **Donovan, William** – Founder of the Office of Strategic Services (OSS) in 1942, which was the U.S. spy agency in WWII and forerunner of the CIA.

17) **Wallendas** – Circus family of high wire daredevils originated by Karl Wallenda (1905-78); several members of the family, including Karl, have perished during dangerous performances; the family continues its high-wire tradition to the present day.

18) **Scattolini, Virgilio** – Italian journalist who began spying for Mussolini in 1939 as a money-making endeavor; switched to the Allies' side later in WWII; nearly all of his results were fabricated, including fanciful tales involving Vatican personnel and politics.

19) **Burma** – Former name of present day Union of Myanmar, though some countries continue to recognize only the name "Burma" for the country.

20) **Foggy Bottom** – Neighborhood of Washington, DC dating to the Seventeenth Century; reputed as an area of fog and industrial smoke due to its low-lying location along the Potomac River; often refers to the U.S. State Department because of the agency's office building in the area and the agency's reputation for obfuscation and befuddlement.

21) **Ramar of the Jungle** – The lead character in an early syndicated television show of the same name (1952-54) set in Africa and India; Ramar was the natives' name for scientist-adventurer Dr. Tom Reynolds.

22) **Krystal** – Chain of fast-food restaurants located generally in the

South, featuring small, inexpensive hamburgers; patterned after the older White Castle chain in northern states.

23) *Keystone Cops* – Comical policemen in silent films produced by Mack Sennett; often featured a wild, uncoordinated, and usually unsuccessful car and foot chase.

24) *July 26, 1953* – The date of the attack on the Moncada Barracks; though a complete military failure, the battle is celebrated by the Castro Government as the beginning of the Cuban Revolution.

25) *British Guiana* – The colonial name for present day Guyana on the north coast of South America.

# AUTHOR'S NOTE

Older natives of Havana will fail to recollect the High Amateur League (HAL) of Cuban baseball, as it operated solely in the author's imagination.